PRINCESS VAYLE

A NOVEL

by: Timothy Swiss

First Novel in the Princess Tales Trilogy:

Princess Vayle

Tale of the Vanished Princess

Plea to the Warrior Princess

Table of Contents

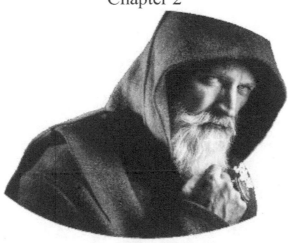

Chapter 3

Noble Intentions

Chapter 4

Solitary Endowment

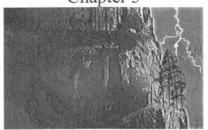

Chapter 11

Astonishing Deliverance
220

Chapter 12

The Encounters
247

Chapter 13

Feast of Consummation
262

Chapter 1

Homestead Calamity

Giralda mused over the fundamentals of midwifery. She sat in a wooden chair at Lady Monica's feet. It was not likely that she would forget anything about birthing an infant, not after ten years of experience.

"Good, it's starting again. Take a deep breath and push."

Lady Monica drew a breath. She was mentally prepared for a sixth son, but her heart yearned for the appearance of her first daughter. She had always wanted a daughter. And besides that, King Wildon and Queen Aracia's infant son was promised to Sir Marticus's newborn daughter, if only Sir Marticus's wife could birth a female.

"Ahh!" grunted the virtual queen of a comely homestead. Her head cocked forward with flushed cheeks as both hands clenched a feather-stuffed mattress.

Giralda scooted to the front edge of her chair and leaned forward. She placed the open palm of her right hand upon an emerging crown, exerting just enough counter pressure to prevent tearing of tissue. A smile broke out on her face as her hands caught a petite female's slippery body.

The baby cried.

"I didn't even have to slap this one," commented Giralda. She slipped one end of a hollow straw into the baby's mouth and sucked out fluid. Her deft hands utilized felt scarves to wipe moist skin. Her right thumb and forefinger milked blood from the umbilical cord until the baby's skin was pink. The cord was clamped twice using wooden pins, with one pin positioned close to the baby's abdomen. Clean scissors bisected the cord.

Lady Monica raised her face and observed Giralda for several hopeful seconds. But then her head plopped back into the feather pillow. She surmised that her midwife's silence signified a sixth son.

"I suppose I shall name him Joel, if my husband likes the name."

Giralda was preoccupied. She glanced toward the upturned face of the woman who had just birthed the most fascinating infant she had ever looked upon, but then her eyes returned to the object of her fascination.

"I do not think, ma'am, that Joel would quite do, not for the likes of this dainty."

Lady Monica's mind cleared. She snapped her head back up and stared upon Giralda's visage. "What do you mean? Is my baby a girl?"

Giralda cradled the newborn in the folds of her skirt. She raised her face and smiled, but then she gazed back downward. "Oh, yes, your baby is a little girl…but…"

"But what? Is something wrong with my baby?"

Giralda looked back up. The expression on Lady Monica's face made it easy to guess what she was thinking, namely that the baby had some terrible defect. Giralda was perplexed; she had not meant to suggest that anything was awry. She tried to think of how to apologize, but before she could formulate a response, Lady Monica broke her gaze and wailed toward the ceiling. "Oh! My baby! Marticus! Help! I want you here! Marticus!"

Pounding footsteps sounded from wooden floors and stairwells. Giralda found herself in an awkward position. She collected her wits just in time to throw a sheet over Lady Monica's legs as the latch to the master bedroom sprang upward. The door swung ajar. Sir Marticus and his five sons filed into the room with widened eyes and tense muscles.

At the side of Lady Monica's bed stood the makings of a small-scale army. Sir Marticus was a hardened farmer and an accomplished swordsman—the best swordsman in Gaul besides his eldest son, Zake, age twenty. Luke, second born, was a deadly archer; and Joshua, though two years younger at seventeen, was Luke's equal at releasing arrows. Zephanoah, mature for a four-year-old, stood barefooted beside his father. And then, demurely positioned behind the others, stood Baruk. No man in all the kingdom of Shareen could match the brawny might of Sir Marticus's fourth-born son, Baruk. He was built like a bear and possessed the strength of an ox—yet he was so warmhearted that children crawled onto his lap to hear stories of woodland creatures, dwarves, and elves. Though only fifteen, he was by far the largest member of the family.

Despite their magnificence, the six males appeared sheepish—standing speechless as they stared upon the three disquieted females.

"Um," began Giralda. She swayed her knees from side to side to calm the infant. Her eyes rose to address Sir Marticus. "I'm afraid I've misconveyed a message to my lady. I mean, I think I've made her think something was amiss."

Sir Marticus scrutinized Giralda's face, and then he turned toward the troubled visage of his wife. He had sat in councils that weighed the fates of kingdoms, but such experience did little to mollify his fatherly concerns. It was Giralda's facial expression that eased his mind. He smiled to reassure his wife and then focused imposing eyes upon Giralda. "So then, the baby is all right? I mean, no major concern?"

"Oh yes, quite all right, sir. The baby is fine." Giralda glanced toward the drape covering Lady Monica's legs. "But I was not entirely ready for visitors yet. The delivery is not altogether complete."

Sir Marticus's eyes popped open. "There's another one?"

Giralda released a soft chuckle. She was tempted to ask Sir Marticus if there had ever been triplets among his ancestors; but instead, she shook her head. "No, just the finishing up. You know—what comes after."

Recollections from past births jostled Sir Marticus's mind. He did not fancy explaining the phenomenon of afterbirth to Zephanoah. "Well, boys," he began, "I…"

"Father," interrupted Zake, nudging his father on the shoulder, "the baby's a girl."

There followed a look of astonishment. Sir Marticus had been through similar experiences several times before but never with the opportunity to associate such an experience with the term *girl*. For a while his face appeared blank, uncomprehending, as if he expected to awaken from some sort of dream. But then his features transfigured into a portrait of exhilaration. He leaned forward, with all five sons huddled about him, and peered downward upon his newborn child. After several seconds of suspenseful silence, he reared back to his full stature and whooped. "Woaoo! Did you hear that, Monica! A girl!" He moved to the head of the bed and bowed with his face close to his wife's face. "We have a baby girl. No doubt about it, not like the other five— definitely a girl."

Lady Monica's eyes sparkled. "A little princess," she declared.

"Great lands!" exclaimed Luke, capturing everyone's attention. He stared at his newborn sister with a look of awe. "What's that on her hair?"

Giralda made no comment. She wrapped the baby in a soft blanket and lifted her for everyone to view. Lady Monica flexed her back and peered over draped knees. For several seconds no one spoke—every eye was transfixed.

"She's lovely," stated Lady Monica, "but is that golden bang natural?"

Giralda drew the newborn back into her arms and stroked the child's crown. Additional grooming only made the golden lock more stunning. It grew above the child's forehead, to the left of center; and it was dazzling in contrast to otherwise dark brunette hair.

"It's surely natural, ma'am. I don't know of anything that could turn hair the color of pure gold."

Stillness followed. Eight onlookers stood in mesmerized silence— marveling at the beauty of the newborn female and entranced by the extraordinary lock of golden hair.

"You know," spoke up Zake, "I learned a Euphratian word for a golden-hued dawn—*colesia*. What about naming her Colesia?"

While the others continued staring at the infant's hair, Sir Marticus turned his eyes upon his eldest son. For two years Zake had studied under the tutelage of a mysterious philosopher. No one knew where the philosopher came from or why he settled in Shareen. Zake befriended the gentleman and helped him secure a job spinning goats' hair into fabric. This kindness was rewarded—the gentleman adopted Zake as his sole pupil. Never before had such an astute teacher set foot in the mountainous regions of Gaul. Zake gained knowledge that astounded everyone in his family.

"Colesia," echoed Sir Marticus, looking back at his newborn daughter. "Yes, that would make a fitting name." He turned and met his wife's eyes. She nodded her approval. He then stood tall and drew a breath. "I hereby proclaim that this child, my only beloved daughter, shall be named Colesia."

"And may her *golden-hued dawns* be blessed with true love—love such as her father has given her mother these many years," added Lady Monica.

Giralda flushed with emotion, but she was never one to overlook practicalities. "The baby has not even had a drink yet," she fussed. "Now if you men can get back to manly businesses, we women can proceed with nature's business. And, remember," she added, looking at Sir Marticus, "there is still what comes after."

"Oh, yes, right," said Sir Marticus, nodding and motioning for his sons to exit.

As clumsily as would be expected under the circumstances, the males shuffled out the bedroom door. Sir Marticus stood and held the door open until Zephanoah, looking back with inquisitive eyes, ambled out behind his brothers. Then Sir Marticus faced his wife. His face beamed every whit as radiantly as when his first son was born; and before he pushed the door closed, he honored the women inside with a respectful bow.

Everyone in the family knew there was a special reason to celebrate the arrival of a baby girl. It was no secret that Sir Marticus and King Wildon agreed that the baby would become the promised bride of the eight-month-old Prince of Shareen—Prince Zarkanis—provided that Lady Monica birthed a female. Sir Marticus could have more easily thrust the blade of his sword through the solid oak wall circumventing his house than to dissolve the smile that adorned his face.

While the business of childbirth recommenced in the master bedroom, the six males slapped, hugged, and congratulated one another. The matter of having a family member destined to be a princess was elating. Sharean law forbade the practice of forcing persons into matrimony, but infants who were promised in marriage almost always consummated the arrangement. The father and sons made their way into the kitchen and sat down at the dinner table, and then each of the five brothers took a turn describing the golden lock of hair on Colesia's head. When finally Zephanoah finished speaking, Sir Marticus folded his hands upon the table and looked from face to face with an expression of fascinating contemplation.

"You have heard me tell stories of my homeland, the Kingdom of Southern Ivoria within the realm of Subterrania."

There were nods and grunts of affirmation. All of the boys loved hearing stories about the world beneath the earth's surface; and although none of them had ever visited that world, not one of them doubted a single word of their father's tales.

"Well, something I've never told you is that my mother was part Ivorian."

"Ivorian?" returned Zake. "Weren't the Ivorians the native people in Southern Ivoria? Wasn't Southern Ivoria their kingdom before men invaded Subterrania from the earth's surface?"

"Yes, and you have heard me describe the Ivorian race."

"They have skin the color of new-fallen snow, and their hair appears as golden as rays of sunshine," remarked Luke.

Sir Marticus issued a soft laugh as he mused over his second-born son's description of the Ivorian race. "And I will tell you this," he said. "I have never seen hair upon any man or woman that matches the color of Ivorian hair—that is, not until this day."

There was a ponderous pause.

"If that be true, then our newborn sister carries the mark of a race from beneath the earth's surface," proclaimed Baruk.

Sir Marticus nodded.

Meanwhile, Giralda leaned back in her chair and took a deep breath. With all aspects of birthing completed, she noted with satisfaction that Colesia nourished herself with her mother's milk. The entire affair seemed the composition of a delightful dream.

"She's strong for such a dainty child," reported Lady Monica.

Giralda wiped her hands. "It is a good sign when an infant takes to the breast. I think she will do well, especially being born in the spring. I think all women should have their children during springtime."

Lady Monica did not argue, despite the fact that only one of her sons was born during the spring, namely Zephanoah—though his fifth birthday was still a month away. She was in a euphoric mood, prone to agree with anything Giralda might say. Her mind focused upon the little person lying upon her bosom. "It seems that all I could ever want on this earth is now fulfilled," she declared. "Nothing but heaven could be better than this."

A warm smile formed upon Giralda's face. But then the smile dissolved... She sensed something. She was well known for possessing a sixth sense—an uncanny premonition of impending circumstances—and now she sensed something disquieting, something from without. She jolted as knocking sounded on the front door to the house.

"Who might that be?" questioned Lady Monica.

Giralda made no reply. She arose and stepped past the bed, and then she opened wooden shutters on the outside wall, swinging them inward. Morning air drifted over a flowery garden and entered the room. The window faced east, and light from lanterns on the inner walls yielded to rays of sunshine. She leaned her head out the window and looked toward the southeast corner of the house. "Oh my, it's the king's horse—King Wildon's horse. I would know that buckskin anywhere, with or without the purple and gold caparison."

The news put Lady Monica in a dither—both pleased and excited. "The king...oh...the king..."

"I wonder why a page is not tending his horse," commented Giralda. Her uneasiness persisted.

Lady Monica ignored the comment. "Giralda, in the second drawer of my bureau, fetch my golden silk scarf. It will complement Colesia's golden lock."

Outside the maternity room, Sir Marticus and his five sons responded to the knocking. The front door was situated on the south side of the home. After passing down a rugged hallway, they emerged into a den embellished with deerskin rugs, mounted antlers, marble statues, decorative rocks, and unusual pottery. Crafted furniture lined the walls—Sir Marticus was well known as a builder and an artisan. A limestone fireplace was centered in the den's northern wall.

Zephanoah was first to reach the oak door and heave it ajar. His eyes grew large as his face tilted upward. There, tall and valiant, stood the bearded king of Shareen.

"King Wildon!"

The king smiled, looking downward into Zephanoah's eyes. "Aha, my brave little knight!" His expression sobered as he lifted his gaze toward Sir Marticus. "I would enter to warn you," he spoke with a staid voice, "but I lack the strength. I fear that Dragus is launching an attack against Shareen."

Gravity beset Sir Marticus's face.

King Wildon continued. "A band of demons fell upon my party as we rode to pay your family a visit, namely to see if Zarkanis has a bride."

"Yes, a beautiful little girl," interjected Sir Marticus.

A brief smile appeared before panged weakness overcame the king's countenance. "I thank God Queen Aracia was not with us. Dragus has surprised us, and my attackers are close behind—you must act quickly to defend yourselves."

The king stopped speaking. He wavered and toppled forward. Sir Marticus and Luke caught his body, but the king no longer inhabited the limp frame—he was dead. A crude shaft protruded from the back of his bloodied jerkin.

"Zephanoah," Sir Marticus spoke while he and Luke dragged the body into the room, "close the door and bolt it." After positioning the king's body in the southwest corner of the den, Sir Marticus stood and faced his older sons. The sounds of Zephanoah bolting the door lent gravity to the span of silence that followed. After a few seconds of looking from face to face, Sir Marticus spoke again.

"I have no doubt that Dragus is attacking, and I have no doubt that he will strike our home at the same time that he launches warfare against Shareen." The four older sons watched their father's face harden. They listened with respectful silence. "You must flee at once. There is no chance of escaping in company with a woman and her newborn daughter, and your mother would prefer dying in her own home. The chances of escape will be increased if you flee in separate directions. Flee into the forest on horseback, and I want one of you to take Zephanoah. I will stay and defend my wife and daughter."

Zephanoah stood in silence. His face wore an expression of overwhelming apprehension. The expressions on the faces of the older brothers were much different—they were the expressions of trained fighters—the expressions of mature and courageous men. The four of them looked at one another for several seconds, and then the eldest brother nodded and set his eyes upon his father.

"We have lived together for many wonderful years," said Zake, "and we can all enter the eternal realm together. Do not ask us to incur the dishonor of leaving our own mother and sister to their fates. We will all stand before our Creator someday, if not this day, and not one of us desires to stand before him bearing a soul that is blighted with cowardice."

Baruk, Joshua, and Luke all uttered affirmations.

The face of Sir Marticus blanched; but then the color returned to his cheeks. A proud smile formed beneath his tearing eyes. "Our lives upon this earth's surface are brief. You have chosen well." He turned and took hold of Zephanoah, and then he positioned his youngest son before him. "By my own right as this boy's father, I bestow upon him a second name—the name of Ferando."

All four older brothers gazed at their father with questioning eyes.

"And by that same right I bestow the name of John upon whichever one of you will volunteer to take my youngest son to safety. You may take him to his mother's sister in the south of Shareen—it may hardly be noticed that Myrtle has a seventh child. What you do thereafter is between you and your Creator. But now, I want John and Ferando to travel in swift silence, unencumbered by weapons of any kind, keeping hidden insofar as possible and taking on the guise of two simple farm boys."

The four young men broke their gaze with their father and addressed one another with uncertain expressions. No one was volunteering. At last Baruk stepped forward.

"I fear that my axe and hammer would be sorely grieved to part with me," said Baruk. He slammed a fisted forearm against his breast. "In allegiance to my dear weapons, I must respectfully decline. I stay and fight."

The three remaining brothers looked quickly at one another, and then both Luke and Joshua stepped forward. "There is only one amongst us who can creep upon a rabbit and snatch it by the tail," said Luke.

Zake said nothing, but he slowly shook his head.

"That is most certain," averred Joshua. "And I give my sneaky eldest brother this parting wish—after delivering Ferando safely into the hands of Myrtle, I wish for him to set out in search of the princess who was recently deported from Shareen, namely Princess Alania."

Zake's head grew still. Though she was eight years younger than him, it was no secret that Zake dearly loved the only daughter of King Wildon and Queen Aracia—Princess Alania.

Sir Marticus smiled in relief. He had feared that none of his sons could be coerced into fleeing with Zephanoah, but Joshua had used the perfect strategy—the mention of Alania.

"Quickly then," said Sir Marticus, nudging Zephanoah toward the firewood hatch in the northwest corner of the room. He opened the hatch. "Come Zake, be off! Now!"

Sir Marticus kissed his youngest son and peered into his eyes. "I love you. The Creator be with you." He produced a courageous smile and rubbed Zephanoah's head. Zephanoah realized much of what was happening, but he still managed to smile in return. Then Zake was beside them, kneeling and assisting Zephanoah through the hatch. He faced his father.

"God be with you," said Zake.

Sir Marticus nodded. "No doubt he will. Now go with my blessing."

No more was spoken. Zake ducked through the hatch. Sir Marticus closed the hatch and stood to face his three remaining sons.

"Joshua, Baruk, gather our weapons and bring them here. Luke, bar the back door and all the windows—have Giralda bar the window in your mother's room."

Joshua, Luke, and Baruk strode from the room. Sir Marticus stepped to the fireplace and removed a sword that hung above the mantel.

Giralda and Lady Monica were unaware of the king's death; they only knew that his horse stood outside. The bureau was on the opposite side of the bed from the window, and as Giralda pulled the second drawer open to search for a golden scarf, Lady Monica sat up and laid Colesia on the bed. She slipped to the floor and stepped to the window for a look outside—she wanted confirmation from her own eyes— confirmation that the King of Shareen was honoring the birth of her newborn daughter. She knew that Giralda would not approve of such activity so soon after delivering a baby, so she waited until Giralda's back was turned. Extending her head well beyond the windowsill, she scrutinized the buckskin that was now grazing at the edge of shrubs near the northeast corner of the house. A pleased smile formed across her lips. The king had indeed come to acclaim her newborn child.

Giralda heard a knock on the bedroom door at the same time she heard a crackling thud and a gasp—sounds that drove a chill through her breast.

"Father says to bar the window," Luke's voice announced. "We're under attack by Dragus."

Giralda wheeled around. For a moment she froze in horror. One of the most gratifying days of her life transformed to one of terror. Lady Monica's body slumped to the floor with a round shaft extending from the back of her head. Giralda could force no sound from her throat, but she sprang across the room and slammed the wooden shutters closed, sliding an iron bar to secure them.

She dropped to the floor and examined Lady Monica's body. The arrow was fatal. Then she raised her eyes, gazing upon the innocent baby girl who lay upon her slain mother's bed. She knew that Sir Marticus and Dragus were archenemies. There was no doubt in her mind that the evil dictator of Pithrania would murder every member of Sir Marticus's family, including a helpless newborn. Her heart sank toward the pit of her abdomen and her limbs weakened. She slumped downward and dropped her face into her hands.

All at once a shock of inspiration brought Giralda to her feet. Her eyes burned with determined passion as she again turned her head and faced Colesia. An idea had sprung to life within her mind. It was an incredible idea—an idea that seemed far beyond her mental capacities—and she deemed it a summons from heaven. She prayed with desperate hope as she exchanged clothing with Lady Monica's slain body, adorning herself with garments that bore the evidence of birthing a child.

"Help me, my God," Giralda prayerfully whispered as she adjusted a cloth belt around her waist. She lifted her eyes and gazed upward. "I will not lie...I know you shun lies, but please grant that these murderers may fall prey to my ploy. From this day hence, this girl is my own—I take her as my adopted daughter, and I will therefore speak no lie when I claim her as my newborn child."

Joshua and Baruk returned to the den, followed by Luke. Joshua carried two longbows, two quivers, and twenty arrows. Baruk held an axe, a sword, and an enormous sledgehammer—all toted within the huge hands of his two-hundred-and-seventy-five-pound frame.

Sir Marticus faced Baruk and smiled. "How about letting Luke have that sword? You can wield the hammer better with both hands."

Baruk handed the sword to Luke and set the axe on the hearth. Luke positioned the sword against the wall and then raised both hands to accept a bow, quiver, and arrows from Joshua. Then he took a position beside Luke. They both strung their bows and nocked arrows. All four men were armed and ready for battle. They were bound together in bold commitment to defend Lady Monica, Colesia, and Giralda.

There was little waiting. Loud clopping and the squeaking of wagon wheels sounded and grew louder.

Wham! Sphitt! Bam!

A battering ram burst the oak door from its frame. The door fell inward and slammed against the floor. A Pithranian warrior appeared in the entranceway—ready to leap inside with drawn sword. Luke released an arrow that drove deep between the warrior's eyes. The warrior toppled backward and lay motionless. Several others planning to follow drew back.

"On, you cowards! Don't give him time to nock another arrow!" a gruff voice hollered.

The Pithranian warriors, accustomed to massacring families with little resistance, regained composure and charged forward with loud yelling and curses. The first to reach the doorway had to stomp over three fallen comrades, and then he focused across the room upon Luke and Joshua. Joshua had just released an arrow, and Luke was nocking one.

"Yah!" screamed the warrior as he slang an axe in Luke's direction. Like the other attackers, he wore a pewter helmet with a three-inch spike atop the crown. Most of his garments were leather, and he was further equipped with a knife and a sword. Luke abandoned shooting and dove to the floor beneath the flying axe. The sound of the axe rebounding from the wall and plopping onto the floor echoed throughout the house. The warrior then drew his sword and leaped through the doorway, and two more Pithranians, one with a raised axe and the other with an arrow nocked on a bowstring, also rushed into the room.

Joshua released an arrow simultaneously with the Pithranian archer. There were dull thuds that wreaked spasms of nausea through Sir

Marticus's abdomen—both shots were accurate, and both archers crumpled to the floor. The first warrior met Sir Marticus's sword with his Adam's apple and was decapitated. Baruk separated the remaining warrior's head from his neck with the sledgehammer, sending the bodiless head and helmet bouncing back through the ranks of Pithranians outside. An astonished hush fell over the attackers. Murmuring erupted, followed by frantic cursing and furious orders.

"On, you cowards! Attack! Now!" came an agitated voice from amidst the Pithranian ranks. Luke regained his feet and stood with a nocked arrow, but then he dodged to one side as two archers appeared and shot arrows in his direction.

"To the front wall!" yelled Sir Marticus.

Luke understood. Two more archers replaced those who shot at him, and one stepped inside to cut off Luke's retreat, but Sir Marticus's sword split the warrior's skull before the warrior could loose an arrow. The second archer, a coward, remained outside and shot an arrow into empty space. No sooner was his arrow released than Luke stepped into view and zipped an arrow through his breast.

A loud bang came from the rear of the house.

"Baruk! The back door!" directed Sir Marticus.

Baruk lunged across the room. An arrow and an axe, poorly aimed, streaked through the open doorway and ricocheted from the walls and fireplace. Pithranian warriors charged again. The first to enter turned toward Sir Marticus with a drawn sword, and the second faced Luke. Luke surprised the second by shooting past him and dropping the first, freeing Sir Marticus to swing his sword and behead the second. Fallen Pithranian bodies cluttered the floor, but still more warriors clambered through the entranceway. As Luke drew back his bowstring to release a seventh arrow, an axe pierced his cranium. Even as the shock knocked him backward and unconsciousness closed upon him, his skilled hands directed the seventh arrow through the heart of his assailant.

The walls of the house quivered as heavy thuds sounded from the rear of the house. Sir Marticus knew that Baruk was pounding assailants with his hammer. Another warrior fell beneath his sword, but then three more appeared—one an archer. Sir Marticus continued battling until an arrow pierced his chest. As he crumpled to his knees, he launched his sword—zipping it through the chest of his killer. The last thought to flash through his mortal mind was the hope that Zake and Zephanoah escaped.

With the guardians in the den slain, three Pithranian warriors pressed forward through the hallway that led to the kitchen. Loud bellowing, screaming, and the clashing of weapons made them think there was a small army to contend with; but what they found was a single giant. Baruk held a wooden door as a shield and brandished a prodigious sledgehammer. There were numerous arrows in the door, one in Baruk's left boot and another in Baruk's right leg; but this seemed little damage compared to the collection of heads, helmets, and bodies representing those who dared charge through the kitchen doorway.

Baruk's back was turned to the approaching warriors. A smartly thrown axe struck him in the posterior skull, whacking his cranium with a thick portion of the blade. There was a crack like the sound of wind wrenching a limb from a tree, and then Baruk crashed to the floor. Silence followed.

The three Pithranian warriors stood aghast. Two wary faces peered through the back doorway.

"There were only four of them," commented Kahl, the warrior who launched the axe.

A lapse of silence followed. Three warriors stepped through the rear doorway and joined their comrades in the kitchen. Approaching footsteps became audible from the den.

"If all Shareans fight like these, it is fortunate we outnumber them," said Bennill, one of the two warriors who witnessed Kahl take down Baruk. He grasped a gash in his left arm.

"No other Shareans will fight like the sons of Sir Marticus," a huffy voice interjected from the hallway. Sir Wixton strode into the kitchen where Baruk's body lay before the group of Pithranian warriors. He wore a golden helmet, signifying higher rank. "How many were there?"

"Four," reiterated Kahl, "not counting the king."

Fear flashed across Sir Wixton's features. He looked around as if expecting a surprise attack. The warriors sensed his apprehension and began fidgeting.

"Are there more?" asked Kahl, kneeling to retrieve his axe.

Sir Wixton assumed an air of composure and eyed each of the six warriors in the room with him. "I've ordered everyone else to remain outside. We will search every room, every closet, and every cupboard in this house. There are still three more members of Sir Marticus's family to be slain, a mother and two more sons. But take care—one of the sons will be old enough to fight. Kahl and Thran, come with me. The rest of you split up. Call me if you find anyone."

There were no expressions of surprise when Sir Wixton selected the best two fighters as bodyguards. Two other warriors headed for a stairway on the opposite side of the kitchen, and the remaining two warriors, Lyhn and Bennill, turned back down the hallway toward the den. Lyhn stopped and pulled on the latch to a door halfway down the hall. He fiddled with the latch for several seconds, and then he turned his face toward Bennill.

"Bennill!"

Bennill spun around and strode to his comrade's side. "What is it?"

"This door is jammed."

The commotion caught Sir Wixton's notice. He motioned for Kahl and Thran to follow him, and then he stepped closer to watch as Bennill took Lyhn's place in attempting to open the door.

****

When sounds of fighting erupted from the den, a feeling of dread surged through Giralda's body. She knew what manner of men would release an arrow through the back of an innocent woman's skull. She faced such men before on the darkest day of her life. Ten years past, on a small farm near her home village of Marne, she was pinned to the ground as her husband and daughter were slaughtered by a band of drunken Pithranian marauders. Her daughter was an infant, only three months old. The rapacious barbarians then abducted her, and they would have killed her if not for a band of Sharean soldiers that intervened as she was being stolen away along a mountain trail.

After securing the door, Giralda took up her adopted daughter and lay down in the featherbed. The newborn was brought to her breast, and was soon suckling as before, though now drawing milk from a surrogate mother—Giralda was a wet nurse.

Outside in the hallway, Bennill determined that the bedroom door was barred on the inside. Sir Wixton motioned for Thran. Thran wielded his axe and burst the fasteners that secured an iron bolt. The door creaked open. Raising his axe, Thran stepped through the doorway. Kahl followed close behind. Several seconds later they were joined by Bennill, Lyhn, and Sir Wixton.

All five men stood and stared down upon a well-proportioned woman with disheveled amber hair. She stared back at them with golden-brown eyes as she nursed a newborn baby. Blood and amniotic fluid stained her garment. Placental afterbirth filled the bottom of a pan beside her feet. Lady Monica's slain body lay in plain sight on the floor beneath the window; it was garbed in Giralda's clothing.

Giralda swept her eyes across the group of Pithranian warriors and then settled her gaze upon Sir Wixton. "You...you wear a golden helmet." She spoke with a brusque accent that was typical of persons from Marne. The village of Marne lay about three days' march northwest of Shareen and one day's march northeast of Pithrania. Due to rugged terrain between Marne and Pithrania, it was easier to get from Marne to Pithrania by way of Shareen, even though the distance was greater. The route through Shareen was the way a pregnant woman on horseback would be expected to travel.

"That's right," returned Sir Wixton.

Giralda then asked, "Do you know a man who wears a helmet just like yours but with three red rubies inlaid over the brow?"

There was silence. The other Pithranian warriors looked at their warlord's face. For a moment Sir Wixton appeared baffled by the woman's inquiry, but then he recovered his bearing. He stared hard at Giralda. Then he turned his head toward the slain woman on the floor.

"Who is this?" he inquired, pointing to Lady Monica's body.

Giralda turned her head toward the slain body and then looked back at Sir Wixton. Her face depicted no great concern. "Her name is Monica."

Sir Wixton looked back and forth between the body on the floor and the woman on the bed.

"It's got to be," asserted Thran. "This woman is much too young to be Lady Monica."

Sir Wixton nodded in response, but his eyes remained fixed upon Giralda. "So then, who are you?" he inquired.

Giralda paused, looking into Sir Wixton's eyes. Her mind wandered back to the appearance of a Pithranian officer who strode past her as she lay upon the ground after her husband and child were murdered. The officer stopped and gazed down upon her. She remembered his callused expression, and the cold look in his pale blue eyes, and she also remembered three red rubies that were lined across the brow of his golden helmet.

"My name is Giralda, and I come from the village of Marne."

"I see," returned Sir Wixton, "and why do you ask me if I know a man who wears three rubies in his helmet?"

Giralda looked down at Colesia and then back at Sir Wixton's face. "Will you take us to him?"

Sir Wixton's brow rose and fell. "I would not wish to disturb a Pithranian captain unless it were a matter of great importance. Why should I take you to him?"

Giralda coaxed Colesia from her breast and pulled her dress together, and then she held Colesia up for view. She turned Colesia's face toward Sir Wixton. "Has not nature borne witness to the fact that this child is of noble blood? How else would an infant's crown manifest gold?" She glanced toward Thran and then looked back at Sir Wixton. "I would not expect one of your pewter-topped minions to engender such a child as this one."

"She's insulting the legion," Thran blustered. He approached the side of the bed and raised his axe. Giralda's eyes widened, and she pulled Colesia back into her arms; but she did not say a word. She was resolved to rescue the child or die. She knew that she would rather be slain than fall prey to a band of wanton flesh mongers.

"Stay!" ordered Sir Wixton.

Thran cursed under his breath, lowered his axe, and backed away from the bed. Sir Wixton stepped forward to examine the infant. Giralda had no choice but to allow him to lift Colesia in his hands. He studied the infant's eyes and hair, staring for quite some time at the golden lock, and then he placed her back into Giralda's arms. Just then the remaining two warriors in Sir Wixton's search party entered the bedroom. They each wore a knife and sword that were pilfered during rummaging, and they both gawked at the strange woman and baby.

"No one else, sir. We checked everywhere," spoke one of them.

A look of puzzled alarm swept Sir Wixton's features. He turned his face toward Giralda. "We'll be back." Then he faced the warriors. "Come with me, and make sure the door is closed behind us."

The warriors followed Sir Wixton back to the den. He motioned for them to gather around him.

"I don't want that woman to hear us," he remarked, speaking in low tones. Then he faced one of the two warriors who had searched the home. "You are positive that no other human being is alive within this house?"

"Not even a rat could have escaped our notice," answered the warrior.

Sir Wixton paused and strode about the room, examining the fallen bodies. He stopped at the body of Sir Marticus. "This is Sir Marticus, he's too old to be one of the sons." He turned and faced the warriors. That means that the youngest son is missing, merely a child, and one of the older brothers. No matter, the report to reach Dragus shall be that Sir Marticus and his entire family, including all five sons, have been slain; and this report is what we shall share with our comrades outside. We shall burn this house to the ground to erase any evidence to the contrary. I can assure you that this company will never be allowed to reenter Pithrania until Dragus receives such a report."

Kahl faced Sir Wixton. "Shouldn't we see if we can track down the other two?"

Sir Wixton eyed Kahl sternly. "I've been counseled in regard to Sir Marticus, and I've been counseled in regard to the sons of Sir Marticus. One of the older sons is no doubt fleeing to a safe haven with the youngest child, and I can assure you of this—there is no chance that any man in Pithrania could track down one of the older sons of Sir Marticus. If either of the sons shows up, we'll just stick to our story—five warriors and a boy were slain in this house, in addition to finding the slain bodies of King Wildon and Sir Marticus' wife, and quite naturally, we assumed that we slew Sir Marticus and his five sons."

There were no rebuttals. The warriors knew that Dragus possessed an extravagant lust for vengeance, whether just or unjust; and they knew that Dragus had forbidden their return to Pithrania until Sir Marticus's entire family was exterminated. And in addition to that, they knew that challenging the instructions of a Pithranian officer was tantamount to suicide.

"All right then, you two stay here," directed Sir Wixton, addressing the two warriors who searched the house. "The rest of us will join you in a few minutes." He turned and led Thran, Kahl, Bennill, and Lyhn back into the bedroom with Giralda and the infant. Kahl, who was the last to enter, closed the door and then turned and folded his arms. Thran,

Bennill, and Lyhn stood toward the foot of the bed, looking back and forth between the woman and their commander.

Sir Wixton stood beside the bed and stroked his chin as he scrutinized Giralda and Colesia. Then he clasped his hands behind his back and cleared his throat to speak.

"There are four Pithranian captains. Did the captain tell you his name?"

Giralda did not flinch. "This child's father did not grant permission for me to tell anyone his name. Will you show me each of the captains in turn?"

At first Sir Wixton made no reply, but he did not appear to consider Giralda's request preposterous. "Can you describe him for me? I may find it easier to assist you if I have a description of the child's father."

"I'll never forget his blue…"

Giralda's speech faltered; she paused with her mouth open, staring into Sir Wixton's eyes. "Are you tricking me? If I do not have permission to give the father's name, then do you think that he would want me to identify him by describing him? I will tell you no more about him."

Pensive seconds passed. Sir Wixton leaned over to reexamine Colesia's eyes. Then he raised himself and addressed Giralda in a low voice. "You will be allowed to live, and the infant also, but I advise you to repeat nothing of what you have spoken to me—not to anyone—not unless I instruct you to do so. I will assist you in finding your captain."

Giralda responded by sighing and kissing Colesia's brow.

Sir Wixton turned and faced the four warriors who were in the room with him. "This woman and child are my personal consorts, and until I find out who fathered this child, you will not molest either of them, and you will guard them with your lives."

The warriors understood. Captains were of highest rank in the Pithranian army, subject only to the king, and they were addressed as lords. Sir Wixton could gain notable advantage by rescuing the mistress and child of a captain.

"Furthermore," added Sir Wixton, "nothing spoken in this room shall be made known to anyone. I issue this warning as a warlord, and in addition to that, I speak on behalf of a captain—namely the captain who fathered this child."

Sir Wixton's threat was not questioned. He stepped to the bedroom door and opened it.

"All right, you two may join us," hailed Sir Wixton, speaking loudly.

The other two warriors reentered the room. They knew better than to ask questions.

"We shall set up camp. Our mission is accomplished," declared Sir Wixton. "We can report that Sir Marticus and all five of his sons have been slain," he reiterated, facing each warrior in succession to emphasize his proclamation. "Furthermore, Lady Monica's dead body lies before you, and King Wildon's corpse shall be delivered to Dragus without delay."

Giralda's heart was bruised by Sir Wixton's words. She did not know that Zake and Zephanoah had not been found. Her outward countenance, however, displayed little emotion.

Sir Wixton eyed his warriors for several more seconds and then resumed speaking. "This house is to be set afire. The woman and infant were prisoners held by Sir Marticus, but they are now my personal consorts, and they are to receive the highest respect. Guard their safety with your lives, and assist them in preparing to travel to Pithrania with us." Sir Wixton again looked at the infant, and then he strode from the room.

Giralda felt confident that she and Colesia were safe from immediate harm. "I'll gather up some things before this place gets burned—that woman won't be needing them," she said, nodding toward Lady Monica's body. "And besides that, I need to change clothes."

"Very well," said Kahl. "I'll stand guard in the hallway."

The room was cleared of men, and then Kahl pulled the door closed.

Giralda looked downward at Colesia. "Well, child," she whispered, "I guess I'm a mother again. We'll just have to find some way to escape."

Lady Monica was well prepared for a baby. Giralda found plenty of linens. She selected a gown and a dress from a bountiful wardrobe, but she discovered that her feet were too large for Lady Monica's shoes. That was not a problem—her own shoes were made of leather and were in good condition. She packed clothing and supplies in a bag, and then she lifted Colesia to her shoulder and faced the door. "I'm ready," she announced.

The survivors in Sir Wixton's company included two officers and thirty-one warriors. The officers had mounts, and the warriors traveled afoot. Giralda was placed on one of five horses found in the stable northwest of the house, and the other horses were assigned to favored warriors. The bag of goods Giralda collected from Lady Monica's bedroom was tied to her horse's saddle. A chill swept her ribcage as she contemplated the carnage that expunged the family of Sir Marticus and Lady Monica from the earth—all except for the tiny infant cradled in her arm.

Giralda sat upon her mount and watched as fires were started at all four corners of the oak house. An inversion in the atmosphere pressed thick gray smoke downward and spread it outward like a heavy fog. Though most of the smoke drifted north, it also billowed eastward where Sir Wixton's regiment was gathered. It irritated Giralda's eyes and lent an excuse for tears.

"Enough! Mount up. Let's set up camp in the field to the southwest," hailed Sir Wixton. "Thran, see to it that the fire doesn't spread to the forest. Troy…Bastion…stay and help Thran."

A cheer rose through the ranks. The warriors knew that their assignment was accomplished, and they all expected Sir Wixton to stay and revel in success. His regiment would wait to rejoin the main force until after the battle in Shareen was concluded. Shoots of oats carpeted the fertile field where they set up camp; the sprouts provided food for horses and padding for bedrolls.

Giralda was assisted in dismounting from her horse, and then she was led to a spot where she could sit on the ground. She sat down and held Colesia close to her bosom as tents were raised. It seemed apparent that she and her adopted infant would be treated well—at least for a while. Black smoke churned above the blazing house. Giralda watched the house fall prey to pitiless flames. She thought about how wonderful Colesia's life might have been if tragedy had not befallen the infant's noble family.

Meanwhile, a giant human frame jerked in a fit of coughing. Half awareness crept into a mind aroused by the feel of fiery heat, the smell of charred oak, and the sound of collapsing timbers. Baruk peered upward as a supporting beam shifted above him. The second floor was a searing inferno. Chunks of incinerating wood fell and exploded near his feet and legs. He crawled through the doorway, paused on his hands and knees to gain his bearings, and then rose and dashed into the forest to the northeast, passing beyond the vacated stable. His escape was shrouded from view by dense smoke, and his footsteps were muffled by sounds of fiery demolition. Seconds later he collapsed amidst thick shrubs.

Chapter 2

Seclusive Ally

Zake paused after reaching for Scarletmane's saddle. He was thinking. Big Blue was almost as fast as Scarletmane and possessed greater stamina. He turned from Scarletmane and saddled Big Blue. He mounted with Zephanoah positioned before him—Baruk's saddle was spacious. The stable's main doors faced southward, but he exited through a smaller door to the north. He directed Big Blue into the forest until they were concealed by foliage, and then he turned eastward and headed toward Shareen.

Pithranian soldiers could be heard from time to time on the main road farther north—a stone and cement thoroughfare built by the Romans— but Zake and Zephanoah were safely concealed as they traversed a clandestine pathway. Big Blue, accustomed to bearing Baruk, easily bore the weight of Zake and Zephanoah. The forest grew dense with pine, spruce, and cedar. Once they were able to course farther from the northern trail without venturing onto open fields, Zake worried less about stealth and urged Big Blue to a faster pace. He wondered if fighting had already started in Shareen and whether or not he would be able to reach the city wall without encountering enemies.

"Are Father and Mother dead now?" asked Zephanoah, ending an intense silence.

Zake pulled his youngest brother close to him and reined Big Blue with one hand. There was no obvious trail along the shortest course to Shareen, but he was familiar with the trees, gullies, and hills en route to his destination. He pondered a response to Zephanoah's question. Of all his brothers, Zephanoah was most like him—contemplative and sensitive, yet apt to seem stoic. "People like your mother and father never die, Zeph. Sooner or later they leave their mortal bodies behind them, but they never die."

Zephanoah did not doubt his brother's words. "Why can't we go with them?"

Packed conifer needles padded the ground beneath Big Blue's hooves. Ahead appeared clusters of pink and purple flowers where trees stood farther apart and sunshine splashed into miniature glades. It seemed that nature offered a token of floral sympathy to the two orphaned passersby. "We can, and we will, but not until we are taken to them. It is our duty to live our mortal lives until the breath is drawn from us, and to fight for all that is good."

Zephanoah considered his older brother's words. "Like Father?"

"That's right Zeph. Just like Father."

Zake straightened and pulled up rein. Big Blue halted and perked his ears. A deer bolted across a clearing to their right and then vanished into a clump of cedars.

"It's fine—just a deer," said Zake.

Big Blue resumed a hurried pace beneath Zake's prodding. On they rode through the mountainous forest with both riders deep in thought. There was little additional conversation before Shareen broke into view below them, scenically situated in a mountain valley. Through the heart of the city flowed the Great Stag River, a majestic waterway that provided ample irrigation for crops and livestock. A great rectangular wall surrounded city dwellings.

An eerie sensation rose through Zake's breast as he prodded Big Blue along the tip of a rocky promontory. The fields south and west of the city should have been bustling with activity, but not a soul was in sight. Then he turned his eyes to the north. Glints of light flashed from place to place within the flatland between the forest and the northern city wall—glints caused by sunlight reflecting from apparel that encased the bodies of fallen combatants. Sharean soldiers lined the inside of the northern wall while Pithranian warriors stood along the base of a cliff that rose at the far edge of the northern field. War between Pithrania and Shareen was underway.

Big Blue stepped beyond the concealment of sagging branches.

"Zake, draw back!"

Zake wheeled Big Blue back around. His teacher's voice was unmistakable. He held Big Blue steady until a gaunt figure stepped into view. His teacher's countenance was generally cheerful, but now it seemed the visage of a weather-beaten mariner. The robe his teacher wore was rusty brown, as were his leather sandals. Zake had never seen him wearing any color but gray.

"I see you have your youngest brother with you."

Zake nodded, studying his teacher's eyes. "Yes. Father commanded me to flee with him. The king warned us of attack, but there was no time."

A look of keen interest mounted the teacher's face. "The king? Have you seen him?"

"He was killed, and the same must now be true of my family, including my newborn sister. Only Zephanoah and I escaped."

A thoughtful gaze responded to Zake's words. The teacher lingered in respectful silence until Zake spoke again.

"My sister was born before the attack. She was promised in marriage to Prince Zarkanis. We gave her a name meaning *golden-hued dawn* because of a golden lock in her dark hair. Her name is a word you taught me from the Euphratian language—*colesia*. I have never before seen such golden color in any living creature, neither in the hair of a man nor in the fur of an animal."

Zake spoke with forced composure, though his arms tightened their embrace around Zephanoah and his eyes tore into Dametrius's soul in lamentation.

Sensing the depths of Zake's grief, the teacher found himself in awe of the steadiness in Zake's voice. But the circumstances at hand warranted urgent and focused attention. He chose to redirect the conversation.

"Is anyone following you?"

"No. I am certain that we escaped without being seen."

There was a pause. "Do you remember what you told me about Danvurst? Do you remember how Dragus captured the city years ago and prevented any uprising by keeping the king's only son in prison?"

"Yes," replied Zake, "I remember."

"The citizens of Danvurst honored the prince's right as heir to the throne, and they would not elect another king so long as the imprisoned prince survived. Is that not correct?"

"That is correct."

"Well then, does not Shareen share the same custom? Would not any leader be denied the title of king so long as the rightful heir to the throne survived?"

Zake studied his teacher's face. It seemed evident that the wizened old man was planning to engage himself in the war.

"Yes," Zake responded.

"So then, even if the rightful heir to the throne were an eight-month-old infant, would he not be raised and esteemed as king? And if he were captured and imprisoned, would not his imprisonment hamper or prevent another individual from being inaugurated as King of Shareen?"

The teacher's line of reasoning was obvious. "So then, Dragus will try to capture Prince Zarkanis and confine him."

"Quite so."

"Then we must rescue Zarkanis and flee. Is that not your plan?"

The teacher looked upon his sole pupil with steady eyes. "That would be a fine plan, if it were possible; but Pithranian warriors are making their way southward along the eastern and western borders of Shareen. It will not be long before the city is surrounded."

"But you have a plan," prompted Zake.

"Yes, a very good plan. You must trust me, though, and do exactly as I say. The future of Shareen rests upon the successful execution of a sophisticated stratagem."

Zake had confidence in his teacher. "Surely. What is the plan?"

"It is important that you do precisely what I tell you."

Zake proffered a curt nod. "I will."

The teacher relaxed furrowed brows and smiled.

Zake studied the look on his teacher's face. He found himself wishing that he could withdraw his last two words. He sensed that his teacher had duped him into making a virtual vow. His father had compelled him to flee combat; and now, he was in no mood to play the role of a coward by retreating from another battle.

"There is no chance that Dragus would allow you to live, and your presence here would interfere with my excellent scheme to—"

"Oh no," interrupted Zake.

"I must insist," recommenced the teacher, raising an open palm to bid Zake's silence. "As much as I admire your abilities, any connection between you and me would foil my plan. Your father was the only man that Dragus hated and feared more than he hated and feared King Wildon. For my good as well as yours, and for the good of Shareen, you must take Zephanoah and ride south to Glamster."

Zake shook his head. He faced his teacher with fearless resolve. "I am younger, stronger, and faster. Take Zephanoah to Glamster for me. I will do what I can to rescue Zarkanis."

The teacher's eyes grew imperious. "Is the first-born son of Sir Marticus one who would break his word? I assure you that the speed and strength of one man's youth are not sufficient—only an old man's craftiness holds the chance of success. I have a plan that may thwart Dragus's evil reign, and I need you to heed my words so that my plan may come to fruition."

Zake shifted his eyes. Pithranian forces were advancing. The elder's words were inarguable—the physical prowess of one youth proffered little hope of liberating Prince Zarkanis. He peered downward upon his youngest brother, realizing that his teacher's instructions were Zephanoah's best hope for survival. He also gave thought to Princess Alania—what future might she face if he did not find her?

Zake dismounted and lifted Big Blue's reins upward to Zephanoah. "Hold him steady," Zake instructed. Then he turned and clasped his teacher's shoulders. No words were spoken until he released his embrace and stepped back.

"We will flee as you request. God be with you. Can you use Big Blue? Zephanoah and I can make it afoot."

A relieved smile was irrepressible. "Thank you, but no. I have no need of a horse, and it is four days' travel to Glamster, even on horseback." The teacher untethered a bag that hung at his side and handed it to Zake. "Take these provisions and be on your way; and when you reach Glamster, seek out a blacksmith named Sorgon. Let him know that you need a home—at least for a while. He is a good man, and he owes me a great favor—I once saved his life. Just tell him that you are the adopted son of Dametrius the Wise."

Zake's eyes widened. He had given up hope of ever learning his teacher's name. The secretive tutor had never revealed his name to anyone in Shareen—he was simply referred to as the teacher. Dametrius seemed a suitable name, a noble name, and Zake felt honored at being proclaimed the *adopted son of Dametrius the Wise*. He nodded and mounted Big Blue behind Zephanoah. Something about hearing his teacher's name made his mission seem momentous. *Dametrius*, he spoke to himself as he reined Big Blue away from Shareen.

"A safe journey to you," said Dametrius, but then his brow wrinkled. He lifted his right hand toward Zake with his index finger extended. "Wait!"

Zake tugged back on Big Blue's reins. "What is it?" he inquired, looking back over his shoulder.

Dametrius dropped his hand and faced Zake. "About your sister. Sometimes infants are stolen and sold to slave traders. In turn, the slave traders sell them to families in Rome. Such families assign the task of raising these infants to their servants, and the infants are raised as slaves."

"You think they may have spared Colesia's life?"

Dametrius's face sobered. "I think Dragus would want any child born to Sir Marticus slain. But Dragus is undoubtedly with his army at the northern border of Shareen, and a greedy warrior may not follow orders when his commander is engaged elsewhere. I do not want to raise your hopes to an unreasonable degree, but…"

"But you think there may be hope?" coaxed Zake, anxious to gain any information that might suggest that his sister escaped death.

"In the event that Colesia was stolen rather than slain, it might be crucial to prevent Dragus from ever learning that she was born."

Zake had no problem following his teacher's reasoning. "So what should I do?"

"Never tell anyone what you have told me. Your mother was pregnant on the day that Dragus attacked. Is that not true?"

"Yes."

"Very well, Colesia's best chance of survival, if she still lives, may be to keep her birth a secret. Dragus may not have known that your mother was due to deliver another child. And if he did know, and if your sister was stolen, then Dragus will be told that your sister was slain, whether or not it is claimed that she was within your mother's womb."

Zake pondered his teacher's words for several seconds and then nodded his understanding. "I will explain this to Zephanoah during our journey. We will keep our sister's birth a secret."

Dametrius nodded. "Go with God," he said.

Zake loosened Big Blue's reins. "My prayers will be with you," he averred. Then he turned his face away. He sensed that he would never see the face of Dametrius the Wise again—not during his years of mortal existence. The massive steed carrying two orphaned riders stepped forward and disappeared amidst branches of spruce and cedar. The forest swallowed all sounds of escape.

****

Dametrius drew a breath and then released a sigh. He had surmised that the house of Sir Marticus would be attacked when he learned that Pithranian soldiers were pitching camp against Shareen, and he hoped to see survivors emerge from the western forest. He had climbed to the secluded hilltop where he and Zake often met, guessing that Zake would come that way if he were able to escape. And now, with Zake and Zephanoah riding beyond sight, he was hopeful that his prized pupil would survive Dragus's ruthless attempt to annihilate the entire family of Sir Marticus and Lady Monica. He had no doubt that Sorgon would honor his request to give the two boys a home, and Glamster was so near the northern reaches of Roman jurisdiction that Dragus would surely leave the village alone.

With the goal of safeguarding his pupil accomplished, Dametrius turned his eyes toward Shareen. The Pithranian emperor wielded a powerful army, and the Sharean forces would be no match, but there were other ways to fight battles, and Dametrius was resolved to engage Dragus in a battle of wits—a battle through which he hoped to achieve the dissolution of Pithranian oppression. Dragus was clever, but Dametrius aspired to be cleverer. Beneath his calm countenance blazed an ardent hatred of evil and a desire to see wicked plans foiled. He planned to wage war with Dragus in a way the tyrant would never suspect; and though his plan would take time, he knew it held the hope of ultimate victory.

With his face still fixed upon Shareen, Dametrius took a minute to reflect upon the expression that overcame Zake's countenance when Zake heard the name Dametrius. The discretion he practiced pertaining to his identity stemmed from disagreements between himself and such persons as the Emperor of Rome and the Pontifex Maximus. The emperor would have him crucified, and the Pontifex Maximus would have him burned at the stake; so a reclusive life in regions far north of Rome proffered the hope of physical survival. Having settled comfortably in Shareen, the present disruption of his life by a proud and unscrupulous dictator was exceedingly unwelcome. King Wildon's fair and principled rule was refreshing, and Dametrius had hoped to inhabit Shareen for the remainder of his years. So in addition to all else, he considered the attack against Shareen a personal affront.

Distant yelling drew Dametrius's notice. Shouts and curses became mixed with the clashing of armor. He descended the hillside with dexterity incongruous to his grayed hair.

Pithranian warriors were charging the northern wall of Shareen, so an old man traversing a wheat field southwest of the city drew little regard. Sharean sentries spotted him, but he received only occasional glances—the sentries were intent upon watching the forest line for signs of enemy forces. He walked to the nearest gate unimpeded.

"You'd best stay inside these walls," said a sentry who hoisted a bar and opened the gate. "Dragus's demons would kill an old man for sport, just like you or I would slap a gnat."

"Thank you for that advice," said Dametrius. He pulled his brown hood up over his head.

The wall surrounding Shareen was fifteen feet tall. The stony road inside the wall showed little wear; the city was less than a century old. Dametrius walked past dwellings that were spaced along both sides of the road, most of them two-story houses of gray limestone. He continued through an arcade and reached an open area with a marble fountain that featured water spewing from the lips of a mermaid. People were gathered around the fountain, fleeing homes in the northern section of the city. There were few adult males among them.

The city of Shareen surrounded an island that sat in the middle of the Great Stag River. The island rose from the center of the river like a giant turtle. A white marble castle glistened upon the summit of the island— a perfect pearl set atop an earthen pedestal. The royal palace was smaller than most castles, but it was sufficient for its purpose, and it was hailed the most beautiful castle in Gaul. Eye-catching turrets at each corner encircled a central, cerulean tower that soared above all else in Shareen and stirred citizens of Shareen with aspirations of being selected to accompany a royal escort to an encircling balcony near the tower's peak.

Dametrius made his way to the southwest bridge which led to the royal palace. Four guards stopped his progress.

"Sorry, the palace is closed to visitors," spoke a guard. He wore leather breeches, a leather vest, and a leather cap. The leather was choice ox hide with toughness that served as flexible armor. This particular guard's cap was green rather than tan, indicating that he was an officer of the guards.

"Sir," Dametrius replied, "I have just received news of Sir Marticus and King Wildon. I must speak to the queen."

The officer stood motionless and eyed Dametrius. All of Shareen had been awaiting news of King Wildon—ever since learning that he rode off with a small party of soldiers toward the homestead of Sir Marticus. It was in hopes that King Wildon would return that Sharean soldiers fought against overwhelming odds.

"Does the king live?"

Dametrius knew that gaining entrance into the palace was vital to his plans. "The queen should be first to hear the news that I bear. If you will accompany me, then you may hear also."

Curiosity seized every aspect of the officer's face. "Who are you?"

Dametrius motioned the officer aside, bringing his lips near the officer's ear. "I am the private tutor to Zake, eldest son of Sir Marticus. I wish to keep my identity a secret from all but Queen Aracia, for I hope to wield the secret of my identity as a weapon against the Pithranian King."

The officer's features eased. He backed away and faced Dametrius. "I have heard of you—you fit your description." He stared at Dametrius as if he were gazing upon a legendary figure from an ancient chronicle. Although he had seen Dametrius walking down the streets of Shareen in a hooded robe, he had never seen the reclusive tutor's face. It was a weathered face with vibrant and congenial eyes. It seemed a trustworthy face, and though the officer had no idea how a single old man intended to use secrecy as a weapon against the Pithranian King, he decided to honor the old man's request. "Come with me."

The limestone bridge arched over the water and adjoined a blue chalcedony walkway. The walkway led to white marble steps. Grasses, shrubs, and flowers along the walkway were so meticulously tended that they yielded the impression of a three-dimensional painting. Guards at the palace entrance gave way to the green-capped escort. This was the first time Dametrius had ever set foot within the palace—he was not inclined to draw attention. The officer led him through a grand reception room and up marble steps to a corridor that led to the Queen's chambers.

Dametrius's eyes became transfixed to a figure at the end of the corridor—the silhouette of Queen Aracia. She was kneeling in the confines of a small balcony that jutted outward from the eastern wall of the palace. Her back was turned toward them.

As the green-capped officer and Dametrius came closer, the queen rose and turned to face them. A turquoise robe draped downward from her neck to the tops of matching slippers. Her long golden hair enframed emerald eyes that captured both men. She peered at Dametrius, and as he drew nearer, her eyes seemed to pore through his mind. Her cheeks glistened with tears—cheeks more accustomed to the rosy tint of laughter. Then she turned her face toward the green-capped officer.

"Emric, my friend, what news do you bring?"

Emric bowed, and then he stepped to one side and motioned toward Dametrius. "This man is the tutor to Sir Marticus's eldest son, and he brings news of King Wildon."

The queen's gaze departed from Emric and met the eyes of Dametrius. Dametrius possessed little admiration for royalty, having made acquaintance with decadent rulers in the southern regions, but beholding the eyes of Queen Aracia imparted a sense of sanctity. There was an aura of affection about her, and composure governed every movement of limb and lash, even though it was obvious from the look in her eyes that her heart pulsed with passion.

"You are Zake's teacher?"

"Yes, madam."

The queen turned and braced her hands on the balustrade. "My heart has told me what news you bring of my husband, and judging by what

I see on the battlefield, I do not think that I will be kept from him for long."

Emric peered toward Dametrius. Dametrius nodded, wondering at the queen's perception.

"There are other matters I must consider now," resumed the queen, releasing the balustrade and turning back around to face Emric and Dametrius. "My only daughter, Alania, was sent to visit my cousin in Glamster. She has been gone for two weeks. Sorgon has strict instructions regarding her management."

Dametrius's brows rose. Could Zake and Zephanoah be en route to the home of Queen Aracia's cousin? Sorgon was not a friend he had visited often, but he was a dear friend—a friend he occasioned to meet while fleeing north from Rome. A charging boar threatened Sorgon's life, and it was Dametrius's handily wielded staff that prevented the boar from rending Sorgon's body with grim tusks. After the rescue, the two men spent several days together in Glamster and became close friends, but Sorgon had never mentioned anything about having royal relatives.

"I know that Alania is only twelve years of age," resumed the queen, "but she is mature for her age, and she has been infatuated with Zake for two years. I think she truly loves him. The family of Sir Marticus always received the warmest welcome in our palace, but I told Alania that it would not be appropriate to disclose her love for Zake until she was thirteen. And what is more, I think Zake thinks fondly of my daughter." Queen Aracia focused upon Dametrius. "I wish there were some way that Zake, if he lives, could be informed that my daughter loves him."

Despite somber circumstances, Dametrius came close to smiling. "Would it be appropriate to describe your cousin Sorgon as a robust blacksmith with a bushy black moustache?"

The queen appeared startled. "Yes, that describes him perfectly."

"Your cousin owes me a favor, and I have sent Zake to his house for safekeeping, along with Zephanoah."

Queen Aracia stared at Dametrius. Her countenance transfigured into an expression of delight. "Well, it sounds as though at least one of my prayers has been answered. I only wish I could see Alania's eyes when Zake arrives." For several seconds she maintained a mused expression, but then her face grew sober. "Perhaps I shall, if such privileges are granted from heaven. But I am worried about Zarkanis—they will not kill him, they will imprison him."

Emric listened to the conversation between Queen Aracia and Dametrius without comment. His face grew stolid when the queen spoke of seeing Alania's eyes from heaven.

"Is Zarkanis nearby?" asked Dametrius.

"Yes." Queen Aracia raised her left hand and pointed at the wall to the right of Dametrius. "He is sleeping in that room. We could not send him into exile—it would have been an open declaration of defeat."

"I understand that," stated Dametrius, "and I also understand the custom that will keep Dragus from killing him. That is why I am here. I have come on behalf of Prince Zarkanis."

For a second time Queen Aracia appeared startled. She gazed into the mysterious messenger's eyes—a messenger who had delivered favorable news in regard to her daughter, and who now spoke of aiding her son. With an enemy army surrounding the city walls, there seemed little chance that the frail-appearing fellow standing before her could offer any appreciable help. But she would grant him the courtesy of listening.

Dametrius sensed his license to proceed. "I know that your son will be imprisoned, and I know that Dragus will want to keep him from becoming a future threat. But Dragus will not want him to die."

The queen nodded.

"I intend to be imprisoned with him. Dragus could not hope to keep an infant alive without a caregiver. I am an accomplished tutor, and I—"

"But Dragus would never place a tutor from Shareen in a prison cell with an heir to the Sharean throne," interjected Aracia. Her assertion was undeniable, and yet an inkling of hope began shaping within her mind. She peered into the eyes of the man who was volunteering to serve as guardian to her son—volunteering to be imprisoned with Zarkanis.

"True enough, but what about a deaf jester who cannot speak a comprehensible word, and yet a jester who is an experienced caregiver."

The queen tilted her head to one side and stared at Dametrius with drawn brows. After a few moments of contemplation, her expression cleared. A smile bloomed upon her face, and there appeared a gleam in her eyes that was fostered by the emergence of unforeseen hope. She stepped forward and grasped Dametrius by both arms. She peered into his eyes. It seemed to Dametrius that she surveyed his very soul. "You would do this? But why?"

Dametrius paused. His eyes were locked with those of the queen. The question was profound. She was not asking how he would manage such a scheme, but rather she was asking why he would commit himself to such a purpose. Formulating a response to this question required a minute of introspection. The queen waited, motionless, peering into his eyes. At last he spoke, and he spoke with bared sincerity. "I serve a King other than Dragus, a King above us all; and my King does not approve of evil dictators. I believe that nurturing the heir to the Sharean throne would provide a worthy cause for an old man's last years—an old man who wants to do something useful with the remainder of his feeble days upon this earth."

Aracia stepped back and stood in silence. After staring long and hard, she nodded her understanding, seeming to draw as much from Dametrius's eyes as from his words. She drew a breath to speak. "There are some jester outfits in the third room to your left. I'll show you where they are." She turned to address Emric. "Do you understand? He plans to play the perfect imbecile so that Dragus will place him in confinement with Zarkanis."

Emric formed a dubious expression. "Will they even allow a jester from this castle to live?"

"Please," the queen pleaded, "it is my only hope. Will you not help us?"

Emric looked from the queen to Dametrius and then back to the queen. He felt certain that no mortal man could resist an appeal from Queen Aracia. He also knew his queen well enough to guess what plans she held for her own future. He grasped the hilt to his sword. "Whatever role I may be able to play in preparing for this charade, I am at your service. I only proffer one request in return—if you are determined to engage in mortal combat, then I plead that you grant me the honor of fighting at your side."

****

A few hours after Emric escorted Dametrius into the castle, a party of Pithranian warriors accompanied their king to the crest of a cliff. The cliff formed the southern face of a hill north of Shareen. From that vantage point, mounted upon a coal-black stallion, Dragus surveyed a body-strewn battlefield outside the city walls. The metal helmets on his fallen warriors contrasted with the leather headgear of his fallen adversaries; and to his loathing, the number of slain combatants wearing metal helmets was greater than the number wearing leather headgear. He muttered an unintelligible curse and spit. He expected the Sharean soldiers to fare better than his warriors, but foreseeing such progression of battle did little to mollify his vexation. King Wildon had declared him a depraved fiend and an unworthy general, and Dragus could not bear rebuke.

"Lord Barkot has arrived from the battle front," announced Barnum, one of Dragus's appointed bodyguards. There were fifteen select warriors surrounding Dragus, and their sole duty was to shield him from harm. Each rode upon a choice steed, and each demonstrated exceptional fighting skills. It was a high honor to achieve such assignment. Dragus's bodyguards were granted first-rate rooms in his castle, and they were given first choice of bounty from pillaged villages.

"Bring Lord Barkot to me."

Barnum turned his horse and made his way past fellow bodyguards to the edge of a steep decline. He peered downward and made an abrupt signal with his right hand; and in response, Lord Barkot rode up the hillside.

"Dragus will speak to you now," said Barnum. He spoke with a haughty air. For five long years he had served as an underling warrior, taking orders from officers such as Lord Barkot. Since his selection as a bodyguard, however, he answered to no one but Dragus. The pewter helmet he had once worn was replaced by a golden helmet with three diamonds lined horizontally above the forehead. Dragus wore no helmet; he considered helmets uncomfortable, and he had no intention of engaging in combat.

Lord Barkot walked his horse up beside Dragus. "At your service, Sire."

Dragus did not remove his gaze from the battlefield. "How many have we slain?"

"About two-hundred and twenty, not counting the wounded. Our losses are about—"

"Never mind," snapped Dragus. He turned dark eyes to address his highest-ranking officer. His face wore an expression of tyranny, a look that reminded his subjects that their lives were in his hands and that a spoken word from his lips could bring an axe to their necks. He bore a sinister charisma that stemmed from an air of self-assigned deity. "That means we have eliminated about a quarter of their fighting force?"

"Yes, Sire."

"That is sufficient. We shall proceed as planned. Sir Kramsky shall move into the white palace, and the Shareans shall furnish us with generous portions of wheat and barley. We shall leave all the women, at least for now. I understand that you are prepared to confront the Sharean commander with the news that we possess the slain body of King Wildon, and I assume that the terms of surrender have been rehearsed. Is that correct?"

"Yes, Sire. Everything you have spoken has been written and reviewed, and our emissary has been cross-examined."

"Then proceed with our plan. The death of King Wildon shall force the Sharean commander to surrender." Dragus turned his eyes back toward the city. "That is all."

"Yes, Sire."

Lord Barkot turned his horse and rode back to the edge of a slope that led down to an encampment of Pithranian warriors. He withdrew his sword and waved to an officer below.

Dragus dismounted and walked to the edge of the cliff to observe the execution of his orders. A Pithranian emissary rode onto the battlefield, brandishing a long spear with a green scarf fluttering from its upper end. This was the recognized signal for requesting a peaceful exchange of dialogue. Dragus knew that the Shareans would respect the gesture and allow his messenger a safe approach. What concerned him most, however, was not the safety of his emissary but rather the successful delivery of his message—a message he prepared with an unmitigated sense of spite.

From his vantage point atop the northern wall of Shareen, Captain Lark signaled his archers to hold fire. He was the highest-ranking Sharean officer yet alive. The dispatched Pithranian messenger stopped before the northern gate and awaited response. Captain Lark descended the wall and opened the gate. He walked out on foot, after which the Pithranian messenger dismounted and faced him, lowering the end of the long spear until the green scarf rested upon the ground.

"What news do you bring?"

The messenger stared at the Sharean Captain and tottered as he tried to speak. He regained his balance and drew a deep breath. "News from King Dragus."

"What news?"

Looking from Captain Lark's eyes to the line of archers along the wall, the messenger swallowed hard. He withdrew a parchment from an inner shirt pocket and read over it, and then he replaced the parchment and again faced Captain Lark. "We have the body of King Wildon. King Dragus says that if you surrender at once and allow a Pithranian governor to occupy the palace, then King Wildon's body will be delivered without mutilation. He also says that no prisoners will be taken with the exception of Queen Aracia and Prince Zarkanis. He further requests that you relinquish all weapons."

A grimace swept over the captain's countenance. "And if we do not surrender?"

The young Pithranian warrior cast a worried glance toward the archers. He cleared his throat twice before speaking. "If you do not surrender, King Dragus says that King Wildon's body shall be sliced into pieces and hurled over the walls of your city; and after you are defeated, you will only be left with such women as none of the Pithranian soldiers deem worth having."

Captain Lark looked upon the messenger with disgust. "Wait here." He turned and walked back through the city gate, closing it behind him.

Dragus fidgeted. He watched for nearly an hour, annoyed by the length of time that elapsed after Captain Lark retreated within the city walls. The long wait tempted him to order another attack, but there was a valid reason to exercise patience—his army was growing stronger through the recruitment of farmers from northern villages, and he needed the supply of grain that subservient Shareans could provide for his army. Dead men could not till soil. After calling for a makeshift chair, he seated himself and stared toward the northern gate of Shareen.

The fields west of Shareen were streaked with shadow when Captain Lark reopened the northern gate and approached the Pithranian emissary. The tremulous youth had felt Dragus's eyes upon him during the entire wait; his legs ached from maintaining a dignified stance. There was a noticeable alteration in the officer who now faced him. Captain Lark's eyes reminded him of great brown orbs he once observed as a buck bled to death from arrow wounds. Still, there was something about the Sharean officer that decreed nobility.

"The queen is packing a few supplies. She agrees to submit to King Dragus's custody, provided that her son, manservant, and jester accompany her. The jester will neither speak nor follow verbal orders, but he cares well for Zarkanis, and he responds to hand signals as would be expected of an obedient deaf mute. If her simple demands are met, then my army will relinquish all weapons other than one sword or axe per man. A Pithranian governor will be permitted to inhabit the palace."

The youth stood motionless, reviewing the points of Captain Lark's message. "Very well." He raised his spear, holding the green scarf aloft, and mounted his horse. A sense of supremacy swept through his breast as he turned his back on the subdued Kingdom of Shareen. He rode across the northern field with a bearing of grandiosity. At the far reaches of the field, he drew back on the horse's reins. Before him stood a line of Pithranian warriors. They were gathered at the foot of a cliff—the cliff where Dragus and his bodyguards waited above.

Lord Barkot came forward on horseback and received the emissary's report, and then he turned and trotted his horse up the western slope of the hill. There were many curious eyes cast upon him. He steadied his horse to a canter as he topped the hill, and then he slowed the horse to a dignified walk as he approached Dragus.

"Have they chosen to preserve their lives, or do they prefer to nurture their fields with their own blood?" Dragus inquired.

Lord Barkot waited to reply until he dismounted. He stood before Dragus. "The queen agrees that she and Zarkanis shall submit to your desires, provided that they may be accompanied by two persons—a manservant and a deaf jester who is trained to care for the infant."

Dragus cocked his head, pondering Lord Barkot's statement. "What of their army?"

"Their commanding officer agrees to surrender all weapons other than one sword or axe per man. He does not ask to retain bows, arrows, or spears. And in addition he agrees that we may occupy the palace."

Sinister embers appeared within Dragus's eyes. "How thoughtful," he pronounced with ironic indulgence. "Such an amiable offer merits consideration. I accept the terms." His face hardened. "See that our best archers are stationed at all five castle towers. Post additional archers on the bridges and at all entrances to the city and in the corner watchtowers of the city walls. If any man resists, have him beheaded. Bring the queen to me."

"As you wish, my lord."

Lord Barkot stepped back to his horse and mounted. He was relieved to learn that the terms of occupation were acceptable. It was disconcerting to think of taking Shareen by force—the Sharean warriors were well trained and they fought with courage. He walked his horse down the slope to the grounds below, and then he called for the spear that displayed a green banner. He took up the spear in his own hand. The Shareans were trustworthy people, so he considered it safe to accept the final statement of surrender himself—a sure way to boost his vainglorious reputation. A company of warriors followed behind him.

It was past nightfall when Lord Barkot returned. Late March winds drove clouds across the face of the moon. Dragus and his personal bodyguards were gathered about a campfire when Lord Barkot's horse emerged from the pathway leading to the hilltop. A few tents were raised north of the fire.

Dragus schemed as he sat and waited for Lord Barkot to arrive at the campfire. Taking control of a subjugated city was nothing new for him, but Shareen proffered something different—he was brewing over plans for possessing the most beautiful woman in Gaul, namely Queen Aracia. He was trying to figure out an honorable means of ousting his jealous spouse, Lady Eldra. Lady Eldra was bold and beautiful, but Queen Aracia surpassed her, and the thought of marrying the former wife of King Wildon appealed to Dragus's lustful pride.

Lord Barkot was instructed to dismount and join Dragus for a semiprivate conference. Barnum directed him to have a seat before the fire.

"I trust everything went well," spoke Dragus.

Lord Barkot and Dragus sat across the fire from one another, each crouching forward in a collapsible chair comprised of a wooden frame and wicker seat. Flickering flames fostered darting shadows in the recessed hollows of Dragus's eyes.

"Everything went exactly as you planned, Sire," answered Lord Barkot. "We shall finish procuring weapons at daybreak, and we shall also secure the palace. We have complete control of the city walls, including all guard stations and entrances. Sir Kramsky and his ménage shall be escorted to the palace tomorrow at noon."

Dragus stared without blinking. "Why did you leave the palace unoccupied tonight?"

Lord Barkot stammered uncertainly, "It…ah…well, Sire, the queen insisted that the royal house be given one night to mourn her husband's death, and she said that she preferred preparing for her future life in privacy. She said it would take time to put herself together suitably for presenting herself to the King of Pithrania."

Dragus's firelit image seemed an enchanted statue—an eerie idol absorbing each spoken word like a zombie imbibing blood. His mannerism lent the haunting impression that his soul skulked out and invaded Lord Barkot's mind in order to extract any unspoken parcel of information. There was a hint of frustration at the news that the castle would not be secured until dawn, but his visage melted into a devious smile as Lord Barkot relayed the message from Queen Aracia. "And when shall this future life for the queen begin?"

"They will meet us at the northern gate after daybreak."

Without additional speech, Dragus rose to his feet and stepped south of the fire. His shadow stretched out toward the conquered city. He stood like a reincarnation of Caligula. "Our new province is quite comely, and I hear that my new queen is the most beautiful woman in Gaul. Lord Barkot, see that King Wildon's body is delivered tonight— we want to keep our end of the bargain."

There was a tense pause. Lord Barkot was taken off guard by the mention of a new queen. Lady Eldra was well established as the reigning queen of Pithrania, even though she had only held the position a few months. "Yes, Sire."

"That is all— you are dismissed," asserted Dragus.

Lord Barkot turned to carry out his master's orders.

Chapter 3

Noble Intentions

Zarkanis rolled over in his goose-feather bed and peered at rays of sunlight streaming through the bedroom window. Tiny flecks of dust danced and twirled, coming into view as they entered luminescent beams. He yawned as he stretched his arms and legs. "Araah," he grunted, which was his eight-month-old manner of summoning his mother.

It was the young prince's custom to initiate activity within the palace at the first inkling of dawn. The previous night, however, had been stressful and tiring; so the sun was higher than usual when he awakened. He remembered being roused from sleep by a din of wailing that came from the room below his bedroom floor. There were awful sounds, sounds of grownups crying. He recognized the voices of his mother, her lady-in-waiting, and one of the cooks who fed him oatmeal to supplement his mother's milk. There were other voices too—less familiar voices.

It took a fair amount of time to get back to sleep when the wailing ended. And then a second interruption aroused the sleeping prince, the reverberating sounds of steel clanging against stone. The sounds resonated upward through the floor. Within a few minutes, the sound was repeated, and then it occurred over and over again at ever-increasing intervals. By the time the clamor ceased, he was exhausted. No wonder the dawn grew older than usual before his eyes drew open.

Queen Aracia entered the bedroom and closed the door behind her. She introduced Zarkanis to goats' milk and was pleased to see that he took it readily.

Once his hunger for milk was satiated, Zarkanis began looking for the lady from the kitchen—the lady who fed him cereals and fruit. "I'm going to feed you breakfast this morning, my little prince," said his mother. Zarkanis was pleased. He could not understand all of his mother's words, but he knew that she was providing an extra dose of affection. After eating his fill and being garbed in clean clothes, Zarkanis was placed on a wool rug. His mother sat beside him.

"You're too young to understand me, I know," Aracia spoke as she gazed down into his uplifted face, "but your father and I are leaving you much earlier than we intended." Zarkanis's steel blue eyes delved into the green orbs above him. "I hope that somehow you will remember us and that you will remember that we both love you very, very much." Aracia pulled a ring and necklace from the right pocket of her robe. "This was your father's ring," she said, and then she dropped both the ring and necklace into a doeskin bag at her side. "Your father was a good man and a good king. I pray, my son, that you may someday wear this ring as your father before you, and that you may be as good a man as he."

Zarkanis was quiet. He sensed the austerity of his mother's demeanor. Aracia kissed him on the brow, and then she rose and donned traveling clothes. A long-sleeved leather blouse and leather gloves were garments Zarkanis had never seen worn by his mother before, but the split leather riding skirt and leather boots were familiar. She packed some of his things in the same bag with the necklace and ring. There was nothing packed for herself.

"Come, little Prince, it is time to do what must be done." Aracia lifted Zarkanis in her arms and held him, praying with closed eyes. Then she opened her eyes and picked up the doeskin bag with her left hand while continuing to hold Zarkanis in her right arm, and then she used the same hand to open the bedroom door. Dametrius and Emric turned and faced her as she entered the hallway. She closed the door behind her, knowing that she would never open it again. She stepped to the northern balcony where her two friends were engaged in ardent conversation.

"My queen," began Emric, "the wise tutor and I have been discussing the matter. It is simply not necessary—"

"Please," Queen Aracia interrupted, "I appreciate your loyalty and your concern, but no one else shall have the opportunity that will be mine—and no one else would have to face the fate that is mine if I desist. Our plan is a good one, and we will follow it—all of it."

"My queen," began Dametrius.

"No more," she declared. "We must carry out the plan as devised. You may consider these words to be a direct command from the reigning queen of Shareen. The throne is mine until surrender is complete."

Dametrius was silenced. He found himself reflecting upon the orders he gave Zake the previous day. Now he was the one receiving orders. He understood the reasoning behind the queen's plan, and he respected both her royal office and her noble intention. He could not bring himself to resist further. "Yes, my queen. It shall be as you wish—you can trust me wholly."

Aracia shifted her eyes to Emric.

"I am at your side," stated Emric, dropping his right hand to the hilt of his sword. "I will carry out our plan."

"Good. Now remember, from the moment we leave this balcony, Dametrius will only be referred to by the name we are giving him, Tonan. Also remember that he will act as if he hears nothing, and he will speak no intelligible words." The queen looked long and hard at Dametrius and then at her son and then back at Dametrius. "He takes the goats' milk well. God be with you."

"And with you," returned Dametrius. He wore the winter attire of a court jester.

"Let us do what must be done," stated the queen.

The doeskin bag was given to Dametrius, and then after giving the little prince a final kiss, Aracia lifted Zarkanis into the caregiver's arms. Emric led the way from the palace, followed by the queen. Dametrius and Zarkanis came last. There were Sharean soldiers waiting outside the palace door. The soldiers held the reins to saddled horses. Emric had his own mount, as did the queen. They both mounted. Dametrius and Zarkanis were placed on the king's second horse—a buckskin much like the stallion King Wildon rode to the home of Sir Marticus. There were waving hands, dabbed tears, and farewell bids as Sharean soldiers accompanied the group to the gate in the city's northern wall. Dametrius looked dumbly around him as though he heard nothing, and his facial expression suggested that he had little comprehension of what was transpiring.

Beyond the gate were Pithranians. The little party was escorted northward. Sounds of farewell faded behind. Armed warriors traveled alongside the four captives without speaking, but there were numerous glances at the renowned queen. Now and then the king's spirited buckskin tossed his mane and whinnied, but Dametrius had a way with animals and kept the stallion under control. Zarkanis was all eyes—he always enjoyed outings on horseback. The metal helmets worn by the soldiers glistened in the morning sunlight and elicited vociferations from his infant throat.

Before long, the party reached the edge of the northern hills. A band of Pithranians awaited them, including four of Dragus's bodyguards.

"Welcome. You may dismount and come with me," spoke Diakus. He was the largest of the bodyguards, standing about six and a half feet tall and weighing over three hundred pounds. Emric and Aracia dismounted, and then warriors stepped forward to take custody of the horses. Aracia turned and motioned for Dametrius to follow suit.

Diakus led the way up the hill to Dragus's encampment. The other three bodyguards followed behind the captives. Everyone was on foot. As they climbed higher, they were able to see tents at the back of a clearing where pines served as props. At the foreground of the clearing stood Dragus, Barnum, and another bodyguard; all looking down upon the subjugated city of Shareen. Five additional bodyguards intercepted the group as they topped the hill. Four more bodyguards, all accomplished archers, were positioned along the circumference of the clearing where they could keep a watchful eye on Dragus. Emric's eyes narrowed as he caught sight of the archers.

"The prisoners are here as you directed, Sire," Diakus announced with unmitigated hubris.

Diakus's arrogance was overshadowed as Dragus turned and scrutinized the captives, eyeing each of them with pretentious demure. His eyes roved over Aracia as if she were an Arabian mare and he were a stallion. "No, not *prisoners*...bring my *guests* closer," he crooned.

Aracia turned and faced Dametrius. "Stay," she commanded, drawing attention to the movement of her lips and making obvious gestures with her arms and hands. She then addressed Diakus, speaking loudly enough for Dragus to overhear. "The caregiver and infant may remain. Emric and I will meet with Dragus."

Diakus looked toward Dragus. Dragus nodded his approval. The queen was to be his, whether willingly or unwillingly, but any show of flattery was welcome. Bodyguards walked behind and beside Emric, watching his every move. In addition, Barnum positioned himself between Emric and Dragus where he could intercept any advance that might get past his comrades. Emric wore a single sword, as was allotted to vanquished Sharean males. The queen was permitted to approach Dragus, and Emric followed closely behind, though surrounded by bodyguards.

"I am honored," spoke Dragus, staring upon Aracia as if Emric did not exist.

"The honor is mine," Aracia spoke coolly. "This is my manservant, Emric." Only by turning her head and holding one hand toward Emric did Aracia succeed in loosening Dragus's riveted stare. Emric bowed in feigned deference.

Dragus acknowledged Emric's presence with a brief glance and then readdressed Aracia. "I assure you, my queen, that your safety shall henceforth be a matter that need not trouble your regal mind."

The words *my queen* served to settle Aracia's intentions more surely than anything else Dragus could have spoken. Emric sensed the intensity of Aracia's silence; his heart quickened, and tiny beads of sweat emerged upon his forehead.

"Thank you, King Dragus," replied Aracia. The alluring tone of her voice astonished Emric. She exercised more self-control than any soldier he ever accompanied into battle. "Perhaps we may be granted some privacy."

Emric glimpsed an evil glint in Dragus's eyes. Dragus signaled the nearest bodyguards, including Barnum, to take the queen's manservant and move away. Aracia watched Emric's feet. When he turned and took his first step, she began counting within her mind.

Dragus had never before spoken to Aracia; in fact, he had never even seen her—but he had seen paintings portraying her beauty. He had intended to keep her in the manner one might keep a wild bird or an exotic cat, if such treatment were necessary. But now, in light of her pleasant disposition, he wondered if more amiable arrangements might be in the making. Perhaps the widowed queen's principles were more suitable to his tastes than those of her departed husband. He waited as his bodyguards issued Emric toward woods on the eastern side of the clearing. "They will soon be too far to overhear," he spoke in confidence.

Aracia did not reply. Dametrius held her only son at the edge of the clearing, but she had completed her goodbyes. Her mind focused upon the rhythmic counting that she and Emric had rehearsed time and time again in the great reception room of the palace…eighteen, nineteen, twenty, twenty-one, twenty-two…

Emric shoved Barnum to one side and drew his sword. Within three seconds, four guards surrounded him and drew their own swords. The two nearest archers looked on with little concern—Emric was at great disadvantage. The commotion drew Dragus's attention, and he was shocked to see Emric launch his sword through the air toward Aracia.

"Take heed!" exclaimed Dragus, stepping back to the edge of the cliff. He figured the queen's manservant had gone berserk, attempting to assassinate Queen Aracia. Although Dragus had little time for contemplation, the presumed act of treason pleased him—defection on the part of the queen's manservant suggested that the widowed queen wanted to retain her royal stature even if it meant defaming her former husband by submitting to her husband's murderer. These thoughts raced through his mind during the same brief moments that Aracia took a stride in the direction of the flying sword and then caught it in midair. She turned fiery green eyes upon the King of Pithrania and raised the sword above her head, stepping forward with the hilt of the sword grasped in both hands. A demon banshee could not have stricken more fear through the heart of Dragus than the look in the noble queen's eyes.

"No!" Dragus shrieked. With the cliff behind him and an angel of death before him, the dark lord crumbled in a fit of terror, dropping to his knees and lifting both arms. Archers on either side of the clearing reached for arrows. Aracia's leather-clad hands brought a sharpened blade crashing downward with determined force. Bloodcurdling screams erupted as the blade lodged itself through the bones of Dragus's right wrist and his torso slammed back against the ground. The back of his head abutted the upper edge of the cliff.

Aracia planted a foot against the ground and pulled backward in an attempt to withdraw the sword. The sword's steel blade was wedged deep in bone. An arrow zipped from the east side of the clearing and pierced her right side, driving through her lung and into her heart. Another arrow tore through her back. She leaned forward against the sword. Dragus's wrist was sliced clean through as her body collapsed upon him; and his severed hand fell to the ground like a stunned spider.

Spellbound moments of silence arrested the entire group of onlookers. Dragus jolted to an upright position, sitting and staring wide-eyed as blood gushed from the amputated stub of his wrist. Aracia's body dropped to his side. "My physician!" he yelled. "Summon my physician!"

Emric felt hands fall upon his shoulders as he sought to approach the slain body of his queen. There could be no doubt that the arrows protruding from her body were fatal. The archer who released the first arrow called down the eastern slope for Piardro, Dragus's physician. Piardro was a Grecian-trained surgeon, and he was quartered with menial servants in an encampment at the foot of the hill. Dametrius continued playing his role, standing at the edge of the clearing where a single bodyguard watched over him and Zarkanis. The infant in his arms remained silent; his wide blue eyes were fixed upon the tragic scene before him. *Look well and remember, little one*, Dametrius thought.

Diakus and two of his companions dragged Emric before Dragus. Dragus pressed his left palm against the stub of his right wrist to curb the bleeding.

"What of this assassin?" asked Diakus.

Dragus jerked himself to a standing position and kicked Aracia's body over the edge of the seventy-foot cliff that comprised the southern side of the hill. "Let him join his queen."

Emric faced Dragus. There was no hint of fear in his eyes, and his voice did not falter as he spoke words that would haunt Dragus forever—"Her body has fallen, but her soul rises to heaven while your severed hand sinks to the infernal pits of hell before you."

Dragus shrank away from Emric's eyes. "Now! Do it now!"

Emric fought for several seconds before the three bodyguards managed to push him over the cliff's edge. He voiced no cry during his fall—a fact that riled Dragus. Dragus thought of retrieving the fallen bodies and launching them over the walls of Shareen, but such thoughts were interrupted by Piardro's arrival.

"You are bleeding profusely, my king. The loss of blood must be stopped," Piardro proclaimed. He recognized his dependency upon Dragus, just like the close-knit group of bodyguards, but there was no man Piardro considered his superior. Dragus had the tendency of enlisting the vainest of men to his service. "I'll heat the cauterizing iron and return. Keep pressure on the stub of your wrist."

Dragus grew pale and dropped back to his knees. "Not without strong wine." He turned his face toward the nearest bodyguard. "Barnum, my wineskin—bring it quickly."

Zarkanis emerged from statuesque surveillance and cried. Dametrius wondered to what degree the prince's mind perceived the dreadful circumstances. Dametrius was directed to sit down, and supplies were issued upward from a bag on his horse. Included with the supplies were silk scarves and a corked gourd filled with goats' milk. Fortunately for Dametrius's plans, he soon had Zarkanis sucking milk from a silk scarf. He needed to gain acceptance as a capable caregiver.

Dragus gulped down fermented wine and stared toward Dametrius and Zarkanis. After several minutes Piardro returned. Despite the wine, Dragus screamed as Piardro cauterized his severed wrist. It was a sullen king who began the victorious journey back to Pithrania. His plans for Zarkanis were exactly what Dametrius predicted, so the young prince's life was spared. No mention was made of the queen's fallen body.

Dametrius and Zarkanis rode upon the same buckskin as before. This would not have occurred if Dragus had known that the captured prince was mounted upon a king's horse. The two of them were included in a party of soldiers preceding Dragus and his bodyguards. Dragus chose not to lead the procession in case of an ambush; but with Shareen subdued, there was little chance that any power in northern Gaul would confront him. Meanwhile, Dametrius was treated just as he behaved, as a simple and obedient idiot. The name Tonan was sometimes spoken as guards issued simple directions, but Dametrius pretended to not perceive any verbal cues. He only responded when hand-signals were executed before his eyes.

As the day wore on, Dragus's drunkenness diminished—though he still imbibed adequate boosters of fermented drink to dull the pain in his severed wrist. By early evening he was reflecting upon the hero's welcome he would receive in Pithrania, and he was contemplating his undisputed supremacy as emperor of Gaul. The loss of his right hand was unfortunate, but he was left-handed, and he fancied that many of the greatest military leaders throughout history were maimed in war. It was with his customary arrogance that he ordered encampment before nightfall.

Due to the pace of foot soldiers, the journey from Shareen to Pithrania required three days' travel. Therefore, the army would camp twice before reaching the gray stone castle that loomed at the base of Mount Thrandor—the stronghold of the Pithranian hierarchy. Dragus directed two of his bodyguards to watch over Zarkanis and Dametrius as camp was set up the first night. He was determined to prevent anyone from kidnapping or killing the heir to the Sharean throne—he would imprison the prince and thereby guarantee that no new king would arise in Shareen to challenge Pithranian domination. The march to Pithrania resumed the following morning.

The course of events encouraged Dametrius. He was with Zarkanis, and Dragus gave no indication that he suspected any sort of trickery. These circumstances made it improbable that anything remarkable would happen during the journey, but, to the contrary, something exceptional transpired after camp was set up the second evening. Dragus's party was situated on the side of a hill, with Dametrius and Zarkanis assigned to a tent where Dragus could keep an eye on them. Just when the business of the day was drawing to an end, and just as the sun was dipping into the edge of the western horizon, a Pithranian officer was escorted into Dragus's presence.

"What is it?" Dragus demanded. He stood facing the officer. Dametrius was sitting outside the small tent provided for him and Zarkanis. He was feeding Zarkanis cows' milk obtained from a nearby farm, and Zarkanis seemed to savor cows' milk as well as goats' milk.

"It regards a matter on which I felt you would want to—"

"What matter?" demanded Dragus.

The officer swallowed nervously. He hoped that what he had to say would warrant the act of imposing upon the king's privacy. "It seems, Sire, that a woman has birthed a remarkable child that was fathered by Lord Gardgeon, who as you know was killed. If you remember, Lord Gardgeon—"

"Lord Gardgeon?" interjected Dragus. His countenance transformed from a look of annoyance to one of interest. He was fully aware that Lord Gardgeon had fallen during an attack against a Sharean patrol—an unsuccessful attack that took place seven months earlier. Dragus did not regret Lord Gardgeon's death. Lord Gardgeon was one of the better field officers in the Pithranian forces, but his wife was beautiful, wicked, and ambitious, and she had succeeded in seducing Dragus. At the time of Lord Gardgeon's death, she possessed a one-year-old child whom both she and Dragus knew was Dragus's son. Thus, it was only two weeks after Lord Gardgeon's death that Dragus married Lord Gardgeon's widow, Lady Eldra—the reigning queen of Pithrania.

"That is correct, Lord Gardgeon," confirmed the officer.

"I know all about Lord Gardgeon," remarked Dragus. "Now, tell me about this woman."

The officer was obviously encouraged by Dragus's show of interest. He took a small step forward and resumed speaking. "The woman claims that the man who fathered her child did not give permission for her to tell anyone his name. We figured this would make sense if the man's wife were the type that might do something hurtful."

"Hurtful?" inquired Dragus, again interrupting.

"Yes, well, some women might be capable of inflicting injury over a secret mistress."

Dragus raised no objection to the officer's remark. There was not a wife in all of Gaul more capable of bloody murder than Lady Eldra. Her temperament prompted him to keep bodyguards posted outside his bedroom throughout nights that he slept in the castle, and there were no weapons of any sort permitted within the walls of his bedroom. Such precautions were niggling, but they permitted uninhibited indulgences with a woman who was both gorgeous and vain.

"Go on," directed Dragus, now intrigued with what the officer had to say.

"Well, one of the warriors in my company happened to mention that the best captain he ever served under had a big scar across his forehead, just as he himself does, so he figured the scar on his own forehead must be a sign that he will someday be a captain. And, well, the warriors listening to him all knew that he was talking about Lord Gardgeon."

The officer paused and looked for a response from Dragus. Dragus did not reply; he just glared.

"Well," continued the officer, "after that was said, another warrior laughed and pointed out that the captain with the scar on his forehead was killed by Sharean soldiers in a battle last summer. He said that he was glad he did not have any such scar on his forehead—a sign that he would soon be dead. And when the woman heard this..."

"She heard this?"

"Yes, Sire. They just happened to be sitting and talking near the woman's tent, and..."

"Very well," interrupted Dragus, "so the woman heard. What happened next?"

"Well, after hearing that the captain with a scar on his forehead had been killed, the woman let out a hideous howl and ran over to the warrior who had just mentioned it, and she demanded that he describe the captain."

"And then?"

"Well, Sire, the warrior began describing Lord Gardgeon, mentioning how tall he was, how he dressed, the color of his hair...and then all of a sudden the woman clutched the warrior by his shirt and asked if the slain captain had blue eyes."

Dragus's eyebrows shifted upward. He was well aware that Lord Gardgeon had striking eyes. "If I remember correctly, Lord Gardgeon did have bluish eyes."

"Yes, Sire, and when the warrior answered the woman and told her that Lord Gardgeon's eyes were blue, which was the first time he had mentioned Lord Gardgeon's name, well, she fell to weeping and wailing again. She collapsed to the ground in a fit of sobbing, clinging to the foot soldier's pant leg until we dragged her back to her tent. And when we reached the tent, her infant was crying. So the woman picked up her infant, and they both settled down a bit, and then we managed to get some more information out of her. It seems that she's no longer interested in traveling to Pithrania since she does not expect anyone there to provide for her and her infant, given that the infant's father is dead, namely Lord Gardgeon. I thought you might be interested in knowing about this, so we ordered her to stay put and tend to the infant while I informed you that Lord Gardgeon fathered her child."

Dragus's lips drew into a sardonic smile. "Are you certain that the warrior had not already mentioned that Lord Gardgeon had blue eyes prior to the woman's asking if they were blue?"

"Yes, Sire. And besides that, Sire, I had already found out that the infant's father wore a golden helmet with three rubies."

"Really? And did you mention the three rubies first, or did she?"

"Oh, she did, Sire."

Dragus could not hold back a decadent utterance of spiteful indulgence, though his words were not intelligible to anyone who overheard him. His relationship with his queen was such that he relished tormenting as well as ravishing her, and the fact that her late husband had apparently bred an illegitimate child would provide ample fuel for taunting. "Hum, most interesting. Bring this woman and her child to me."

"Yes, Lord Dragus," the officer acquiesced, congratulating himself upon reckoning that the matter would interest the king. He turned and walked several paces toward the foot of the hill, and then he stopped and called to a warrior standing twenty yards beyond him, "Bring the woman and child."

Since Tonan was thought to be deaf and mute, Dametrius had to guard against any show of intelligent awareness of matters that he happened to overhear, but that did not keep him from listening. The discussion between the Pithranian officer and Dragus took place less than twenty feet in front of him, and his ears attuned themselves to every word. He was captivated by the fact that Dragus demonstrated intense curiosity regarding an illegitimate child—it suggested some sort of personal involvement. Zarkanis finished taking his fill of cows' milk, and Dametrius lifted Zarkanis to his shoulder for customary burping. Had timing been different, Zarkanis may have experienced his first glimpse of Colesia. As it was, however, his back was to the clearing when a young warrior entered the camp escorting an amber-haired woman who carried a newborn child.

No one witnessed the look of surprise that swept Dametrius's face when Giralda appeared. Dametrius knew this woman for who she was—a Sharean midwife. He remembered seeing her only a few days back, and she had been much too slender to be in late pregnancy. Zake's description of his newborn sister played in Dametrius's mind as he gazed upon the infant in the woman's arms. The setting sun cast rays upon the infant's crown and highlighted a golden lock. The baby, it only made sense, was none other than Colesia, Zake's sister, the daughter of Sir Marticus and Lady Monica. Giralda did not look at him, and even if she had looked, she would not have recognized him, for he had always moved about Shareen with a gray hood shrouding his face, and he had never spoken to her.

Dragus motioned for the woman and child to be brought before him. Though the woman was unarmed and held an infant, Barnum stood close to Dragus's side, and two other bodyguards escorted the woman and child. Giralda acted the part of a proud, bereaved mistress. She cast defensive glances at the bodyguards. When she arrived before Dragus, she looked into his eyes, but then she cast her gaze downward. Cold shudders swept through her spine. She had never seen such eyes— demonic, charring coals.

A smile formed upon Dragus's face. He even laughed. Giralda positioned herself so that the infant's exquisite features and wondrous lock of golden hair were in plain view. The evil king's laughter puzzled her. She was unaware that Lord Gardgeon was the Pithranian queen's former husband. Ominous eyes gleamed as they perused Colesia's beauty. "This is your child?" inquired Dragus.

Giralda pulled Colesia against her bosom. "Her father has been slain. She is my family. He was a great man, and I have no doubt that he would have cared well for her. But I am a strong woman. We will survive."

Giralda's mind raced in anticipation of questions Dragus would pose next. It had been a fortunate surprise to learn that Lord Gardgeon had blue eyes. She was also pleased to learn that Lord Gardgeon had dark hair—lending further support to her insinuations that he was Colesia's father. She had been closely guarded along the journey to Pithrania, and it seemed unlikely that she would be able to escape. There were two Pithranian captains traveling with the forces that attacked Shareen, and she had denied that either of them fathered Colesia. She was dreading the prospect of meeting the other two captains; and therefore, being able to lead the Pithranians to believe that Colesia was fathered by a deceased captain was much in her favor.

"The infant is a female?"

"Yes."

Giralda's answer accentuated Dragus's smile.

"Well then, let's have a look at her."

Giralda felt as if she were surrendering a helpless fawn to a rabid carnivore. Dragus grasped Colesia, cradling her in his left hand and forearm and lifting her to his face. He examined her eyes, and then he stared hard at her hair as he stroked her golden lock with the cuff that covered the stub of his right wrist. "Most impressive," he commented, and then he handed her back to Giralda. He straightened and faced Giralda with a look of inquisition.

"And where, may I ask, did you and Lord Gardgeon meet with one another?"

The woman standing before Dragus reacted as one would expect. Her eyes squinted in a defensive glare befitting an adulteress under interrogation. She stared down at Dragus's feet. "The child's father was a virtuous man. I would prefer, by your mercies, to decline answering that question. But I was born and raised in the village of Marne."

"Of course, and where was your cottage?"

"North of Marne."

"I see," remarked Dragus. "Your cottage must have sat under the shadow of the two ragged hills."

Giralda had suffered much during her youth, but the tragic dichotomy of her life now proffered an advantage. "You must be referring to the three ragged hills," she corrected Dragus. "Several dwellings align the bank of a stream within the shadow of those hills."

Dragus's face sobered with satisfaction. Very few persons outside the village of Marne knew that a clandestine band of prostitutes subsisted in cottages along a stream north of the village; that is, very few persons other than members of the Pithranian military regiment. The ill-fated women who inhabited those cottages were largely supported by Pithranian officers. Dragus was most pleased to deduce that Lord Gardgeon was no more faithful to his wife than she had been to her husband. He could hardly wait to see the look on his queen's face when she discovered that her late husband left a beautiful addition to the royal household—for he saw definite possibilities in the physically endowed infant before him.

"That is enough," declared Dragus. He turned his face toward the officer who first brought the woman and infant to his attention. "Sir Wixton, I congratulate you; a promotion shall be in order. I place this woman and her child under your personal protection. They shall be delivered to Master Edmond with the instruction to see that all of their needs are taken care of, and they shall be housed in the royal tower. This woman shall be allowed all the privileges of a royal lady-in-waiting, and she shall raise the child as a Pithranian princess. Henceforth the child shall be addressed as Princess Vayle."

Dragus turned his gaze upon Giralda. "The child need never know her unfortunate origin. If you are willing to keep that origin a secret, you may raise her and care for her, serving as her assigned lady-in-waiting. On the other hand, if disclose the fact that you are Princess Vayle's mother, I will be forced to banish or execute you. Do you understand?"

Giralda, who had merely hoped that Colesia's life would be spared, was struck dumb by Dragus's words—just as dumb as Dametrius pretended to be as he peered at them while holding Zarkanis. Her eyes were still cast downward. New thoughts raced through her mind... Would she still try to escape? If she did not flee, would she be able to train and raise the daughter of Sir Marticus under the nose of his foremost enemy? What kind of fate would she face as a lady-in-waiting in Dragus's castle? Would anyone ever know who the child was? She collected her wits and nodded before Dragus.

Dragus turned and strode back to his tent. Sir Wixton grasped Giralda by the arm. "You are a fortunate woman. Let us return to our tents."

Giralda permitted Sir Wixton to lead her away from Dragus's quarters. She followed him back to a central campsite where she and Colesia were given their own tent among the officers. As word passed throughout the camp concerning what had transpired, a perceptible change took place—Giralda and Colesia were, indeed, treated as royalty. Giralda had just finished feeding Colesia and was tucking her in a blanket when someone called to her from outside the flap that hung over the entrance to her tent.

"Who is it?" asked Giralda. A blonde-haired officer with his helmet removed pulled back the flap. Soft rays of moonlight entered the interior. "For you," he said, placing a bowl of preserved strawberries at her feet. His eyes strained for a glimpse of the proclaimed princess. "Sir Wixton thought some dried fruit might improve the quality of your milk, for the princess."

"Thank you."

The officer withdrew and closed the flap. Giralda ate the berries and lay down beside the sleeping princess—Princess Vayle. Though her body relaxed, her mind remained active. She pondered all that had happened since the attack on Colesia's family, and she contemplated the words spoken by Dragus. It was hours past midnight before she decided to embrace the role of lady-in-waiting. As personal guardian, she would have the opportunity to educate Colesia in a proper manner—hopefully without Dragus's ever finding out—and it made sense that Colesia would be no safer anywhere in Dragus's domain than within the fortified walls of his castle. Rays of moonlight pierced through imperfections in the goatskin tent and danced upon the golden lock in Colesia's hair.

"Sleep well, my little princess," whispered the newly acclaimed lady-in-waiting.

Back in Dragus's camp, Dametrius also passed much of the night contemplating the future. It was most remarkable that the daughter of Dragus's archenemy would be housed in the royal tower of the Pithranian castle. He knew enough about Giralda to presume that she would inform Colesia of her true identity; that is, she would do so when the child reached an appropriate age for being trusted with such dangerous information. He also knew that Giralda would be aware that Sir Marticus's daughter was promised in marriage to Prince Zarkanis. He turned his attention to Zarkanis and gazed upon the prince's sleeping face. His thoughts ranged from teaching the prince the difference between right and wrong to properly communicating theories of metaphysics and biometrics. He fancied that perhaps, someday, a Sharean prince and a Pithranian princess would be joined in the matrimony their parents intended. He prayed more fervently than ever that Dragus would imprison him with Zarkanis.

Chapter 4

Solitary Endowment

Z arkanis stared from place to place as dungeon guards led Dametrius down dank recesses beneath the castle of Pithrania. Dametrius cradled the young prince against his chest with the prince's head raised above his left shoulder; and while being held in this position, Zarkanis had a good view of the surroundings. The ceiling, comprised of great cedar planks, stretched onward like the roof of a cave. The walls and floor were limestone slabs fit together with mortar. There were three guards escorting Dametrius and Zarkanis, one carrying a torch in the lead, another carrying a torch in the rear, and a third without a torch who followed directly behind Dametrius and prodded him onward.

The corridor coursed eastward. Odorous compartments aligned both sides of the passageway, each with a heavy wooden door. The cell doors

68

had small openings where food trays could be passed in and out. Barred windows in the outer walls of the southern compartments permitted inklings of daylight to permeate a virtual grotto between the rows of cells. There were large lanterns in the corridor and smaller lanterns in some of the cells, but most of them were unlit. It was late afternoon, three days following the fall of Shareen.

Fewer captives inhabited the dungeon than Dametrius expected. It seemed evident that Dragus executed more captives than he imprisoned. Among the few inmates were Prince Ewando of Aquari and Prince Lanier of Danvurst. Aquari and Danvurst both held similar customs to Shareen, and there was little chance that kings would rise to challenge Dragus in those cities so long as the rightful heirs to the thrones were detained in the Pithranian dungeon. As Dametrius and his guards continued walking, the rows of prison cells ended and the corridor narrowed. Darkness thickened. The only visible light came from the torches carried by the guards.

Dametrius was directed onward, but only two of the guards advanced with him, one leading and one following. Both guards carried torches. The lead guard withdrew a key, unlocked a solid door, and heaved the door ajar. They passed through the doorway and continued onward, coursing through a dank, secluded tunnel until they came to another solid door. Again the lead guard inserted the key, unlocked the door, and shoved it open.

The castle of Pithrania was constructed in the side of a rugged mountain, Mount Thrandor. The mountain was presumably named after a Viking king who established Pithrania centuries before, and Dragus boasted that he was a direct descendent of King Thrandor. The castle was built by King Braham, a harsh dictator who rose to power some fifty years earlier. King Braham ruled the realm northwest of Shareen for over thirty years. Toward the end of his reign, King Braham fell to madness, and Dragus replaced him. Dragus promised fairness and freedom to all Pithranians, but in time his entire kingdom was cowed into subservience. During the tenth year of his reign, a year renowned for savagery and conquest, he proclaimed himself supreme emperor of Gaul. Nonetheless, an additional year would pass before he dared to attack the solitary city in Gaul that did not yield to his jurisdiction—the kingdom of Shareen.

A picturesque lake lay east of the Pithranian castle. This lake, Lake Manassa, was deep and blue, fed by underwater springs. At the southeast corner of the castle, the lake released excess waters to form the source of the Requain River. The Requain River flowed beside the south wall of the castle and served as a natural moat. Cliffs rose north of the castle, topped with jagged rocks and indented by deep crevices, making it impossible for an army to approach from the north. After coursing thirty feet past the castle, the Requain River poured over the upper lip of a cliff and plunged twenty feet downward as the Requain Falls. Seventy feet west of the Requain Falls stretched a wooden bridge linking the northern and southern shores of the Requain River.

A second, smaller waterway flowed westward from Lake Manassa and passed beneath the castle. After passing beneath the castle it curved southward and joined the Requain River. This smaller waterway divided into three channels before it reached the castle's eastern wall— a northern channel that provided drinking and bathing water; a center channel for sewage; and a southern channel that served the dungeon for both drinking water and for sewage. Such configuration of the smaller waterway resulted in isolated patches of ground on the east and west sides of the castle—patches of ground surrounded by water except where the patches adjoined the castle walls.

Above the point where the smaller waterway's southern channel passed beneath the eastern wall, there sat a lone prison cell. King Braham ordered the construction of this cell for a single purpose—to reprimand members of the royal household. He called this cell the *chamber of chastisement*. Incarceration within this chamber was supposed to encourage reflective repentance. In some ways it was not as brutal as the common prison cells, being much larger and providing a beautiful view of the outside world through an eastern window, but it was dreadfully isolated. One who was imprisoned within the chamber of chastisement could not communicate with anyone, not even with other prisoners.

After the second door opened, Dametrius again followed his guide down a narrow passageway. It was only after a third door was unlocked and opened that a room appeared—the chamber of chastisement. Dametrius was no fool. He deduced that he and Zarkanis were being placed in solitary confinement. This wrought a surreptitious smile, for he knew that solitary confinement would serve his purposes well. The guards fixed their torches in notches in the wall, and then Dametrius followed the lead guard into the room.

A barred window was situated in the far wall. Dametrius was pleased to see that the room had decent natural light. The room was larger than he expected, twenty feet from north to south, and fifteen feet from east to west. The gray stone wall that framed the window was a foot in breadth, and the window's iron bars were thicker than a man's thumb.

The second guard unfastened two goatskin bottles from his belt. The bottles were filled with milk. He presented these to Dametrius and pointed to the child in Dametrius's arms. Dametrius nodded and sat down beneath the window, leaning back against the eastern wall. He withdrew a silk scarf from a pocket in his outfit and began feeding Zarkanis. The guards watched for a while and then faced one another.

"Well then Grehg, what now?" asked Duardo, the guard who gave Dametrius the goatskin bottles.

Grehg broke eye contact and stepped toward the captives. He tapped Dametrius on the arm and pointed to an oak bucket sitting upright beside a hole in the stone floor. The hole was situated near the northeast corner of the cell. Once he had Dametrius's attention, he demonstrated how water was withdrawn from the canal beneath the cell.

The bucket was rigged with a chain handle that was looped through opposing holes near the bucket's rim. Strands of wire were wrapped around wooden slats comprising its sides. A twine rope about ten feet long was tied to the chain handle. Dametrius noted all of these components with interest. A splash sounded after half the rope dropped through the hole, indicating that the surface of water was five feet below the upper surface of the floor.

After hauling a bucketful of water up into the cell, the guard toted the bucket to Dametrius and demonstrated that the water was fit for drinking—something he would not have done at the western end of the dungeon due to sewage contamination. Dametrius made various gestures with his lips and forehead to indicate cognizance of the guard's directions. He maintained an expression of worry and concern but still portrayed composure. It was important to keep the guards from suspecting that he was happy with the circumstances of his imprisonment, yet he needed to convince them that he was capable of keeping Zarkanis alive. The guard seemed satisfied with Dametrius's performance.

The only object in the cell besides the bucket was a huge, rectangular stone with a flat surface—a limestone bed. It lay adjacent to the southern wall. A rough cedar ceiling was dimly visible twelve feet above the floor. The height of the ceiling surprised Dametrius, especially since the passageway leading to the cell was no more than seven feet high. The two guards were just about to exit through the doorway when approaching footsteps halted them. A third guard entered carrying four wool blankets.

"Wilken," spoke the guard who showed Dametrius how to draw water, "what are you doing?"

"Following orders—Bruxtas handed me the blankets himself."

Bruxtas was chief prison guard. Grehg, the guard interrogating Wilken, had never known Bruxtas to issue more than two wool blankets to a cell, even during winter. He stepped to Wilken and counted the blankets.

"Bruxtas ordered four blankets delivered to this cell?" queried Grehg.

"The order came from higher up—from Dragus himself," declared Wilken. "He wants this infant to have ample provisions."

"In a prison cell?"

"Well, at least he wants to keep the tot from dying. And that's not all."—Wilken pointed back to the passageway—"Commencing at dawn tomorrow, any man who speaks a word beyond the first door to this tunnel forfeits his tongue—it will be cut out and fed to the dogs. I will post a sign on the first door."

Grehg cast a puzzled look at Dametrius and Zarkanis, and then comprehension swept his face. He looked back toward Wilken. "He doesn't want the tot to learn how to talk."

"That must be," concurred Wilken. "All three doorways are to be kept closed except when food is delivered; and even then, each door is to be opened and closed separately—no two doors are to be open at the same time."

"If it's me delivering food, then I'll want a torch," remarked Grehg. "I don't want some rat biting my ankle in a pitch-black snake pit."

Wilken ignored Grehg's remark and continued his exhortation. "Each day's supply of food is to be delivered one hour after sunrise. And other than that, no one is to enter the tunnel. And one more thing—

Dragus does not want the name *Zarkanis* spoken after today. The Sharean prince is to be referred to as *the Captive from Shareen*."

Grehg started to say something, but then caught himself. He motioned with his head for Wilken and Duardo to follow him back up the passageway. The thought of having his tongue hacked out dissolved all desire for further conversation within the isolated cell—he would not speak again until he reached the opposite side of the first door to the passageway. Wilken and Duardo were also disinclined to speak. Three heavy doors, all built of iron and walnut, were closed and locked as the three guards secured *Tonan* and *the Captive from Shareen* within a cell of silence.

The first two doors leading to the cell were solid from top to bottom, built to squelch all sounds from reaching the chamber of chastisement. The door that opened into the cell had a rectangular hole near its bottom edge. This hole could be used for sliding plates of food into the cell. Stillness followed the departure of the guards. Sounds made by Zarkanis sucking goats' milk from a silk scarf were louder than all else.

After taking his fill of milk, Zarkanis was ready for sleep. Dametrius tucked him inside one of the woolen blankets. He rose and walked to the window in the eastern wall. Beyond the crude bars lay a scene of enchantment. The craggy foot of Mount Thrandor nestled conifer-laden toes along the northeastern shoreline of Lake Manassa, and the lake itself presented an image of grandeur.

Looking south, Dametrius scrutinized the architecture of a soaring tower. It had a rounded exterior protruding twenty feet farther east than the primary castle wall. Several small windows bedecked its surface, revealing that the tower was five stories high. Three balconies were visible. The largest and highest balcony, extending from the fifth story, was elegant, with Corinthian balusters connecting a seamless railing to a smooth base. The balcony was composed of white marble, and was situated so that one could stand at its balustrade and behold the glorious sights of nature as if standing at the edge of a mountain cliff.

A distant cart drawn by oxen drew Dametrius's attention. It approached along a roadway south of the lake. Beyond the roadway were fenced pastures and fields of grain. Dametrius watched until the cart passed from view, and then a grateful sigh concluded his circumspection of the world outside the cell window. There was much within eyesight that a teacher could expound upon while tutoring a child.

One of the wool blankets served as Dametrius's bed. He wedged the bucket sideways in the well opening, just in case Zarkanis crawled from his makeshift cocoon and explored the cell floor without awakening him. The well opening was small enough to prevent an adult from squeezing through, but a small child was a different matter. Nightfall was approaching, and three days on horseback left Dametrius sore and tired. He cuddled up in his blanket beside Zarkanis with the intention of sleeping, but then he found himself lying awake and thinking.

Dametrius's plans regarding Zarkanis had focused upon achieving shared imprisonment. That was now accomplished; and in fact, it was accomplished with better circumstances than Dametrius imagined. Being cut off from Pithranian guards and fellow prisoners was ideal for maintaining his guise as a deaf mute. But now his mind deliberated the next task—that of raising a fit and capable king. He peered through the darkness toward the sleeping prince. It was hours later before he finally succumbed to sleep.

For several days Dametrius maintained silence. He continued to peruse the world outside the cell window. The triangular patch of land below the window was so inaccessible that no one ever set foot upon it. He figured that unless he yelled to someone through the bars in the cell window, no one in the outer world had any chance of hearing him. The door to the cell opened an hour after sunrise, and it never opened otherwise.

The goats' milk was fresh each morning. Although Dametrius continued finding time to gaze out the window while Zarkanis napped, he generally stayed busy—feeding Zarkanis, caring for Zarkanis, and inventing games to play with Zarkanis. A large pan of food accompanied the goats' milk—a heap of bread, meat, fruit, and vegetables. Dametrius surmised that his meals consisted of leftovers gleaned from royal tables. Though he ate his fill, much of the food got dumped into the channel below. Fish swarmed to the surface for whatever morsels of food were discarded. The well opening was close enough to the eastern castle wall to permit sunlight to penetrate the channel waters and provide a view of aquatic creatures, and this was especially true at daybreak.

After several days of silence, Dametrius decided to begin speaking out loud, although he still maintained silence between sunrise and the delivery of rations. A medieval painter would have relished the opportunity of portraying the renowned scholar engaged in verbal exchange with an infant less than a year old. The garments of a jester made Dametrius look much less mysterious than he appeared in his long, gray robe; but the same vibrant eyes captured and engrossed the inquisitive mind of his pupil. During his toddler years, Zarkanis tumbled and stretched on wool blankets; finger-painted in moistened dust; learned to recite rhyming poems and lullabies; and received lessons in singing as well as lessons in making various animal sounds and bird calls. He learned the alphabets of several languages and was instructed in the proper etiquette for courtly conduct. Little wonder, then, that Zarkanis was engaging in sophisticated conversation by five years of age.

The prison guards never discovered that Zarkanis could talk. The clopping of boots and the creaking of iron hinges warned of their approach each morning. It was helpful that the guards never spoke—that way Zarkanis was not prompted to respond to their speech.

Dametrius always grabbed hold of Zarkanis and positioned one hand near the child's mouth when food was delivered. He staged this practice as a manner of being protective. The guards considered such actions natural, like a caged bear protecting a cub. They did not esteem Dametrius, whom they knew as Tonan, to be more intelligent than a confined animal. Dametrius taught Zarkanis over and over again that he must never speak in front of the guards, but he determined never to leave Zarkanis out of his grasp when the guards approached—at least not before Zarkanis reached seven years of age. It was his understanding that children were not capable of assuming serious responsibilities before age seven.

As Zarkanis grew, a formal schedule developed—eight hours a day of teaching and mental games, three hours of physical exercise and play, four regular meals followed by naps, and nine hours of sleep each night. This rigorous schedule demarcated the lifestyle Zarkanis experienced between ages two and five. By six years of age, Zarkanis possessed an elementary grasp of mathematics, botany, natural philosophy, biology, alchemy, geology, history, geography, and astronomy, plus an extensive vocabulary and flawless diction. He also attained the ability to climb the prison wall and secure a position on the stone ledge of the window. And in addition to mental and physical training, Dametrius encouraged Zarkanis to develop in spirit and character. He aimed to manufacture a king who was not only intelligent but also respectable. Zarkanis matured far beyond his years.

After reaching age five, Zarkanis expressed the opinion that naps were a waste of valuable time—time that could be employed in studies. Intellectual exchange, he felt, would not interfere with digestive processes—especially not if he and his teacher reclined on their blankets while conversing. Dametrius could not help but smile and concede. Never had his life been more enjoyable than in confinement with such an exuberant and inquisitive student. There began to occur nights during which Zarkanis got by with only eight hours of sleep.

It was shortly past Zarkanis's fifth birthday when he confronted Dametrius with a thought-provoking question. It came just as Zarkanis finished drawing a partially filled bucket of water from the canal.

"Do you suppose I might learn to swim like the fish that eat bread crumbs off the surface of the water? I have seen Colesia's guardian permitting Colesia to swim in the southern cove of Lake Manassa. I have seen them several times when I was looking out the window while you were napping."

Under Dametrius's tutelage, Zarkanis had learned that Colesia was a girl who had been promised as his bride—though this fact did not occupy so much of his reverie at five years of age as it would later. One thing that did occupy his thoughts, however, was the prospect of playing in the waters of Lake Manassa. Within the confining walls of his simple home, he learned to engage a vivid imagination. Little wonder, then, that he came to realize the possibilities presented by the well opening through which he and Dametrius obtained water—a well opening large enough to permit the passage of his body—and he did so without Dametrius proffering a word of suggestion.

Dametrius gazed at his enthusiastic student. He was well aware that Zarkanis's lithe body could slip through the circular hole that coursed through two feet of solid stone and adjoined the free air of the outside world. He had considered the possibility of Zarkanis escaping through this outlet, but such an escape would need to be delayed until Zarkanis was more mature—perhaps nine or ten—depending upon the growth rate of the prince's body and his sustained ability to fit through the hole, and depending upon Dametrius's assessment of the prince's ability to escape and survive.

"Well," returned Dametrius, looking worried.

"I know that I must not be discovered," coaxed Zarkanis, his eyes beaming with boyish zeal, "but you have taught me that a prince must develop every conceivable talent to best serve the causes of truth and justice."

Dametrius contemplated an appropriate response with mixed emotions. He considered swimming an important skill, but would it be worth the risk?

Zarkanis sensed that his tutor was softening. "If the princess, a girl, is taught the art of swimming, then should a prince be lacking in such accomplishment?" he argued. "I observed her behaving like a swan, venturing so far from shore that her guardian beckoned her return."

Such a beseeching look mounted the prince's face that Dametrius could not help but laugh. "You must have the eyes of an eagle to recognize Colesia swimming in the southern cove," he mused. He faced Zarkanis, but before approving his student's request, he forced himself to assume a stern and authoritative expression. "This will be the most dangerous undertaking we have ever attempted. Not only must you avoid drowning in water deeper than your height, you must also avoid detection."

****

Much more slowly than usual, or so it seemed to Zarkanis, the sun completed its journey behind the western wall of the castle. The moon appeared and edged upward above the eastern horizon. At long last Dametrius averred the presence of nightfall. Frogs, snails, snakes, salamanders, and fish of every description crawled, hopped, and darted within Zarkanis's imagination. He was anxious to enter their world.

The rope was removed from the bucket handle and tied around Zarkanis's chest. He wore a loincloth and undergarment fashioned from wool, silk, and doeskin—materials that were present within the cell during his infancy. This sophisticated article of clothing, sewn together as one piece, was hidden from the guards who served food—it was concealed beneath a bulky outer robe fashioned from a wool blanket with a hole cut in its center. One of the few items Dametrius had toted into the cell besides infant clothing was a small razor used for shaving. With this instrument he sliced a hole in the center of one of the blankets that Wilken delivered on the day that he and Zarkanis were imprisoned. Zarkanis wore the makeshift robe every morning when food was delivered. This way Dametrius's tailoring was kept a secret—tailoring accomplished using wire from the sides of the bucket and strands of wool from the blankets. There were other secrets too, such as the use of wire as a fishhook and the employment of strands of rope as fishing line.

"Are you ready?" queried Dametrius. He held the loose end of the rope and pulled it snug. The boy's excitement was contagious; it transcended the rope like heat through metal.

Zarkanis smiled in the moonlight. "Ready," he confirmed. His nimble fingers grasped the outer edges of the well as he dropped downward. A thrill rose through his chest when he realized that his feet dangled below the level of the dungeon floor—down where open space connected to the outer world—down where there was freedom from stone walls and iron bars. Dametrius held the rope taut and lowered Zarkanis. Fish nibbled Zarkanis's toes when his feet first touched the water. He gasped, but voiced no cry. Dametrius had warned him that his toes might be mistaken for breadcrumbs. The fish scattered as Zarkanis felt the invigorating water envelop his feet, legs, trunk, and arms.

The early September water was warm, though by no means too warm, and the sense of buoyancy was exhilarating. The current caressed Zarkanis's body. He used his hands and arms to turn his face toward the mouth of the channel. Beyond was the outside world. There was nothing to prevent his entering that world except the rope tied around his chest, but for now he was thankful for the safeguard—he had not yet learned to swim. A silvery ribbon lay upon the outer channel and reached inward toward him, piercing downward through the water with illuminating rays.

Three tugs on the rope aroused Zarkanis from enchantment. This was the signal for him to hold his breath, a feat that he had practiced within the dungeon cell. The rope slacked, and Zarkanis ducked his head beneath the water. Three seconds later he raised his face and sputtered. Dog paddling came by nature, and Dametrius kept enough tension on the rope to keep the prince afloat. Plunging his face back into the water, Zarkanis opened his eyes and was delighted to discover that he could see beneath the water's surface—just as Dametrius said he would. He observed a school of minnows darting at the edge of the moonlit channel like a swarm of tiny comets, and it was with reluctance that he finally raised his head for a breath of air.

When Dametrius finally drew Zarkanis up into the cell after his first lesson in holding his breath beneath the water, Zarkanis was startled to discover wrinkled fingertips and toes. Dametrius had not thought to tell the young prince about the temporary appearance of waterlogged skin. The next morning, however, Zarkanis's skin was back to normal, and the next night he returned to the channel. Dametrius recognized swimming lessons as an excellent form of exercise, using muscles that would be less engaged during physical training within the cell, so Zarkanis was permitted to enter the water every night. The art of swimming was something Dametrius mastered during three years of residence in a monastery that was situated near the Port of Ostia, and after a few days of instruction, Zarkanis advanced from dog paddling to a variety of strokes. Dametrius directed him to swim against the current in order to develop skill and endurance, all the while remaining secured to the rope.

Following three weeks of swimming lessons, Dametrius was not surprised when Zarkanis posed another question. "May I remove the rope and swim unassisted?"

The answer had been premeditated. "Yes, when you are seven."

There was no rebuff. The tone in Dametrius's voice informed his five-year-old pupil that the decision was final. Nonetheless, the following two years were happy and venturous ones. The daily schedule outlining Zarkanis's activities was altered to permit two hours of swimming nightly—generally commencing after practicing writing skills in moistened dust near the well opening. Within a few months, Zarkanis was able to hold his breath beneath the water for over ninety seconds, and the rope permitted him to plunge downward in the six-feet-deep channel until he was within two feet of the mossy bottom.

****

On the morning of her tenth birthday, Princess Vayle rose and made her bed—though she did so with customary caution. She knew it was contrary to the wishes of Dragus and Lady Eldra for a royal princess to perform menial labor. Giralda was presumed to accomplish all such tasks as making beds, washing clothes, cleaning up after meals, dusting, and sewing. But Vayle also knew that a conscientious human being should develop intellectual pursuits, hone physical skills, become attuned to the emotional needs and expressions of other persons, and seek spiritual maturity. She knew these things because of tutoring from Giralda. Thus, at a tender age, she came to realize that King Dragus regarded females as senseless objects to be coveted and abused, and she perceived the tragic inclination of Prince Borgar, the only child of Dragus and Lady Eldra, to espouse the views of his father. It was no secret that Lady Eldra had her eye on Princess Vayle as a potential bride for the Pithranian prince, but there was no eleven-year-old in all of Pithrania who Vayle abhorred more than Borgar.

Giralda made no attempt to conceal her own name. Using her own name posed little risk since *Giralda* was a common name in northern Gaul. She decided, however, to keep Colesia's real name secret, even from the princess. Dragus had declared that the princess would be named Vayle on the night that he decreed she would be a Pithranian princess, and Giralda feared that telling Vayle her real name might prompt questions that she did not want to answer—at least not yet. She also withheld the princess's ancestry, determining that such revelation should also be postponed until Princess Vayle grew older.

No one knew why Dragus chose the name Vayle. Lady Eldra inquired about it, but when Dragus responded by saying that Vayle was the name of a legendary dragon rider from the faraway realm of Urmoonda, the queen scoffed and never asked the question again. Giralda learned about Dragus's response from one of the castle servants, and the servant assured Giralda that Dragus spoke matter-of-factly without any hint of sarcasm. Giralda had heard some strange and wonderful things while working in the home of Sir Marticus, and she often wondered about Dragus's odd comment when brushing the princess's golden lock of hair.

After making her bed, Vayle turned and walked toward the antechamber adjoining her bedroom. Her royal quarters were spacious, occupying the entire fifth floor of the royal tower. The antechamber was where Giralda slept—a quaint room with a small featherbed, two draped closets, and various homemaking devices. Giralda used these devices in serving the princess's needs and whims. Princess Vayle's bedroom was lavish, featuring a silk-encased featherbed cradled in a walnut frame. The frame was carved roundabout with ferns and fairies, and matching ferns and fairies were carved into corresponding furniture. A special tapestry hung on the eastern wall above the fireplace, a tapestry presenting a young princess being courted by a dashing prince. It was this tapestry that Giralda referred to when telling bedtime stories of love and romance.

The furniture in Vayle's room was more exquisite than any artisan in Pithrania could have fashioned. Dragus's empire was stretching farther and farther eastward, and the castle reaped treasures from vanquished territories. Vayle was never informed about the origins of her material assets; and, thanks to Giralda's influence, she never fell subject to material lust. Her favorite portion of her royal quarters was the balcony, a marble platform accessible through a doorway in the eastern wall. The doorway was situated in the northernmost portion of her bedroom, near the wall separating her bedroom from the antechamber.

Two engraved doors swung inward to permit entrance onto the balcony. They were usually standing wide open, even during nighttime. Vayle often stood outside, rested her hands upon the balustrade of the balcony, and gazed into the forest or peered down upon Lake Manassa—an aquatic world that infatuated her. On cloudless mornings, dawn's rays played colorful tunes upon the surface of the water, and many such dawns found Princess Vayle gazing in awe.

"Good morning," greeted Giralda as Vayle peeked into the antechamber.

"Good morning," returned Vayle. She turned and walked out onto the balcony, but she did not remain there long before reentering the royal bedroom and then stepping into the antechamber. Giralda sat at a loom where she was weaving flaxen thread into scarves. "May I help weave again this morning?"

Giralda smiled. She rose and stepped to a closet. She reached inside and withdrew a golden dress with purple lace. "Happy birthday, my little one! There will be no weaving today. The cooks are preparing a special surprise for you, and there will be other surprises too."

"Other surprises?"

Dancing eyes addressed the inquisitive child. "I think I may have heard Master Edmond mention something about a boat ride on Lake Manassa."

Radiance bloomed upon Vayle's countenance. Heretofore Master Edmund, majordomo of the royal household, had deemed Vayle too young to risk venturing out upon the lake in a flat-bottomed rowboat that was little more than an oversized canoe. The princess demonstrated such remarkable swimming ability, however, that there was little doubt that she could swim to shore from anywhere on the lake. Giralda had noticed the princess's strong attraction to water almost as soon as Vayle could crawl, and it was due to fear that Vayle would plunge into the nearest reservoir and drown that Giralda began teaching her to swim before she could walk. Vayle rarely missed an afternoon or evening swim unless lightning or severe cold interfered. The thought of her first boat ride launched the princess into a state of emotional exhilaration.

Food was already set out on a long oak table when Giralda and Vayle entered the royal dining room. Children were seated along both sides of the table, and each child was provided with a glass plate, a glass cup, a cloth napkin, and pewter utensils. Numerous servants were present. Vayle was adored by the cooks, maids, butlers, and other castle residents who performed menial tasks. Her favorite playmates were children whom Lady Eldra considered lower class, namely children of the servants, and Giralda managed to gain permission for these children to attend the party. Lady Eldra did not approve of this—she rarely approved of anything Giralda suggested—but Dragus granted permission. He had no qualms about differing with Lady Eldra.

The party progressed well. Servants laughed and teased while children made merry over cream, berries, omelets, and pie. Even Borgar was behaving decently. Then Lady Eldra appeared on the scene.

"All right, everyone, it is time for the princess to receive a gift from her king and queen," announced lady Eldra as she entered the dining room. With the appearance of his mother, Borgar withdrew from interacting with peasants and stood in company with two of his cousins. Lady Eldra assumed a smug look of disgust as she surveyed Vayle's guests, and then she summoned Borgar to her side.

"Prince Borgar, heir to the throne of Pithrania, shall present a gift of good favor to Princess Vayle," Lady Eldra proclaimed. She placed a silk bag into Borgar's hands.

Borgar was tempted to examine the contents of the bag before relinquishing anything to Vayle, but the formality of the occasion forced him to exercise better manners. He toted the bag around the table to Vayle, placed it in her hands, and stood hovering over her. He reminded Giralda of a vulture that was watching for the opportunity to snatch a bite of carrion. Vayle had grown accustomed to Borgar's obtrusive disposition and paid him no mind. She untied silk strings and opened the bag, peeping inside. Her hand reached inside and withdrew a perfectly wrought necklace of pearls. Half the pearls were white, and half black, arranged so that each black pearl was positioned between two white ones. This was not the sort of gift that appealed to the eleven-year-old Borgar—he grunted his disapproval and returned to the company of his cousins.

"Oh, how pretty!" exclaimed Marlda, Master Edmond's youngest daughter. She was the same age as Vayle. Although not a member of the royal court, she was attributed higher rank than the children of most servants and was permitted free access to the royal tower. Vayle considered Marlda her dearest friend apart from Giralda.

Although Dragus forbade Giralda from revealing that she was Princess Vayle's mother, he took great pleasure in making that fact known to Lady Eldra. Lady Eldra, in turn, instructed Giralda to claim that she was a servant from Marne. This was no problem to Giralda because it was the truth. In fact, Giralda was thankful for the instructions she received from Dragus and Lady Eldra in regard to her identity. She would have deplored leading the daughter of Sir Marticus and Lady Monica to believe that she was the princess's biological mother. Meanwhile, Lady Eldra told Vayle that her parents had ruled a kingdom far to the north and that they were both killed by Vikings. When Vayle questioned Giralda concerning Lady Eldra's story, Giralda responded by saying that *time can be a remarkable teacher.* Though she could get nothing more out of Giralda, Vayle concluded that the truth about her parents was something different than what she heard from Lady Eldra.

"Would you like to wear it?" Vayle responded to Marlda's exclamation, holding the necklace outward toward Marlda.

Lady Eldra was appalled. The princess's generosity was an act of debasement—an effacement of royal dignity—and she was about to interject her disapproval when Marlda spoke up. "Oh, no! It is your necklace, my princess, and you must wear it."

Marlda's words aborted Lady Eldra's criticism, leaving the intolerant queen standing with an open mouth and rutted brow. She watched Marlda and Giralda fix the necklace around Vayle's neck, and she also noted that Giralda whispered something into Vayle's ear.

"Thank you very much for the beautiful necklace, Your Majesty," Vayle stated as she stood and curtsied. Then she sat back down.

Lady Eldra straightened her face and nodded in approval of the compliment. Then, without even glancing at Giralda, she turned and departed. As soon as she was gone, celebration recommenced.

Long hours and a late lunch came to pass before Vayle and Giralda boarded a small boat constructed of pine and pitch. There were three wooden seats. Wool-covered pillows lay upon the wooden seats where Giralda and Vayle situated themselves. Vayle sat toward the bow, and Giralda sat in the middle. They boarded at the bank of the southern cove where Vayle often swam; it was a tamer sector of the lake about a quarter-mile east of the castle.

Once the ladies were situated, Master Edmond boarded the boat and sat down at the stern. He lifted a paddle from the bottom of the boat and stroked outward from shore. The responsibility of keeping watch over the princess during her first boat ride was something he would trust to no one else. He was a man of unusual caliber among those in the service of Dragus—honest, hardworking, and highly esteemed.

All three occupants faced forward as the boat glided over the surface of the water. The southern shore grew distant behind them, and a sense of adventure swelled within Vayle's breast. The center of the lake seemed much larger and deeper when looking over the side of the boat than it did when gazing out from her balcony—and so alive!

"Oh!" gasped Vayle as a trout leaped for a moth a few feet to her left and then splashed back down into the water. She laughed with delight. "Are we crossing to the other side? Can we paddle along the north shore and go all the way down to the cliffs?"

Master Edmond grunted. "If you wish, princess. But we will have to beach this craft at the mouth of the river and allow servants to return it. I have duties that I must attend to at the stables, and I will not have time to paddle all the way back here if we venture to the cliffs."

"Thank you," said Vayle.

Across the heart and depths of the lake drifted the exultant princess. She piped up with excitement whenever she sighted a fish or turtle or frog or any other form of aquatic life. Drifting closer to the wild northern shoreline seemed like passing through a veil of enchantment. From time to time she lifted her eyes toward the cliffs—sheer walls of limestone that rose north and northeast of the castle. She noted that the castle grew more shadowed as the sun dropped toward the western horizon. What the princess could not see, however, were two blue eyes that were fixed upon her—eyes that gazed out from beneath bushy auburn hair.

****

Zarkanis knew by the glint of gold amidst dark hair that the child sitting in the bow of the boat that was being paddled toward his cell was Colesia; and as the boat drew nearer, he recognized her face. By the time he reached ten years of age, the princess had become a major factor in his life. Dametrius taught him that Colesia was his chosen bride; and if she consented, no one could rightfully dispute his claim for her hand in marriage. Dametrius had also taught him that Colesia had another name, a name he overhead as it was given to her by Dragus—namely Princess Vayle. Colesia occupied a significant proportion of Zarkanis's thoughts, and that proportion increased with time.

Standing upon an overturned bucket within the darkness of his cell, Zarkanis was hidden from Princess Vayle. She came within thirty-five feet of him without even glimpsing him. Master Edmond had turned south and was paddling close to the bank, making his way along the western edge of Lake Manassa. "This is where currents are diverted to provide water for the castle," he explained as the boat passed by the mouth of the waterway that flowed west and coursed beneath the castle.

"Can we swim beneath the castle and let Bimrod draw us up to the royal ladies' bathing room?" queried Vayle with a smirk, glancing back toward Giralda and Master Edmond. Bimrod was the primary servant responsible for drawing water and filling wooden tubs for bathing. The tubs were mounted on iron stands and were heated with burning logs.

"Never, never... Oh my... Don't you dare think of swimming beneath the castle," retorted Giralda, gasping at the thought, "I have heard that lizard-like creatures with horrendous teeth slither along the mud beneath the castle, and some are gigantic!"

Master Edmond grinned following Giralda's report, but he said nothing to contradict her extraordinary account. He did not want to say anything that might encourage the bold little princess to actually swim into the channels beneath the castle.

A young prince with attuned ears grinned also. The channel beneath his prison cell was his second home, and he had never seen a lizard-like creature with horrendous teeth. He knew to be careful with snakes,

85

having learned from experience that their teeth could be as sharp as those of rats, but he had never been pursued by a giant lizard.

"Well then, dear Master Edmond, since we cannot swim beneath the castle, may we pass down the river and dangle our feet over the waterfall?" Vayle requested with roguish zeal. She was fond of teasing Giralda in Master Edmond's presence; he seemed to relish good-natured buffoonery, and he produced entertaining responses.

"I think not, at least not with Giralda aboard," returned Master Edmond. "Her feet might dam up the falls and cause a backwash to flood the castle."

Giralda squawked but said nothing. She was thankful that the conversation was moving to matters other than the prospect of swimming beneath the castle.

"And besides," added Master Edmond, "what if the boat passes over the falls? Giralda cannot fly like you, my princess."

As Master Edmond continued paddling, Zarkanis turned toward Dametrius. "Must I now learn to fly to keep up with the princess?" he asked with a concerned furrow cast across his brow, though a wry smile revealed that he was joking.

Dametrius did not answer for several seconds. He was thankful that his ten-year-old protégé had a sense of humor. "If anyone could learn to fly, my prince, I am sure that you would be among the airborne. Nonetheless, you may rest assured that the gentleman merely bantered. I have never seen a man, woman, or child who could ascend into the atmosphere after the manner of a swan."

"Then I shall have to be content with buoyancy in a denser substance—I look forward to my nightly swim."

Dametrius chuckled. "Very well, but beware of gigantic lizard-like creatures with horrendous teeth."

The prince joined his teacher in laughter.

The remainder of the day seemed uneventful to Princess Vayle after her passage over Lake Manassa. As she soaked within a tub in the royal ladies' bathing room on the third floor of the royal tower, her mind played upon the feelings she experienced while gliding over a world of liquid wonder. The lake had such dimension, such body, such vibrancy… She fancied herself slipping over the side of the boat and swimming through aqueous realms of fascinating flora and incredible creatures, and such reverie made her feel like a virtual mermaid.

Two spiral stairways led up the royal tower from one floor to the next, with one set of stairs rising inside the tower and another set of stairs encircling the outer wall of the tower. Both sets of stairs continued upward to the roof where lookout guards were posted. After bathing, Princess Vayle and Giralda began climbing the inner stairway to the fifth floor—the level of Princess Vayle's bedroom. They wore long, furry robes that served as appropriate attire while passing royal guards.

Due to thickening clouds, it was already dark outside. Giralda escorted Princess Vayle into the princess's bedroom and tucked her into the large featherbed. An oil lamp was burning on a table in the antechamber, and the drapes dividing the two rooms were drawn open, so the bedroom was dimly lit.

"It looks as though I should shut the balcony doors tonight, dear one," Giralda apologized. "I think a nasty storm is coming."

Vayle voiced no objection as Giralda walked to the balcony doors and closed them. Rather, she made a request as Giralda began stepping back through the draped passageway to the antechamber. "Could you tell me the story about the prince? Please?"

Giralda halted as Vayle began speaking. A smile creased her lips. She turned and walked to the bed and sat down beside the princess.

"Once there was a handsome and strong young prince…"

"Who was also kind and thoughtful," inserted Vayle.

"Indeed so, and this young prince grew up, dreaming that someday he would find a charming young princess to marry him."

"Who could cook, and work the loom, and swim like a salamander!"

"Of course, but the young princess was held captive by an evil sorcerer who only wished to possess her for her outer beauty. He wanted to brag that the most beautiful princess in the world belonged to him. The sorcerer knew that someday a prince would come looking for a suitable princess, so he devised a wicked plan to raise the young princess in such a manner that she would be spoiled and no prince would want her."

"By not teaching her anything, and making her stupid and lazy."

"But a good fairy came to visit the little princess at night, and the fairy brought looms and brooms and cooking utensils."

"As well as many interesting books to read—and she would waft the princess away to an enchanted pool where she gave the princess singing lessons and taught her to swim like a salamander!"

Giralda smiled. The enchanted pool was a new addition to the story. "Yes, so, when finally one day a handsome and kind prince came looking for a suitable princess to marry, he chanced upon the princess while she was weaving material for a cape. She sat at her loom in a gazebo beside a brook. He watched the princess with much interest, and she was not aware of his presence. Then she stopped weaving and picked up a book to read. She often did these things when the sorcerer was away."

"And the prince was much impressed by the princess's skill, and by her interest in reading books, and he approached her to ask her name. But this startled the princess, and she jumped into the brook and swam to the other side like a salamander."

Giralda nodded before she resumed speaking, squinting to see the princess's face in the sparse light. It was delightful to observe Vayle's dynamic imagination come to life in her aqua eyes. "After reaching the other side of the brook, the princess climbed up the bank and stood, dripping wet, upon the shore, facing back toward the prince. He called out to her, telling her that she need not be frightened, and then he dove into the brook and swam to her. He climbed ashore and stood beside her. And then he knelt before her, took her by the hand, and asked her to marry him."

"And she did."

Giralda leaned toward the princess. "Indeed she did." She brushed back thick brunette locks and one golden lock, and then she kissed Vayle upon the brow. "Sweet dreams, my little princess."

"Sweet dreams."

Giralda rose and stepped away, but Vayle did not close her eyes. She appreciated the wonderful adventure on the lake, and she decided to do something special for Giralda's birthday; and it so happened that Giralda's birthday fell upon the following day. Once the oil lamp was extinguished, it did not take long for the exhausted lady-in-waiting to fall asleep. Vayle slid from her bed, pulled leather slippers onto her feet, and crept to the door to the stairwell.

Princess Vayle knew that her lady-in-waiting liked flowers, and there were purple irises that had captured Giralda's fancy earlier that day. Giralda spotted them while they were boating. They were growing high upon the face of the cliff northeast of the castle. Even Master Edmond said that he had never seen more magnificent irises.

Imagining how pleased Giralda would be to awake and see the irises in her antechamber, Vayle paused at the door and peered back through the darkness. Her lady-in-waiting did not stir. She opened the door just wide enough to slip out, and then quietly closed it. Next she crept up the stairwell to the lookout station. She knew there would be sentries, but she hoped to sneak past them and make her way down the steps that spiraled around the outer wall of the royal tower.

The upper hatchway to the interior stairwell was left open to facilitate the ventilation of fumes from oil lamps. Peering with her head raised above the top of the stairwell, Vayle noted that there were three guards. Two guards were reclined upon the roof of the tower, apparently sleeping; and a third guard stood facing southward between two stone slabs in the crenellated battlement. The top of the exterior stairway commenced a short distance from where the interior steps ended. Vayle exited and crept to the exterior stairway without being detected.

After descending the royal tower's exterior stairway to the top of the southern wall, Vayle circled around the tower and then turned northward along the eastern rampart. She continued to the northeast tower and then circled around to the northern rampart and walked westward for several yards before halting. The northern rampart was constructed without a battlement since it abutted the northern cliff, and it was easy for Vayle to feel out the presence of a particular jutting boulder and slide down the western surface of the boulder to a rocky ledge. Then she crawled back beneath the boulder to a secret opening.

The secret opening was the mouth of a tunnel excavated years before by King Braham. The tunnel was meant to provide a last means of escape in case King Braham found himself threatened within his own castle. A large portion of the tunnel was a natural cave, and this made excavation of the tunnel much less laborious. Borgar had shown Vayle the location of this tunnel on an occasion when he felt compelled to boost his ego, and he had claimed that the tunnel led to higher ground above the cliff. They did not enter the tunnel and Vayle wondered if Borgar really knew what he was talking about. Now she was going to find out... Her only real hope of obtaining irises from the upper face of the cliff depended upon the veracity of Borgar's claim.

By the time Vayle reached the opening beneath the boulder, the storm Giralda had predicted was brewing. Whistling winds gusted around the castle walls; springtime leaves rustled above the cliff; and deep black clouds, almost invisible in the darkness, stirred like brewing porridge in a low sky. Everything calmed, however, when Vayle crawled into the pitch-black tunnel.

It was quiet—quiet to the point of eeriness. The opening grew larger, and Vayle was able to stand. By feeling along a cool limestone wall, she progressed without mishap. Her feet shuffled across a stone floor. An uncanny sense that she was illicitly trespassing swelled within her breast as she ventured deeper into the mountain's gullet. The silence seemed to harbor countless eyes that peered through the darkness and stared at her. "Just my imagination," she spoke, and the sound of her voice calmed her nerves.

After a while she realized that the tunnel was longer than she had anticipated, and twice she paused with thoughts of turning back. Any thoughts of retreat, however, were quelled by the mental image of Giralda discovering an arrangement of irises. At one point something soft and slimy squirmed between her hand and the stone wall, but after a gasp and quick withdrawal of her hand, she continued on—touching the wall with more caution. There was a faint sound of dribbling water and an earthy smell of limestone. By and by the tunnel began ascending. Her feet discovered that steps had been carved into the stone floor, and the steps made moving upward easier. A wisp of air penetrated the fabric of her gown and drew her attention to an opening overhead.

At last, she emerged from the opposite end of the tunnel; but to her surprise, she surfaced into an environmental nightmare. Erratic webs of lightning streaked through a black sky like fluorescent, pulsing veins in a bat's wing; and the thunder that followed sounded dull and distant, muted by fierce winds. Bursts of light revealed tree limbs jerking in all directions—spasmodic appendages jutting from the swaying bodies of frightened forest sentinels. Cool mist whipped against her face. Moist air dampened her nightgown.

It seemed certain that heavy rains would soon follow. She was glad she had not come later. Guided by glimpses of her surroundings— glimpses that came during bursts of heat lightning—she made her way along the jagged edge of the cliff until she reached the point above the irises. Here she lay flat on her stomach and looked downward, waiting for another flash of light. It was not long before she espied several irises. They were about four feet down the surface of the cliff.

Just then the sky let loose a torrential onslaught of rain. Vayle hastened forward and clasped a handful of irises. The ground beneath her body grew slick. She dug her fingers into a thin layer of earth but to no avail—her body slid downward. A short-lived scream was absorbed by wind and rain, and was cut short by a dull whack. Then came a splash.

Chapter 5

Enchanting Rescue

A fter a strenuous afternoon of academic pursuits, Zarkanis was anxious for a swim. His studies had been mollified by the appearance of Colesia as she passed before his cell window in a boat, and this left him with the desire to enter the waters of Lake Manassa.

"Can I go now? I believe the clouds are sufficiently condensed to increase the darkness and prevent visible detection," Zarkanis remarked, using the most impressive diction he could muster.

There were a few seconds of silence before Dametrius responded. "The enhanced dimensions of cloud cover may bid well for the adventuresome wishes of a young prince."

Zarkanis peered through the blackness for a glimpse of Dametrius's droll smile—the smile he knew his teacher assumed when bantering.

"So then, by now my thumbs and toes should be as wrinkled as dried apricots."

"Well now, it is thought by some sages that learning puts wrinkles upon a man's brain. Perhaps thumbs and toes wrinkle more easily than do brains."

Zarkanis laughed. "Perhaps so, but if the sages are correct, then it would seem certain that my thumbs and toes shall never grow as wrinkled as the brain of my teacher."

Dametrius was flattered by the praise of his intelligence, and he was also awed by the wit Zarkanis displayed at ten years of age. He knew that Zarkanis was far more mature than most boys of comparable age. "If lightning strikes the ground, you are to return immediately. Up to this point there has only been heat lightning. A clap of thunder that indicates cloud-to-ground lightning will be your signal to return, and I have taught you how to differentiate between the sound produced by heat lightning and the sound produced by cloud to ground lightning. Furthermore, it has started raining heavily, so be careful of swift currents."

"Yes, sir."

Zarkanis looked toward the window long enough to see heat lightning redden the sky. He made his way to the well opening. When he was eight years old he developed a technique for lowering himself into the channel without assistance.

Dametrius sat nearby. Zarkanis maneuvered headfirst through the two-foot long opening through the limestone floor. With his hands and arms dangling toward the water, he hung, suspended by his lower legs and feet. Next he slid his hands back up along the rough stone until his fingertips found crevices. He faced the water as he searched for a hold. He intended to grip with his fingertips while he withdrew his legs and feet, and then he intended to drop into the water feet first—but he did not carry out his intentions. No sooner had he secured a grip with his fingertips than a bright flash filled the atmosphere, followed by a veritable explosion.

"Dametrius!"

It was understood between Dametrius and Zarkanis that loud talking was prohibited. Dametrius, therefore, sprang to the well opening when Zarkanis yelled. The young prince was brave, but such a shattering blast of thunder would be expected to frighten any ten-year-old, especially one who was hanging upside down and facing water that could transmit the shock of lightning. Dametrius chastised himself for letting Zarkanis talk him into swimming on a night like this one. Why had he permitted such a thing? He gripped Zarkanis by the ankles.

"I'll pull you out," he said while tugging on Zarkanis's ankles. But the prince resisted.

"No, listen, when the lightning flashed I saw a little girl's body floating beneath me in the canal. I must go after her."

Alarmed lines of concern drew across Dametrius's brow. He had little time to think. "Then go!"

No further words were spoken. Zarkanis dropped beneath the water. He did not take time to use his usual method of entry; he released his legs and feet and plunged straight downward. The canal was familiar territory. Even in almost pitch-blackness he was able to stroke swiftly downstream and then surface in contact with the girl's body. A limp arm draped over his shoulder and a soft face brushed his cheek. He turned back toward the entrance to his cell, but with the torrential downpour, the current was growing stronger by the second.

Although he could have fought his way against the current by releasing the girl and swimming upstream on his own, the thought of doing so never entered Zarkanis's mind. He turned back around and endeavored to keep the girl's head above the surface of the water as they flowed downstream. The girl was alive—her warm body hinted to the fact, and intermittent coughing left no doubt.

The isolated corridor stretching between Zarkanis's cell and his nearest imprisoned neighbor was eighty-five feet long. He knew the canal beneath this corridor well, but he had never ventured past the point where the canal split into two parallel canals coursing westward. One canal passed beneath prison cells situated along the castle's southern wall, and the other canal passed beneath prison cells to the north. Dametrius had warned against exposure to human waste that dropped into the waters of these canals—waste that might confer illness. After selecting the southernmost canal, Zarkanis continued downstream. This canal coursed another hundred feet before reaching the western side of the castle. Light from oil lamps filtered downward through well openings; and although the light was faint, Zarkanis's eyes were adjusted to the darkness and he was able to see.

While passing beneath the brightest opening above, thirty feet from the castle's western wall, Zarkanis took an inquisitive look at the girl in his arms. By this time her coughing had ceased. His eyes widened. There could be no mistaking the glittering gold upon dark hair. It was Colesia. Her eyes were closed, and tiny droplets glimmered upon her eyelashes. Her face seemed that of a marble goddess—a goddess such as Dametrius described when extolling Roman statues. She was even more beautiful than when viewed from a distance, but her skin was pale. His strokes quickened.

Upon exiting the channel, Zarkanis grabbed the southern bank and pulled Colesia onto the grassy turf next to the wall. He knew that castle guards would not be able to see them without leaning over the edge of the lookout tower, and even then it would require the light of lightning to reveal their presence. Drops of rain fell like pellets from the sky. He placed his face above Colesia's face to shield her mouth, nose, and eyes. She was breathing, and the feel of her warm breath was enchanting.

****

Consciousness returned slowly. First Vayle was aware that she lay upon her back and that she was wet and cool. She remembered sliding from the cliff, so she surmised that she was lying upon the bank at the base of the cliff. But then—this seemed odd—she could not recall any bank existing at the base of the cliff. Slowly she opened her eyes. There was darkness, and she could hear the sound of rain; but there was more. She felt liquid missiles striking her naked legs and feet—her slippers having washed away—and she felt rain pelting her gown-covered thighs and abdomen, but something hovered over her upper chest and face, something that pressed against her right side; and it was not just something… It was someone.

Colesia's breathing altered, no longer slow and deep but rapid and uneven. It was too dark for Zarkanis to note that her eyes had opened, but he sensed her consciousness. Tingling crept up his spine and magnetized his neck and face. Her breath seemed a draught of charm.

"You are awake, my princess."

The voice was unfamiliar, dreamlike. Vayle could tell from bodily contact that she lay in company with a child, and the tone of the voice was male. The words *my princess* were captivating and inspiring—not like words spoken by a servant or guardian, but something different…something wonderful.

"Who are you?"

Her voice sparked an ecstatic explosion. For a time Zarkanis was as mute as Dragus intended him to be, but at last the pounding in his chest diminished and the rigidity in his lips eased. "I am Prince Zarkanis. I found you in the water—you were unconscious."

Prince Zarkanis. The boy's words entered Vayle's ears and then penetrated her heart. The stories and dreams she shared night after night with her guardian emerged from the world of fantasy and personified themselves in the person above her. Her prince had come. For a time she was speechless, but she would not remain speechless. This was the moment she had wished for and hoped for, and she would not be bereft of the courage to speak.

"Prince Zarkanis, I am Princess Vayle. I fell from the cliffs behind the castle—and I can swim, but—"

"Vayle!" a woman's voice sounded, disrupting Vayle's explanation of her predicament. It came from the south, from across the river moat. Thunder had awakened Giralda, and she had made a trip to the royal ladies' bathing room. It was her custom to check on Vayle whenever returning to the royal quarters, and when she did so, she discovered that the princess was missing.

"Princess Vayle! Princess Vayle!" a man's voice hailed more strongly. The rain was subsiding, allowing voices to carry farther through the atmosphere. Light from torches cut through the darkness.

Zarkanis dropped his lips to Colesia's ear. "I know you can swim well, Princess Vayle, so you must have been rendered unconscious. But your real name is not Vayle. Your real name is Colesia, which means *golden-hued dawn*. Remember what I am telling you. Your name is Colesia. When I am older and stronger, I will come for you; and if you will have me, I will marry you. Tell no one about me, though, or I might be killed before I grow strong enough to defend myself. Dragus is my enemy. God be with you. I love you."

Zarkanis had spoken without pausing for a response. He had spoken as Dametrius's tutoring guided him, and as his own fantasizing prepared him; and he had spoken by inspiration of his own heart as he hovered within the wondrous aura of the girl lying beneath him.

Vayle's head reeled. Her heart throbbed in astonishment. A bright flash of lightning branched out below the clouds and lit the atmosphere for one spellbinding second—a second that introduced Colesia's eyes to those of the prince. The name, the face, the eyes… They all etched themselves indelibly within her virgin mind. Then he was gone, with only a faint splash to mark his departure.

Vayle sat up, expecting to discover that she was awakening in her bed. But she was not dreaming. She felt thick grass and solid earth. Whirlwinds danced over her legs, and sounds of rushing water filled her ears. The prince was real—a flesh-and-blood boy who told her that he would come back for her and marry her. He said that he loved her. Her heart pounded against her breast.

"Vayle!" hailed Giralda's voice, but Vayle could barely hear it. Giralda was trekking south. There were farms south of the river, including the farm where Marlda lived.

Vayle sat in mystified wonder. Cliff-top silhouettes grew discernible as clouds moved westward and moonlight broke through a thinning canopy. She looked around her. It was puzzling. She was sitting on the west side of the castle—the waterfall roared before her. How had she ended up on the west side of the castle? She stood up and stepped around the southwestern corner of the castle. The strip of earth beneath her feet became narrower as she advanced, and soon she reached a point where rushing water lapped against the castle wall. The drawbridge was still several yards away.

The idea arose in Vayle's mind that postponing contact with anyone who was searching for her would give Prince Zarkanis more time to escape. She wondered where he lived. It did not seem surprising that Dragus was his enemy; she expected the prince of her dreams to be contrary to Dragus. Then something happened that changed her strategy—several guards debarked from the castle, carrying burning torches. They walked fast and scattered in all directions. She did not want them to stumble across Prince Zarkanis.

"Help! I'm over here! Help!"

As for Zarkanis, he had surmised that a search party would rescue the princess. He reentered the same outlet from which he emerged and progressed upstream with breaststrokes and scissor kicks. The strokes and kicks were executed without breaking the water's surface. He thought about Colesia's eyes as he swam… They looked blue, or green, or perhaps bluish green—he wasn't sure. There wasn't much time to discern color during the flash of light that revealed her face and eyes. It was not the color of her eyes, however, that infatuated him; it was their essence. There was something about her eyes that was fathomless…alluring…wonderful.

Despite swimming against the current, his return trip took no longer than the one he made downstream while supporting Colesia. Dametrius waited and listened at the upper opening to the well. His young pupil had either experienced contact with a dead body or had interacted with a living human being. The risk of detection from attempting to rescue a drowning girl was obvious, yet Dametrius had let Zarkanis go. His own ethical convictions would not permit him to ignore a hapless child, and such ignoble abandon would be inconsistent with all the hours, days, months, and years of training that Zarkanis had received since infancy. Still, it was with great concern that the sole guardian of a young prince sat in anticipation of the youth's return.

Following a few light tugs, Zarkanis felt himself lifted from the water as he clung to the rope. Dametrius was stronger than his years and appearance suggested—the Captive from Shareen was not the only one who performed exercises within the prison cell.

"She was alive. It was Colesia," Zarkanis spoke as his head rose above the level of the well.

Dametrius waited until Zarkanis was secure within the cell before responding. He draped a dry wool blanket over his excited pupil. "You mean the little girl was the princess?"

"Yes, I saw her golden lock while passing beneath a lighted opening, and her dark hair, and her face. It was her."

Dametrius sat down beside Zarkanis. His eyes were accustomed to the darkness, but there was not enough light to discern Zarkanis's expression. "And she was breathing?"

"Yes. She was unconscious when I pulled her from the canal, but she woke up."

Dametrius's brow furrowed. "What was she doing out at night?"

Zarkanis hesitated. He had not given this question any thought. "I do not know. I did not have much time to talk with her. They were out looking for her."

The furrow in Dametrius's brow deepened. "You spoke with her?"

"Yes."

"Did you tell her who you are?"

"Yes, but I told her that they might kill me if she told anyone about me. I do not think she will tell. Her eyes seemed most virtuous."

Dametrius glanced toward the cell door. "Did you tell her where you stay?"

"No."

"You are certain?"

"Yes. We spoke very little. There were searchers. I left before they detected me."

Silence ensued. Zarkanis peered toward his teacher. He wondered what pronouncement would follow. Surely Dametrius would have something to say about his sole student's conduct.

"You did well," spoke Dametrius. "I could not have hoped for better behavior from a Sharean prince." He opened his mouth to speak again but changed his mind. He decided to keep his other hopes to himself—first, the hope that Giralda had done well in raising Colesia, and, second, the hope that Colesia would make choices that were honorable to the daughter of Sir Marticus and Lady Monica.

****

In the grand hall—an immense chamber just within the portcullis to the drawbridge—commotion and chatter erupted when the missing princess was returned by three guards. She had been lifted to the drawbridge from a small boat. Giralda followed close behind, sobbing in relief and joy. She was accompanied by Master Edmond and Marlda. All inhabitants of the castle were gathered in the great room.

Standing in the midst of the congregation was Lady Eldra. The queen had sworn that Giralda must have mistreated the princess or else the child would have never sneaked from the castle on a stormy night. Such an accusation could have proven very serious if Vayle was never found, but Giralda had not given any heed to Lady Eldra's accusation—her mind was solely possessed by apprehension over the princess's well-being.

"Dear child!" Giralda cried as she made her way forward, clasping the princess in her arms. She was almost as wet as Vayle.

Lady Eldra knew that her accusation against Giralda was improbable, so she made no attempt to prevent contact between the princess and her lady-in-waiting. Nonetheless, she strolled to the forefront and stared imperiously downward upon Vayle. Then she lifted her face and addressed Elmar—the nearest of the three guards who were credited with rescuing the princess.

"Where did you find her?"

99

The commotion in the vast room died. Elmar became the focal point of attention. More than a hundred pairs of ears cocked to hear his reply. "Well, it was most mysterious."

"Go on."

Elmar was more than willing to take center stage. He shifted from foot to foot several times and lifted his face like a thoughtful savant. When at last he spoke, he faced Lady Eldra, and he spoke loudly enough to address the entire assembly. He was not a bad orator.

"She called out to us from the forsaken wedge of earth between the moat and southern wall of the castle. As it is quite unsafe to swim west of the drawbridge lest one be swept over the falls, we had to fasten a rope to a boat and use a winch on the drawbridge to retrieve the princess in the boat. It was our good fortune that there was a small boat at hand on the southern bank. We—"

"You rescued the princess, that is obvious," interjected Lady Eldra, interrupting Elmar's spellbinding narrative. "Now, tell me, how do you suppose the princess came to be on the forsaken wedge of earth against the southern wall?"

The atmosphere thickened. Sounds of breathing grew perceptible as all other sounds were hushed; and all eyes in the grand hall became riveted upon Elmar.

Elmar shrugged. "The castle wall is forty feet high, the moat and canals are flowing too swiftly to swim across the moat from the southern shore, and the cliffs to the north are steep and dangerous."

"So what are you saying?" pressed lady Eldra.

Elmar implemented a dramatic pause. When he spoke next, he did so like a Greek actor projecting his voice from the stage of an amphitheater. "So far as one can reason, it was impossible for the child-princess to reach the wedge of ground against the southern wall without falling forty feet from atop the castle wall."

Lady Eldra took half a step backward and stared hard at Elmar. "Are you saying that the child fell forty feet without injury?"

Again Elmar shrugged. He proffered no further explanation. Low murmuring commenced among the onlookers.

Lady Eldra gave a slight shrug and assumed a casual and condescending posture, hiding the fact that she was disconcerted by Elmar's words. "Perhaps we should inquire of the princess herself," she redirected, and the murmuring ceased. Turning to the princess, Lady

Eldra bent downward. Vayle nudged deeper into the enfolding arms of her lady-in-waiting. She faced Lady Eldra. "Now tell us, dear, don't be afraid. Why did you wander out into the nasty storm?"

Vayle hesitated. She did not want to say anything that would get Giralda into trouble.

Giralda observed a worried little face turn upward. "It's all right. Please answer Lady Eldra's question," she coached.

Vayle respected the advice of her lady-in-waiting. Lady Eldra sensed as much and flinched with jealousy. Rubies, diamonds, and furs were at her disposal, but Princess Vayle was subject to a woman she despised.

Vayle's voice quaked as she looked back at Lady Eldra and responded. "I waited until Giralda was asleep, and then I tiptoed past the guards to pick some irises. It started raining, and I fell. It was stupid, Your Majesty. I won't do it again."

"But there are no irises growing west of the castle," Lady Eldra retorted.

"That may be true, Your Majesty, but I fell from the cliff on the east side of the castle. I must have been rendered unconscious, and when I woke up I was lying on the ground on the west side of the castle."

Lady Eldra straightened and stood speechless. The silence besetting those gathered in the grand hall of the Pithranian castle thickened into an aura of mystery. Hairs on the backs of necks began tingling and rising. Most knew the charming princess well enough to consider prevarication foreign to her mind. That she spoke the truth, or what she believed to be the truth, was an assumption that not even Lady Eldra challenged.

"Perhaps she has amnesia," suggested Briam, one of the guards who escorted Vayle into the castle.

"Perhaps an angel bore her to safety," stated Giralda.

Giralda's remark was unsettling. With the exception of several servants, few of those among Dragus's retinue were religious—spiritual cognizance was deemed something that could threaten licentious indulgence. Nonetheless, it was not difficult to believe that an angel might intervene on behalf of the courteous little princess.

Lady Eldra was transfixed. The suggestion of a supernatural phenomenon disquieted her conscience. She was the first, though, to shake her head refutably. "I hope, child, that you have learned a lesson from this."

"Yes, ma'am," replied Vayle, relieved that the interrogation was concluding.

"Will you use better judgment in the future?"

"I will try to use good judgment, Your Majesty."

"Very well. Let's get some sleep."

Giralda took Vayle by the hand and departed without another word. They never hesitated during their five-story ascension up the royal tower. After reaching the fifth level, Giralda used a candle to transfer flame from a lantern in the stairwell to a lantern in her antechamber, and then she blew out the candle and closed the door to the stairwell. She set the candle on a table.

There was little talking while Giralda and Vayle wiped themselves with towels and slipped into dry nightgowns. Then Giralda led the way into the princess's bedroom. She tucked Vayle within lush sheets and blankets, and then she sat down in her usual spot on the side of the bed. The light in Princess Vayle's bedroom was too scant to disclose tears streaming down Giralda's face. She knew Vayle well enough to guess why the princess was picking irises in the dark of night—she knew that Vayle had not forgotten her birthday.

"I'm...I'm sorry I caused you so much trouble," said Vayle. She had started to simply say *I'm sorry*, but then she realized that such a statement would not be true. The most wonderful experience of her young life would not have taken place if she had not ventured beyond her castle walls, in the face of a storm, to acquire a gift for her beloved guardian. She was, however, sorry that the venture caused so much worry for Giralda.

"No measure of trouble has matched the joy of having you back with me, dear princess," said Giralda.

There was a pause, and then Vayle sat up. Her arms shot upward and wrapped themselves about Giralda's neck. "Oh, I love you so much, my lady; and I so wanted you to have some lovely lavender irises on your birthday morning." As she held the only mother she had ever known, Vayle felt a burning desire to share her extraordinary experience—the experience of being rescued by Prince Zarkanis—but the young prince's words resounded within her heart and mind, words warning her to keep his existence a secret.

"It is the purpose of one's intent that truly counts, princess, but you must avoid endangering yourself like this again. There could have been wolves atop the cliff."

Vayle had seen a number of wolves over the years, usually while she was surveying the sights of nature from her balcony. One time a wolf came to the eastern shore as she swam in the southeastern cove of Lake Manassa. The wolf lapped up some water, raised its head to look at her, and then slunk back into the woods. Giralda, who was sitting on the southern bank, had not seen the wolf, and Vayle chose not to mention it—she was afraid her evening swims would be curtailed if Giralda found out that a wolf had been nearby. At present, though, her mind was engaged with something other than a wolf, namely the recollection of a boy's charming eyes.

"Would you please tell me the story of the prince again?"

Vayle's request startled Giralda. "Of course, princess. If you wish."

After again tucking Vayle beneath soft sheets and blankets, Giralda rose and stepped across the room to the drapes between her antechamber and Vayle's bedroom. She opened the drapes wider to let in more light, and then she returned and sat down on the side of the bed.

"Once there was a handsome and strong young prince," began Giralda, and then she continued on with the story.

The story progressed as usual except for one notable difference—Vayle lay in silence and listened. Usually she ended up telling about a third of the story herself, but not this time. She seemed so absorbed in listening to the story that Giralda began wondering if the princess were awake or just sleeping with her eyes open.

Finally Giralda neared the end of the story, coming to the part where the prince approached the princess while she was reading a book in a gazebo beside a stream: "When the prince came closer, the princess was startled. She jumped into the stream and began swimming like a frightened swan…"

"No!" cried Vayle, springing to a sitting position as though someone had jabbed her with a sewing needle. Giralda's stomach seemed to leap into her chest. She sat stiff and stared at Vayle with her breast pounding. "No," Vayle repeated more serenely, turning her torso toward Giralda and grasping her by the arm. She then began speaking with mesmerizing passion. "The prince approaches. The princess is reading—engrossed in a tale of romance while perched atop a quaint bluff. She does not see him approach, but a curious sensation bestirs her breast. Her mind dreamily wanders, and her eyes shift from lines of prose to crisscrossing rainbows of light that dance upon the surface of the flowing stream beneath her."

Giralda was astonished. Vayle was bright, but such eloquent articulation seemed beyond her years. Giralda wondered what could possibly inspire such polished sentences to pass from the lips of a ten-year-old girl. And then came more.

"Suddenly she is aware of footsteps—the solid footsteps of a man. She rises and turns, and then she faints at the sight of a smiling prince with blue eyes—eyes that seem to penetrate her heart and caress her soul. Toppling backward, she plunges, unconscious, into the stream, but before her satin gown is saturated with water, the prince is with her. He takes her in his arms and carries her to the bank. He lays her on the spongy flora, kneels, and gently kisses her lips. When she awakens he asks her to marry him, and she does."

Giralda sat and stared. She was dumbfounded. It was a beautiful story told with captivating fervor—but who was the sophisticated young woman doing the telling? How had Vayle suddenly become so romantically refined? What had happened out in the wilds of the stormy night to induce such quixotic maturation? Giralda's mind was still swirling when Vayle spoke again. "Good night, my lady. I love you very much." Vayle kissed Giralda on the cheek, released the grasp on Giralda's arm, and then dropped back against her down-filled pillow.

"Good night, princess. I love you too," Giralda managed to speak. She began rising from the bed, but then she stopped, half-raised, suspended in thought. She sank back down onto the bed.

"Vayle?"

"Yes, ma'am."

"Did you see someone before you fell from the cliff?"

"Oh, no, ma'am."

"You are sure?"

"Yes, ma'am."

There was a pause. "Do you know how you ended up on the west side of the castle?"

Again there was pause…a longer pause. "That is a thought-provoking question."

Silence followed. Vayle said no more. Giralda felt as if the walls and ceiling became transparent and a thousand ethereal eyes turned upon her—as if she were prying into a matter too hallow for human interrogation. A part of her wanted to ask more questions, but she sensed a supernatural dissuasion, and she was not prone to discounting spiritual epiphanies. "I see, well, good night."

"Good night, my lady."

There were no more words. Giralda leaned and kissed the princess on the forehead, and then she rose and stepped into her chamber. Soon she was situated in her bed. There was an aura of enchantment permeating the room, and Giralda drifted into sleep laden with heartwarming dreams.

Chapter 6

Challenge and Adventure

The sound of trickling water played upon Zarkanis's ears as the great Mount Thrandor shed his winter coat. Reminiscing upon past years, Zarkanis recalled that it was only during the bitterest and coldest weeks of the year that he deferred nightly swimming; the running water beneath his cell rarely froze. A major difference in his schedule of activities occurred during his thirteenth year when he discovered that he had grown too large to fit through the well opening. Now, age fourteen, he leaned on an outstretched arm and gazed downward through the well opening upon the moving water beneath his cell.

Sunlight blazed the surface of the channel as a dazzling orange globe peered above the eastern forest. Sometime later the surface succumbed to shade while deeper water glistened in brilliant illumination. Aquatic life was most visible during the mornings after sunrise. This was the silent period preceding breakfast—a time when Zarkanis sat in mock dumbness, wearing a wool blanket. Dametrius taught him to utilize this period of silence for meditation and prayer, but on sunny mornings Zarkanis found it fascinating to gaze into the natural aquarium below the cell and observe fish, amphibians, eels, minnows, snakes, turtles, and crawdads.

The prince's aquatic surveillance was interrupted by the sound of grating metal. A guard's footsteps became audible. Duardo opened the cell door and stepped inside, lugging a bucket laden with leftovers.

After emptying the bucket near the well opening, Duardo took a long look at Zarkanis. He grinned at the prince's gifted imitation of a swine. Then he turned and departed.

Enormous quantities of food began appearing after Dragus received reports that the Captive from Shareen was growing fat. Dragus never visited the dungeon chambers himself due to his fear that a prisoner would somehow inflict bodily harm upon him while he passed by the cells, but he delighted in reports he received concerning the portliness of King Wildon's son.

Zarkanis turned the morning acceptance of victuals into charades. When a guard entered the cell with a bucket of food, he held his eyes fixed to the bucket and grunted. Dametrius had warned him not to make eye contact with the prison guards, explaining that a man's eyes can betray intelligence more readily than words. The grunting was Zarkanis's idea, and in truth he had no objection to the excess ham, beef, cheese, and poultry that his antics procured.

Morning after morning, Dametrius stared blankly as Zarkanis impressed guards with swine imitations. Inwardly he laughed. His pupil was cunning and was a gifted actor. Life in confinement with the Prince of Shareen, who needed only the decree of public sanction to become a king, was entertaining.

A clang echoed through the opening in the lower section of the cell door, indicating that the second door in the corridor was closed.

"We are fortunate today," announced Zarkanis. "Seven boiled goose eggs and two not even cracked. And, here, chicken liver! We shall dine on fresh catfish tonight."

Dametrius smiled. He was not fond of raw fish, but acquiring aquatic protein provided amusement for his captive student, and fresh meat was nourishing. And besides that, it seemed appropriate for Zarkanis to learn the art of scaling and filleting fish by utilizing a chunk of sharpened flint that he brought up from the bottom of the canal when he was nine years old.

"Here you go," said Zarkanis, handing over three choice goose eggs.

Dametrius gazed downward at the eggs. His morning meditations had been far reaching and staid—there were far weightier matters on his mind than either goose eggs or catfish fillets. "Perhaps you should have fled two years ago before growing too large to fit through the well."

It was rare that Dametrius spoke any word that was not optimistic. Zarkanis looked up, staring at his comrade. "It was my decision, and I do not regret it. Someday I will grow strong enough to breach the bars and walls that contain us, and then I will be much more capable of fending my way to Shareen and assuming kingship. And when that day comes, I will not wish to leave a capable and irreplaceable advisor behind."

Dametrius raised his face and met Zarkanis's eyes. He knew that his schooling fostered cognizance of free will, and he had no doubt that the imprisoned Prince of Shareen spoke with sincerity. To witness his student choosing to exercise charity warmed Dametrius's heart and spurred his resolve. He had already lived longer than the expected lifespan for inhabitants of either Rome or Gaul, and he determined to apply the remaining years of his life shaping Zarkanis into an instrument of righteous justice that would strike terror through the heart of evil dictators such as Dragus. Perhaps he was an old idealist, but why not be? When he looked upon Zarkanis, it was easy to be an idealist.

"You have spoken wisely pertaining to readiness, but I would advise you to reconsider your proposed manner of approaching Shareen," remarked Dametrius.

The prince's blue eyes gleamed with interest. "Do you have an idea?"

"Certainly," consented Dametrius, "but let us not delay breakfast. The first meal is important to all subsequent activities of the day."

The prince had long since mastered the virtue of patience. There was bread and ham to go with the eggs, and he passed generous portions to Dametrius—far more than the lean scholar would eat. He also lowered the bucket into the canal, drew out fresh water, and set the bucket between himself and Dametrius.

It was not Dametrius's custom to eat in silence. "You must consider," he said after washing down egg and bread with water sipped from the rind of a gourd, "that Shareen will have been a captive city for several years." Before hearing more, Zarkanis had to wait until his teacher finished some ham—and so it went throughout the discourse. "What I suggest, therefore, is that you establish a stronghold elsewhere. There are bound to be Shareans scattered throughout the villages and countryside surrounding Shareen who would band together to redeem their city if their rightful king showed up."

Zarkanis nodded. "Yes…well…you know…" he said, and then he took several bites of barley bread before resuming speech, "I think that is excellent advice."

Dametrius could not help but smile.

When breakfast was completed, Dametrius and Zarkanis sat side by side on the floor and leaned back against the stone bed.

"Have you any questions regarding the latest series of lectures?" posed Dametrius.

"No, sir, I believe you covered the motivational and emotional entities common to the human race quite satisfactorily."

"Good. Now for a miscellaneous quiz."

Zarkanis perked up. He liked miscellaneous quizzes.

"By what vector," began Dametrius, "may a village become subject to the plague of pestilence?"

"Flea-infested rats," answered Zarkanis, relaxing the back of his head against the stone bed.

"Good." There followed a short pause. "Why does water turn to ice upon the surface of a lake rather than forming ice at the bottom of a lake?"

Zarkanis thought for a minute. "Water shrinks in volume as it grows colder, but at the point of freezing it expands. This causes heavier liquid to be drawn beneath the ice by the force that draws all things towards the earth's core. The downward movement of the water presses the ice upward, so ice floats above water." This was an adequate response to the question, so Zarkanis refrained from exhibiting his further knowledge that surface ice provides insulation and helps prevent lakes from freezing into solid blocks. *A wise man*, Dametrius taught, *does not boast of his own merits or intelligence but rather leaves such praise to others.*

"Good. Now answer this—by what means may one decipher north versus south on a dark night in the forest when black clouds efface the moon and stars?"

For a few moments, Zarkanis feared he was stumped, but then the solution popped into his mind. "By feeling around the trunks of trees. Moss grows on the north side of tree trunks in Gaul."

"Excellent," averred Dametrius, and then he paused longer than before. Zarkanis knew that three correct answers in a row meant that the next question would be formidable. "Here is a question that poses a different sort of challenge."

"I knew it," Zarkanis murmured, though he was enjoying the entire affair.

"What animal that walks upon land has the longest tail?"

Dametrius knew that he had mentioned some interesting facts regarding animals long ago, back when Zarkanis was learning to speak. The disclosure of such facts came during bedtime stories about wonderful and faraway places. He did not expect to hear the correct answer to his question after so many years, but it was not his custom to permit more than three correct answers in a row.

Zarkanis delayed his response. He was chuckling inside. He loved those bedtime stories. "The longest tail…the longest tail… Now, let me think…hum… I've never seen one, as I've never been to Africa, but that must be the animal that also has the longest neck—the giraffe."

"Yes," stated Dametrius. He was baffled by the prince's recollection. There was a very long pause this time. "If there is an underground world called Subterrania, as is rumored in Glamster—that is, if there is a world beneath the ground with skies of rock— then how must the atmosphere of such a world support plant and animal life?"

Subterrania was a conjectural matter Dametrius often pondered but seldom mentioned. Although the reality of such a place seemed implausible, he had a valid reason to believe in its existence—Sorgon himself avowed that the underworld was authentic. Sorgon said that he once visited there, and he described a land of fantastic flora, peculiar wildlife, and unique races of men. If not for the confidence Dametrius placed in Sorgon, he would not have given the matter much regard. Sorgon, however, was an honest and intelligent man. For this reason, when his thoughts were his own, Dametrius entertained hypotheses as to how an underground world could subsist. He was challenging Zarkanis with a question that he had contemplated for many years.

Zarkanis remembered Dametrius mentioning Subterrania years before. The underground world was discussed during a lecture that also addressed the lost city of Atlantis. Such places appealed to Zarkanis's adventuresome spirit, but until hearing this question pertaining to Subterrania's atmosphere, he had not thought that his teacher took the existence of either Atlantis or Subterrania seriously.

"You mean there really is an underground world?"

"Perhaps," Dametrius acknowledged. "Whether such an entity exists, however, does not alter the question."

Zarkanis grew excited. Here was yet another reason to someday escape his cell—to investigate the mystery of Subterrania.

"Do you resign the question? I have new activities to discuss that may compensate for the absence of swimming."

Zarkanis turned his head toward Dametrius. "No, I have an idea," he replied, though his mind was obsessed with guessing what Dametrius meant by *new activities*. "Perhaps the atmosphere is maintained by the circulation of air through openings that connect with the outer surface of earth."

"Good assumption," said Dametrius, "but there are a few problems with it. Sorgon, the blacksmith in Glamster to whom I sent Zake and Zephanoah, told me that there is only one opening into Subterrania. That opening is reached through a cave found deep within a mountain crevice, and it enters Subterrania at a point where the vaulted sky of the underground world rises much higher than at any other site. It would be impossible, therefore, for sufficient air to circulate from the outer world."

Zarkanis thought for a minute before responding. "Do you surmise, then, that there are forms of life with different atmospheric needs than in the outer world?"

"A stimulating concept, but Sorgon visited Subterrania and survived. He described thick foliage with edible fruit, and he did not return to the outer world for two weeks."

"Foliage! The underworld is a biosphere with its own equilibrium," blurted Zarkanis. "There must be some form of natural energy, something that emits light, and the light must promote the propagation of botanic life, and the botanic life must in turn supply nourishment and a proper atmosphere for animal life."

There was little Dametrius could add. "Half credit," he granted. "The source of light must be phosphorescent rock, namely the rock forming the vaulted ceiling of the underground world. The only other viable theory is that Sorgon received a blow to his head and dreamed the entire experience."

Zarkanis was disheartened by Dametrius's alternate theory. "But two weeks? How would you explain his missing for two whole weeks?"

"Amnesia."

Zarkanis realized that his teacher had a point. One man's incredible claims did not proffer overwhelming evidence to the supposition of an alien world. "I guess such a conclusion is sensible," he pined.

Dametrius could see that he had raised reasonable doubt within Zarkanis's mind. With this accomplished, he presented a confession. "Nonetheless, I believe in Subterrania's existence."

Zarkanis recouped his excitement. If Dametrius the Wise believed that Subterrania was a real world, then no other proof was needed. "Did Sorgon tell you where the opening to Subterrania is found?"

"No," answered Dametrius, "he said that the entranceway into the underground world is a secret, and he said that he could never divulge that secret to anyone. I can only think of one logical explanation for such reticence."

"What?"

"He spoke of human inhabitants whose spoken language is bizarre but beautiful, and whose written language includes peculiar symbols interspaced with images of birds, plants, and animals. Those inhabitants must have forbidden Sorgon from disclosing the means of access to their world. In fact, it would be logical to surmise that they would not release him to return to his home until he promised to keep the entranceway a secret. I have often pondered upon this, but you are the only person to whom I have disclosed the existence of Subterrania. I never even mentioned the underground world to Zake, though I probably would have…eventually."

Zarkanis's imagination soared as he contemplated the existence of an underground world. "Did Sorgon know how to write in the Subterranian language?"

"Some."

"Did he teach you?"

"Yes. He had parchments that he brought back with him, and he jotted down translations on the parchments while he was in Subterrania. He permitted me to copy all that he had written, and I took pleasure in teaching myself, to what extent I could, a language spoken by the inhabitants of an underground world."

Zarkanis stared in wonder. "Will you teach me?"

"Of course."

Zarkanis smiled, deep in thought about all the marvels that might exist within a world beneath the earth's surface; but then his mind returned to his present circumstances. "I believe you said something about some new activities?"

Dametrius also smiled. He rose and stepped to the window. Zarkanis was at his heels, following Dametrius's gaze toward the northern shore of Lake Manassa. The imprisoned Prince of Shareen no longer needed the aid of a bucket to stand and peer out the cell window.

Most of the lake's surface had already thawed, but ice persisted along the northern edge. Early spring dabbed the tips of twigs with tiny green orbs, and evergreens shrugged cottony tufts from their limbs. Birds flitted from limb to limb and tweeted flirtatiously.

"There are quite a number of limbs, branches, and cones lying upon the ice," pointed out Dametrius.

Zarkanis focused upon debris at the base of the northern cliffs. "I see them."

"I'm sure you have noticed that most soldiers coming and going along the road south of the lake wear swords on their belts."

Zarkanis turned toward Dametrius. "Yes, and not only swords but also knives, and sometimes they carry bows and tote quivers of arrows."

"And what do you suppose these items are made of?"

Zarkanis glanced back toward the debris. "The bows and arrows are wooden."

"And the knives and swords may be simulated with wood."

For the third time that morning, the Prince of Shareen became excited. "So you will teach me to use weapons! You will instruct me in the arts of defense!"

Dametrius was well trained in swordsmanship and archery, having learned from accomplished masters in Roman schools. "It is necessary for good men to become proficient in such matters, lest the wicked rule and the innocent suffer."

"So when do we begin?"

"As soon as we obtain materials."

Zarkanis looked toward the well. His inability to fit through the opening seemed dire. "But how?"

"It is a cloudless day. Sunshine is melting the ice. I will loosen the rope from the bucket, and then I will tie adjacent corners of a blanket to the two loose ends of the rope. I will then hold the middle of the rope in one hand and grasp the other two corners of the blanket in the other hand—forming a pocket. I will then lower the blanket down the well and partly submerge it beneath the surface of the water. This will serve as an improvised net to capture items that nature sends our way. Watch from the window, and when limbs or cones are drawn down the channel by the current, inform me."

The entire enterprise sounded like great sport to Zarkanis. "Why cones?"

"You must also learn to throw."

"But I have been throwing bits of stone since I learned to crawl."

"Cones will give you different aerodynamic perspectives."

Zarkanis pondered his teacher's remark. "May I trade tasks with you from time to time?"

"Of course. I will show you how to loop the rope around your wrist so that it will not slip off your hand."

Zarkanis took his position at the window while Dametrius fixed his makeshift net. No sooner was the task completed than a long branch with several small limbs was carried by the current so that it passed down the waterway leading to the castle. "Here comes one!" Zarkanis whispered loudly. Dametrius lowered the blanket into the channel below and Zarkanis watched the branch float toward the castle wall. It was a miss... The branch floated down one of the other two channels. As time passed, however, another branch was carried down the waterway, and the two inmates hoisted a sizeable limb with two twigs and several cones.

By late afternoon there were sticks, limbs, cones, and twigs strewn about the floor near the well opening. Dametrius chose which items to keep from the hodgepodge and the selected items were hidden behind the stone bed. Discarded items were returned to the canal.

The space between the southern wall and the stone bed was four feet in width, and it was where Zarkanis slept—it had been his bedroom since seven years of age. It was also where secret items were cached, stashed between the limestone floor and the uneven edges of the great bed. When the prison guard served breakfast the following morning, he saw nothing out of the ordinary. The wool blanket that was used to secure virtual treasure for the two inmates had been wrung out and hung on the wall to dry, and then it had been placed back on the floor.

****

On the same morning that Dametrius the Wise would begin carving weapons in a dungeon cell, a cheerful princess donned riding attire in anticipation of an adventure. Master Edmond, after pleading on Vayle's behalf, gained permission from Dragus to take the princess on an overnight camping trip, along with Marlda and Giralda. The foursome was supposed to camp in a forest that grew northwest of Mount Thrandor. It would be the first time for either Vayle or Giralda to travel such a far distance away from the castle.

The princess was alone. She and Giralda ate an early breakfast in the antechamber, and then Giralda gathered up dishes and departed. Natural leather boots, a suede riding skirt, and a suede jerkin all blended together to highlight the golden lock in Vayle's hair. A silver mirror reflected the sporty outfit for perusal. Beneath the long-sleeved jerkin was a silk blouse that was dyed emerald green.

Princess Vayle was proficient in dressing and behaving as a royal lady, but she was incalculably different from other members of the Pithranian monarchy. It was a well-kept secret among the castle servants that she tended the ill, counseled the brokenhearted, and assisted with castle chores. The servants knew, just as she knew, that such behavior on the part of a Pithranian Princess would incite ill regard from Dragus and Lady Eldra, and it was a collective effort on all of their parts to conceal Princess Vayle's gracious nature from the self-absorbed king and his pretentious queen. Giralda sometimes wondered if the princess were taking too many risks, but on the other hand, she could not have been more pleased with Vayle's maturity and compassionate disposition.

The princess had just finished donning her jerkin when the door to the stairwell opened. The drapes between the antechamber and her bedroom were already drawn apart, so she was able to turn and see who entered.

"Marlda!" exclaimed Vayle, remaining seated as she pivoted around on the stool that sat before her mirror. Giralda came in behind Marlda and closed the door.

"I can't believe it," said Marlda, holding one hand to her chest as she hastened into the bedroom with her dearest friend. "Lady Eldra threw a tantrum when she found out that Dragus is letting us do this. Giralda and I came up the outer steps to the lookout post and then came down through the hatch just to make sure the queen wouldn't see us." She stopped speaking and looked hard at Vayle, inspecting every article of clothing from the leather boots to a golden hairpin fixed in the left side of Vayle's hair. For a moment she glanced back toward Giralda, who was gathering a few last-minute items and placing them into a wool bag, and then she turned back to Vayle. Approaching closer, she leaned and whispered into Vayle's ear. "Perhaps your prince will see you and come snatch you from us."

Vayle leaned back and snapped her eyes at Marlda. She had warned Marlda to never mention her prince unless they were alone; and even then, Marlda was only to do so with utmost caution. She had never mentioned the existence of Zarkanis to anyone else, and even Marlda did not know his name—Vayle simply referred to him as *my prince*. Sometimes Vayle regretted telling Marlda, but it was hard to keep such a thing to herself—dwelling upon her prince night after night, evoking the feel of his body and envisioning the look in his eyes as moonlight flooded her room through open balcony doors—and not share his authenticity with at least one other person.

Marlda produced a teasing smile, and then she changed the subject. "Father says I can ride Sandy, and you can ride Black Pearl."

"Yes, I know," said Vayle, "Giralda told me."

Vayle preferred a white mare named Littlehooves, a horse she often rode about the castle grounds, but the upcoming journey was considered too strenuous for Littlehooves. Both girls were assigned larger and sturdier mares.

"Have you ridden Sandy before?" asked Vayle.

"Once."

"I rode Black Pearl twice. She's as gentle as a ewe. No one's ever been thrown by her, except, of course, for Borgar."

"Borgar!" scoffed Marlda. "He probably pulled Black Pearl's tail to try to get the mare to walk backward."

Vayle laughed.

"Now, girls," crooned Giralda as she walked into the bedroom, "it is a lovely day. Would it not be good to think and speak of good things?"

Giralda spoke these words for Marlda's sake. She had overheard Marlda verbally lashing Prince Borgar on previous occasions when the girls were together, and she knew that harsh punishment could befall a commoner if Lady Eldra learned about it. It seemed best to dissuade such dialogue.

"A good point, my lady," replied Vayle. She turned toward Marlda and winked. "I suppose there will be some lovely scenery."

Marlda peered into Vayle's eyes and smiled. She was much more sophisticated than Giralda imagined. "Have you ever heard of Poolglade Forest? My father says it is altogether rugged and downright beautiful. He says no one lives there—the region is all rocks and trees and waterfalls and wild animals!"

"How marvelous!" rejoined Vayle. "I've heard of it, but no one has ever told me much about it. Have you ever been there?"

"Never."

"Ready, girls?" interjected Giralda, turning toward the passageway to the antechamber while toting the wool bag.

"Yes," they replied in unison.

Vayle and Marlda followed behind Giralda. They stepped outside the antechamber and climbed to the top of the tower. Three guards nodded. "Take care on those steps… Stay close to the castle wall," one of them instructed when he noted that Princess Vayle had joined Marlda and Giralda.

The three females stepped down a spiraling staircase until reaching the level of the castle roof. Giralda then led them to a western stairwell and down into the grand hall.

There was much commotion. Dragus and his troops were back after a drawn-out campaign that wrought expansion of the eastern reaches of the Pithranian Empire. Soldiers sat at wooden tables, bartering and bragging, while officers assembled loot for Dragus's inspection. No doubt there would be brawling and carousing before the day ended. Vayle was thankful to be leaving.

Giralda led the girls to the castle entranceway without much notice. They crossed the drawbridge and turned southwest toward the primary castle stables. Only under threat of attack would horses be moved into small limestone stables within the castle itself—stables known as the *battle stables*—and there was no passageway to the battle stables except through the grand hall. Master Edmond, as majordomo of castle affairs, was granted the privilege of boarding horses in the primary castle stables.

The countryside south of the castle was very different from mountainous realms to the north. The north was rugged and wild; whereas, the south was cultivated and civilized. Other than Esther, the daughter of a castle cook, most of Vayle's friends inhabited homes in the southern farmlands—including Marlda. The culture in these farmlands seemed detached from Dragus's decadent regime.

A distance of three hundred yards separated the far edge of the drawbridge from the stables. Giralda was wistful as they walked through an intersecting apple orchard. The outing presented a possible opportunity to flee from Pithrania with Princess Vayle, but Giralda had already determined that attempting to flee was a bad idea. Dragus was in control of every kingdom and village that she had ever inhabited, and he was certain to hunt down Princess Vayle and her lady-in-waiting should they take flight. It seemed safest to wait and see what opportunities for escape might arise in the future, and it also seemed safest to continue withholding Vayle's true identity, even from the princess herself. Meanwhile, she and the princess continued to live as Dragus's pampered protégées.

"Hail, ladies! Welcome!" hollered Master Edmond. He stood waiting before the stables. In line beside him were four saddled horses, all tethered to a rail. The saddlebags on the first two horses were tied shut, and the first horse had a bow, quiver, and arrows secured upon blankets behind the saddle. The saddlebags on the other two horses still hung open, awaiting paraphernalia that Giralda toted in a wool bag. Heavy blankets were secured behind each saddle.

"Dragus is allowing us to travel without escorts?" questioned Giralda.

"Yes, but only because the northwest region is uninhabited, and because we are returning tomorrow, and because no sojourners have been seen in the northwestern realm for weeks," replied Master

Edmond. "And besides that, none of his soldiers want to miss tonight's festivities."

Giralda thought the term *festivities* was a misleading description of the drunken revelries that took place at Dragus's homecoming celebrations. Nonetheless, she appreciated the rare treat that Master Edmond arranged—a trip free of Pithranian warriors. "You have my sincere thanks," she remarked.

Master Edmond smiled. He was of different timber than most men serving Dragus. Giralda figured that the only reason Master Edmond remained living within Pithranian territory was because his family had lived there for generations. His oldest daughter, Geneviere, was married to a Sharean farmer; and his only other child was Marlda.

"Well, ladies, the sun has been begging us to get started for an hour. If we want to see the demented king's castle before nightfall, we must leave right away and make good time," remarked Master Edmond.

"Oh, wow, we're going to see that! You didn't tell me that!" decried Marlda. Both she and Vayle had heard Master Edmond tell the story about the strange castle, but neither one of them knew that they would get the opportunity to see it.

Vayle said nothing, but she faced Master Edmond with interest.

"You mean there really is such a thing?" asked Giralda. Master Edmond accepted Giralda's bag and began transferring goods into the open saddlebags as he answered her inquiry. "There is indeed, though I will tell you ahead of time that it is inaccessible—we will be able to look, but we will not be able to enter. No one has set foot within the castle for well over a hundred years. But even so, it is a sight worth seeing."

Master Edmond turned and left the ladies talking among themselves. He finished packing and tying the saddlebags, and then he untethered Giralda's horse. Giralda was to ride a large mare palomino named Starlight. He led the horse to Giralda. "Have you heard the full story about the demented king's castle?" he inquired.

Vayle and Marlda looked toward Giralda. If she responded in the negative, then they would get to hear the story again. It was one of their favorites.

"Well, no, I've only heard it mentioned in passing conversation."

"Very well then. Since we are going to see the eccentric edifice, you may as well hear the entire tale."

The girls both whooped.

"But first let us embark upon our journey," said Master Edmond. "We need to get going before Dragus changes his mind."

Master Edmond's offhand remark about Dragus induced prompt activity. Giralda mounted Starlight, and Master Edmond handed her the reins. Then he untethered Sandy and signaled for Marlda. Once Marlda was mounted, it was Vayle's turn to mount Black Pearl. The stirrups were set the same length as Marlda's and were therefore adjusted well—both girls were petite. She mounted with ease.

Giralda and Marlda wore wool slacks. Vayle was fitted with brown, soft-leather breeches that came into view as the hem of her suede skirt slid upward to her thighs. Such breeches and skirts were adjudged fashionable by royal ladies in Gaul.

"Have we forgotten anything?" asked Master Edmond.

Giralda shifted in her saddle and looked at the two girls, and then she faced Master Edmond. "I think not."

"Very well. I will take the lead, followed by Princess Vayle and Marlda. Giralda may guard against any bear attacks from the rear."

Giralda was accustomed to Master Edmond's sense of humor, but she still cast him a remonstrative glare as he coaxed Jasper past her.

"At times," resumed Master Edmond, halting Jasper and looking back toward the women, "we will all have to ride single file. When we do, Princess Vayle will follow me, and then Marlda, and then Giralda. This will prevent Black Pearl from stepping on Sandy's heels, as she is prone to do. She will not bother Jasper."

Vayle gazed toward Jasper. He was a spirited Arabian stallion, and he would not permit anyone to ride him other than Master Edmond.

"And in the event that any of you see a threatening carnivore, do not yell or scream or do anything that would frighten the horses. Just calmly say, 'Pardon, Master Edmond, but a dragon has just devoured the bear that was stalking Giralda.'"

The girls laughed while Giralda staged another look of admonition.

"Now, let's get going, and when we reach the ridge beyond the cliffs, I will tell you the story of the demented king and his peculiar castle."

Master Edmond turned and prodded Jasper forward. The four travelers headed west and coursed down an embankment, and then they crossed the wooden bridge that spanned the Requain River below the falls. Hollow, clopping sounds echoed from the face of the mountain.

Vayle and Marlda conversed as they rode side by side. Giralda trailed close behind. The horses climbed to a ridge that circled the west side of Mount Thrandor and the travelers seemed to depart the reaches of civilization. Sights and sounds of chirping birds, squawking squirrels, and rustling pine needles engulfed them. The wild fragrances of a pristine forest aroused their sense of smell, including scents of cedar, spruce, and windswept limestone.

Tufts of green mountain grass pierced through white sheets of snow. A hare bounded from beneath a spruce tree and splayed snowflakes through sunbeams. The dispersed snowflakes looked like a swarm of tiny fireflies rising from the snowy ground and then relighting on the frosty floor of the forest. Relative warmth belied the wintry landscape. The girls got so caught up in the surrounding scenery and stimulating sounds of nature that Master Edmond's story, for a while, was crowded from their minds. Giralda, who was curious about the demented king's castle, exercised patience as she followed in the rear.

The atmosphere dimmed as they entered the late morning shadow of Mount Thrandor. The higher reaches of the mountain were to the northeast. More time would pass before the sun topped the mountain's peak. On they rode, with the girls conversing about natural wonders along the way.

Then Vayle redirected everyone's train of thought. "Oh, say," she remarked, "Giralda has not yet heard the story about the odd castle."

"Father, you should have reminded us!" scolded Marlda.

Master Edmond continued facing forward and replied in a tone replete with innocence. His voice was full and resonant, and Giralda had no problem hearing him from the rear. "I did not have the heart to disrupt your inspiring conversation, my dear. And, besides, we will have plenty of time for stories before this day's ride is over."

"How about now?" Marlda persisted. She was well accustomed to her father's teasing.

Master Edmond's voice rose to a new level of magnificence. "About two hundred years ago, give or take a few years, there arose a powerful monarch in the Asperian Mountains—some distance to the northeast of Mount Thrandor. He was cunning and crafty, luring many men into his service with promises of riches and prestige. It is said that he gave every man who joined his ranks an exquisite black pearl—meaning a gem rather than a horse such as Princess Vayle is riding."

The girls chuckled.

"Where any man could come up with such a number of exquisite black pearls is a mystery unto this day, for it is said that he never ran out of them, even though more than a thousand men enlisted in his service. Of course, he kept the biggest pearl for himself—it was the size of the eyeball of an ox."

Giralda emerged from a state of infatuation and smirked. Up to this point she had thought the story might be true, but she had never heard of a pearl being anywhere near the size of the eyeball of an ox. Still, there was something about the manner of Master Edmond's presentation that made her question her doubts. She found herself engrossed as he recommenced speaking.

"In time the monarch was declared King of Asperia. King Spero he was called, though no one ever knew if Spero was his real name. He built a fortress where the town of Asperia now sits in the Vanube Valley. Many think that his success as a ruler stemmed from the mystery surrounding his origin. He seemed to appear from nowhere, with no past and no native country, and it was rumored that he was some sort of sorcerer."

"Was he?" asked Vayle.

"I doubt it. Nonetheless, he was eccentric. He demanded that his diet include raw eel at least twice weekly, and he kept lanterns burning outside his bedroom window at night so that it would not appear dark outside."

"Outside his window?" inquired Giralda, accentuating the word *outside*. Like Master Edmond, she possessed a hearty set of vocal cords and was easily heard.

"Yes, there were special shutters and a canopy built to protect the lamps from wind and rain, and during the winter a silk tarp was fitted in the window to resist cold air."

"It seems to me that a small night-lamp would have been less trouble," said Giralda.

"True, but for whatever reason, King Spero could not bring himself to accept the reality of nighttime darkness."

The horses fell into proper sequence, walking single file along a narrow ridge that cut across the western slope of Mount Thrandor. A radiant crown sat atop the peak of the mountain, heralding a cascade of brilliant rays that would soon pour over the mountain's white mantle.

Master Edmond knew the northwestern territory well and he had no trouble staying on course, even though the region was so seldom traveled that there were no obvious paths. He paused from his storytelling and gazed up at the peak of the mountain, anticipating the moment when sunbeams would brighten the landscape.

"Wow," breathed Vayle as the upper rim of the sun rose above the peak of the mountain, "it's so wonderful."

Everyone's silence assented. They rode along and gawked up and down the mountain. Forest trees, rocky promontories, and snow-covered slopes took on new dimensions of splendor as they were bathed in an ocean of sunlight. Granite cliffs that rose above green conifers transformed from shaded tones of gray to brilliant pinks, purples, reds, and blacks—like the necks of colossal hummingbirds reflecting iridescent rays above glistening green feathers. And the mountain's pinnacle pointed upward toward the heavens like a great white pyramid.

By and by Giralda grew impatient. She was impressed by the majestic scenery, but she was caught up in Master Edmond's discourse. "All right, go on with the story," she urged.

Master Edmond obliged. "King Spero proved to be a great military leader, which was not such a great thing for folks in surrounding villages. He presided over his army in a reign of conquest and pillage. As time passed he grew more and more arrogant and imperious. He was feared as far as his name was known, and there was no one who dared challenge his dictatorial supremacy. Then one morning, for no apparent reason, the pompous tyrant went berserk. It was early in the morning, about three o'clock, when this bizarre transformation occurred. Of course, on the other hand, I have heard it said that it may have been more like two o'clock, or perhaps even one o'clock…"

"No matter! What happened?" erupted Giralda.

The girls giggled. They had heard stories told by Master Edmond before, and they were familiar with his suspense-laden divergences. They knew that Giralda had been lured into a digression.

"The thing that happened was most bizarre."

"Yes, you've said that," Giralda retorted, "but what happened?"

"It happened sometime during the very early hours following midnight."

A pause followed. Giralda was a fast learner. After a few seconds of taunting silence, her patience was rewarded.

"As the soldiers, servants, jesters, and royal Asperians were sleeping in King Spero's castle, a horrendous scream echoed throughout the fortress. Guards rushed into King Spero's bedroom, and they found him sitting up in bed with his mouth drooped open and his eyes nearly bulged from their sockets. He was staring at the window and screaming. It took several minutes to quiet him down and get him to talk. When he did talk, he claimed that blue men had climbed the wall to his window—a feat that would have required scaling a vertical rock wall that was thirty feet tall—and he claimed that these blue men intended to kidnap him. The guards checked the window. It was summertime and the window was uncovered, but they saw no evidence of any abductors, much less blue ones."

There were a few seconds of dramatic suspense. The horses' hooves plopped across the snowy ground and the group continued coursing single file along the mountainside. The women were all silent, waiting for Master Edmond to resume his tale.

"After that, the king was feared more than ever. Some folks thought that the blue men were sent by a sorcerer, but most deemed them a figment of the king's imagination, and so it was then that many folks began calling him *the demented king.* He refused to sleep without at least two guards at the bottom of the castle wall outside his window, and each guard was required to make sure that the other guard did not fall asleep. But even this was not enough to calm his fears—he began to think that an entire army of blue men would march upon his fortress. And that was when he decided to build an unassailable edifice where he could flee to safety."

By this time Giralda was convinced that Master Edmond was a master storyteller. The inflections of his voice, his timing between words, and his charismatic personality all worked together in a captivating manner. Whether or not she granted veracity to the existence of blue men, she was transfixed by Master Edmond's narrative style. She found herself leaning forward in her saddle whenever he paused.

"Several search parties were sent out from the Asperian fortress to find the perfect site for an unassailable edifice. A large reward was promised to whichever party found a site that suited King Spero's fancy, so you can be sure that an earnest exploration ensued. But it was nearly a year before someone was crazy enough to suggest the site that appeased the king's apparent insanity—a secluded shelf high in the face of a sheer cliff, a shelf set back in the cliff so that objects dropped from the top edge of the cliff could not strike it. There was a natural spring that surfaced through the floor of the shelf and formed a brook that poured over its edge; so with preserved food, a group of people could survive upon the shelf for long periods of time without outside aid."

A hawk let out several cries as it appeared from between two soaring pines and then swerved back eastward. All eyes followed the hawk until it dropped behind the top of an evergreen, but there was no comment from among the women—their silence cued Master Edmond to continue his story.

"Since there was no access to the high stone shelf, the king ordered that huge steps be carved in the smooth face of the cliff. These steps were completed, and then men toted building materials up to the shelf. In time a small castle was constructed. This undertaking took years, and meanwhile the king remained on the lookout for blue marauders—or, more specifically, for blue kidnappers."

Master Edmond paused. Again there was silence.

"As the castle was being constructed, the king directed a choice group of laborers to dig a secret tunnel that led up to the shelf—a tunnel with stone steps. The tunnel was to begin behind a thicket at the base of the cliff and emerge inside the castle, seventy feet above. Like the castle, the tunnel took years to complete. The arduous excavation required workers to chisel with iron hammers that were used to strike forged steel wedges. These workers made their way through solid stone, and the tunnel was hardly a secret by the time it was finished."

"You mean that we can actually climb up to the castle through a tunnel?" Giralda queried, startling both the girls in front of her. "So what did you mean when you said that the castle was inaccessible? What's to keep us from going up the steps in the face of the cliff or up the steps in the tunnel?"

There was a well-timed break in speech. Master Edmond drew a belabored breath, and then spoke with the mannerism of a priggish steward. "Princess Vayle, please advise your illustrious lady-in-waiting that if she can manifest some well-mannered bridling of the tongue, her seemingly insatiable curiosity will be served."

Vayle cast a glance rearward, looking past Marlda at Giralda. Then she turned back around and broke out laughing. Seeing the look on

Giralda's face made restraint from mirth impossible. Marlda also glanced back and then joined Vayle in laughter. As for Giralda, she felt inclined to say something, but since an appropriate rejoinder would not come to her mind, she decided to bid her time and wait for another opportunity to banter with Master Edmond.

"Very well," pronounced Master Edmond after the laughter settled. "I will take leave to continue my tale. So, with the completed construction of both the castle and the tunnel, King Spero directed his warriors to destroy the outer steps and make the face of the cliff as smooth as one of his black pearls. And like his previous demands, accomplishing this task was laborious. By the time the entire project was finished, the undertaking had cost more than half of the Asperian treasury, but the odd castle was fashioned just as King Spero desired."

Master Edmond shifted positions in his saddle. Marlda and Vayle, who had heard this story before, waited in anticipation of the climax. Giralda was simmering with curiosity, but she sealed her lips and waited for Master Edmond to resume speaking.

"Then one day the king disappeared—right from his own bedroom. A party of warriors journeyed to the castle in the cliff to see if the king had withdrawn to his newly-completed hideaway. When they reached the airborne structure, which was two days' ride from Asperia, they discovered that the secret tunnel, which was really no secret at all, had collapsed. They hollered to see if anyone was in the castle above, but there was no response.

"So then, a new king was chosen from among the Asperian officers, and Asperia became a village of goat herdsmen and wood craftsmen— a much happier village than before. And thus the castle sits to this very day—never having been lived in. And hereby ends the story of the demented king and his peculiar castle."

As he finished his story, Master Edmond turned at the waist and faced his audience. His right hand still clasped Jasper's reins, but his left hand was extended in formal salutation. He bowed with uninhibited flamboyance. His head nearly touched Jasper's tail, at which both Vayle and Marlda clapped loudly. With the outbreak of clapping, Jasper reared up on his hind legs, and it was only by ludicrous maneuvering that Master Edmond retained his position on Jasper's back—he looked like a squirrel clutching to a limb on a blustery day, and then he almost flipped over the top of Jasper's head as the stallion thumped back to his forefeet.

The girls, who stopped clapping at once, were alarmed and silent. Giralda, on the other hand, burst into a spontaneous fit of hilarity, and her laughter was long sustained. The girls found themselves laughing with her. For his part, Master Edmond righted himself in the saddle and rode along the mountainside as if all were quiet behind him. It was his goal to amuse the ladies, and Jasper merely lent a helping hoof.

With the story of the demented king completed, and having recovered from laughter, Vayle and Marlda resumed chatting back and forth. Giralda said little, but she remained in a jolly humor for hours. The four travelers stopped twice for food and drink. It was mid-afternoon when they began making their way down a steep ridge on the northwestern side of Mount Thrandor.

North of the travelers there spread a rugged and magnificent terrain. Rocky peaks jutted upward like snooping giants that peeped above treetops for a view of passersby, and most peaks wore white, snowy caps. The group crossed a stream with a bed of multicolored pebbles, pausing long enough for the horses to drink. Then on they traveled, heading west to northwest. Towering trees swallowed horses and riders as Jasper, Sandy, Black Pearl, and Starlight stepped downward into a sea of cedar, spruce, hemlock, fir, and pine. Springtime was more evident in this lower region, and there was little snow. Vayle drew the surrounding atmosphere into her lungs. Vitalizing air permeated her body.

"Oh, look!" said Marlda, pointing southwest. The forest opened into a circular meadow bounded by cedars. Five stately elk were clustered in the middle of the meadow—a bull, two cows, and two calves. The cows and calves continued grazing as the strange intruders passed by, but the bull raised his massive antlers and stared.

"You can tell that few men pass this way," remarked Master Edmond. "Otherwise, spears and arrows would have trained those elk to flee at the sight of man."

They left the elk undisturbed and passed on into the forest. The scenery grew more beautiful as the journey progressed. As evening drew closer, more wildlife appeared. Chipmunks and rock squirrels scampered to and fro across the forest floor, and Vayle spotted an owl staring at her from the hollow of a walnut tree.

The coniferous trees outnumbered the deciduous. Nonetheless, the few oak, walnut, maple, elm, birch, and sycamore trees standing from place to place had grown into preponderant giants. Spring leaves budded at the tips of far-reaching branches. Vayle was certain that any one of the mammoth oak or walnut trees would house and feed a hundred squirrels.

Deeper into the forest they ventured. Shadows lengthened and the sun became a glowing orange ball above the distant silhouette of Mount Zeborah, a great mountain to the west.

Then the environment changed. The change was not simply due to the onset of evening, but rather, as the group traveled farther northwest, stunning topographical variations appeared all around them. Red and gray monoliths shot upward from the ground, standing as sentries over gushing springs and miniature waterfalls. Pink granite bluffs encircled fern-laden hollows, and terraced pools reflected elvish conifers. Vayle could have easily imagined she was dreaming.

"We have entered Poolglade Forest," proclaimed Master Edmond. "Soon the greatest choir of frogs in all of Gaul shall laud our presence with merry song, provided that they have come forth from hibernation."

Giralda had an inspiration. "This must be where you learned to sing!"

Master Edmond laughed along with the girls at Giralda's teasing, and then he broke out singing. Though both Marlda and Vayle knew that he was an accomplished singer, Giralda found herself listening in astonishment. His voice was rich and resonant, pouring into the wild environment and seemingly welcomed by the trees and forest denizens.

The song Master Edmond sang was a hilarious ballad about a bullfrog who decided that he should be king—a song Master Edmond composed impromptu as he serenaded the ladies. The pompous frog boasted the many qualifications and achievements by which he merited kingship. As the song progressed, the women found themselves laughing until they nearly toppled from their mounts, and their laughter inspired verse after verse. It soon became noticeable that frogs were indeed singing along with Master Edmond—cued by the advent of eventide. By the time the ode drew to completion, the ladies were gasping in gleeful hysteria. Giralda was especially entertained by the comparisons Master Edmond made between the frog and Dragus, though he never mentioned Dragus by name.

When laughter subsided to the level of whimsical chuckles, Marlda asked if the frog had a son; and then laughter broke loose again as Master Edmond commenced a new set of verses about an ostentatious tadpole. Giralda could scarce believe that Master Edmond was so daring, for it was more than obvious that the tadpole was a caricature of Prince Borgar; but, nonetheless, she had never enjoyed a bard more. And when Master Edmond finished his singing, the girls began telling funny stories. Giralda joined in, and it was a long while later before anyone giggled without generating additional laughter. By the time the last anecdote was completed, the group was deep within the heart of Poolglade Forest. All traces of the setting sun had vanished—for all three women were adept storytellers. Soft white light beamed from a full-faced moon.

"We are almost there," stated Master Edmond.

Vayle was ready for a rest. She had never ridden so far from the castle. With a clear sky and full moon above, the landscape was still visible, though it appeared as a monochromatic masterpiece dabbed across a three-dimensional canvas via the tip of an eccentric artist's paintbrush. Sheer cliffs rose in the distance to both the left and right with additional cliffs far ahead. The barren cliffs seemed disassociated from the lush forest and meadows, like gargantuan stone guests standing as aloof observers.

The travelers continued onward into a secluded gorge that was about seven hundred yards wide. The sound of splashing water caressed the environment. Nighttime instilled the atmosphere with a sense of mystery, as if creatures unbeknown to daylight peered out from behind every boulder and from around every tree. Vayle observed the silvery surface of a small lake through thick boughs to her left, but the lake was obscured from view as they trekked deeper into the gorge. Nighttime sounds continued. An owl hooted in rhythm with frogs and crickets, like a flute playing harmony to bagpipes and maracas.

"There it is!" exclaimed Vayle.

"What? Where?" asked Marlda.

"There," said Vayle, pointing forward and to her right.

All four riders drew back on their horses' reins and came to a halt. Marlda and Giralda peered toward the distant cliffs. Master Edmond knew the location of the castle and realized that they were approaching within viewing distance, but he chose to allow one of the ladies to make its discovery.

They all stared at the moonlit caste. It sat within a natural indention in the face of a stone cliff. The front wall, twenty feet tall, was capped with a battlement; and the castle had small towers on either end. The edifice spanned about thirty yards from tower to tower, running from southeast to northwest, parallel with the face of the cliff; and a small stream spilled over the edge of the ledge on which the castle sat—a gleaming tail dangling to the ground below.

"Do you know how far back the castle goes?" asked Giralda.

"No, there's no place to climb up for a look, and I've checked all along the base of the cliff for a means of access," answered Master Edmond. "I would guess, though, that the hollow in the side of the cliff is about fifty feet deep."

"And to think, no one can get inside. It just sits there, wasted," said Giralda.

"Oh, I don't know that I would call it wasted," responded Master Edmond. "The birds must enjoy it, and I imagine that some lizards can scale the cliff."

"Perhaps," Giralda conceded, though she spoke with a tone of satire. "And maybe there's an old dragon curled up behind the front wall."

"Dragon? Are there dragons up here?" inquired Vayle.

"I was just teasing," returned Giralda, though her voice carried a note of uncertainty. She peered from place to place about the multidimensional landscape. She had never seen a dragon, but if there were any dragons to be found, this seemed the sort of region a dragon might inhabit.

"Don't worry princess, dragons only eat cows or larger women," commented Master Edmond.

"Larger women?" posed Giralda.

The girls both laughed.

Master Edmond did not proffer a response. The group grew quiet, gazing upon the mystical castle.

"Are we going to sleep here, Father?" Marlda inquired.

Master Edmond turned Jasper around and began riding back past the ladies. "We will camp beside Crystal Pond."

"Oh, is that the little lake we just passed?" asked Vayle.

"That it is, and a very nice thing about sleeping at Crystal Pond is the waterfall. It pours from a fissure in the cliff, and the gushing water plunges into the pond. The sound lulls you into dreamland like a sleeping potion."

"I'm ready for a dose of that," said Giralda, nudging Starlight off the pathway so that the girls could more easily follow after Master Edmond.

Vayle and Marlda turned their horses, and Marlda let Black Pearl come up beside Sandy, motioning for Vayle to come close. She leaned and whispered into Vayle's ear. "Do you suppose your prince can climb like a lizard?"

Vayle's eyes snapped with admonition and she brought her right index finger to her lips. Then she prodded Black Pearl forward. But she was thinking. The implication of Marlda's words aroused her mind. She turned and peered hard at the little castle. The prince's origin was a mystery that she often contemplated. She knew he must live somewhere in the vicinity of Pithrania, or at least she supposed he must. And if that was so, then why couldn't he live in the clandestine chambers of a secluded castle?

"Catch up, girls, before a bear decides he needs a bedtime snack," called Master Edmond.

"Maybe there are no dragons around here, but there really are bears," said Marlda, speaking forward toward Vayle.

Vayle tore her eyes from the castle. The strange fortress was alluring. She found herself looking back over and over, and she seemed to see the distant face of a young prince staring down upon her from atop the castle wall.

A few minutes later, with the horses tethered so that they could graze, Master Edmond spread blankets upon the soft grass north of Crystal Pond. Moonlight transformed the waterfall, which poured down the face of a cliff on the far side of the pond, into translucent silver—a great nightlight that played upon the surface of the water with titillating toes. Frogs croaked boldly, and crickets chirped unabated, but none of the four travelers were kept awake; the soporific song of the waterfall worked its spell. Deep and restful sleep settled upon them as peacefully as the mist from the waterfall settled upon the surface of Crystal Pond. In her dreams, Vayle saw Prince Zarkanis climbing down a stone cliff and walking across a flowery gorge. A wishful smile formed upon her unconscious face.

****

Appealing fragrances coaxed Vayle to wakefulness—fragrances of sizzling cured bacon and venison. A gasp of delight rushed past her lips as she sat up and beheld Poolglade Forest dressed in the light of dawn. Multicolored stone jutted upward into miniature mountains that overlooked botanical gardens, and it seemed that every species of flower in the world bedecked the ground, displaying hues from sunset pink to midnight violet.

Master Edmond and Giralda were busy cooking and preparing breakfast. They worked beside a fire at the edge of a nearby stream. Vayle leaned several feet to her right and shook Marlda. As Marlda sat up and looked around, her face exhibited the same awe that had struck Vayle.

"This is unbelievable," said Marlda. "I have never seen any place like this. What a perfect site for a little castle."

Vayle had not yet reexamined the castle in daylight. Once Marlda mentioned it, however, she turned for a look. "You can hardly see it."

Marlda peered along with Vayle. "You're right. The gray wall blends in with the cliff. If I didn't know it was there, I don't think I'd have noticed it."

The two girls stared for a while, and then they rolled up their blankets—something that Lady Eldra would have frowned upon since she did not consider it appropriate for Vayle to engage in manual labor. Then they joined the two adults for breakfast. Bread, jam, bacon, venison, and apples tasted sublime when partaken in the depths of Poolglade Forest. Marlda caught Vayle staring at the soaring castle while eating. It made perfect sense to Marlda that a mysterious prince would live in a mysterious castle, though she was not at all certain that such a prince existed. It seemed more likely that the prince of Vayle's reveries was an angel sent from heaven—a likelihood that went along with Giralda's theory about Vayle's rescue; or maybe the things Vayle remembered were the result of a concussion.

"This land is so beautiful," Vayle remarked. "Why do people not live here?"

Master Edmond washed down a mouthful of bacon and bread with water from Crystal Pond. The waterfall that fed the pond issued from a subterranean spring, and the water was clear and pure. "The land is uneven and rocky, not good for farming, and herding goats would be difficult. Besides that, the terrain would make transporting goods a preposterous undertaking. And most people consider this region to be infested with ferocious beasts. Some even believe that blue men roam the forest, such as those in the story of King Spero."

"At least you waited until morning to tell us all that," commented Giralda.

"Quite so, and I did not even mention the Bear King."

"The Bear King!" Marlda and Vayle exclaimed in unison. Marlda visually consented for Vayle to speak first as the two girls exchanged excited glances. "You mean this is where the Bear King lives?" asked Vayle.

"Just a minute," inserted Giralda. "Why is it that everyone here, or at least everyone besides the large woman who serves as dragon bait, knows what Master Edmond is talking about? Who is this Bear King?" She turned her face toward Vayle. "Have we been keeping secrets?"

"It has been less than a week since Master Edmond told us the story of the Bear King," Vayle apologized. "With all that has been going on, well, I have not chanced upon the opportunity to mention it to you—or at least I have not thought to do so."

The princess seemed so sincere that Giralda did not have the heart to continue bantering. "I was only teasing," she said. "Besides, I think I would rather hear about the Bear King from Master Edmond, especially if he proposes that this *Bear King* is real." She looked upon Master Edmond with challenging eyes.

Master Edmond appeared unabashed. He replied with a nonchalant tone of voice. "It has been several months since report of the Bear King passed amongst the warriors. The tale is a strange one, but it is not the type of story that warriors would invent to cloak some misdeed—no warrior guilty of a crime would fabricate something that drew so much attention."

"Drew so much attention? What happened?" asked Giralda.

"A Viking prisoner was caught reconnoitering in a western Pithranian province, and he was imprisoned in the castle dungeon. Dragus kept him alive for questioning, worried that the Vikings were planning to pillage within the borders of his acclaimed empire."

"Afraid he would get some of his own medicine," mumbled Giralda.

Master Edmond looked startled. He stared at Giralda. "You know that you must never say such things back home, do you not?"

Giralda feigned an insulted expression. "Why, of course. Any goose would know that."

Master Edmond returned to his story, though not before glancing back at Giralda with a look of interest. "The very night of his capture, the Viking somehow opened the door to his cell and dashed past the guards. He was swift and strong, and he fought his way out of the castle and scaled the cliff beyond the northwest tower. It was a dark night, and no one attempted chasing him. The next morning, six warriors set out on horseback to track him down. Tracking was not difficult since there was snow on the ground, and they found that the tracks led northwest around the western side of Mount Thrandor."

"Isn't that the way we came?" asked Giralda.

"Yes, much the same. Anyway, the Viking had journeyed all night, and it was not until late afternoon that the six warriors spotted him. It was several miles northwest of here, in a mountainous region lying north of the Zeborah plain. He fled when he saw the Pithranians, and for a while he eluded them, but then they spotted him again—this time running across the northwestern tip of the Zeborah plain, toward Mount Zeborah. Mount Zeborah, as you know, is the largest mountain in Gaul, and the tallest mountain visible from Pithrania."

"Yes, we know," gibed Giralda, but she was infatuated with the story—she listened with her eyes glued to Master Edmond's face.

"So then, the warriors prodded their horses to a gallop and overtook the Viking as he neared the brink of several boulders at the foot of the mountain. Just when they had the Viking in hand, a giant of a man rose atop the nearest boulder. He had a russet beard and coarse hair, and he wore furry clothing made from wolf hides. In one hand he held a shield of hammered iron, and in the other hand he wielded a huge sledgehammer. As he rose to full height on top of the boulder, he bellowed out, 'I am the Bear King, and I warn you to release this man and depart.'

"The warriors dismounted and fired upon the stranger with arrows— no one desired to engage him in hand-to-hand combat. The Bear King roared and leaped from the boulder, and at the same time two fully-grown bears charged from behind the boulder and bore down upon the warriors, wreaking havoc—though the bears wrought no more havoc than the Bear King himself. Any arrows released seemed to bounce off, miss, or fail to cause any significant harm. All six warriors tried to escape, but only two returned to the castle. Neither of the two warriors knew what happened to the Viking."

"Oh my," said Giralda, breaking her gaze from Master Edmond's face and peering to the west, "perhaps we'd better get started—we want to get home before it gets dark."

"Indeed we'd better; we have another long ride ahead of us. And today I will tell the story of the princess who slew a dragon."

"Princess?" queried Vayle.

"Indeed, and a young princess, at that."

Chapter 7

Solo

An ember of inner strength pierced through the steel-gray surface of aged eyes. Dametrius sat wrapped in blankets in the northwest corner of the prison cell. Satisfaction and pride for the paramount product of his life's vocation swelled within his breast as he watched the eighteen-year-old Prince of Shareen climb upon the stone wall. A snowy beard was tucked beneath the edge of the blanket that encircled his neck—Zarkanis had persuaded his venerable comrade to grow the beard as insulation against wintry cold. It was now more than Dametrius could do to feed or care for himself, but his devoted pupil proved a capable and meticulous attendant. The intrepid and outspoken sage of Rome, who was sentenced to death more than twenty years before, was dying of nothing more than old age.

Though his skin grew colder each hour, the heart of Dametrius still throbbed in warm memory of the conversation that transpired the previous evening. "You are now strong enough to break free of this prison," he told his beloved pupil, "and when you do, what you choose to do with your life is between you and your Creator. No man, including myself, has any right to be your god."

"I know," Zarkanis replied. "I have possessed sufficient strength to rip the bars from the stone for over a year."

"So, why do you stay?"

There had been a long pause. Moonlight was sufficient for Zarkanis and Dametrius to meet one another's eyes. "I have made sport of causing the prison guards to think that I am a great swine," Zarkanis declared. "And if not for you, I would be as my charade depicts. I will never leave you here alone."

A gleam had appeared in Dametrius's eyes as he opened his mouth to respond, but Zarkanis resumed speaking first. "And besides that, I told a little girl that I would come for her and that I would marry her. If she will have me, then I intend to honor my words. That little girl is now the woman I watch each morning as she steps out upon her balcony to greet the break of day. I do not wish to venture far from her presence."

Dametrius made no reply. Zarkanis's nobility was everything that Dametrius ever envisioned. Affectionate memories now played upon Dametrius's mind as he continued observing Zarkanis climb around the inner walls of the cell like a nimble lizard.

The evening frigidity of mid-February increased the difficulty of feeling for nicks and seams in the rock walls. Despite the cold and despite his scant attire, tiny beads of sweat popped out on Zarkanis's forehead as he advanced to his right. Dametrius had determined that Colesia's rescue would require Zarkanis to scale the royal tower during the black of night. Zarkanis would then have to descend the tower with the princess on his back. To develop the skill for such an achievement, Dametrius directed the prince to practice climbing upon the inner walls of the cell and to do so after dark. Dametrius figured that when Zarkanis attained the ability to maneuver his way around the entire circumference of the inner cell without touching the floor, then he would be ready to scale the royal tower.

For over a year Zarkanis had been able to climb around the surface of the cell walls, even scaling the span of stone above the door. More recently, though, Dametrius suggested a new challenge—that of passing across the span of the cell door rather than climbing above it— a span of about three feet. Zarkanis was supposed to do this without touching the door. Now he approached the door with zealous determination, and there was good reason for his resolve—he felt certain that his teacher would not survive another wintry night. Crossing the gap of the doorway was a goal he yearned to fulfill prior to the inevitable—prior to the moment in time when the only human friend he had ever known would be issued into eternity.

Cracks and crannies on the wall north of the door were few and shallow, increasing the difficulty of passing across the doorway. Zarkanis began this night's journey just north of the doorway, so crossing over the doorway would mean success—it would mean that he had mastered Dametrius's most recent challenge. With the toes of both feet and the fingertips of his left hand all but embedded in the limestone south of the doorway, Zarkanis stretched out his right hand and leaned across the doorway. His right fingertips caught fast in tiny crevices; then he extended his right leg and searched out a fault in the rock with his toes. The next move was the most delicate. While pushing off with his left hand and foot, he brought his entire body to the right side of the doorway–and clung with fervent determination. He was only inches above the floor.

For a fraction of a second, Zarkanis's left foot seemed to catch on a slightly elevated patch of stone while his left hand searched for a crevice; but then his left foot slipped, and when the strain of this slippage was added to the momentum of launching his body across the doorway, the kinetic force dislodged his right fingers and toes from their minute niches. The powerful youth slid painfully to the floor, but his anguish was not physical—it was mental. Dametrius only permitted one such attempt per night, and Zarkanis felt certain that there would be no additional attempts—not with his teacher alive and able to witness his success. He had been so close… He had tried so hard… And the last-second failure loomed cruel and unfair—his teacher deserved better. He turned and walked to Dametrius, and then he sat down. It was dark inside the cell, but not very dark. Starlight and moonlight poured through the cell window from a clear winter sky.

"So you succeeded," the old man spoke. His voice was weak.

Zarkanis looked up. Dametrius was exerting a great deal of effort to smile. The temptation crept into Zarkanis's heart to leave the dimming mind of his teacher with the erroneous belief that he had circumvented the entire wall and crossed the doorway, but this was not consistent with the tutoring he had received since eight months of age, and he would not speak a lie. "You are gracious," he said, "but in truth I slipped before securing a hold on the right side of the doorway."

Dametrius's face beamed, reminding Zarkanis of merry moments when he and his teacher fenced with one another using long sticks capped with pinecones. "I know you slipped," said Dametrius, "but true success transcends physical circumstances. You did your very best, putting forth maximum effort, and that is success." There was a dramatic pause, and then Dametrius spoke again. "And now, an even greater success—you resisted the temptation to leave a pitiful old man in ignorance, or what you thought was ignorance, rather than enduring the pain of honesty." He faced Zarkanis with as serious a mien as Zarkanis had ever seen. "There is power and blessing in truth, my son, and it is a wise young man — a student who makes an old tutor proud—who cherishes truth."

Then again, Dametrius smiled.

Zarkanis smiled in return.

"Tomorrow night," resumed Dametrius, "when you again reach the doorway, first feel for grooves where you intend to move your left hand and left foot, and then place your right hand and right foot in farther grooves. That way you will know where to aim your left hand and left foot during the final transfer of your body across the doorway."

The effort that Dametrius exerted in speaking brought tears to Zarkanis's eyes. Even the teacher's final words were encouraging and enlightening. Despite tears, Zarkanis continued to smile—he could sense that Dametrius was dying.

"I love you, my beloved father," spoke the prince. He knew that King Wildon was his natural father, but Dametrius was certainly his intellectual father.

"And I love you, my son."

Several reverent moments passed, and then Dametrius's head dropped to his chest. Zarkanis made no attempt to prolong his dear friend's departure. He sat still for several minutes, and then he closed the eyelids on a lifeless body.

The next morning brought little surprise to Duardo, the prison guard. He had been expecting to find Dametrius dead for several days. He dumped rations from a bucket and then went to fetch his chief, a burly brute named Schark. Schark had replaced Bruxtas two years before. Zarkanis had seen Schark on several occasions due to the fact that

Schark occasionally brought a friend to the chamber of chastisement to guffaw over Zarkanis's presumed obesity and piggish manners.

There was still no speaking permitted in Zarkanis's cell, and the penalty for doing so remained the same as when Zarkanis was an infant. Duardo reentered the cell, followed by Schark. The gruff chief kicked Dametrius's stiff body to ascertain death, and then he signaled for Duardo to grab the body's shoulders while he picked up the feet. The wool blanket, which was kept wrapped around Dametrius's timeworn body during most of the winter, was left behind on the floor. There was little evidence that the tattered rags that remained upon the corpse had once been royal fabric. Zarkanis, who sat with bowed head in the northeast corner of the cell, was ignored. The brilliant and sensitive prince was deemed subhuman. As always when food was delivered, he wore the wool blanket that Dametrius fashioned as a robe.

The door closed. Zarkanis did not move. He sat in thought. During the last few months, Dametrius had required a lot of care and had been in pain much of the time, so his death seemed more merciful than tragic. And besides that, Zarkanis did not doubt that Dametrius was transported to a better place. Still, it felt odd to be left alone within the cell.

Then Zarkanis rose to his feet. He gazed out the window at the wintertime scenery, and then he seated himself beside the mound of food. Once breakfast was consumed, he lay upon the stone bed and engaged himself in mental gymnastics, electing to recall some of the things that Dametrius taught him concerning woodcraft and outdoor survival. And after that, for a while, he simply rested.

After allowing his digestive system to begin incorporating his morning meal, Zarkanis reached to the floor south of his bed and picked up the straight razor he inherited from his teacher. He was adept at keeping the drawn folds of the wool blanket cradled in his arms as he worked with his bare hands. Dragus was troubled, years before, when he learned that Tonan taught the Captive from Shareen to shave, but Bruxtas assured him that any wild animal might be trained to perform tasks of equal difficulty. With only the reflection of his face from the surface of the water in the bucket to aid him, Zarkanis held the razor at the correct angle and proceeded with care. It was a wonder that learning to shave left him no permanent scars, or at least none that were noticeable. From time to time he also used the razor to trim his hair; he kept his hair short enough to prevent it from dangling into his eyes while he exercised.

With shaving accomplished, Zarkanis replaced the razor and commenced warming up with stretch exercises, sit-ups, push-ups, and rapid squats. Next he decided to practice one of his skills. He walked to the rock bed and leaned over to scrutinize the manufactured weapons and training devices he and Dametrius contrived. He first had to lift a wool blanket that covered the items—a shroud against discovery of the treasure by one of the prison guards. This was precautionary, for up to that point in time, none of the guards had ever walked far enough toward the southern wall of the cell to visualize the clandestine space behind the bed.

From the concoction of stashed goods, Zarkanis withdrew a hardwood sword and then selected a few pinecones. Starting with only three, he tossed the pinecones into the air and then whacked them with his sword, one at a time, before they hit the ground. This was too easy, so next he tossed up four pine cones. Four cones proved more difficult, but he still proceeded to five cones. Whacking five pinecones seemed impossible. At last he managed by tossing the five cones higher and striking with short, quick strokes.

Even in midwinter, Zarkanis built up enough body heat to shed his improvised robe. Dametrius warned the prince against performing many exercises upon the blankets, since accelerated wear might raise suspicion among the guards, so the prince's firm body was accustomed to solid stone. Since it was an extremely cold day, Zarkanis dared not linger in idleness. His shorts, which he once considered fashionable, were now tattered and provided little insulation. He lay upon his back and raised one leg so that he could grasp a foot in both hands, and then he pulled with his arms and pushed with his leg so that one or the other would be overpowered. His leg proved stronger. After a few seconds of rest, he raised the other leg and repeated the procedure. Then he rolled to his stomach, bent one leg at the knee, and clasped his ankle with his hand. Again he employed one group of muscles against another.

After an hour, one third of the day's isometric strength exercises were accomplished. Zarkanis intended to exhaust half the muscles in his body by sunset, leaving the other half of his musculature to be keyed upon the following day. Sweat was emerging from the pores of his skin.

He donned his robe before the perspiration chilled, and then he sat down for his second meal.

While eating an early lunch, the prince's eyes fell wishfully upon the large stone bed—the only object of appreciable size and weight within the isolated cell. Isometric training, namely engaging muscles against one another—was the type of strength training that Zarkanis had performed for years. Dametrius taught Zarkanis that isometric training could theoretically strengthen muscles without limit, and yet such exercise posed much less threat of injury than attempting to lift the huge stone that sat like a petrified behemoth upon the prison floor. He had agreed that Zarkanis might be able to lift the bed, which probably weighed about six times the prince's body weight; but he felt that such a feat would not be within safe limits for Zarkanis's capabilities before the prince reached at least nineteen years of age, which was still a year away. Turning his eyes from the bed, Zarkanis lifted the bucket—the same bucket that was in the cell when he and Dametrius were first imprisoned—and then he gulped down a quart of revitalizing mountain water. He would heed his teacher's advice. Lifting the bed would have to wait.

****

As Zarkanis continued eating lunch within his cell, Princess Vayle sat before a loom in her lady-in-waiting's antechamber. She was seated upon a solid cherry stool that she borrowed from her adjoining bedroom. Unlike the wooden bucket, stone bed, and wool blankets within Zarkanis's cell, her environment had undergone notable changes over the years. Her walnut bed frame was replaced on her fifteenth birthday with an extravagant, canopy-topped frame featuring cherry wood posts carved as slender nymphs. The frame enclosed a plush mattress packed with over two hundred pounds of down, and the canopy and bedspread were both woven with purple silk. The borrowed stool, upon which she was seated, came with the cherry wood bed frame.

Giralda sat in a nearby wicker chair and knitted on a pair of socks. She was not making much progress. The skill and style that Vayle exhibited in her handiwork at the loom was too distracting. Giralda was certain that Vayle loomed more adroitly than any other female in the castle.

The past two weeks had been especially enjoyable for Vayle and Giralda, for they constituted one of those rare segments of time when both Dragus and Lady Eldra were absent from the castle. The Pithranian king seldom took his wife with him when he traveled abroad, but in the bitterest weeks of winter her presence provided a source of nighttime warmth. The Pithranian warriors were none too pleased when the irksome queen accompanied them, but there was no objection to Lady Eldra's departure among the castle servants.

A faint sound of footsteps from the stairwell touched Giralda's ears. She was positioned near the closed door to the antechamber.

"Quick, princess! Someone is coming!"

There was a lock on the door to the antechamber, but it required a key, and Lady Eldra was overseer of the key; so the door was unlocked. Vayle rose and grabbed the stool. She dashed into her bedroom and set the stool before a vanity dresser that was positioned in the southeast corner of the room. After seating herself, she picked up a brush and assumed the posture of a self-admiring monarch. A silver mirror hung on the stone wall above the dresser, and by looking into the mirror, she could gaze back through open drapes and into the antechamber.

A gentle knock sounded on the door.

"Who is it?" inquired Giralda.

Iron hinges creaked as the door opened. Vayle turned her head to observe. To both her surprise and Giralda's surprise, Diana, who was Lady Eldra's current lady-in-waiting, stepped into the antechamber. Her left hand held a bowl of dried fruit. She looked at Giralda, and then she closed the door.

Diana was a newly acquired slave of Grecian descent, and she had been Lady Eldra's lady-in-waiting for two months. Neither Vayle nor Giralda had ordered any fruit, and it seemed evident that the fruit was merely a ploy.

"Hello, Diana," said Giralda as the dark-complexioned girl turned and stood before the closed door. "What brings you to visit us?"

"I...I need to talk to you and to the princess," said Diana. Her ebony eyes roamed the surroundings and espied Vayle in the bedroom.

Giralda doubted that a newcomer to the castle staff would be a cohort in some sort of sinister scheme on the part of Lady Eldra; but for Vayle's sake, as well as her own, she sustained an aloof air. "Does Lady Eldra approve of such?"

Diana appeared frightened by Giralda's inquiry. "No, but she will not return until tomorrow, and what I have to say pertains to your safety."

Diana's statement startled Giralda. She stared in silence.

Diana resumed speaking, "You and the princess have treated me with gracious kindness since my arrival. I feel that we share kindred spirits. I feel that I must warn you. I have information that pertains to the safety of Princess Vayle's lady-in-waiting."

Vayle rose with resolve. The queen had always disliked Giralda, of that Vayle was certain; and Lady Eldra's dislike for Giralda seemed to bloat into vindictive hatred as Vayle matured into womanhood. Vayle stepped forward through the passageway dividing her bedroom from the antechamber. Both Diana and Giralda faced her as she halted and stood before them.

"Come into my room. There are chairs where we can sit and talk."

Diana's posture eased. She set the bowl of fruit on a small table and followed Vayle into the royal bedroom. Giralda gave Vayle a wary look and then trailed behind Diana, but she voiced no objection. Vayle had become a mature and strong-willed young woman, and Giralda knew it would be futile to protest.

There were five wicker chairs clustered together so that occupants faced one another. The chairs were situated in the northeast section of Vayle's room, near the closed doors to the balcony. Although Vayle preferred the balcony doors open, they were sometimes closed during the coldest days of winter. Vayle motioned for Diana and Giralda to be seated next to one another, and then she sat down across from them. Light was provided by lanterns on the walls, as well as by fire in the fireplace. She first addressed Diana, meeting her eyes with candor.

"You must excuse our elusive manner, Diana, but as we have held nothing but highest regard for your safety and happiness, we hope that we can trust that your visit here is not intended to work against us or to spy on us."

Giralda's eyes widened. Sometimes Vayle's frankness made her a little nervous—or even very nervous.

"Oh, no, I am not spying for Lady Eldra," returned Diana. Her reply was so spontaneous that there seemed little room for dissimulation, and the fact that she mentioned Lady Eldra's name weighed against her serving as the queen's spy. "It is I who must beg your confidence, for I

144

am only a slave. My mortal life will be in jeopardy if the nature of our meeting is made known to the queen."

Diana looked back and forth between Vayle and Giralda. Her pleading countenance broke through Giralda's defenses.

"You have our empathy, and you need not fear any disclosure to the queen from us," said Giralda.

Diana looked toward Vayle.

"Giralda has spoken truly," said Vayle.

Diana dropped her face into folded hands, generating sufficient courage to proceed. She then raised her eyes with the expression of one who has passed beyond all points of possible retreat, resigned to whatever fate that carrying out the convictions of one's heart might proffer. "I know that my time spent with you has not been long. It has only been two months since my imprisonment here."

Giralda's eyes widened again, this time in response to Diana's outspokenness. She glanced incredulously at Vayle. It was taboo to refer to service under a royal monarch as imprisonment.

Vayle tried to hide an amused smile—she was growing fonder of Diana by the second.

"Nonetheless," continued Diana, "I have come to believe that Princess Vayle and her lady-in-waiting are kind and noble ladies." She sat and thought for a few moments before proceeding. "It is no secret among the cooks, waiters, and other servants that Princess Vayle has been raised to be an affectionate, industrious, and intelligent young woman. She is altogether different than the conceited and slothful vixen that Dragus foreordained."

At this Giralda's mouth dropped open. Vayle's mind flashed to Marlda; the words were too much like those of her best friend for Diana's statement to be free of Marlda's influence. As she thought about it, she remembered seeing Diana and Marlda together quite a number of times.

"For this reason, and because I admire those virtues to which you adhere, I must warn you that Lady Eldra has become aware of the princess's upbringing, and she has informed Dragus."

"You heard this?" asked Vayle. Her face grew serious.

"Yes, before they departed. I was returning some gowns to the queen's chamber after washing them, and when I approached the door, I heard the king talking with her. I decided not to interrupt, and just as

I was turning to leave, I heard the queen raise her voice and say that Giralda had to go. Two bodyguards were standing nearby, so I dropped the gowns and then picked them up one by one to give myself more time to listen. The queen told Dragus that Giralda was making a mockery of him behind his back, teaching Vayle to behave like a peasant and a slave, and then she demanded that Dragus get rid of Giralda. And those were her exact words—*get rid of Giralda.*"

Apprehension beset Vayle's countenance. "Go on," she spoke.

"The king said that it could wait until after the trip. That's all I heard. I had to leave because I was finished picking up the gowns and both guards were staring at me."

The verbal account drained Diana. She dropped her face back into her hands. Vayle and Giralda addressed one another with troubled eyes, but they waited in silence to see if Diana had more to say. She again lifted her face, drew a deep breath, and resumed speaking. "I would have come sooner, but…well…this will surely mean my execution, but…"

Vayle rose and crossed to where she could lay her hands on Diana's shoulders. She gazed into Diana's eyes. "Your regard for Giralda's safety is most honorable. And be assured of this, I will not see you slain for this deed without risking my own life on your behalf."

Diana drew reassurance from Vayle's eyes. The princess's approval granted validation to her efforts, and she was convinced that the princess spoke with sincerity of heart. She marveled that such a virtuous heart could beat within the breast of a Pithranian monarch.

"Now, did either Dragus or Lady Eldra disclose what was meant by *getting rid* of Giralda?" asked Vayle.

Giralda looked on and listened with increasing trepidation. Her personal plight was being discussed, but something else concerned her more… What would all of this mean for Princess Vayle?

"No, or at least I did not hear; but I believe they are both most heartless."

Vayle nodded. "I agree with you." She stepped back to her chair and sat down where she could again face Giralda as well as Diana. "Perhaps we should all three flee at once."

"No," asserted Diana, "if what I have learned from my fellow servants is correct, and I believe that it is, escape would be impossible. The guards have orders to prevent my leaving the castle—I have not yet served long enough to be granted the freedom to wander beyond the castle grounds. So at least for now, I am captive here." Diana assumed a deeply solemn expression as she continued speaking. "And you, my princess, are under more rigorous surveillance than me. Dragus has commanded that his guards keep you within the bounds of the castle walls unless two Pithranian warriors escort you outside, and even when you are accompanied by escorts, you may only venture upon short excursions.

"Furthermore," resumed Diana, "the guards have been warned not to let you sneak past them through the hatches at the tops of the towers—under threat of their very lives. The doors to all levels of the royal tower are watched constantly. I had to explain that I was delivering you some fruit in order to get past a guard when I came here."

Vayle nodded. For the past two years, she had noticed guards escorting her whenever she stepped beyond the castle gate. She knew it was boasted by Dragus's ignoble hierarchy that they housed the most beautiful woman in Gaul, and she knew the Pithranian monarchs would not want such an acclaimed possession to escape their jurisdiction. She was aware that the escorts appeared to be providing royal protection, but such an appearance was a sham—they were assigned to prevent her escape. "What about Giralda?" she asked.

"I have not heard that she is under observation."

"Wait," interjected Giralda. There was a tone of dread in her voice. She had no trouble ascertaining where the conversation between Vayle and Diana was leading. "I cannot leave you here alone, Princess."

"You will have no choice when Dragus returns," Vayle replied matter-of-factly. "I would prefer to choose your manner of departure rather than leaving that to Dragus."

Giralda gaped at Vayle. "Perhaps Dragus will have changed his mind by the time he returns."

"Lady Eldra has been with him the entire trip," Vayle stated in a low voice. "It is most certain that he will not have changed his mind."

Giralda began fidgeting. She knew that she would lay down her life to protect Vayle, but it seemed that laying down her life would accomplish nothing.

Diana noted that Giralda seemed lost in a world of desperate deliberation. She turned her face toward Vayle and stared with questioning eyes.

"I have an idea," said Vayle, primarily addressing Diana. "I'll banish Giralda from Pithrania." Vayle paused and glanced toward Giralda's astonished face, and then she turned her eyes back to Diana. "Giralda will argue this point, I am sure, but that is all the better because then I can tell Dragus and Lady Eldra that my lady-in-waiting and I quarreled. If I know Lady Eldra, such news will please her—she would relish my being at odds with my lady-in-waiting. You, Diana, can just go about your duties as though nothing happened."

There was a moment of silence, and then Giralda found the ability to speak. "No, Princess, you must not do this."

"Oh, yes, I must," Vayle declared, facing Giralda with staid sincerity. She smiled and looked back toward Diana. "See, now we've quarreled."

Giralda paled. "But, Princess, you should not dwell within this room alone."

"I know," said Vayle, looking back and forth between Giralda and Diana. "I will approach Dragus and request Marlda as my new lady-in-waiting."

The princess's brow rose and fell conclusively.

There was further discussion, but Vayle's plan was not altered. Giralda's mind was discombobulated and her heart was in turmoil. She had little to say that was coherent, much less did she proffer anything dissuasive to Vayle's plan. Diana thanked the princess for sparing her from danger and then departed with an empty bowl—the fruit had been poured out and covered with a napkin.

Vayle and Giralda continued in conversation for quite some time after Diana departed, deciding that Master Edmond, whom both of them trusted, should be informed. They were certain that he would prove helpful. Giralda wondered if she would awaken from a nightmare, but she did not. Instead she and Vayle began packing clothing and supplies, selecting those items deemed crucial. They conversed while packing, discussing what to wear, what to eat, and other practicalities.

"I will bring you some lunch from the kitchen," spoke Vayle. Most of the packing was completed. "I will also arrange a rendezvous with Master Edmond. When Dragus returns, I can tell him that I gave you a horse to accomplish your banishment, which will be true."

Giralda drew a breath to say something, but then paused. Her facial expression melted into one of resignation. "It is a good plan, Princess."

Vayle closed the door as she departed. Giralda collapsed into her well-worn chair. The princess insisted that Giralda take several precious jewels, pointing out that they would probably never be missed. Giralda knew that the jewels would supply means for her to subsist, and she accepted them; but as she sat alone in the antechamber that had been her room for over seventeen years, her thoughts turned to a matter that weighed more heavily upon her mind than either food or clothing—she had never yet told Vayle that she was really Colesia, the daughter of Sir Marticus and Lady Monica. It would be a shameful tragedy if the princess never learned her true identity, so she had to think clearly and quickly, for such a tragedy could not be permitted—Vayle had to be informed.

When Vayle returned with a liberal lunch and a flask of water, most of which was intended for Giralda's journey, she found her lady-in-waiting finished with packing. All of the provisions and goods, along with the jewels, were stowed in a leather riding bag—a gift from the princess.

"I brought food for your journey, wherever you may be going," Vayle remarked after closing the door. She was permitting Giralda to decide whether or not to disclose the journey's destination. "Master Edmond says that you should meet him at the stables as soon as you are ready. He says that Dragus may return later today."

"I am packed," said Giralda. She accepted the food from Vayle and secured it in a side pouch on the leather bag, and then she tied the flask of water outside the pouch. Vayle's eyes glistened with moisture as she stood watching. When preparations for departure were complete, Giralda turned and enveloped Vayle in a motherly hug. "I will miss you, Princess."

"I will miss you too," replied Vayle, "more than I can begin to say. I shudder to think what kind of woman I would have become without your tutoring and guidance. I truly love you."

Giralda loosened her embrace and held Vayle's shoulders at arm's length. "Come sit down in your bedroom. There are a couple of things I must tell you before I leave."

Vayle pursed her lips. She was anxious for Giralda to depart before Dragus returned.

"Please," coaxed Giralda.

There was such a pleading look in Giralda's eyes that Vayle reluctantly yielded. She followed Giralda into the royal bedroom. Both she and Giralda sat down in the same chairs where they had conversed with Diana a couple of hours before, only this time Giralda repositioned her chair so that she sat directly in front of Vayle.

"What I have to tell you may be shocking," began Giralda, "but it is something you absolutely must know." Her eyes addressed Vayle with a look of unabashed sincerity.

Vayle's expression softened and then deepened. She returned Giralda's regard with puzzled interest. There were so many things going on—Diana confiding in them, Giralda preparing to flee, and Master Edmond abetting escape—that it hardly seemed likely that Giralda could say anything that would be *shocking*. Nonetheless, she resolved to listen to whatever her virtual mother had to say. Her aqua eyes gazed into the beseeching brown orbs that beckoned her attention.

"Dragus and Lady Eldra have taught you that you were rescued from death following the murder of your royal parents—murder that took place in a city to the north, a city that no longer exists."

"Yes," replied Vayle, "they claim that the city was ransacked by Vikings." There was an obvious note of disbelief in her voice.

"Well, that report is false, and I know your true origin."

Vayle took a moment to absorb Giralda's words, but then her facial expression transformed to a look of perplexed awe. She sat, speechless. The last five words Giralda spoke seemed incomprehensible. She had never imagined that her assigned lady-in-waiting, who was purportedly from Marne, might know who she really was. Why had the woman who she loved as her own mother kept her identity from her? She peered into Giralda's eyes with a mixture of alarm and wonder.

"Calm yourself, Princess," said Giralda, reading the expression on Vayle's face. "I have not held back the secret of what I am about to tell you without worthy cause. Now listen to me… You must not, by either words or actions, disclose to the king or queen the knowledge of what I am about to tell you; such would only increase their tenacity in guarding and retaining you—that is, if they did not immediately execute you, which would be more likely."

Vayle was bewildered. Though she did not speak, her eyes pled for Giralda to continue.

"Now I will free my heart and mind of the burden they have borne for years, for I have often yearned to disclose what I am about to tell you," said Giralda. Her eyes drew Vayle's utmost regard as she leaned closer and drew a breath. "Your father was Sir Marticus, and your mother was Lady Monica—both respected citizens in the kingdom of Shareen. Your parents were murdered by Dragus's cutthroats on the day that you were born, but your birth was kept a secret. No one alive, other than me, knows that you were born. I was the midwife who delivered you. Your mother was killed by an arrow while looking out the window, and I exchanged clothing with her before the Pithranian warriors broke into the bedroom. The warriors assumed that you were my child."

Vayle's eyes widened. A thousand questions flooded her mind, but her tongue remained still.

"Dragus and your father were bitter enemies," resumed Giralda, "which is why Dragus must never learn that you are the daughter of Sir Marticus. If Dragus ever learned this, he would almost certainly kill you, or worse. Do you understand?"

Vayle managed a nod. She knew that Shareen was overthrown by Pithrania around the time that she was born.

"Very well then; while your mother was pregnant with you, a wonderful king ruled Shareen. His name was King Wildon. King Wildon and his beautiful queen, whose name was Aracia, had an infant prince whom they hoped would someday be married to the daughter of Sir Marticus and Lady Monica—provided, of course, that Lady Monica gave birth to a girl."

Giralda opened her mouth to say more, but then she froze in silence. The look of astonishment that sprang up within Vayle's eyes immobilized her lips. She remained dumb for several seconds. Finally she discovered that her lips could move again. "What is it, Princess? Why do you look at me like that?"

Princess Vayle brought her right hand to her breast and leaned backward in her chair. Her heart fluttered. "Me? They hoped the prince would marry me?"

"Yes."

Vayle sat in silence, but the expressions of her face and eyes transformed—passing from one state to another like the visage of a dreaming child.

Giralda was mystified. She stared at Vayle with intense curiosity.

Vayle's eyes turned away and lost focus; but a few moments later, her eyes turned back toward Giralda and ignited in passion. She sat back up and leaned forward.

"And was the prince named Zarkanis?"

Giralda reeled. She steadied herself by grabbing the edge of her chair. She knew better than to mention that name… Dragus forbade the mention of that name, and she had never heard it spoken since the day she moved into the castle. How could this be? How did Vayle know? She drew her tongue from the roof of her mouth, staring at Vayle in sheer astonishment. She had no choice but to respond.

"Wherever have you heard that name?"

Vayle surmised that the prince was indeed named Zarkanis. That was all she wanted to know; that was all she needed to know. She could not hide the ecstasy that rose within her heart and bloomed upon her countenance. Dearly held dreams passed from hope to reality—dreams that rested upon words spoken to her in confidence when she was ten years old, words that now pulsed through her being like the rush of thawed waters heralding the coming of spring.

"And…and do I not have another name? My real name?"

Giralda was transfixed. What was going on? Did Vayle know the name proffered by her eldest brother and bestowed upon her by her father and mother? How could this be? No one knew that name, no one alive, no one but the midwife who served Lady Monica in the delivery of her sixth child. Giralda stared at Vayle, scarcely breathing. She nodded.

"Colesia?"

Colesia…the princess spoke the name so naturally, as if she had known her name since the day she was born. The skin at the back of Giralda's neck began tingling, and goose bumps rose upon her limbs. She stared at Colesia from far beyond the bounds of utter bewilderment. The only other human beings who heard Sir Marticus bestow the name Colesia upon his daughter were the immediate members of Sir Marticus's family, and they were all slain on the day that the name was given…or were they?

Giralda leaned as far forward as she could without falling from her chair. "How? How do you know? How could you possibly know?"

Colesia, who from that moment onward thought of herself as Colesia rather than Vayle, bowed her head. The long years since her fascinating rescue from drowning lent ample time to question whether that experience were reality or fantasy. Still, her heart held fast to the belief and hope that her senses did not lie, that her prince was real, and that he would someday return for her. Now she became as certain of the prince's reality as she had been on the night that he knelt above her and spoke awe-inspiring words into her ear. He was a bona fide, genuine, flesh-and-blood prince, and he had saved her life, and he had vowed to marry her. And as she contemplated the truth of her origin; and as she pondered the origin of her prince; her heart grew more charmed than ever.

"Perhaps I have spoken more than I should, I do not know," said Colesia, not yet looking up. "Zarkanis told me his name, and he told me my name, and he said that he would come for me. He said not to tell anyone about him or he might be killed. And…and he told me that he loves me."

Giralda stared upon the princess's bowed head. Her heart swelled with wonder. She had supposed Prince Zarkanis dead unless he were the dumb and corpulent Captive from Shareen about whom the warriors jested. It now seemed that her suppositions regarding Prince Zarkanis were impossible. One must be alive to speak, and one must also possess the ability to communicate verbally—and the princess, whom Giralda knew to be sane, claimed that Zarkanis told her his name. But still, even if the prince somehow survived, and even if he knew that Vayle was the daughter of Sir Marticus and Lady Monica, and even if he managed to communicate with Vayle without being apprehended; still, how could Zarkanis know the princess's name?

Giralda drew a deep breath and straightened in her chair. The only reasonable course of action dawned upon her mind in a manner remindful of the inspiration that prompted her to exchange clothes with the slain body of Lady Monica on the day that Colesia was born. If the Prince of Shareen managed so many unthinkable marvels, then both she and the princess should heed his words.

"Tell me no more, Princess," said Giralda, speaking like a divinely inspired prophetess. "It is a man's place to protect the woman he loves, and a virtuous woman should honor his words." Curiosity imploded her mind, yet she spoke with resolution. New hope for the princess welled up within her bosom. Was communication between Zarkanis and Colesia anything less than celestial providence? Did not the princess's knowledge of her own name denote the employment of powers greater than the faculties of mortal men? Her soul rose in reverence.

Blessed divinity, Giralda prayed in silence as she continued gazing upon Colesia's bowed head, *I know not whether my path may lead to torture and interrogation, but if it does, no adversary can extract information from my mind that does not exist there. So in respect to this consideration, I will quell my curiosity and curb my tongue. Notwithstanding, my heart desires to dwell yet longer upon this earth so that my eyes may behold this young woman's dreams unfurled, for I cannot believe that her future holds any course apart from the nuptial fulfillment of the amorous devotion that fills this room with the aura of her love.*

Colesia needed no further admonition. Now that the reality of her prince was ascertained, his few words to her became hallowed canon. She raised her face. "Thank you, my lady, for telling me these things."

Giralda sat for some time without movement or comment, and then she shrugged and shook her head. "My mouth has proffered little in comparison to what my ears have partaken. Yet still, there are a couple of other things I want you to know. First, you must never speak the name Zarkanis. Dragus has forbid anyone from speaking the name of King Wildon's son."

Colesia nodded. She remembered Zarkanis telling her that Dragus was his enemy.

"And second, although I lived in Marne until I was seventeen, I lived in Shareen thereafter. And as I mentioned before, I was the midwife who assisted your mother when you were born. Dragus and Lady Eldra believe that you are my natural-born daughter, and they also believe that Lord Gardgeon, who was the queen's previous husband, is your father. Lord Gardgeon was slain in battle before you were born, so no one was able to question him about you, and the mistaken belief that he is your father has endured. And although Dragus believes that I am your natural mother, he commanded me to raise you without ever telling you that I am your mother, and he threatened to banish me from Pithrania if I did not heed his commandment."

Again Colesia nodded. Many things were falling into place within her mind, including why Lady Eldra had never liked Giralda.

"Now, with God as my witness, I tell you with sincerity that I took you as my own adopted child on the day that you were born, so you may assert with all honesty that I claim to be your mother, for I am your mother by willful adoption, and I now claim such motherhood without reserve. You must tell both Dragus and Lady Eldra that we quarreled and that you decided to replace me with Marlda and that I resisted you—and that I openly averred to be your mother. You will be speaking the truth, and I advise that you act insulted about the fact that a mere servant claimed to be the mother of a princess. You should be able to insinuate that such a claim prompted you to banish me from the kingdom—and you should be able to do so without speaking a lie, for I would never ask you to speak a lie, not even upon threatened pang of death. The insinuation that you banished me because I claimed to be your mother presents a plausible excuse for my banishment. Do you understand?"

There were several questions floating in Colesia's mind, but she understood Giralda's suggestion, and she knew that Giralda needed to escape before Dragus returned. "Yes, I understand."

"As far as my home goes, Dragus thinks that I am from Marne. When I leave here, I will travel northeast through the Asperian mountains, which is the shortest route to Marne. There is no danger of my meeting Dragus that way. His forces will be coming back along the road from Shareen. In Marne I will seek temporary lodging, but I will not remain long. If no one seems to be spying on me, I will journey southeast to Shareen and seek to live a quiet life among old friends. Perhaps someday you will have the opportunity and means to pay me a visit. If so, just ask where you can find a midwife. Any midwife in Shareen should be able to direct you to me."

Colesia looked into her guardian's eyes. "Perhaps someday I shall bring you to live with a prince and princess who will love you as a mother. For now I know that you are, forsooth, my mother."

For several silent seconds, the eyes of a mother and her adopted child conveyed depths of love that no words could communicate. Then, when speaking resumed, it was decided that Giralda should depart from the room alone, thus supporting the ruse of conflict. She walked through the doorway to the royal stairwell, knowing that she would never return. Her arms held a large bag containing most of her personal possessions and several valuable jewels, and her heart held reciprocated affection from a dearly beloved daughter.

After the sounds of Giralda's footsteps faded from detection, Colesia closed the door to the stairwell. She strode to her bedroom, opened the doors to her balcony, and stepped outside.

Master Edmond met Giralda at the stables. A large mare, one that would not be counted a great loss, but one that Master Edmond knew to be sure-footed and hardy, was saddled and ready for the journey. Master Edmond bid Giralda farewell. She rode off alone.

Colesia watched her surrogate mother pass down the roadway south of Lake Manassa. After circumventing the lake, Giralda coursed northeasterly. Forest evergreens extended green boughs as if hailing farewell—boughs that were tipped with white clumps of snow. Colesia continued staring from her balcony long after Giralda disappeared.

The door to the stairwell opened and closed. Winter wind whipped through the princess's hair and muted the sounds that Marlda made as she entered.

"Princess," Marlda called, standing at the doorway to the balcony.

Colesia turned and faced Marlda. Within seconds both girls' eyes glistened with tears. Colesia stepped inside and closed the doors to the balcony. After a comforting embrace, Marlda assisted her bereaved friend to one of the five wicker chairs in the northeast corner of the bedroom. After seating the princess, Marlda sat in the chair to Colesia's left, turning in the chair to face her.

"My father told me the whole story. I came as soon as we saw that Giralda made a safe escape."

"Thank you... I..."

"I will be honored to serve as your lady-in-waiting during Giralda's absence, if that is what you desire—that is, if Dragus will allow it."

Colesia reached out and grasped Marlda's hand and then released it and peered into Marlda's eyes. "Dragus will consent, I am sure. Your father has served him well, and there is no other man alive whom Dragus would permit to trim the hooves of his favorite stallion."

Marlda smiled in thoughtful silence. It was true that her father had earned a reputable title in the Pithranian hierarchy, but she had other knowledge concerning her father's activities—knowledge that she dared not reveal, not even to Princess Vayle. Dragus was not worshipped by all men in Pithrania; in fact, there were men who abhorred the evils that befell the kingdom after Dragus rose to power.

Some of those men were even willing to put their lives at risk in hopes of someday delivering the land from tyranny.

Marlda continued facing Vayle. She marveled at the fact that such chaste beauty could bloom in the nefarious environment of Dragus's household. Her face sobered. The challenge of following in Giralda's footsteps was awesome.

Colesia broke the silence. "I hope my bringing you into the walls of the castle will not change you; I mean, you are a good person, Marlda."

"Thank you, Vayle."

Colesia's brows furled as she continued facing Marlda.

"Why are you looking at me like that?" asked Marlda.

"There is something I just learned. I already knew it, but now I really know it, and I want you to know too."

It was easy to incite Marlda's curiosity. "What is it?"

Colesia lowered her voice. "My name is not really Vayle. My parents were citizens of Shareen. In fact my father was a close friend of King Wildon."

Curiosity poured from Marlda's eyes. "Really?"

"Yes, my father was Sir Marticus."

Marlda's expression transformed to one of startled amazement. "Sir Marticus the builder?"

"I do not know if he was called *the builder*."

"Do you know your mother's name?"

"Lady Monica."

"That's it!" Marlda exclaimed in a loud whisper. For several seconds she just sat and stared, looking upon Princess Vayle with weighty mien.

"That's what? What are you talking about?" pressed Colesia.

"You must have been born after all... I mean..." Marlda paused and looked downward. She drew a breath and then again faced Vayle. "Sir Marticus was Dragus's most feared enemy. It is rumored that Dragus postponed his attack upon Shareen for almost a year because he feared some sort of military stratagem on the part of your father." Again Marlda paused. Her expression deepened. "Dragus must never know that you are Sir Marticus's daughter. Tell no one else—please promise me that you will not tell another living soul."

"I will be careful," conceded Colesia, but Marlda had aroused her curiosity. "You seem to know quite a bit about my family. Did I have any brothers or sisters?"

Marlda grew still. "It is said that you had five brothers and that they were all slain along with your parents."

There was something suspicious about the tone of Marlda's reply. "Is that what truly happened? Were all five of my brothers slain?"

Marlda's countenance grew distraught. There were certain secrets that her father charged her to protect. "Princess, please question me no further. You must trust me. We must speak no more of this, nor should you ever mention any of these things to another—it would be too dangerous. Dragus hated your father, and there is no doubt in my mind that his vicious hatred would lash out upon any child born to Sir Marticus, whether male or female. Perhaps, in the future, when the time is right, we can speak more freely."

Colesia's mind raced. It seemed incredible that she was of kindred blood to Dragus's archenemy. What else did Marlda know? What had happened? Was anyone else in her family still alive? She thought about Giralda—Giralda must have been flirting with death to nurture the offspring of Dragus's foremost enemy. Her heart beat fast. She peered more deeply into Marlda's eyes. "If you say that we should wait to speak more of this, then I accept your counsel; but when the time is right, I want you to tell me more."

"Oh, I will," avowed Marlda. Her facial expression eased. "But you said your name is not really Vayle. Do you know your real name?"

"You do not know?"

"No. All I know is that you died in your mother's womb on the day that your home was burnt to the ground…I mean…that's what everyone thinks. My father never mentioned that you had a name."

"Someone gave you a false report?"

Marlda looked taken aback. "Oh, no, I would not think so, princess. It was presumed that you were slain along with your mother, I mean, the house was burned to little more than a pile of ashes, and…" Marlda stopped and looked apologetically downward. Then she raised her face in silence. Her eyes pled for permission to omit further details.

"That is horrible; and to think that I must again face Dragus and conceal disgust and abhorrence from my eyes."

"I have said too much," Marlda spoke. Her voice carried a note of dread.

"No, I want to know everything. Thank you." Colesia granted a consoling smile. "My name is Colesia."

"Colesia," repeated Marlda. "That is a lovely name. Giralda knew your name?"

Colesia paused in thought. "Perhaps I should refrain from answering that question until I can be more certain that the time is right, just as you have said that you must do in regard to my question about my brothers."

"As you wish," said Marlda. She was experienced in keeping secrets, and she knew there could be crucial reasons to exercise discretion.

Thereafter the girls redirected their conversation toward other matters, such as arrangements for Marlda to take up occupancy as Colesia's lady-in-waiting. Master Edmond and his wife had already given approval. At supper the two girls sat together at the royal dining table, with Marlda sitting in Giralda's former seat. By the time of Dragus's arrival that evening, the news of Giralda's replacement was widespread. The princess and her new lady-in-waiting were in the princess's chamber on the fifth floor of the royal tower when Dragus and his entourage arrived.

A chill of apprehension swept Colesia's spine as loud footsteps sounded from the stairwell. She and Marlda were seated on the floor between her bed and the fireplace, absorbing warmth from a glowing fire. They were both fully dressed in anticipation of visitors. It had just turned dark outside.

A knock came on the stairwell door.

"I will answer," said Marlda. She rose from an elkskin rug where she and Colesia had been playing a game of knucklebones. It was a trite game, and just the sort of game to play when weightier matters engaged the mind.

Colesia watched as Marlda crossed through the antechamber and opened the door. There appeared Jarak, Dragus's largest bodyguard.

"Dragus requests the presence of Princess Vayle in the grand hall," Jarak stated with as much eloquence as he could muster.

Colesia felt apprehension swell within her abdomen.

"The princess will comply at once, I am sure," Marlda replied.

Colesia rose and strode toward them. She and Marlda followed Jarak down the stairwell. The stairs spiraled downward until ending in a small chamber dividing the grand hall, to the west, from Dragus's private meeting room, to the east. Jarak led the ladies into the grand hall.

As was usual after a military conquest, there was hustle and bustle in the grand hall. Several conversations ceased and many eyes stared as the two ladies passed into the room behind Jarak. Most tables in the grand hall were toward the sides or rear of the room, but one large table sat just back of center. Behind this table sat Dragus, and to his left sat Lady Eldra. Warriors standing across from Dragus stepped aside as the princess, Marlda, and Jarak approached.

"What is this I hear about Giralda being banished from the castle and replaced with Marlda?" inquired Dragus. His voice was firm but without notable emotion.

Colesia was thankful that Dragus confronted her, rather than commissioning Lady Eldra to the task—she thought it would work out better for Marlda that way. "I am afraid it is true, Sire, but perhaps my decision was hasty. If you wish to recall the kind lady, I will be more than glad to make amends with her."

Lady Eldra's face skewed. She could not bear Vayle speaking a favorable word regarding Giralda.

"What was the nature of your disagreement?" Dragus inquired. He served as supreme judge within the precincts of his empire.

Princess Vayle paused and tossed her head, flipping gold and brunette locks back toward her shoulders. She drew a breath with an expression of smug contempt. Her outward bearing presented a well-practiced ruse—she was long accustomed to acting the part of a vain monarch in the presence of Dragus and Lady Eldra. "Suffice it to say, Your Lordship, that she did not readily agree with my decision to banish her from Pithrania," she expounded. Then she cast her eyes downward as if agitated by the thought of what she would speak next. "I beg your forbearance, Sire, but permit me to pose this question"—she raised her eyes and faced Dragus before continuing her dialogue—"I ask you, how should a royal princess of noble blood respond when a common lady-in-waiting speaks of being that princess's mother?"

The eyes, nose, and mouth upon Dragus's face hardened like stone, and the skin upon his cheeks and forehead blanched. Colesia avoided looking at Lady Eldra, but Marlda witnessed the queen's upper lip draw back into the visage of vicious vixen.

"You are justified in reacting to such an atrocious and disrespectful assertion," stated Dragus. "It sounds as though the poor old fool went berserk. I will try to contact her, but do not hope too dearly that she will return. She is a proud woman, and she will be highly regarded after serving in my castle."

"Your attention to this matter is exemplary of Your Lordship's character," said Colesia, hiding the irony in her compliment. She knew that Dragus's words were deceitful and that there would be no attempt to summon Giralda back to Pithrania. She curtsied as she finished speaking.

Dragus was pleased by Princess Vayle's seeming flattery. He turned his attentions toward Marlda. "Your father has served well as majordomo. I trust you will serve the princess with more respect and consideration than that shown by her previous lady-in-waiting."

Marlda curtsied also. "My hands and heart are at the princess's feet. It is a great honor to serve my royal lady."

Lady Eldra's eyes narrowed as she stared at Marlda. She had never approved of Vayle's befriending a commoner.

"Very well," proclaimed Dragus, "I assign Marlda, daughter of Master Edmond, to serve as lady-in-waiting to Princess Vayle." He turned his face toward Jarak. "Escort the princess and her lady to their quarters."

Chapter 8

Reunion

Pithranian guards atop the wall surrounding Shareen were alerted to the presence of a rider after Giralda prodded her horse onto the field northwest of the city. She reined the horse toward the northern gate. Thick cloud cover had not yet reached the western horizon, and the setting sun tinted the underside of a skyward canvass with iridescent orange and pink. A lengthy shadow was cast across the snow alongside her, clinging to the horse's hooves and accentuating her approach. She continued walking her horse after spotting two Pithranian warriors above the gate. The presence of sentries did not disturb her;

soldiers and guards had been ordinary elements of her life in Pithrania. She sensed that Shareen had changed, but she hoped to find at least a remnant of the mirthful community she had previously inhabited and loved. The guards stared without comment until she drew rein outside the closed gate.

"Who goes there? And what is your business?" one of the guards called down. He wore a coarse fur coat over leather attire. A silver-colored helmet adorned his head, revealing that he was of lower rank. An identical helmet sat upon the head of his companion.

"My name is Giralda. I am a midwife. I come from Marne." Giralda reached to a leather purse hanging at her right side. She withdrew a couple of coins and held them aloft. "It is cold, and I request admittance into Shareen."

There were no additional words. The guards descended and opened the gate, and the guard who hailed Giralda from atop the wall accepted the coins from her hand, giving one to his companion. Giralda passed into the city. She gazed ahead. The royal palace rose in the distance.

Stacks of firewood were piled against the outside walls of dwellings that Giralda passed as she nudged her horse forward. This was a residential quarter. She recognized the mortar and rock structures; they were the same homes that lined the road when she began working as a midwife. She turned east before reaching the palace and then continued across a wooden bridge that passed over the Great Stag River. Most of the river's surface was frozen and covered with snow. There were few people outside their homes. Snowflakes began floating downward from a dark canopy of clouds.

Smoke ascended from chimneys and drifted upward, leaving the lower atmosphere clear apart from snowflakes. The air was flavored by odors from numerous stables, but the smell of hay, feed, and manure did not offend Giralda. After coming within twenty yards of the city's eastern wall, Giralda stopped before a sizeable structure that sat on the north side of the road. It was a quadriplex—a four-home edifice constructed of limestone and oak. Each of the four living quarters had a kitchen, a living room, and two bedrooms. There were two bathing rooms, each one shared by two of the living quarters.

Giralda wondered if this were still headquarters for midwifery. She prodded her mare forward to an adjacent stable. After dismounting, she led the mare beneath a leather awning and tethered her to a hitching post.

Snow began falling in clumps as well as flakes. Clouds obscured the fading sunset, and daylight yielded to nightfall. Giralda trod past the southeast apartment where she had lived for ten years, stepping on to the next apartment—the southwest apartment. Conelle was living in this apartment when Shareen was attacked over seventeen years before, and if she did not live there now, the tenant might know her whereabouts. Light seeped through the seams of the door and window shutters.

Giralda knocked on the door. There were movements inside—shuffling sounds suggesting the presence of children.

"Who knocks?" a woman inquired from inside the door.

Giralda's heart leaped. The voice was Conelle's. "It is your long-lost next-door neighbor."

An inside bolt flew back and the door popped ajar. A widened eye stared through a crack, and then the door swung wide open. There, before Giralda, stood a middle-aged woman wearing a robe and slippers. The woman leaped out into the falling snow and clasped Giralda in a bear hug, and then she pulled Giralda inside and shut the door. A crackling fire lit the room. Flames danced within an open fireplace that sat back in the north wall, nestled behind a large stone hearth. Giralda was impressed to see two young girls standing before the hearth. They both stared at her.

"Giralda! You're alive! I just cannot believe it! Where have you been?"

Giralda grinned. Conelle was still her old self—an elfin bundle of enthusiasm. "It is a long story." Giralda again looked at the two girls. They both had the same blonde hair as Conelle. "Perhaps you might tell me what you have been doing."

Conelle's expression grew staid. She turned and faced the two girls. "This is a good friend. Her name is Giralda. Now come and tell her your names."

The two girls bounded forward. They positioned themselves in front of their mother. The older one spoke first.

"My name is Dwindalin. I am nine years old."

"Nice to meet you, Dwindalin," returned Giralda.

The younger girl then spoke up. "My name is Jamie, and I'm five."

"Very nice to meet you too, Jamie."

"Did you travel alone?" asked Conelle.

Giralda turned to face Conelle. "Yes."

"Is your horse outside?"

"Yes, tied to the hitching post in front of the stable."

Conelle walked to a closet in the southwest corner of the room. It was next to the front door. "Your horse will need fed and boarded in a stall," she said, pulling out a fur coat. "I'll help you."

"Oh, no, I can take care of that," said Giralda.

Conelle ignored Giralda's protest and donned the coat over her robe and then pulled leather boots over her feet. Giralda noted that the coat was ermine, a very expensive item to purchase—something that clashed with the fact that Conelle was residing in the midwifery quarters. The boots had an inner lining of the same fur. Both the coat and boots appeared to be a few years old, but they were in good condition.

"Girls, you can play until we get back. We are going to the stable."

A blanket of snow was thickening atop the ground. Giralda and Conelle stepped outside and then Conelle pulled the door closed.

"There will be plenty of snow for iced fruit in the morning," remarked Conelle as she began leading the way to the stable.

"And if my memory serves me right, you store up ample dried fruits for wintertime," said Giralda.

It was dark enough to conceal facial expressions as the two friends conversed. "I suppose you are wondering about my husband."

There was a pause before Giralda responded. She noted a quiver in Conelle's voice.

Conelle walked around the mare and opened the stable door.

"Yes," replied Giralda.

"What is the horse's name?"

"Penelope. I was just introduced to her a couple of days ago," answered Giralda. She sensed that Conelle was mustering the nerve to talk about her husband.

Conelle untethered the mare and led her into the stable. "I forgot a candle. Come hold Penelope, and I will return with one." Giralda walked forward and received the reins from Conelle. "Before I leave, though, I will tell you about Sir Reynold."

"Sir Reynold of the royal guard?" inquired Giralda. She remembered a tall, polite officer by that name.

"Yes. He was wounded when Shareen fell to Pithrania, and I took care of him during his recovery." Conelle drew a deep breath. "After regaining his strength, he decided to pursue the art of healing, and within a matter of months he became a respected physician. Over the next year we developed a deep friendship, and then we married, and the next nine years were the happiest of my life." There was a break of silence, and then Conelle tried to recommence speaking, but she broke down crying. Giralda, who held Penelope's reins in her right hand, stepped to Conelle's side and put her left arm around Conelle's shoulders.

Conelle leaned into Giralda's side and wept.

Giralda knew, without asking, that Sir Reynold was dead. She said nothing, holding Penelope and supporting Conelle until the crying eased.

Conelle straightened, maintaining one hand on Giralda's shoulder. "We moved to a home south of the palace. Our lives seemed a charming dream—though for the first five years I wondered if I would ever get pregnant. And then Dwindalin was born, and our lives grew even richer—and richer still when I learned that I was pregnant for a second time. Our house was full of cheer and laughter, despite the foul cloud that always hovers over Shareen—ever since the fall of King Wildon."

There was a respectful pause after mentioning King Wildon's name, and then Conelle resumed speaking.

"One summer night Sir Reynold and I were taking a stroll beside the palace. The white marble reflecting upon the surface of the Great Stag River is a gorgeous sight in the moonlight. Three Pithranian warriors were patrolling the south side of the palace. It was a balmy evening, and I was wearing my most attractive gown."

Giralda felt a lump form at the base of her throat.

Conelle's voice fell low and constant. "The three guards stopped us, and one of them invited me to see the reception room inside the palace. I declined, but then I was informed that I had no choice. My husband drew his sword, which he always wore when we left our home, and then he fought for my honor. He fought well—two of the guards were slain by his sword, and the third fled for his life."

Conelle hesitated. Giralda waited in quiet dread to hear what Conelle would say next.

"My husband thought that Sir Kramsky would be behooved to advocate a man's defending his pregnant wife from errant guards. What my husband did not know, however, was that one of the slain guards was Sir Kramsky's nephew. The next day my husband was publicly executed by archers. I was there. His eyes were fixed upon mine to the last. It must have been a painful death, but just before collapsing he smiled at me. It was a loving, consoling smile."

Again Conelle drew a deep breath. "I can say with all sincerity that I have never known a more wonderful man than Sir Reynold. I will love him forever."

Silence followed. Giralda waited to make sure that Conelle was finished with her story, and then she fell to weeping. Conelle joined her, and it was several minutes before their tears abated. It was a brief mourning—a hallowed ceremony between two close friends. The years that had separated them dissolved.

"How old was Dwindalin?" asked Giralda.

"Three years old. I was only two months pregnant with Jamie. But now tell me your story."

"Ma...my story?" Giralda stuttered. For a few moments she stood tongue-tied in the darkness. She had planned to be reticent toward sharing information about her years in Pithrania; but in Conelle's presence, she felt a strong desire to confide. She trusted Conelle without reserve. "It is a long story," she remarked, beginning to ponder what should be told and what should be kept secret.

"I will bring a lantern so that we can tend to your horse. Then we can go inside and help the girls get tucked in their beds. After that you can take all the time you need to tell me your story."

Giralda consented. The thought of sharing the most important matters in her life with Conelle was heartening.

Before long the horse was stabled and the girls were tucked in their beds. Conelle closed the door to the girls' bedroom and turned toward Giralda. Her face wore an expression of curiosity.

There were numerous wooden chairs in the living room, eight altogether, and Conelle positioned two of the chairs before the fireplace. Giralda sat down across from Conelle. She had been contemplating what to say. She prayed in silence as she peered into Conelle's eyes, and when at last she opened her mouth to speak, it was to tell everything. She decided that if she were to die or be slain, it would be important for someone to know the truth about the princess.

Two hours passed before Giralda finished sharing her story. As she disclosed the truth about Colesia, Conelle's face took on an expression of astonishment. Then when Giralda divulged the fact that Colesia claimed to have been spoken to by Prince Zarkanis, Conelle's eyelashes parted and she audibly gasped. At last Giralda came to a conclusion... "And so then, after I left my brother's house in Marne, I came down here, hoping to find some old friends and a place to stay."

The look on Conelle's face remained one of wonder. "Wait here," she voiced while rising from her chair. She stepped to the hearth and put two more logs on the fire.

Giralda was puzzled. It seemed odd that Conelle was not asking questions. She remembered her friend having more curiosity than a rummaging fox.

Conelle turned from the fireplace and scurried into her bedroom. Shortly afterward she emerged with a blanket and a pillow. She laid them out before the hearth. "You may use the wash basin in my bedroom, and you know where the outside facilities are."

"Thank you," Giralda replied, bewildered by Conelle's lack of inquiry.

Conelle reseated herself across from Giralda. "The tenant who was living next door, Lenanne, recently married and moved out, so your old apartment is unoccupied, and you can move back in. Sir Kramsky will tax you from the day you take up residence, but I think one of the jewels you mentioned will cover several months of tax."

Giralda's puzzled expression eased and her face acknowledged thankful approval. She decided that Conelle was waiting until later to ask questions. "Thank you, I could not have hoped for more."

"One more thing before we sleep." Conelle folded her hands on her lap and leaned forward. Her face grew solemn and imploring. She stared into Giralda's eyes. "I have a friend—a trustworthy and virtuous friend—to whom I would like to tell all of the things that you shared with me."

Giralda shifted position in her chair. She was wary for her princess's safety. "Well, I don't know. Why?"

"For the sake of Shareen and for the sake of Colesia." Conelle could have also said, *and for the sake of Prince Zarkanis, who we believe is imprisoned beneath the Pithranian castle*, but she refrained.

Conelle's words drew Giralda's interest, especially at the mention of Colesia. "Who is this friend?"

"He is a spy for the Sheranites. A military spy. Have you heard of the Sheranites?"

"No."

"The Sheranites are an intricately organized fellowship. Their goal is to overthrow Dragus and free Shareen."

Giralda sat back in startled contemplation. The news, although unnerving, was pleasing. "I suppose, no doubt, that you are a Sheranite?"

Conelle leaned back also. "One of the first."

Giralda slowly nodded and peered into Conelle's eyes. "That does not surprise me. How many of you are there?"

"Only a few, at present. We must be careful in regard to whom we disclose ourselves. If our existence became known to Dragus, he would stop at nothing to search us out for public execution, and he would take drastic measures to intimidate the populace against joining our ranks."

"And you are sure it will not imperil the princess for you to reveal her identity to this friend of yours?"

Conelle gazed back into Giralda's eyes. It was apparent that she gave serious consideration to Giralda's question. "What will happen to your princess if no one delivers her from Pithrania? My friend may be able to arrange her rescue."

Giralda sat in thought, but she did not have to think for long. She knew that it would be almost impossible for the princess to escape without assistance; and if the princess did not escape, then her fate could be worse than being devoured by a dragon.

"You may tell your friend."

Conelle smiled. She rose and stepped to the door to the girls' bedroom. She eased the door open, and then stepped back across the room and disappeared within the confines of her bedroom. No more words were spoken. Giralda removed her heavy wool clothing and cuddled up in the blanket before the fireplace. She rested her head upon the pillow. She had much to think about, and she could not seem to get Conelle's inquiring words out of her mind—*what will happen to your princess if no one delivers her from Pithrania*? But despite her many thoughts, she drifted into sleep.

When Giralda awoke the next morning, there were four hazel eyes looking down upon her. A hearty fire was crackling in the fireplace, and light shone about the edges of the door and window.

"Are you awake?" asked Jamie.

Giralda sat up. "Yes, I'm awake, and it looks like I should have been awake a long time ago."

"Mother said that I could open the window when you woke up," said Dwindalin. She leaped across the room and opened the shutters to the window—a square opening in the center of the southern wall. A bright band of light spilled across the wooden floor. Cool, invigorating air whipped into the room.

"There is really, really deep snow; and it is really white," said Jamie.

"Mother made breakfast. She said you like cream and eggs and bread," inserted Dwindalin.

"Breakfast, that sounds good."

Giralda rose, slipped on her wool dress, and stepped to the kitchen doorway. She peered into the kitchen. Burning lamps were mounted on the southern wall. A black iron oven sat in the east wall, and a black chimney coursed upward from the oven. The oven's iron door was hanging open on sturdy hinges. Giralda knew that the oven had a second door that opened into her old apartment—a door she had opened and closed innumerable times. A smaller door, made of wood, was located just above the floor in the middle of the kitchen's southern wall. It was the door to an outside wooden box that served as a nature-cooled icebox during cold weather—the *cold box*.

Against the kitchen's northern wall sat a long oak table with five wooden chairs that were lined up along its southern edge. Atop the table were pewter plates on heated stones, maintaining warmth for scrambled eggs and fried bacon. Wooden bowls held nuts, a small basket was filled with dried fruit, a block of wood bore bread and butter, and a squat pitcher contained cream. To the right of the table was a walled-off section of space with a slender door—the entranceway to the bathing room.

"Where is your mother?" asked Giralda, looking back toward the girls.

"She went to get barley flour," Dwindalin answered. "She says you make the most delicious barley bread under heaven."

Giralda smiled. Memories of her former life awakened within her mind. "I shall have to try. Have you had breakfast?"

"Oh, yes, we always eat breakfast with Mother. That was a long time ago," said Dwindalin.

"You stayed asleep for a real long time," added Jamie.

Giralda surmised that the two girls exercised praiseworthy self-constraint in allowing her to awaken of her own accord. "Would you like to sit with me while I eat?"

"Yes," the two girls chimed.

"And when I get through eating, perhaps we can go outside and collect some snow for making iced fruit. We can stow the snow in the cold box until your mother gets back."

"Yeah!"

Both breakfast and the collecting of snow were pleasurable experiences for Giralda. Conelle returned home in time to mix iced fruit for lunchtime dessert. There were two pregnant women due to deliver at any time, so she was only at liberty to leave the apartment for short periods. She brought back a bag of barley flour, and after lunch Giralda engaged herself in making the first batch of barley bread she had manufactured in years. This provided an interesting activity for the girls. Both Dwindalin and Jamie insisted upon helping, and such assistance lengthened the time the task required, but Giralda enjoyed every second. She sometimes found herself fretting over Colesia's fate, but there could not have been better medicine for her troubled mind than two ebullient children.

After supper, Giralda sat on the blanket before the fireplace and assisted the girls as they practiced knitting. As it began darkening outside, Conelle closed the window and stacked extra logs in the fireplace. She sat down in a chair to do some knitting of her own—it was a rare treat to have someone else tutoring the girls.

A knock sounded. Conelle rose and walked to the door. The others stopped knitting and watched.

"Who is it?" asked Conelle.

"Hardwick. My wife's time is come!"

"I will be right with you."

Conelle motioned for Giralda to join her before the front closet. As she donned her coat, she leaned and spoke into Giralda's ear. "The friend I mentioned is coming tonight. He hopes to arrive here about two or three hours after nightfall. He will knock three times on the door. Go ahead and put the girls to bed before that. I doubt that I will get back in time to introduce you, but Ferando is friendly. He has brown hair and blue eyes—really nice eyes, eyes that sparkle like starlit sapphires."

"But…what should I…?" began Giralda. She was at a loss for words.

Conelle stooped to grab her boots. She pulled them on and then rose to face Giralda. She placed a hand on Giralda's shoulder and smiled. "Do not fret. Ferando will be most cordial. He is a wonderful young man."

"Yes…but…"

"Don't worry," reiterated Conelle. Then she turned to bid farewell to her daughters. "God be with you, my little angels. I hope to be back by tomorrow morning."

"God be with you, Mother," they hailed.

As Conelle closed the door, Dwindalin jumped up and trotted across the room. She slid an iron bolt into place across the leading edge of the door, thereby securing the only legitimate entrance into the apartment. The only window large enough for someone to squeeze through was the one in the southern wall, and it had already been secured with a bar lock. It was obvious that the girls were well coached on what to do when their mother was away.

"May we have some more iced fruit?" asked Jamie.

Giralda disengaged her mind from pondering the arrival of Conelle's friend and clasped her chin as if contemplating Jamie's inquiry. She was well on her way to becoming an adopted aunt. "I think it would be good for you two to do a little more knitting on your kerchiefs, and then after that, I imagine some iced fruit would be quite proper. Perhaps we shall even have time to play a game before you go to bed."

"Hurrah!" voiced Dwindalin.

"Hurrah!" Jamie echoed.

Giralda squatted to the floor and resumed assisting the girls with their knitting. Caring for the girls left little opportunity for her to fret over the impending arrival of a military spy. It was about two hours after sunset before the girls were tucked in bed. Then Giralda sat down and began agonizing over the prospect of an interview with a stranger.

She rose and put three logs on the fire and then reseated herself, choosing the chair nearest the door to the girls' bedroom. This location would make it handy to close the bedroom door before responding to the visitor's signal—three knocks. She wondered if Ferando would be someone she had ever seen before. Judging from Conelle's description, he would have been a young child at the time she was taken to Pithrania.

Time passed slowly. It was approaching three hours after sunset. Maybe something came up... Maybe he couldn't come...

Knock, knock, knock.

Giralda found herself frozen in place upon the chair. Five seconds passed before she regained control of her limbs. She rose to close the girls' bedroom door. Once the door was closed, she crossed the room to the front entrance. She did not wish to wake the girls, so she opened the front door rather than speaking loudly enough to be heard outside. There was no doubt in her mind that it would be Ferando.

Firelight flickered upon the pewter helmet of a young man dressed in the attire of a Pithranian warrior. A coarse coat of elk hide hung over his leather jerkin, and leather trousers stretched downward over the tops of leather boots.

Giralda squinted and peered at the young man's eyes. Conelle was right—they sparkled like sapphires. He flashed a winsome smile.

"Ferando?"

"Yes."

Giralda was certain that she had never seen such a charming smile beneath a Pithranian helmet. She pulled the door farther open and allowed entrance. After closing the door, she realized that she needed to place a couple of chairs before the hearth. She and the girls had been playing upon a blanket rather than using chairs.

Ferando removed his coat and helmet, laying them on a chair that sat beneath the closed window. He stepped forward and helped Giralda position two chairs before the hearth, and then he motioned for her to be seated. She accepted his courteous gesture. He possessed a calming charisma that she fancied would make him an effective spy, and he placed her in the chair nearest the entrance to the girls' bedroom, which struck her as considerate.

After seating himself, Ferando leaned forward in a cordial posture. "Conelle told me she might be gone tonight, but she assured me that you are not dangerous."

Giralda relaxed a little and smiled; the youth's ironic bantering settled her nerves. He seemed perceptive.

"It is rare that I disrupt my customary duties for a meeting such as this, but what Conelle told me about her interview with you secured my greatest interest. I must not stay long, so I will come right to the point. You were working in Shareen at the time Pithranian forces enslaved this city—is that true?"

"Well, yes, but not exactly. I was not in Shareen itself at the time, I was at the home of a noble gentleman who lived about three miles west of the city."

"Sir Marticus?"

"Yes," replied Giralda.

Ferando's clean countenance grew intense.

"Was this man killed when Dragus's forces attacked?"

"Yes. His entire family was killed, except for Colesia, and his house was burned. I presume that Conelle told you about Colesia."

"Yes, she did. And so what you are saying, then, is that Colesia is the daughter of Sir Marticus and Lady Monica. Is that right?"

"Yes, I assisted Lady Monica in Colesia's birth—I'm a midwife. The Pithranians think Colesia is my child."

"And she has been raised as a Pithranian princess by the name of Vayle?"

"Dragus insisted on the name."

Ferando leaned back in his chair. A look of resolution carved itself upon his face. "It is true then."

Giralda did not know what Ferando referred to, but his comment sparked her interest. "What do you mean?"

"My sister is alive in the house of Dragus."

It took a moment for Giralda's mind to assimilate Ferando's words, but then her eyes went wide. "Your sister! Then you must be…"

"Zephanoah—the youngest son of Sir Marticus and Lady Monica. Perhaps you remember me? I stood with my father and brothers when my sister was born."

Giralda was beside herself. "Remember you!" she spoke with excitement, though still speaking quietly. "Of course I remember you! I'm the midwife who assisted your birth! But it is reported that Sir Marticus and all five of his sons were slain. I heard the Pithranian warlord say so myself—on the very day Colesia was born."

"And so the report must remain," asserted Zephanoah. "But what in fact happened—when attack was imminent—was that my father ordered my oldest brother, Zake, to take me and flee. The rumor that we were all slain was fabricated to appease Dragus."

"Oh my, I had no idea. So Zake is alive too?"

"To my knowledge, Zake is well. If only I could get word to him…"

Zephanoah dropped his face in a downward gaze. The matter of Zake seemed to have cast him into reverie. Giralda was more than curious to know what he was thinking.

"Where is Zake now?"

Zephanoah raised his face and his eyes focused—eyes that captured Giralda's inquisitive gaze. "Have you ever heard of Subterrania?"

Giralda knitted her brows. "Not that I can recall. Is it an island?"

There was a thoughtful pause. "Perchance you have heard the story about a king who lived long ago—King Spero?"

It was startling to hear the name of the ludicrous king from Master Edmond's tale—a tale she heard as Master Edmond escorted her to Poolglade Forest along with Marlda and Princess Vayle. An image of the castle in the cliff and the story about the demented king were indelibly impressed upon Giralda's memory. "Yes, Dragus's majordomo told me the story of King Spero. The majordomo is a fine man, despite his association with Dragus. His name is Master Edmond."

At the mention of Master Edmond, Zephanoah's brows rose, and he opened his mouth to speak; but then he checked himself.

"What?" coaxed Giralda.

Zephanoah appeared flustered. For a few moments he turned his face askance, but when his eyes again addressed Giralda, his former composure was reestablished. Giralda resolved within her mind that Zephanoah withheld something from her—something regarding Master Edmond.

"King Spero came from Subterrania," resumed Zephanoah. "He committed great crimes against a race of people who live there, a race of people with blue skin."

"So there really are people with blue skin?"

"That is correct, an entire race. King Spero feared that the blue people would retaliate against him, so he fled Subterrania and came to Gaul. And after he left Subterrania, a brutal and cunning chief rose up in his place, a chief that became the charftan of a white-skinned race of men who live in Subterrania."

"Charftan?"

"It is a title that means much the same as *king*. The ruler of a given race in Subterrania is called a charftan, and King Spero was a charftan. Next in rank to a charftan is a chief, or several chiefs—depending upon the population of a given race. The chief who replaced Spero as Charftan threatened to turn the white-skinned race into a band of pilfering outlaws, and times of peace in Subterrania are rare enough without a charftan prodding his subjects toward savagery. The charftan's name was Darion, but you know him as Dragus."

"Dragus! So that is where he came from. I never thought he looked much like a Viking. But did you say that Subterrania is not an island? Where is Subterrania?"

Zephanoah looked into Giralda's eyes. "The location is a secret. The white-skinned race in Subterrania originated from a region near here, centuries ago. Hardship and war resulted from their immigration, and as a result, the native races have determined to keep the entranceway into Subterrania a secret from peoples such as ourselves. It is said that an entire race of people, a people with ivory skin and golden hair, was almost annihilated by the immigrants with skin such as our own."

"I guess that doesn't speak well for our race," commented Giralda.

"Well, there are malevolent men and women among several races, and there have been good men who sprang up from our own race. It was a white chief who raised support among his people to bring Darion to justice. His name was Marticus."

"Your father?"

"That is correct. My father became a military leader and came close to capturing Darion, but then Darion decided to escape justice by fleeing. He felt confident that he could rise to power among his own kind in another land. My father suspected as much, and after helping to establish peace in Subterrania, he followed Darion here—to the land of Gaul. He hoped to prevent Darion from desecrating other societies. My father then met the daughter of a Sharean farmer, a maiden by the name of Monica, and he fell in love with her. Much of the rest you know."

"And that is why Darion, who we know as Dragus, was so intent upon killing your father."

"And his entire family." The look on Zephanoah's face intensified. "It is most important that Dragus does not find out that he has nurtured the daughter of his most despised enemy. I understand that my sister has been graced with remarkable beauty. If Dragus finds out who she is, then she will face a fate worse than mortal death before she is granted such death. But even if Dragus never discovers her identity, I still fear that she faces a terrible fate unless we can rescue her."

Giralda was horrified. It was not a new horror, for she had long carried the subconscious dread of Colesia falling into the clutches of depraved Pithranian monarchs, but such fear now blazed in flames of current contemplation. Her eyes plead for words of hope. "What can we do?"

"You have already performed a great service. From what Conelle tells me, it is because of you that my sister lives, and it is because of you that she knows who she is, and it is because of you that she knows the difference between good and evil. I can never thank you enough."

Giralda appreciated Zephanoah's words, but her heart burned with concern over Colesia's future. "But, as you have pointed out, she must be rescued."

"Of course she must," affirmed Zephanoah. He then paused and looked thoughtfully into Giralda's eyes.

"What is it?" asked Giralda.

"You told Conelle that Prince Zarkanis spoke to my sister."

A nervous expression surfaced upon Giralda's face. "Yes."

"When did this happen?"

Giralda shook her head. "I do not know."

"Do you have any idea how it could be possible?"

Giralda lowered her eyes for several seconds and then peered back at Zephanoah. "Your sister is fond of swimming, and she sometimes swims to the far bank in the eastern cove of Lake Manassa."

"East of the Pithranian castle?"

"Yes…and the brush along the northeastern shoreline is so thick that someone could have remained hidden and spoken with her without my knowing it."

A puzzled wrinkle formed across Zephanoah's brow. "Did she ever swim along the western shore, near the castle?"

"No. The water currents are considered too dangerous on that side of the lake—they might draw a swimmer into the moat or beneath the castle."

Zephanoah delved more deeply Giralda's eyes. She felt as if he were reading her mind like the open pages of a manuscript. It occurred to her that Colesia possessed the same ability to peruse one's inner being through the gateway of one's eyes.

"One of the assignments within the ranks of Dragus's Pithranian regiment is that of a prison guard," said Zephanoah, changing the course of the conversation. "Such duty places a warrior inside the castle walls where he might gain favor with Dragus and acquire a promotion."

"So you are planning to become a prison guard in order to gain access to your sister," surmised Giralda.

"Hopefully, yes, but I was already planning to become a prison guard, even before Conelle told me anything about my sister."

"To spy?"

Zephanoah paused. He had learned much from Giralda, and he was willing to share information in return; but certain facts, even among the Sheranites, were only shared with particular persons who were given special assignments. Such discretion was considered necessary in order to safeguard the primary mission of the Sheranite movement. "There is something I had already hoped to accomplish within the walls of the Pithranian castle," he stated. Then he stood up and straightened his jerkin. "I thank you for invaluable information. Should you ever need any kind of help, you can communicate with me through Conelle. God be with you."

Zephanoah's comment about hoping to accomplish something within the walls of the Pithranian castle stirred Giralda's curiosity, but he did not seem open to further questioning. She rose and walked to the front door, opening it for him as he donned his helmet and coat. As he stepped past her, she reached out and took hold of his arm. He turned and met her eyes.

"If there is anything I can possibly do to help free her..." she proffered.

"Thank you. And I assure you that my sister will be rescued, or else my life will be lost in the effort. I may speak with you again."

"Please feel free to contact me anytime. But one more thing..."

"One more thing?"

"Yes. What must I do to become a Sheranite?"

Zephanoah smiled. "Henceforth, you are a Sheranite."

Chapter 9

Escape

The whims and atrocities of nature, sometimes cruel, are known to wreak havoc upon both the just and the unjust. Perhaps a providential hand sometimes chastises evil through means of wind, fire, and rain; but in other instances, earth's unpredictable environment unleashes fateful calamities upon persons least deserving such misfortune. So it was with Mierna, the cordial wife of Master Edmond. Three years following the appointment of her youngest daughter as lady-in-waiting to Princess Vayle, catastrophe claimed her mortal life.

The winter was contrary. Some days were colder than arctic ice, while others masqueraded as harbingers of spring. Along with alternating temperatures came capricious atmospheric extravagances, crystal blue skies invaded by writhing black clouds, and bleak blizzards dispelled by radiating sunlight. Only during such a winter could rain clouds converge above a blanket of snow without eliciting surprise. Still, it was odd to hear thunder in midwinter.

Mierna trod over the packed snow between the stable and her house. She carried a metal pail half filled with cows' milk. One instant she was walking beneath the stormy sky, and an instant later her body lay still upon the snow. Warm milk spilled from the pail and melted the frozen earth.

Master Edmond sat eating breakfast when a flash pierced through open windows. A blast shook the atmosphere and the house shuddered. Then all was quiet. An unsettling sensation swept through his breast. For several seconds he sat without moving, and then he rose and dashed out the back door of his house—leaving the door wide open.

Daybreak was past, and Mierna's lifeless body was visible upon the white landscape. Master Edmond was a strong man, and he would endure—but he was a man who knew what was most dear to him. Tears flooded his eyes as he dashed across the snow and collapsed beside his wife's lifeless body.

The funeral was a simple one. The holy man who delivered the eulogy was a learned farmer who served the spiritual needs of persons in rural regions about Pithrania. Marlda knew how much her father cherished her mother, and her tears during the funeral were as much on his behalf as her own.

Colesia cried no less than her lady-in-waiting. Marlda was her best friend, and she was well acquainted with Mierna. Because the princess was in attendance, Pithranian guards stood on the periphery. Colesia knew that the guards were there to prevent her escape rather than to protect her. They were like a second shadow whenever she stepped outside the castle.

After the funeral, Colesia encouraged Marlda to spend time with Master Edmond. She returned alone to her bedroom and placed a log on glowing coals within the fireplace. Then she stepped out onto the balcony and gazed downward upon the frozen surface of Lake Manassa. The storm that claimed Mierna's life dropped torrents of rain on the southern slope of Mount Thrandor and then fell back to the south, ushered away by arctic air. No snow had fallen since the rain, and the frozen surface of the lake seemed a gigantic, glistening tear.

The sun dropped toward the western horizon. Colesia ordered supper delivered to her room. She did not want to dine with Borgar without Marlda at her side, for her growing reputation as the most beautiful woman in Gaul was beginning to appeal to his ignoble pride. She and Borgar had never been on friendly terms, but she had noticed his eyes gloating upon her in recent weeks, and in those eyes she read the desire for possession.

After eating supper, Colesia occupied her mind by composing a poem. She often dallied in poetry during the wintertime, lying before her fireplace with quill, ink, and parchment. On this particular evening, her pen flowed over cured lambskin with delightful abandon.

In a faraway forest,
little rills make glee.
Glistening pools bloom sprightly,
on a flowery sea.

There a gray escarpment,
cradles safe from harm.
My dear prince's castle,
where he rules with charm.

Robins serenade him,
from the dawn till dark.
Though they pause for solos,
by a skyborne lark.

On a great, winged stallion,
my Zarkanis flies.
Someday I will join him,
'neath those far north skies.

After completing the poem, Colesia lay back on an elkskin rug and mused over the verses. It was in the recesses of her imagination that she exercised romantic proclivities, ever faithful to the young prince who said he would rescue her and marry her. Sometimes sobering thoughts bestirred her daydreaming, such as the possibility that Prince Zarkanis was no longer alive—perhaps he did not even survive the stormy night of her rescue. These thoughts, however, were infrequent and short-lived. Enduring hope sustained her—hope that served as an elixir of life and quelled the oppressive circumstances of her virtual incarceration.

By and by Colesia was roused by a rattling of the latch to the stairwell door. She crumpled the parchment, since it featured her prince's name, and then tossed it across the marble hearth and into the fire. She watched just long enough to see it catch flame, and then she turned her attention toward the individual who was walking across the antechamber. It was Marlda.

"That must have been a good one." Marlda's face looked flushed and tired, but she smiled as she teased Colesia about the little flare in the fireplace. Sometimes the girls wrote poetry together—poems they made sure Dragus and Lady Eldra would never read. Marlda sat down in one of the five wicker chairs on the north side of the room.

"I did not know it was you, or I would have shown it to you…or at least part of it."

Colesia had never revealed Prince Zarkanis's name to Marlda, but the first three verses of her poem would have been fun to share. She had not expected Marlda to come back on the night of Mierna's funeral, and she found herself wondering what words might be most comforting to her bereaved friend. After thinking about it for several seconds, she decided that mere words could not suffice. She rose from the rug and sat down beside Marlda. Her eyes and soul conveyed the depth of her empathy, and her affectionate visage affirmed the priceless worth of their friendship.

Marlda responded to Colesia's eyes. She proffered an appreciative smile and then looked toward the fireplace. Under other circumstances her curiosity would have prodded her to urge Colesia to rewrite whatever prose was turning to ashes, but she was held in check by the gravity of the day. And besides that, she had news for Colesia that was uppermost in her mind. She looked back toward Colesia. "Wait till you hear where my father is going; and he wants me to go too, and you too."

Colesia marveled that Marlda could be so zestful after what had transpired that day—yet she knew that both Marlda and Master Edmond believed that Mierna was alive in a better world.

"Where?"

Marlda was too intent to draw out her exposition. "The demented king's castle!"

The princess's heart fluttered. "Really? In Poolglade Forest?"

"Yes, the same place we went six years ago. What do you suppose it looks like in the wintertime?"

No one other than Colesia knew how often she reflected upon the mysterious castle. It was Marlda who kindled her imagination with the suggestion that her prince lived there. "I think the entire landscape would be like a dream this time of year."

"That must mean you want to go with us...good!" blurted Marlda. "Dragus said my father could have a week off his duties. My father was going to go alone, but I insisted upon going too, and Dragus granted permission for me to accompany him—that is, if it is permissible with you."

"Of course."

"Thanks...so, anyway, I asked my father if you could come with us, and he said that your coming was a wonderful idea, but he said that I should find out whether or not you wanted to go before he asked Dragus."

Colesia's heart sank. "Your father has not asked Dragus yet?"

"Not yet. He did not want to attempt persuading Dragus to let you venture so far from the castle until he found out how you felt about it. He says it can be very cold this time of year, and somewhat dangerous."

The princess shook her head. "That does not matter. I want to go."

Marlda's face beamed. "My father wants to leave tomorrow morning. I will go tell him the good news."

"I will go with you," asserted Colesia, rising along with Marlda.

The two girls made their way down the inner stairwell and into the grand hall. As they passed beneath the raised portcullis at the head of the drawbridge, one of four guards intercepted them.

"Where are you going this late, Princess?" asked Paug.

"To visit Master Edmond. As you know, his wife was killed by lightning yesterday."

"Very well." Paug looked toward another guard named Turon and motioned for him to accompany them. Then he stepped behind Marlda and Colesia. No fewer than two guards ever trailed the princess from the castle, and the guard of highest rank was always one of them. The sky was clear. It was mid evening.

****

Dragus was working later than usual in the meeting room east of the grand hall. He was interviewing warriors from subjugate cities, warriors who sought assignments in the Pithranian stronghold. No warrior was granted duties with access to the Pithranian castle without personal clearance from Dragus. An acclaimed guard from Shareen was sitting at a table in the grand hall. He had been waiting for several hours; and as was the custom with new interviewees, he was blindfolded. He was the last to be called upon for an interview with the king. This was an interview he had been working to obtain for three years. His blindfold was removed, and he rose from his chair. He was directed to leave his sword and dagger on the table.

Zephanoah had seen the ominous King of Pithrania on several occasions when Dragus visited Sir Kramsky at the Sharean palace. The dark king's bodyguards always accompanied him. As Zephanoah stepped into the meeting room, he found Dragus situated behind a large desk with armed bodyguards standing on either side of him. One of the two guards held a bow and arrow. A third bodyguard motioned him onward to the front of the desk, and then the same guard walked back and closed the door, remaining inside where he could watch Zephanoah from behind.

Dragus inspected Zephanoah for a few seconds and then looked down at one of several papers strewn before him. "Ferando, son of a blacksmith in Glamster...good with bow and arrow as well as sword...very dependable and never drunk," he read aloud. Then he perused some further recommendations written on a letter from Sir Kramsky, muttering what he considered key points. When finished, he raised his face and addressed Zephanoah with scrutiny. "So then, Ferando, why do you wish to serve in Pithrania? Were you not happy in Shareen which is closer to Glamster?"

Zephanoah stood in feigned respect. His eyes were directed straightforward. "The pay is better here, Sire, and serving in your castle is more reputable. The fact of the matter is, Sire, that I possess skills beyond those of any other guard in your service. Is there any reason why one with superior skill and merit should not be deemed worthy of an honorable position in the heart of the empire?"

Zephanoah waited in silence. The Sheranites had learned enough about Dragus to know that a haughty attitude was more likely to gain his favor than any other demeanor.

"You reason well. What kind of duty do you prefer?"

The response from Dragus encouraged Zephanoah. "As I am sure you know, Sire, any duty in Pithrania is more gainful than duty in Shareen. I will serve anywhere, to begin with, if you will only transfer me to Pithrania—even if it be in the dungeon."

Zephanoah did not have to see the look of suspicion that Dragus cast upon him—he could feel it. Incarcerated within the Pithranian dungeon were a number of heirs to the thrones of vanquished kingdoms, and none had ever escaped.

"You qualify for assignment as a prison sentinel," stated Dragus, "and I can understand your desire to gain a position here in Pithrania." He leaned forward and folded his left hand over the top of his right forearm. A gold and silver sheath extended from the stubbed end of his right wrist—a sheath that covered a steel blade. "There is another opening, however, as a lookout guard atop the royal tower."

Prison duty was what Zephanoah preferred. His goal was to achieve access to the Sharean prince. Some members of the Sheranite society thought that efforts to free Prince Zarkanis were futile because he was said to be nothing more than a dumb swine—but most Sheranites wanted to free the prince first and then decide whether or not he possessed assets worthy of kingship. King Wildon had been loved and respected, and it was hoped that his son would prove a salvageable heir to the throne.

Zephanoah was admired amongst his fellow Sheranites for his keen insight. Although he preferred prison duty, he surmised that Dragus would never allow him inside the dungeon, and perhaps not even into Pithrania, if he requested prison duty rather than a position atop the royal tower—a position considered much more desirable. He knew that his sister was housed in the royal tower, but the Sheranites felt that her rescue should be attempted when she was outside the castle walls. Raising his chest, he acted as though the prospect of filling a position atop the royal tower pleased him. "Your judgment of my abilities is exemplary. I will be pleased to serve as a member of your royal retinue atop the royal tower."

Dragus had not by any means elevated Ferando to a position meriting the description of *royal retinue.* Nonetheless, such a colorful and conceited acceptance of the suggested alternative to dungeon duty quelled his suspicions. Furthermore, he was in favor of having a guard atop the royal tower who did not engage in drunkenness. "Then it is settled. You shall report tomorrow morning to—"

A sharp rap interrupted the conversation. It came from the wooden door at the back of the meeting room. Such a disturbance was rare; the dark lord did not like disruptions of any nature unless for significant cause. All eyes turned toward the door as Vixro, the rear bodyguard, turned and reached for the latch. Vixro opened the door just wide enough to see who was outside, but then he stepped back and pulled the door wide open. There stood Elmar, a castle guard of high seniority. He stood alone.

Elmar stared across the room and addressed Dragus. "Forgive the interruption, Sire, but the royal lady Princess Vayle requests audience with Your Majesty, along with her lady-in-waiting, Marlda, and along with the majordomo, Master Edmond. They are all present within the grand hall."

In the Pithranian hierarchy, royalty and special privilege went hand in hand. Dragus nodded toward Vixro and motioned toward the northern wall of the room with a sweeping gesture of his right forearm, brandishing the sheathed weapon that replaced his hand.

Vixro responded to Dragus's gesture without a word, pulling Ferando by the arm to an inconspicuous position against the northern wall.

"The princess and her cohorts may enter at once," spoke Dragus.

Elmar turned and walked across the stairwell chamber. He opened the door to the grand hall. "The king will see you at once, princess, as well as Master Edmond and your lady-in-waiting."

Colesia entered first, as was expected. Zephanoah knew right away that his eyes beheld his sister. How different her golden lock appeared amidst thick flowing hair that adorned a mature feminine figure. Dragus glanced at Ferando for the purpose of observing his response to Princess Vayle's entry. When he saw that the young warrior's eyes were affixed to the princess, he smirked. He figured that Ferando would fit in well with his band of lusty minions and would be easily manipulated through corporal bribes.

It was fortunate that Dragus occupied himself observing Ferando, or he may have noticed the look of surprise that swept across Master Edmond's features when he saw Zephanoah. By the time Dragus paid Master Edmond any attention, however, there was no indication that the majordomo had ever before lain eyes upon the new guard. Master Edmond knew that the son of Sir Marticus hoped to achieve assignment in the palace dungeon, but Master Edmond's fellow Sheranites had not yet reached him with word of Zephanoah's transfer orders—orders that were contingent upon Dragus's approval. For his part, Zephanoah did not proffer the slightest indication that he knew Master Edmond. And when Marlda followed behind Master Edmond, Dragus was again pleased to find Ferando engaged in a captivated stare—and this time there seemed to be an interested gleam in the new guard's eyes that had not been there before.

Looking back toward Marlda, Dragus noted a startled blush when she espied the handsome new guard staring at her. The polite chastity of Master Edmond's daughter had long annoyed him; she never participated with other damsels who entertained his warriors during parties and orgies that commenced in the grand hall and spread with lecherous fervor to the barracks, stables, and other hideaways about the castle. Perhaps this conceited young warrior could persuade Marlda to become more open-minded.

Elmar stepped inside behind Marlda and closed the door.

"My humble thanks for your distinguished audience," said Colesia, curtsying as befit a princess. Dragus regretted that he had not raised the lovely creature before him as a slave, for then he would have every right to possess her as a concubine. As it was, he had promised Lady Eldra that Vayle would be Borgar's bride; for despite the fact that Lady Eldra loathed Giralda, she coveted the princess—the most beautiful woman in Gaul—and she fully intended to have Vayle as her future daughter-in-law.

"I am always at your service," Dragus replied with a brazen tone of condescension. "What matter brings you before me?"

"You have granted Master Edmond a week's leave to mourn his wife's tragic death, which is most commendable," complimented Colesia. She knew that Dragus was fond of flattery. "He plans to use this time for a trip to Poolglade Forest, and he plans to begin the trip tomorrow. Marlda has been given permission to accompany him—and I approve of such, under the circumstances."

"I see," interjected Dragus, eyeing Princess Vayle with a look of suspicion, "I would assume, then, that you are concerned about a lady-in-waiting. That will not be a problem. I shall appoint Diana to serve as your lady-in-waiting beginning tomorrow at sunrise, and she shall continue serving in that capacity until Marlda returns. I know that you like the Grecian maiden, and she shall be free from all culinary duties until her services as lady-in-waiting are no longer required."

Colesia winced. She hoped very much to visit Poolglade Forest, and Dragus's words regarding Diana seemed biased against her release from the castle. Diana had not lasted long as Lady Eldra's lady-in-waiting—that position required a determined and accomplished groveler. It was no disappointment to Diana, however, when she was dismissed by Lady Eldra. She was much happier working in the kitchen. She and Princess Vayle had become close friends, and there was no one Colesia would have preferred having as lady-in-waiting in place of Marlda. But the objective of her visit was not to acquire an alternate lady-in-waiting; rather, her objective was to gain permission to travel north with Master Edmond and Marlda.

"Thank you, Your Majesty, but my reason for coming to you regards the trip planned by Master Edmond."

Dragus had already surmised what the adventuresome princess intended to request, and his face darkened. "What reason is that?"

"With your gracious permission, I would like to accompany Master Edmond and Marlda on their excursion."

Zephanoah witnessed his sister's persuasive eloquence with admiration. And then his eyes fixed themselves upon Marlda. Giralda, who he had spoken with on several occasions over the preceding three years, spoke highly of Marlda's character and capabilities, but she had never mentioned that Marlda was strikingly attractive. His rare meetings with Master Edmond had been precarious, and there had been no discussion of the paramount Sheranite spy's daughter.

189

Dragus fidgeted following Princess Vayle's plea. He leaned backward in his chair for several seconds before responding. "I see, well, were it the simple matter of a maiden taking a trip, I would certainly grant your request," he spoke, and before he said another word, Colesia knew that there was nothing she could do or say that would make any difference—she would not be permitted to go. "However," recommenced Dragus, "you are a princess, and what you do, or what you do not do, must be decided upon with serious consideration for your subjects. This trip, at this time of the year, shall be fraught with danger from ice and snow. And, in addition, your well-deserved reputation as the most beautiful woman in Gaul leaves you vulnerable to attack or kidnap by enemy forces. Such an occurrence would result in widespread war and bloodshed. It is for these reasons that I must deny your request. I hope you understand."

Colesia knew the real reason why Dragus denied her request, but she also knew that to reveal such knowledge would be foolish. If she confronted Dragus about the fact that she was a prisoner, then his tactics would likely change for the worse—instead of trying to woo her toward fulfilling his desires, he might force himself upon her, or allow Borgar to force himself upon her.

"I understand, Your Majesty."

Zephanoah was touched by his sister's disappointment. An idea popped into his mind. Had there been time to contemplate possible repercussions, he would have kept his idea to himself, but a force less calculable than mental reason took hold of him—a force stimulated by the presence of the other young lady in the room, namely the daughter of Master Edmond. "Sire," he spoke up, stepping a few feet from the wall.

Vixro looked aghast at the candidate warrior. Interrupting a conversation between two monarchs was unthinkable.

Zephanoah proceeded speaking. "You have granted me the distinction of serving as guardian of the royal tower. Might I offer, as a token of gratitude, my personal services in protecting this party as they travel? Would it not quell any need for worry if Ferando, the best swordsman in Gaul, guards them with his life? I can assure you, beyond any doubt, that the renowned Princess of Pithrania will be safer under my guard than under the protection of fifty other warriors. My years of employment in Shareen have complemented my exceptional skills with keen wisdom."

A pensive hush pervaded the room. Not even one of Dragus's personal bodyguards would have dared such an exploit. But then, to the surprise of all, Dragus produced a wry smile. "One would think that I had assigned you as sole guard over the entire royal tower," he chided. It seemed evident that Ferando's bravado met his approval. His eyes looked over the group, settling longer upon Marlda than upon the others. He again addressed Ferando. "The princess shall remain here, but you shall indeed accompany Master Edmond and his daughter. See to it that they return safely."

"Yes, Sire. As you request."

Zephanoah was disappointed that he had not gained permission for his sister to make the journey, for such an arrangement would have provided an easy means to free her—though it may have erased any chances of his returning to Pithrania as a Sheranite spy. He did not, however, let any hint of disappointment emerge upon his countenance. And in truth, it was not difficult for him to appear contented, for it seemed that the daughter of Master Edmond would be his captive companion for an entire week, and her presence had sparked his interest from the moment she entered the room. He stepped back against the northern wall with a feeling of nervous anticipation, and he could not resist another look at Marlda—a look that lasted much longer than he had intended.

Master Edmond was likewise sorry that the princess would have to stay behind, but he could not have been more pleased about the circumstances placing Zephanoah and his daughter in proximity with one another. His daughter was of age for marriage, and Zephanoah would make a fine husband—so long as the young spy could elude being murdered or executed. He knew, however, that Dragus might grow suspicious if the father of an unmarried daughter did not demonstrate reservations about a strange warrior escorting that daughter on a camping trip. "But Sire," he voiced with a feigned tone of dismay, "is this man fit for such duty? Can he be trusted?"

Dragus turned his face toward Master Edmond. His eyes, though outwardly calm, concealed a blaze of malignant delight. "You have my guarantee. I trust him without reservation."

Marlda shivered. The unfamiliar warrior looked friendly enough, but his egotistical bragging gave her doubts about his integrity with a woman. She hoped her father would further contend his coming with them, but to her surprise, he did not. She looked back at the warrior. He was staring at her. She met his eyes.

"What is your name, guard?" asked Master Edmond, looking toward Zephanoah.

It took a moment for Zephanoah to disengage his eyes and realize that Master Edmond had asked him a question. "Ferando, sir."

"We leave at daybreak, Ferando. I'll have a horse ready for you at the stables. Be there on time."

"Yes, sir."

Master Edmond turned and bowed toward Dragus. "We bid your leave, Sire."

"Granted," said Dragus.

Colesia and Marlda, both befuddled, followed Master Edmond from the room. As the door closed, Master Edmond turned and faced them. Elmar had remained inside the meeting room, and this left the three of them alone in the stairwell chamber. "I am very grieved that you cannot come with us, Princess," said Master Edmond.

Colesia recovered her composure and smiled. "Thank you, sir, but I will be fine. Do not worry—at least not about me." As she spoke the word *me*, she turned and looked upon Marlda.

Master Edmond faced his daughter. "I will meet you in the morning, dear. Be sure to pack warm clothing. I'll take care of other provisions." He leaned and kissed Marlda on the forehead, and then he turned to leave.

"But, Master Edmond," interposed Colesia, postponing his departure. He stopped and turned back to face the princess. "Do you think the warrior is safe?"

Master Edmond stepped forward in close proximity with the ladies. A quizzical look donned his face. Twice he started to say something, but both times he looked toward the closed door, stuttered, and then paused in thought. At last he managed to produce a few intelligible words. "I will keep an eye on him. Do not worry." He shook his head and shrugged. "Do not worry at all… Good night." He turned and departed.

It was a concerned princess who accompanied her lady-in-waiting up the royal stairwell to the fifth floor. Once inside the antechamber, Colesia shut the door and took Marlda by the hand. She led her to the wicker chairs in the northeast section of her room and seated her, releasing her hand and taking a seat beside her.

"Marlda, do you really think you should go?"

Marlda looked askance, but then turned back toward Colesia. There was a look in her honey-colored eyes that Colesia had never seen before, a look that was far removed from fear. "I have to. My father expects me to go, and I told him how much I wanted to be with him, and…"

"But what about the Pithranian warrior?"

"Ah, well…"

Marlda's speech halted. Her eyes were interlocked with Colesia's eyes. For several seconds they stared in silence, and then Colesia's face melted. She assumed an expression of disbelief.

"No, you can't! He's one of them! You are fond of this young warrior, I can read it in your face and eyes as plainly as if you knelt to the floor and swore it. How can you? You don't even know him! Why, you haven't really even met him!"

"Like him? Who says I like him?" Marlda responded, but it was apparent that Colesia was extracting information through her eyes, and there was no denying the perplexing feelings stirring within her breast—feelings far distant from aversion toward the blue-eyed warrior.

Colesia ignored her friend's feeble attempt to evade answering her question. "What if he tries to take undue advantage of you?"

"With my father there? Impossible. You know my father."

"What's to keep him from murdering your father?"

"Dragus's majordomo? He wouldn't dare. I know he wouldn't."

"You know? How?"

Marlda broke her gaze and rocked nervously. What was going on? What was she saying? Who was this man? She reached out a hand, leaning and clasping Colesia's forearm. "Yes, you're right. I'll be careful. But I've got to go." She let go of Colesia and straightened back up, still looking askance, not making direct eye contact. "And besides, Ferando said that he's been working in Shareen. Maybe he's from Shareen. Maybe he's nicer than—"

"Marlda," interrupted Colesia, "You heard him speak."

"I know… I heard him…but…"—Marlda paused and again faced Colesia—"but did you see his eyes?"

Colesia hesitated. She had not seen his eyes, at least not directly. "Why?"

"They were not like the eyes of any Pithranian warrior I have ever seen… They were not like the eyes of any man I have ever seen," spoke Marlda.

Colesia's brows rose. "All the more reason to be on your guard," she said, but her voice carried a tone of uncertainty. A brief interlude of silence ensued, and then Colesia spoke again. "So, his eyes were really different?"

"Oh, yes…very."

"Different in a good way?" she posed, studying the expression on Marlda's face.

"Oh, yes…very good," said Marlda, clutching her arms against her body in a manner that expressed much more feeling than her words conveyed.

Colesia noted Marlda's body language. "Well, still, promise me that you will be careful."

"Of course I will."

Then, for a while, the two girls sat and looked at one another. There was something going on that Colesia could not put her finger on. She thought about Master Edmond's response to Ferando's request, and she thought about Master Edmond's comments in the stairwell chamber. A puzzled wrinkle swept her brow.

"What?" posed Marlda.

Colesia shrugged. "I'm not sure. Just be careful."

"Yes, I will."

"Very well. I'll help you pack for the trip."

The next morning, Marlda and Colesia ate an early breakfast and bid one another farewell. Marlda walked alone from the castle, carrying a bag of clothing. Her father, as usual, took responsibility for food and camping supplies. The two girls had made no further mention of Ferando, but he was on both of their minds, and they both knew that Marlda had never dressed so attractively in her entire lifetime.

The morning was bright and crisp. The first rays of dawn turned icy snow into countless tiny diamonds. Three saddled horses stood before the stable. As Marlda drew nearer, she noted that Jasper's reins were held by her father, but the reins to the other two horses, mares named Moonbeam and Whitefoot, were held by Ferando. A feeling of excitement rose within her breast. Although Ferando wore an abhorrent Pithranian helmet, he still impressed her as strikingly handsome. As she cast numerous glances at Ferando's face, she realized that she was having a difficult time controlling her emotional response to his presence; she would have to be cautious, just as Colesia warned.

Marlda's heart quickened as Ferando brought Moonbeam before her.

Zephanoah noted her spunky bearing. "May I take your bag, my lady," he offered, stepping forward.

"Thank you, but no, I'll pack it myself," replied Marlda, trying to establish a respectable boundary. She walked past Ferando and stood before the saddlebag on the left flank of her horse. She packed her bag of clothing and tied the saddlebag. It seemed more difficult than usual to manipulate her hands and fingers; they seemed to be quivering. Her head swam in and out of an ethereal cloud that threatened her with the embarrassment of collapsing, but she managed to keep upright by leaning against the saddlebag.

"May I assist you to mount?" asked Zephanoah.

Marlda stepped forward and took Moonbeam's reins from Ferando's hands. "Thank you, but I can mount myself," she stated. As she spoke, she raised her face. His eyes seized her and held her. It seemed that her entire being passed from the corporal world into another realm. Her next breath drew a taste of ecstasy from the warmth in his smile. Finally she broke away and pulled herself onto Moonbeam's saddle. She stared downward toward the saddle horn without focusing—moonstruck upon Moonbeam.

Master Edmond looked on without any notable change in his countenance, but he had seen the look in Zephanoah's eyes, and he had witnessed the expression upon his daughter's face, and he was pleased. "It appears that we are ready. I shall lead the way, followed by Marlda. Ferando, you protect the rear."

Zephanoah had no objection to being positioned where he could observe Marlda. "As you request, sir," he spoke as he mounted Whitefoot.

"You have everything you need, my dear?"

Marlda felt flustered at being treated like a child; it had never bothered her before. "Yes, Father," she answered with a note of dignity that Master Edmond had no problem interpreting.

"Very well. Off we go!"

Master Edmond held Jasper to a slow gait as they began crossing the bridge over the Requain River. No one had used the bridge during the past several days, and ice on the wooden planks was thick and slick. Once over the bridge, the little party resumed normal speed toward the western side of Mount Thrandor.

Nature thrived with unmolested vigor in the northern region. Marlda felt something wild and wonderful penetrating her breast, something growing stronger as the society of mankind faded behind. They entered the morning shadow of Mount Thrandor, and a sense of untamed freedom engulfed them. Rocks, trees, ravines, frozen creeks, morning songbirds, and bounding hares all contributed to the stimulating panorama. No one spoke.

After quite some time, the absence of verbal communication became awkward, at least to Marlda. Her father had never started out on a camping trip with such sustained silence. She knew that the death of her mother must weigh upon his heart, as it did upon hers, but she also suspected that the presence of the Pithranian warrior was dampening her father's customary jocularity. When her mind lighted upon the blue-eyed warrior, however, she experienced sensations that were far removed from aversion. She tried to ward these feelings off, but the look in his eyes captivated her thoughts. The memory of his gaze was exhilarating.

Finally, and after they had passed far beyond possible earshot of the castle guards on the western towers, Master Edmond initiated dialogue. He broke the silence with boisterous enthusiasm. "Say, my dear friend Zephanoah, have you ever heard the story of the demented king's castle?"

Marlda furled her brows.

"The demented king's castle?" returned Zephanoah, likewise speaking with hearty zeal.

Sir Marticus had told all of his sons about Subterrania, but Zephanoah had not heard as many stories as his older brothers. Zake eventually told Zephanoah about King Spero, but he never referred to

King Spero by the name the odd king acquired on the earth's surface—
the demented king.

"That is correct," said Master Edmond, "the demented king's castle.
Have you ever heard the tale?"

"No, sir, my comrade, I never have, but I am certain that there has
ne'er been a man nor a woman in all of Gaul who can better narrate the
tale than yourself."

Dear friend? Comrade? Marlda's mind was perturbed. She was not
void of intelligence—these were not words that passed between
strangers. She sat motionless as Moonbeam continued walking behind
Jasper. Her heart began thumping.

"You are too kind—" began Master Edmond.

"Father!" Marlda interjected. Her voice carried a tone of courageous
passion. "You called Ferando by a different name. You called him
Zephanoah."

"Ah! Nothing gets by you, my sweet! Ferando is the name we must
call our friend back in Pithrania, but his real name is Zephanoah. He is
a Sheranite spy, just like you and me. And just so you need not ask,
Zephanoah is an unattached bachelor."

Zephanoah was not able to erase a colorful blush before Marlda
turned from the waist and faced him. Again their eyes met, and this time
Marlda's heart rose unabashed and acknowledged his admiring stare.
He grew lightheaded, taking hold of the pommel of his saddle in order
to keep from sliding off Whitefoot. Marlda noted his response and
flashed him a flirting smile. She then turned and faced forward. Her
own courage astounded her, but it came with willful resolve. This was
a man she intended to know better.

"Now that introductions are completed," resumed Master Edmond,
who had not even looked back, "on with the tale of the demented king's
castle..."

The remainder of the morning passed swiftly. Zephanoah was
intrigued by the prospect of viewing the demented king's castle,
especially after learning that the king's name was Spero. He was much
more intrigued, however, by the girl who rode before him. After Master
Edmond's story was completed, Zephanoah struck up dialogue with
Marlda, and the snow-clad forest provided ample subject matter for
conversation. Zephanoah deciphered animal tracks and espied birds and
other creatures upon which he expounded, and Marlda was delighted by

his tutoring. She was very knowledgeable when it came to birds, and Zephanoah found himself awed by her intellect. Then, when lunchtime came, a simple meal on the slopes of Mount Thrandor seemed grander than a palace banquet.

The more words that passed between Marlda and Zephanoah, the more comfortable they grew in their fond regard for one another. They both sensed a cogent bond—a bond as natural as the forest and yet divine. It seemed like no time had passed when they found themselves entering the southeastern reaches of Poolglade Forest. The sun was dipping toward the upper fringes of the western horizon, and Zephanoah was busy espying additional woodland inhabitants to point out to Marlda. But then plans for camping beside Crystal Pond were abruptly altered.

"Look there!"

The tone in Zephanoah's voice elicited an alarmed response from Master Edmond. He halted Jasper and peered back in the direction Zephanoah was pointing. He rose in his stirrups for a better view. Marlda pulled back on Moonbeam's reins and turned her eyes to follow her father's gaze. Two riders in furry ponchos dropped from sight down the slope of a hillside to the southeast. The riders wore horned headgear.

"And there!" resounded Zephanoah, now pointing due east.

"Viking marauders," uttered Master Edmond. He turned and faced his daughter. She returned his regard with frightened eyes. She did not scare easily, but she had heard stories about the fates of women who fell into the hands of Vikings, and she knew that Vikings murdered men without mercy.

"I think we are clear to the west," said Zephanoah.

Master Edmond looked to the north. He wished that the secret tunnel leading up to the demented king's castle was clear for passage—but it was not, and he dared not lead the group into a gorge enclosed by cliffs. They had no choice; they would have to flee west.

"Make haste, follow me. Zephanoah, watch from behind."

Master Edmond turned Jasper into the thick of the forest, spurring him to a slow trot. It was the fastest pace that the stallion could maintain while maneuvering through dense evergreens. Marlda followed, trailed by Zephanoah. Dread concern tightened Marlda's throat, but the aura of the forest still penetrated her senses. Green boughs gave way and dropped clumps of snow as the horses wove in and out between trees.

Scents of conifers flavored the air. The ground rose and fell, sometimes smoothly and sometimes abruptly. Bizarre rock formations jutted upward from place to place with stark contrasts in color—red, gray, orange, pink, and blue. A few miniature waterfalls resisted freezing. They were about six miles south of Crystal Pond, and they were heading due west.

Now and then the ground crackled beneath the horses' hooves as the stallion and two mares stepped over ice-covered streams or across the thinner edges of frozen pools. There was no talking—all three riders were intent upon a quick and quiet escape. On and on they rode until the sun dropped behind the gargantuan frame of Mount Zeborah. Cumulus clouds edged southward from the north and the atmosphere darkened.

Master Edmond halted Jasper and allowed Marlda and Zephanoah to catch up. He leaned toward them and spoke softly. "There is neither sun nor moon for the Vikings to see our trail. If we go farther west, we will leave Poolglade Forest and enter the Zeborah plain. There are few trees on the plain, and if the clouds break, we could be spotted in the moonlight. Perhaps we should camp here and head south along the edge of the forest at the first sign of dawn."

"Why not travel by night?" inquired Marlda. She was not in favor of allowing the Vikings to gain ground.

"There are ravines and gorges south of here, some steep, and some filled with snow," her father responded. "It would be treacherous to venture that way in blackness. And besides, once the Vikings decide that it is too dark to track us, they might head south to ambush us. I would rather fight Vikings in daylight than in the dark."

"I would prefer camping at the base of Mount Zeborah where enemies would have to cross the plain to reach us," stated Zephanoah. "I have heard that Vikings burn small torches and track by night, and a torch upon the plain would be easy to see. And if they do use torches, what would keep them from finding us here?"

Master Edmond turned his face toward the west, staring into darkness. Mount Zeborah was uninhabited by men, but there were unnerving stories of strange creatures residing upon its eastern slopes. It was not a campsite he favored. Nonetheless, he could think of nothing worse than his daughter falling into the hands of Vikings. He turned back toward Zephanoah. "Good thinking. It is only an hour's ride across the plain. I will lead."

Speaking ceased as Master Edmond led the party out of the forest and onto the Zeborah Plain. Eeriness enfolded them. Soft winds caressed the snow that covered the surface of the ground. Marlda was thankful that there were riders both before and behind her. A harrowing howl rose in the north and dispersed southward. It was the drawn-out wail of a lone wolf—a wail that swept over the plain like the ghost of a lovelorn dragon, gradually fading away as if it were passing by the horses and riders in search of other quarry. Jasper whinnied.

Moonbeam drew a little closer to the stallion before her. The white ground was almost invisible in the darkness, but the mushy sound of falling hooves evidenced snow-covered terrain. Time seemed warped into an immeasurable dimension. The faint silhouette of the mountain appeared near enough to shoot with an arrow, yet on and on they journeyed as if a humongous shadow masqueraded as a solid mass and moved westward before them. More than an hour passed after exiting Poolglade Forest before the level plain met with a line of boulders. They were at the foot of Mount Zeborah.

Jasper halted about a foot from a wall of granite. "Wait here," said Master Edmond. He dismounted and then led Jasper back to Whitefoot, handing Jasper's reins up to Zephanoah. "I will see what lies before us." He turned and disappeared into the darkness. Jasper shook his head as Zephanoah held his reins. Zephanoah and Marlda sat in silence, staring back eastward, looking for any sign of a torch.

Master Edmond made his way around a great rectangular boulder. He figured it was sixty feet long from north to south and five to ten feet thick. It was higher than he could reach. Several pine trees rose behind it. The trees were cradled in a space between the boulder and a steep slope that rose westward. The space was large enough for the party's horses and bedding. He returned to the spot where he left the others and took Jasper's reins, and then he raised his face toward Zephanoah and spoke in hushed tones.

"There is a clearing behind this boulder where we can camp. Maybe you can find a way to climb the boulder and take a look across the plain. With any luck the clouds will drop some snow and cover our tracks. We can circle around the south side of the boulder—the ground is flatter on that end than the northern end. I'll lead the way, and you can follow with Marlda."

"Understood. I'll search for a place to climb after we tether the horses."

Zephanoah prodded Whitefoot to a position beside Moonbeam where he addressed Marlda. "I will lead our horses to a camping spot behind the boulder. Keep your head down in case we pass beneath limbs."

Marlda overheard everything spoken between her father and Zephanoah, but she did not interrupt Zephanoah's speech. "Very well," she responded.

Zephanoah dismounted and took hold of Whitefoot's and Moonbeam's reins. He followed Master Edmond and Jasper.

It was not safe to build a fire with Vikings camped across the plain. After tethering the horses, Master Edmond tossed bedrolls to the ground and instructed Marlda to clear a spot for sleeping. She found a flat stone and began shoveling snow from a patch of ground adjoining the central portion of the boulder. Meanwhile, Zephanoah found rough indentions in the rock where he could climb. He ascended to the upper edge of the boulder and gazed out into the darkness over the plain. He could see no sign of the Vikings, so he climbed back down and helped Master Edmond feed the horses. All three horses were tethered to a pine tree.

The saddles were left on the horses; and after feeding, the bridles were replaced. When finished with the horses, Master Edmond and Zephanoah found additional stones and assisted Marlda.

"I could use a steaming biscuit about now, smothered in yellow butter," remarked Zephanoah.

Despite the dread of Vikings, Marlda found herself smiling. "There is no danger so great that a man fails to heed the summons of his stomach," she commented. "Perhaps we can barter…if you will get me back to where I can take a warm bath in the royal ladies' bathing room, I will fix you the biggest biscuit ever baked in Gaul, served with a slab of butter fit to baste a hog."

Zephanoah chuckled. He had often thought that he would be more nervous than a cornered field mouse if he ever met a girl he really liked; but, to the contrary, he felt right at home with Marlda. "Sounds fair to me."

Master Edmond listened to the conversation without comment. He was delighted by the relationship blossoming between his daughter and Zephanoah. He remembered the first time Mierna offered to bake him biscuits; in fact, he proposed to her the next day. He prayed in silence that Marlda and Zephanoah would live long enough for his daughter to bake biscuits. He rose and strode toward a saddlebag containing food. "I don't know about a basted hog or hot biscuits, but I'll get the cold bread and cured mutton. You two roll out the bedrolls."

Master Edmond lingered at the saddlebags longer than necessary. He wished there were enough starlight to observe Marlda and Zephanoah.

"I suppose we should put you between your father and me, for protection," stated Zephanoah. He was glad Marlda could not see the rosy flush he felt rising in his cheeks.

"How very thoughtful of you," replied Marlda. She could not help imagining herself married to Zephanoah and snuggling into a bedroll with him. It seemed incredible that she had never laid eyes upon him before the preceding night—she was certain that he was the man she wished to wed. "Would you like to sleep on the side nearer the Vikings, or the side nearer the Bear King?"

Marlda and Zephanoah kept bumping into one another as bedrolls were arranged side by side. Neither one of them took precautions to avoid such encounters.

"Let me think," replied Zephanoah. "Since the Vikings are real when one is awake whereas the Bear King is more likely to crop up during a dream, I suppose I would feel safer sleeping on the side nearest the renowned figure of a woman's imagination."

"Imagination!" retorted Marlda, speaking in a forceful whisper. Though she continued teasing with Zephanoah, she realized he was choosing what he deemed the most dangerous spot, placing his bedroll to the south where enemies would be more likely to circumvent the granite boulder. "You will think imagination when you wake up and see three bears hovering over you. My father believes the Bear King is real."

Zephanoah paused. He had heard accounts regarding the Bear King, but he found the accounts difficult to believe—especially since those accounts came from Pithranian warriors. Marlda's father, on the other hand, was a reliable source of information. If Master Edmond believed the Bear King existed, then the matter merited additional consideration.

"You have a point. So then, if I wake up and see three hungry bears staring down at me, I guess I'll have to offer them something that tastes better than I do," he bantered.

Marlda generally responded to jesting with spirited rejoinders, but this time she did not. A sobering thought struck her mind—if it were Vikings that attacked, rather than bears, her fate might be worse than being devoured by carnivores. She sank back on her hips.

Zephanoah sensed her altered mood. He reached a hand through the darkness until it contacted her shoulder, and then he drew his lips near her ear. Her warm presence seemed surreal, as if he were acting out a dream, but as her soft hair brushed his face and her body swayed into his arms, he perceived the genuine reality and significance of their relationship. He whispered with heartfelt affection, "If anything threatens you, my only regret will be that I have but one life to bequeath in your defense."

Marlda realized that she loved a man...this man. She knew his vow was sincere and that there was an awful chance he would have occasion to enact his pledge—to sacrifice his life on her behalf. Her fingertips rose and caressed his face. She kissed him. Perhaps she would be butchered by barbarians, but not before experiencing something she had only dreamed of—a kiss of true love.

When Master Edmond joined Zephanoah and Marlda with the evening meal, he was unaware that Zephanoah's head whirled in rapture. The three conversed with cheerfulness that belied their circumstances, and they consumed their fill of bread and mutton. Snow provided liquid to wash down food. They all craved sleep. Master Edmond and Zephanoah gathered up leftover food and returned to the horses where they repacked the food in saddlebags.

When Master Edmond and Zephanoah returned to Marlda, they each carried a sword. Master Edmond leaned his sword against the boulder within easy reach, and Zephanoah did likewise. They immersed themselves in wool blankets with Marlda between them. Snow began falling in cottony clumps, making pursuit by trackers unlikely. The sensation of contact between Marlda and Zephanoah was blissful to both—it bore them to sleep fraught with pleasurable dreams.

Zephanoah never knew what awakened him, but when his eyes opened, there was something different—moonlight. It was not bright moonlight, such as turns midnight into a white pastel; it was mediocre light sifting through thinning clouds. Nonetheless, it was far more light than was present earlier, and if he could see the environment, then so could the Vikings. Snow was no longer falling.

He rose quietly, taking care not to disturb the sleeping figure beside him. He gazed upon Marlda's profile. She was sleeping on her left side, facing him. Somehow that face and that figure seemed a part of him. He had liked her the first moment he laid eyes upon her, but now he loved her.

His eyes rose to scan the back of the granite boulder. There was a jagged crevice toward its southern end, the same indention that he climbed when they first arrived. He walked to the crevice and began climbing. A loose rock tumbled downward just as his head and neck cleared the upper edge of the boulder.

The moonlight revealed four figures against a snowy background—the figures of Viking warriors on horseback. They were about thirty yards away. Farther back, along the border of Poolglade Forest, there were two blazing red spots—campfires. Zephanoah surmised that the Vikings tracked by torchlight until reaching the Zeborah plain, and then they set up camp. He also surmised that they sent four warriors by moonlight to attempt a surprise attack. This all passed through his mind in a couple of seconds; he did not have time for contemplation—the four Vikings heard the rock tumble down the back of the boulder, and they espied Zephanoah in the same instant that he espied them.

"Haeyah!" yelled the lead Viking. He spurred his horse to a gallop toward the southern end of the boulder. Two of the other Vikings followed while the fourth turned his horse toward the northern end of the boulder.

"Vikings!" hollered Zephanoah. "Prepare for battle!" He sprang from the top of the boulder, landed, rolled to his feet, and then dashed to retrieve his sword.

By the time Zephanoah reached the site where he had lain, Marlda was standing. She held his sword balanced on the open palms of her hands. He took up his sword and met her eyes. The look in her eyes was one of terror, and the sight of them filled him with determination to behead any Viking who dared approach her...but there was also something else in her eyes...something that made him pause...for deeper than the terror in Marlda's eyes shone a burning faith that instilled hope within Zephanoah's heart—faith that vowed to endure any degree of torture without betrayal. *I have loved a man*, her eyes seemed to convey, *and heaven will forever be more glorious because my soul holds that memory*. His eyes bequeathed love in return, and then he turned to battle.

By this time, Master Edmond was up with sword in hand, facing toward the northern end of the boulder with frequent looks back toward his daughter. It was around the southern end of the boulder that the first Viking appeared, shadowed by a second. They charged on horseback with savage abandon, cursing and wielding axes. A third Viking drew Master Edmond's regard from the northern tip of the boulder.

"I love you!" cried Marlda, calling to Zephanoah as he began rushing toward the advancing Vikings with a raised sword. Tears sprang to her eyes.

Zephanoah's heart ached on behalf of the maiden behind him, but adrenalin fueled his muscles and his senses focused upon impending combat

The ground rumbled. With the seeming speed of a branching bolt of lightning there came a monstrous commotion that eclipsed all else. The most unnerving sounds Zephanoah ever heard reverberated through the atmosphere, muting the yells of charging Vikings like the roar of a lion drowning out the purr of kittens. Thoughts such as *earthquake* and *volcano* flashed through his mind. He dropped to his knees and watched in astonishment as the Vikings transformed into caricatures of cowardice. They drew back so dreadfully on their horses' reins that the befuddled steeds crumpled into the snow. The din assailing his ears blended beastly roars with a human war cry—a cry that froze the blood in one's veins—a cry that seemed to embody a great hoary oak, wrenching its roots from the ground and bellowing in rage.

Chapter 10

Impending Peril

It was dawn, and, as usual, Zarkanis feasted. Perhaps half an hour would pass before the guards made their habitual delivery of rations, but Zarkanis partook of sustenance far removed from corporal food. His eyes and soul joined in the amorous consumption of a woman's visage. In every season of the year, the princess stepped out upon her balcony at daybreak to pray, and every morning he stood ready to adore her. He longed to call out Colesia's name—loud and without inhibition so that his passionate cry echoed from one side of Lake Manassa to the other—but he knew that, for the present, he could only voice his love in the silent recesses of his longing heart.

Zarkanis had once asked Dametrius how long he should physically train and increase his strength before attempting to rescue Colesia, and Dametrius had suggested training until twenty-one years of age—so long as there were no signs that the princess was in imminent danger. Zarkanis was now twenty, and he counted the months and days until his next birthday. He had few doubts in regard to his physical ability to break free from the confining stone walls and iron bars, but Dametrius had warned that a failed attempt to escape could reveal the secret of Zarkanis's strength and thwart any future hopes for freedom.

Zarkanis honored his teacher's words and harnessed his longing passion within bonds of patience. He watched as Colesia turned and disappeared, and then his eyes dropped downward upon the face of Lake Manassa.

The midwinter morning was clear and bright, and the frozen surface of Lake Manassa granted a spectacle of sheer brilliance following a freak rainstorm two days past. The heavy downpour melted the snow that lay atop the ice, and the confluent liquid froze into a perfect mirror. Sunlight poured across the ice like the gleaming tail of a comet, and images of trees and cliffs cast themselves upon the icy pallet with detailed perfection.

The morning was beautiful but cold. Wearing his wool blanket, Zarkanis stepped to the center of the cell and began running in place. Already he had warmed up by merely jogging in place, and, in addition, he had already performed stretch calisthenics—even before the first rays of dawn appeared as emissaries of daybreak.

Dametrius had explained that speed and quickness are important physical assets. One of the theories he imparted to his student was the theory of variant muscle strands. He believed that muscle tissue is composed of differing fibers, some contributing to strength, and some contributing to speed. Each type, he advised Zarkanis, should be developed to the utmost potential. Thus, after running in place an adequate length of time to break a sweat, Zarkanis flung the blanket from his body and pumped his legs up and down as fast as he could.

In time the prince's lungs began aching. He pushed his body until pangs seemed to turn his legs to lead, and then he stopped running and donned his blanket. He walked back and forth across the cell like a caged wolf—panting. After about a minute his lungs and legs recuperated and he burst into action again, tossing away the blanket and running in place with vigorous abandon. This pattern was repeated until he had performed stationary sprinting four times. Thereafter he again donned his blanket and continued pacing back and forth until his breathing returned to normal. He pictured himself strolling along the bank of a lake or river, such as the bank he often viewed along the southern edge of Lake Manassa.

The sound of creaking hinges echoed through the rectangular opening in the lower portion of the cell door. Zarkanis knew that the second door in the passage leading to his cell was opening. He sat flat down beside the well and arranged his garment in a manner that concealed his muscular body.

Schark shoved the door open and lugged a food-laden bucket to a spot near the well. Trailing him entered Castor, an infamous member of the Pithranian cavalry. Both men wore sneers—the Captive from Shareen was a popular object of derision. The fact that Zarkanis's name was never supposed to be mentioned made his mockery all the more enduring. Schark became an esteemed confidant, for it was he who granted permission for those of equal or lower rank to view the renowned laughingstock.

Zarkanis fixed his eyes on the bucket and wobbled from side to side, grunting like the swine that were sometimes herded along the roadway south of Lake Manassa. Much of his uncouth reputation was prompted by his creative antics; he took pleasure in theatrical chicanery. Rather than emptying the bucket, Schark picked out a slab of venison and plopped it onto the floor next to Zarkanis. Castor looked on with raised brows and a wide grin—the celebrated prisoner fell upon the venison with his teeth and then shook his head from side to side like a dog with a rat in its jowls. Zarkanis kept his arms and hands beneath the blanket, but he still used his fingers through the fabric to lift the venison and steady it as he continued his ruse of idiotic indulgence.

As usual, Schark was more than satisfied with his prisoner's performance. His popularity would not suffer from the reports Castor would spread in regard to his privileged encounter with the corpulent Captive from Shareen. The previous chief, Bruxtas, had reported that the Captive from Shareen was so stupid that he would perish whenever Tonan died; that is, unless someone else were put in the cell to care for him. Schark, on the other hand, insisted that the prince was a caged pig and would subsist quite nicely so long as he was fed. Dragus chose to agree with Schark; he relished the thought of King Wildon's son being a caged pig.

Schark dumped the remaining food and then motioned for Castor to exit. When the second door closed, Zarkanis set about the task of separating meat, nuts, dried fruit, vegetables, and bread. He preferred his bread dry, but he could down soggy bread when necessary. The vegetables were stacked with the meat, forming the largest heap. Once the food was organized for the day, he ate his breakfast. There were certain foods he found more palatable than others, but his sense of taste was not what dictated his eating habits. Dametrius had taught him what foods, in what proportions, and eaten in what order, would best aid his endeavors toward physical strength and agility.

After breakfast, Zarkanis shaved. The little razor of hardened steel was not as deep from back to front as it had been twenty years before, since now and then it required sharpening on stone, but it still served its purpose well. He thought it best to appear a little scraggly when the guards arrived—a close shave might imply more intelligence and dexterity than he cared to divulge—so he shaved following breakfast. His attitude toward shaving was comparable to that of an aspiring suitor preparing for his first introduction to a female, for his thoughts while shaving dwelled upon Colesia. Dametrius had once mentioned that a princess raised in a castle might prefer the look of a clean shave to that of a shaggy beard, and that single comment resulted in Zarkanis's shaving every morning thereafter.

With shaving completed, Zarkanis lay down on the stone bed for a period of imaginative thinking. While Dametrius was living, the prince was assigned one period of imaginative thinking daily, and that period came just prior to sleep at night. Since Dametrius's death, however, times that had been employed in academic pursuits were merely review, and mental review was not as entertaining as learning under the vibrant sage, so Zarkanis compensated by adding one or two additional periods of imaginative thinking daily. On this particular occasion he concocted several scenarios that all culminated in the liberation of Colesia.

After a period of venturing within the realm of fantasy, Zarkanis's mind returned to his present reality. He rose from the stone bed. The western end of the bed rested fourteen inches from the western wall. After stretching his arms, chest, back, and legs, and jogging for a while until he broke a slight sweat; he reached down to his hiding place behind the bed and picked up a sturdy wooden shaft that was fourteen inches long. It was hewn from an oak branch that drifted below the cell. Holding the shaft in one hand, he stooped and lifted a second shaft. He positioned both shafts on the floor between the western end of the stone bed and the west wall of the cell. Next he repeated the process until there were six shafts aligned between the bed and the wall, and then he moved all of his other cached goods a safe distance from the great stone bed. Again he stretched his muscles.

Off came the cumbersome blanket. Two or three times a week he performed strength training. For the most part he sought to engage one muscle group against another, performing isometric exercises, but for the last couple of years he had included a more daring endeavor. There was only one object inside the cell that was of appreciable weight—the massive stone slab that was meant to serve as a bed.

The stone bed was nine feet long, and there was a span of five feet between the eastern wall and the eastern end of the bed. The bottom surface of the bed was uneven, and the corners were far from square. There were recesses beneath the eastern end of the bed where Zarkanis could place his hands or feet. After loosening and stretching his muscles, he laid a couple of wool blankets on the floor and positioned himself upon them. He lay with his head just inches from the bed, and then he raised his feet and braced them against the eastern wall. His hands, then, were positioned beneath the massive stone.

His eyes stared toward the ceiling but did not focus. Deep breaths filled his lungs and fueled his tissues. His muscles tensed. Beads of sweat popped out across his forehead as he lifted and lowered the enormous stone five times, and then his bulging sinews eased and he lowered the rectangular boulder back onto the floor. He smiled.

Then Zarkanis repositioned himself with his feet propped beneath the great stone. Puissant muscles pressed the slab upward. After eighteen leg lifts, Zarkanis felt pangs besetting his thighs, but he still completed twenty-seven repetitions. It took a minute of pacing around the cell to work pain-inducing acid from muscles, and then he sat down and commenced isometric exercising of his feet, legs, thighs, hips, and stomach. When the strength exercises were completed, his body was exhausted. He donned his blanket and took a long drink from the bucket of water. Then he stashed the wooden shafts in their hiding place and moved his other cached goods back into storage. After this, he picked up the wool blankets from the floor and spread them over the top of the great stone bed, and then he lay down.

At this point Zarkanis undertook academic review. He recalled teachings of Augustine, Cicero, Socrates, Hippocrates, Aristotle, Boethius, and Pythagoras. In addition to being a philosopher, Pythagoras also contributed to the science of mathematics, and Zarkanis's mind drifted from philosophy to mathematics. After a few minutes of mathematical contemplation, Zarkanis's mind again drifted, this time from mathematics to physiology. The light and shade within the cell indicated noontime, and physiology seemed a proper subject to ponder during lunch.

Breakfast, lunch, and supper on any given day consisted of much the same foods. Thankfully, though, there was notable variety from one day to the next. As he ate lunch, Zarkanis leaned back against the western wall and gazed through the cell window. He wondered at the beauty of the sky. Many who lived outside the Pithranian prison did not live such full and rich lives as the captive Prince of Shareen. He thanked his Creator for such an enjoyable day. Dametrius was a gifted tutor, but it was through his own determined will that Zarkanis chose to accept the challenge of living a fulfilling life within the confines of a stone cubicle.

After finishing lunch, Zarkanis rose and walked back to the stone bed. Again he reached downward to the clandestine space behind the lower reaches of the bed. Cached within this space were flint knives used for whittling, pine cones used for juggling, and neatly carved arrows with pheasant feather fletchings and pigskin tips that were used for target practice when the arrows were released from a sturdy yew bow that was hidden along with them. Most of the items were either drawn from the surface of the canal or were previously collected when he was small enough to fit through the well opening, but on occasion he procured an item from outside the cell window during the darkness of night. Such items were snagged with an improvised net or hook and then hauled into the cell.

On this particular afternoon, Zarkanis engaged himself in the art of juggling, and then he practiced releasing arrows while dropping through the air after leaping off the stone bed. Thus he entertained himself until it was time for pre-supper exercises. The sun had driven some chill from the air, but it was still cold. Running in place warmed the prince's muscles, and then he shed the only garment he wore besides scant shorts. He walked to the western wall of the cell and turned his face upward.

Zarkanis ascended the mid portion of the western wall as nonchalantly as a squirrel climbing to a nest in the bough of a tree. He reached out to the ceiling with his left hand and placed his fingers in a recess located about twenty inches from the wall, and then he released his right hand and both feet. Once stabilized beneath the cedar ceiling, he found another recess to grip with his right hand, and then he began pull-ups.

The physiologic demand of completing as many pull-ups as possible did not dampen Zarkanis's imagination. He stared out the cell window with his back toward the western wall of the room, focusing his eyes upon the icy surface of Lake Manassa. Then he let his imagination soar as he executed as many pull-ups as his body could endure; and as always, his daydreams were filled with images of Colesia. After finally releasing his grip from notches in the cedar ceiling, he dropped to the floor and commenced sprinting in place.

Following four episodes of sprinting in place, Zarkanis paced about the cell for a few minutes of recuperation. Then he donned his outer garment and sat down against the western wall, situating himself within reach of food and water. He drank from the rind of a gourd.

Supper was derived from the same pile of provisions as breakfast and lunch. Gazing out the window, the prince observed a hawk circling above the eastern forest. After the onset of evening, he was inclined to daydream; so to avoid such diversion, he selected subject matter for his last topical review of the day and focused his thoughts. He continued eating as he performed intellectual recollection. Only a committed and conscientious student would choose such an arduous mental task at the close of day, for he decided to reminisce upon the two foreign languages Dametrius taught him to speak—Latin and Greek.

Once the meal was completed, Zarkanis extended his academic undertaking to calligraphy. There was always adequate dust about the doorway to the cell, and to this he added a sprinkling of water. It was relatively dark by this time, but the prince was still able to see well enough to decipher letters. Using his right index finger, he wrote first in his own Gallic language, and then in Latin and Greek. As the darkness thickened, he switched to the composition of odd symbols combined with peculiar representations of birds, plants, and animals that comprised prose from beneath the earth's surface; for he had never forgotten Dametrius's teaching of Subterranian script. During some nights he was able to continue writing by moonlight, but not on this night—the clouds were too dense. He poured water onto the rock where he had been writing and wiped away all signs of human intelligence.

****

Aloft in the fifth story of the royal tower, Colesia and Diana were startled by a knock on the door to the stairwell. They were sitting in two of the five chairs in the northeast portion of the princess's bedroom, and they were discussing the worrisome departure of Marlda and Master Edmond in company with the new guard. The departure had taken place that morning.

"Were you expecting anyone?" asked Diana. Her soft, dark eyes probed Colesia's expression. Darkness had fallen, but light was cast upon their faces from flames in the fireplace. The drapes separating the bedroom from the antechamber were drawn closed.

"No, would you mind seeing who it is?"

Diana was still dressed in daytime attire whereas Colesia had already donned a nightgown. Diana rose and stepped through the drapes, allowing them to close behind her. She passed through the antechamber and then opened the door to the stairwell. With oak limbs crackling in the fireplace, it was difficult for Colesia to hear the conversation that ensued. It was only a few seconds, however, before Diana reappeared. There was a perplexed and frightened expression upon her Grecian face.

"What is it?" asked Colesia.

"It's Elmar. He's come after me. Dragus wants to see me in his conference room."

Colesia grew apprehensive. Not once in all of her nineteen years in the Pithranian castle had she ever known Dragus to summon a servant to his martially oriented conference room. She rose from her chair and stared into Diana's eyes.

"I will be fine," Diana declared, troubled by the look on Vayle's face. "I have done nothing warranting punishment. My service in the kitchen has been diligent and consistent."

"Of course," said Colesia, but it was not Diana for whom she feared. Her mind was fretful of another matter—a matter having to do with Prince Borgar. She and Borgar had grown distant over the years, and he was often gone from the castle—either traveling on military ventures with his father or jaunting through subservient kingdoms with a riotous young warlord named Pudok. But at dinner that day, despite Diana's presence beside her, she noticed Borgar staring at her—a bold and lustful stare. Pudok was with him. Borgar did not speak to her, but with the majordomo and his daughter both absent from the castle, Borgar's forward manner seemed ominous.

Colesia stepped closer to Diana, placing one hand on Diana's shoulder. "I do not think he will harm you, but come straight back as soon as he releases you…please."

"That I will, my lady," said Diana. She kissed the princess on the cheek and departed without delay, not desiring to invoke wrath by failing to answer Dragus's summons in a timely manner. She did not notice a figure skulking down the steps that descended from atop the tower. It was not until minutes later, when she stood in the presence of Dragus himself, that she perceived why the princess had asked her to return as soon as she was free to do so, for it became evident that she was called to the meeting for only one purpose—to leave the princess in solitude.

A few seconds after Diana closed the stairwell door, Colesia stepped into the antechamber and stood before a closet. She reached inside and withdrew a black wool dress—the drabbest article of clothing she possessed. She turned to reenter her bedroom and change garments, but then she stopped short and swung back around—the latch to the stairwell door had snapped open. The door creaked ajar. A single oil lamp illuminated the antechamber, and it furnished adequate light to reveal the unwelcome features of Prince Borgar. He stepped into the room and closed the door behind him.

Borgar's attire was that of a warrior—leather breeches, jerkin, and boots—but he also wore garments befitting royalty, including a long-sleeved shirt of golden silk and a purple fleece scarf. Dark curls encased his face and toppled toward his shoulders, and his eyes appeared darker than his hair. His Roman nose and prominent cheeks, inherited from his mother, were deemed traits of nobility, and he was considered one of the most handsome men in the kingdom. There was no trace of inhibition upon his countenance as he gawked at Princess Vayle. It seemed to his liking that he caught her in a compromised posture.

Colesia faced her intruder, holding the wool dress against her gowned figure. "It is not chivalrous to enter a lady's room without knocking," she spoke indifferently, not wanting to exhibit fear.

"Princes and princesses are above petty etiquette," he replied. His demeanor and tone of voice denoted unmitigated arrogance.

"Of course, but I should think the manners of royal ladies and gentlemen should surpass the etiquette of peasantry. Would you not agree?"

Borgar was tall like his father but larger framed. He flashed an oily smile and stepped closer to Colesia, close enough to reach out and touch her. She backed against the stone wall. Her body was positioned just west of the drapes leading into her bedroom. She clutched the wool dress more tightly against her body, ruing the fact that the slim knife she possessed was hidden inside a drawer within her bureau rather than concealed beneath her gown. The pupils in her eyes dilated, but no other sign of fear emerged.

"Father was right," Borgar commented, "you keep more beauty shrouded beneath modest clothing than what is flaunted by all the women in Marne. No doubt you would have found favor in my eyes long ago if you would have dressed half as garishly as your competitors."

A knot formed in the pit of Colesia's abdomen. "Perhaps a princess who wishes for an honorable marriage to a noble prince should attire herself with discretion," she spoke coolly. Her mind raced ahead. If she feigned swooning, Borgar would carry her to her bed. If she screamed and resisted, she would no longer be of value to the Pithranian hierarchy, and her fate would be worse than she dared to imagine. There had to be another way...

Borgar's eyes gleamed with lust, but Colesia's comment about marrying a prince seemed to have gained a degree of respectable contemplation. "Perhaps you are right," he crooned. "Perhaps the future wife of a noble prince should, as you say, attire herself with discretion." He took a step back. His chest swelled. "Father has arranged for a priest to arrive from Aquari in three days. We shall be married that evening, and you shall be destined to rule at my side—the future Queen of Pithrania."

The princess's face paled. She stared at Borgar in veiled horror, speechless.

"Just think, when I become king, you shall be the richest and most powerful woman in Gaul. The entire kingdom shall be at your disposal, and no pleasure shall be withheld from you. What do you say to that? Is that not a prospect worthy of consummation?"

Colesia stared upon the prince's licentious eyes. She collected her wits. When she spoke next, her voice was fluid and resonant. "So how would you describe my proposed destiny? Would you foretell that I am to be exalted above all queens that have come before me and above all queens that shall ever come after, worthy of a king whose fame shall rise above the stars?"

It was apparent from Borgar's expression that he was pleased by Colesia's words. She spoke again before he could conjure a reply.

"Would you not say that my husband shall be a man renowned in stature, in conquest, and in sacrosanct marriage...a virtual god? And would you not think it appropriate that he should forever boast that he wed the most beautiful virgin on the continent?"

Borgar's countenance became a portrait of prideful gloating. He seemed to have no problem deeming himself a god. "Perhaps, given some time to contemplate, I would attest to all of your inquiries in the affirmative," he remarked with pompous indulgence. "But what do you say? How do you respond to your own query?"

Colesia drew a breath. She stared straight into Borgar's eyes. "Of a truth I can say that I bless every day of my hallowed chastity— preserved as a virgin worthy of a sovereign's matrimony and longing to marry a prince who I have held in my dreams since childhood, both in dreams of daytime volition and in dreams of unconscious slumber."

A smug smile erupted upon Borgar's face. He knew enough about Princess Vayle to know that she would never knowingly speak a lie, even upon threat of death. What he did not know, however, was that Princess Vayle spoke of another prince.

Colesia broke eye contact with Borgar lest her eyes betrayed the loathing that fumed within her breast. His eyes dropped and affixed themselves to her body.

"I ask you," recommenced Colesia, "how could an emperor rise in fame above all the kings of the earth if he were not bound in wedlock to a matchless virgin—like a Greek god descending from Mount Olympus and choosing from the fairest virgins of the earth?"

As words meant to fuel Borgar's pride passed through Colesia's lips, her mind drifted back in time…back to the night that she awoke upon the bank of a canal that coursed westward from beneath the castle…back to the night when she gazed up at the face of a boy who told her that he loved her; and although he had only spoken the words *I love you* once, those words had resounded within the dreamful fancies of her heart countless times thereafter. Where was Prince Zarkanis now? Would he come after her? Would he come in time to save her from a horrid fate? She thought again about the knife in her bureau. It would do her no good if she could not reach it. But now she was relying upon a different sort of weapon, a more subtle weapon, a weapon of flattery; and she hoped that Borgar's conceit would prove more powerful than his lust. She prayed that her virginity would endure the night.

Borgar tossed his head back and laughed. "Make ready, my virgin princess," he said. He lowered his face and addressed her with piercing eyes. "Prepare for the greatest of all weddings, and for the fondest of all consummations." He strode back to the door and opened it, stepped outside, and then started to pull the door shut. But then he paused and thrust his head back into the room. "And to think, my father wanted me to inform you that Marlda would be handed over to Jarak if you failed to accept my marriage proposal in a cordial manner."

Colesia stared toward Borgar without comment. There was no alteration in her expression.

"I daresay I'll take pleasure in letting my father know how foully he misjudged your desire to take on your future role as queen. And as for Marlda, I don't think Jarak stands a chance, not from what I've heard about the guard who took her camping."

Borgar broke out laughing at his insinuations about Ferando and Marlda, and then he closed the door. His footsteps and laughter faded as he stepped down the stairwell.

Colesia cringed. She looked about the room with a sense of disorientation. The pretentious walls of security surrounding the Princess of Pithrania lost their dissimulation. Rather than proffering protection, they loomed as fiendish fingers—fingers awaiting a helpless damsel's ripening before squeezing the vital fluids from her body. The chamber that had served as her sanctuary for nineteen years deteriorated into a nightmarish dungeon—a chamber of torture. Her heart felt like ice.

For several long minutes she stood paralyzed against the wall. When animation returned to her limbs, she threw her wool dress upon Marlda's small bed and returned to her bedroom. She withdrew the dagger from her bureau and raised her gown long enough to fasten the dagger to her right thigh with a silk scarf. Then she returned to the antechamber and donned her wool dress. She stepped to the door and cracked it open to peer into the stairwell. Four staring eyes fixed themselves upon her—those of Vixro and Jarak. She surmised that Dragus had assigned two of his personal bodyguards to prevent her escape.

She closed the door and swung her body back around against it. Faintness assailed her head and limbs. The strength of her legs and thighs barely kept her from crumpling to the floor. Using her arms to push off the door, she stumbled across the floor and through the drapes to her bedroom. She managed a few more steps before swooning— collapsing onto the silk bedspread that covered her wool blankets, satin sheets, and down-filled mattress. When she regained consciousness she was weeping. Diana wept with her.

****

Had Zarkanis perceived the agony besetting his beloved princess's heart, he would not have borne a contented smile as he drew a trout up into his cell. It thrashed at the end of a wire hook that was secured to wool twine. After removing the hook, he killed the trout swiftly and washed the hook.

Trout fillets were soon carved and rinsed. Zarkanis sat back against the western wall to enjoy his dessert. He savored the chewy consistency and distinct flavor of fresh fish. The meat was wholly consumed.

Zarkanis yawned. The day had been challenging and eventful. Before lying down in the space behind the stone bed and wrapping himself in wool blankets, there was one more task to accomplish. He rose and jogged in place while holding the wool blanket up about his knees. On the verge of breaking a sweat, he tossed the blanket aside and turned toward the western wall. He stood just north of the door. Then he mounted the wall and made his way around the entire circumference of the cell until reaching the south side of the door.

The night following Dametrius's death, the prince succeeded in spanning the doorway without falling. He accomplished this feat by feeling out depressions and protuberances on the other side of the doorway, just as Dametrius instructed. In time the accomplishment grew trite, so the prince found ways to make the endeavor more formidable. Now, using toes as well as fingers, Zarkanis held his body against the rough wall. He was positioned at the upper, southern corner of the doorway. Then, like a squirrel leaping from one tree to another, he launched across the doorway and clasped to the rocky wall on the opposite side. All four of the prince's extremities participated in securing a hold upon the dark wall, and they held fast.

After passing the point where he had started, Zarkanis lowered himself to the prison floor and retrieved his wool robe. He was accustomed to inclement weather, but this night was exceptionally cold. Attired in his outer garment, he dropped the water bucket into the canal and drew up a fresh drink. Then he gathered up extra wool blankets and nestled down for sleep behind the stone slab. After prayers, his thoughts embarked upon the day's final period of imaginative thinking.

Chapter 11

Astonishing Deliverance

A wave of fury crashed into horses and Vikings, smashing armor and flesh against the western side of the granite boulder. "Stay! Do not move! I'll protect you!" a deep voice bellowed toward Zephanoah, Marlda, and Master Edmond. Zephanoah was spellbound, as were his comrades. A giant figure rushed forward and tossed them into the pit of bedrolls as if they were loaves of bread. Then he stood before them, facing back toward the mountainside and shielding their bodies from attack as well as guarding three petrified horses that were tethered to a pine tree a few feet in front of him. Savage monsters charged about, scattering earth and stone like stampeding dragons. Sounds of bestial panting penetrated the air, broken by episodes of spine-chilling snarls and short-lived screams. Marlda peered outward from within Zephanoah's enfolding arms, espying dripping tongues and bared fangs.

"Nah! Nah! Natah!" hollered the giant. It was evident to all three rescued onlookers that they were beholding the renowned Bear King. His body was encased in layers of animal hides, and loose strips of leather dangled from his raised arms like moss hanging from the limbs of a tree. He seemed a barbaric maestro as he stood and directed his celebrated beasts in bloody battle. One Viking escaped from the northern tip of the boulder, but the other three fell prey to the lethal avalanche of frenzied bears.

Master Edmond rose to his knees and watched in wide-eyed amazement. Marlda and Zephanoah rose to their knees also, but Marlda remained nestled in Zephanoah's arms. Her cheek was pressed to his chest. The soft moonlight caused teary lines on her cheeks to glisten, but she was no longer crying—she was mesmerized. She clung to Zephanoah and stared at the indomitable figure of materialized folklore.

"The Bear King... He is real," Zephanoah spoke.

"Yes," replied Marlda, "and you are here with me...alive."

Master Edmond said nothing. He had narrated stories of the Bear King and had even claimed to believe that the Bear King was real, but his jaw slacked in dumbfounded wonder—and it was a rare moment that found Master Edmond speechless.

"We owe him our lives," said Zephanoah, and then he dropped his lips near Marlda's ear, "and I find myself looking forward to whatever life may bring us."

Marlda melted in affection for the man who held her—she had never felt so exhilarated. Focusing upon Zephanoah's face in the moonlight, she clasped both hands behind his neck and pulled his lips to her own. There followed a long-sustained kiss—a kiss that left no doubt to the depths of her affection. Then she released his lips and faced him. "Yes, but what will he do with us?"

Both pair of eyes turned toward the Bear King. He had stepped a few paces to the south and stood facing a grisly spectacle—seven bears were devouring the slain carcasses of three horses and three men. An eighth bear bounded around the southern tip of the boulder and joined the others. The roars had settled and the killing was over, but sounds of champing, grunting, and crackling bestirred the nighttime atmosphere.

"Chittua! Chittua!" the Bear King hailed toward his beasts, seeming to proffer congratulations. He glanced back at the party of three behind him, and then he turned and walked past the southern end of the boulder. He faced east. His chest rose as he drew a breath. "Aaheeeya!" he roared, shaking a fist above his head. His voice flooded over the plain like the cry of a mythological god erupting from the throat of a volcano. Not one of the three who witnessed his awesome challenge doubted that the Vikings, however many there might be, were fleeing in the opposite direction.

The clouds were whisking away. Visibility improved. The mystifying figure turned and walked toward Zephanoah, Marlda, and Master Edmond. They kept their eyes fixed upon him. The Bear King strode without hesitation until halting a few feet before them. There he stood and propped his hands upon his hips. His ruddy brown hair and beard blended together around his face. His eyes sparkled in the moonlight.

"I am the Bear King," he proclaimed, towering over them like a colossus. On the left side of his waist hung a large sledgehammer, carried as easily as a boy might tote a knife. The head of the hammer appeared to be cast iron. "Who are you?"

Master Edmond recalled verbal accounts depicting the Bear King as a demon who despised Pithrania. It seemed best, therefore, to tell him the truth before he discovered Zephanoah's Pithranian helmet at the base of the pine tree where the horses were tethered. "I am Master Edmond, a Sheranite."

"Sheranite?"

"Yes. Sheranites are spies against Pithrania, and these two are also spies against the evil kingdom."

The Bear King looked hard at each one of them, and then settled his eyes back on Master Edmond. "You allow a woman to endanger her life as a spy?"

"I insisted," Marlda inserted. "The princess needed my protection…"

Master Edmond placed a hand on his daughter's shoulder, letting her know that she had said enough. The Bear King noted the interaction. A look of interest beset his eyes.

"I hope my pets have not frightened you too severely," he spoke with a note of apology. "They have never slain an innocent man. They only slay human beings upon my command." He focused down upon Marlda. "And they have never slain a girl," he added. He then lifted his face and addressed all three. "It is not my pleasure to wage war, but the murderous woman-molesters that tracked you across the plain are little better than the sniveling sycophants that King Dragus enlists as his personal protectors. I can only hope that my pets will not suffer foul eructation and writhe with indigestion."

The great woodsman's face appeared lugubrious as his lips and tongue produced elegant diction in regard to his beastly comrades, utilizing words that taxed the linguistic knowledge of his audience. Marlda began sensing that she was safer in the company of their rescuer than if he and his bears were a hundred miles away. Zephanoah bit his lip to restrain laughter. Master Edmond remained awestruck, but his face hinted of a smile.

"So you are spies, and you call yourself Sheranites," the Bear King resumed. "Are you from Shareen?"

There were a few moments of silence, and then Master Edmond spoke up. "My daughter's name is Marlda. She and I are not from Shareen, but we still hope to see Dragus overthrown. Pithrania was not always a land plagued by wanton tyranny, and we hope to see our homeland redeemed."

The Bear King's eyes peered out from a dark halo of hair and beard. After perusing Master Edmond and Marlda, they turned upon Zephanoah. "And you...are you from Shareen?"

Zephanoah looked toward Master Edmond. Master Edmond nodded, giving his approval for Zephanoah to disclose his origin. Zephanoah again faced the Bear King. "I grew up in Glamster, but I was born on a farm near Shareen, and I lived there until I was four years old."

The giant paused, staring at Zephanoah. "And your name?"

"I go by Ferando, but my real name is..." Again his speech broke and he looked toward Master Edmond, and again Master Edmond nodded. He turned his face back toward the Bear King. "My real name is Zephanoah."

Marlda gasped and grabbed Zephanoah's arm. The Bear King had stumbled forward, stomping a foot into the ground to keep from tumbling onto the snow. His expression changed to one of incredulity—his eyes widened and his brows curved upward. The transformation in his countenance was startling—it seemed as though he were cast into a trance of astonishment. It was thirty seconds before he spoke again, and no one else dared breathe a word. He never removed his eyes from Zephanoah's face. "Zephanoah …that is an interesting name, and not a common one. I hope you will not find it a matter of impropriety if I engage in more personal inquiry. Might I?"

There was something fascinating about the Bear King's eyes. Zephanoah nodded.

"Have you ever seen a two-headed black snake?"

Marlda backed far enough from Zephanoah's breast to gaze upon his face. She could not imagine what prompted such an odd question. Her feminine curiosity heightened as she witnessed his reaction. At first his brows drew closely together, and then they suddenly parted. A distant, reflective expression crept into his countenance. He gazed into the Bear King's eyes. "Yes, I have seen a two-headed black snake, a rather big one at that…or at least it seemed big to me when I was only four years old."

The Bear King, who was larger than any guard in Dragus's service, dropped to his knees and crawled forward. He stopped before Zephanoah, never breaking the link between their two sets of blue eyes. "To whom did that snake belong?"

Marlda's heart beat faster. She watched in wonder as Zephanoah's mouth slacked open, remaining so for several seconds before he was able to speak.

"It belonged to my older brother, Baruk… Baruk!"

"Little Zephanoah!"

Marlda gasped as the two brothers lunged forward and hugged one another, crying and laughing and slapping one another on the shoulders—Baruk being careful not to break Zephanoah's arms. She and her father were both amazed to learn that the Bear King was Zephanoah's brother. Baruk motioned behind him and announced that the group's horses had been spared, and then he insisted that they spend the remainder of the night in his cave. The bears, he added, would stay put at the boulder and enjoy their midnight hors d'oeuvres, and he expected them to remain at their feast until the next morning. He helped Zephanoah gather up the bedrolls as Marlda and her father untethered the horses. They fastened the bedrolls behind the saddles, and then Baruk led the way up the mountain. Master Edmond, Zephanoah, and Marlda led their respective horses by the reins as they followed behind.

Conversation passed between the hikers as Baruk led the way to his cave. The trek was about an hour's climb up the steep mountain; that is, it was about an hour's climb when coursing along a route that could accommodate the horses. Baruk explained that one of his pets spotted a fiery torch upon the Zeborah plain and brought the finding to his attention. He suspected Viking trackers, who were usually up to no good, so he and his bears crept down the mountain to investigate. It had only taken about fifteen minutes to descend to the foot of the mountain, and then they watched the Vikings until they discovered what the vermin were up to. The rest everyone knew.

When Baruk finished speaking, the other three members of the party took turns retelling the events of Baruk's rescue, each sharing details from his own or her own perspective. Baruk laughed at the various mental images that the arrival of his pets incited within the minds of his newfound companions, images that included notions of fire-breathing dragons and cascading boulders. By and by they reached the mouth of a cave that opened toward the east. The interior of the cave was softy aglow with the light of lanterns. They tethered the horses outside the entranceway, and then Baruk led them inside.

All three visitors were astonished as they entered Baruk's cave and followed him about. Whole trees were shaven with an axe and fitted together to make three separate rooms that adjoined end to end along the southern wall of the cave. The cave grew larger beyond the entrance, rising to fifteen feet in height and expanding to twenty feet in width. Wood furniture sat inside and outside the three rooms, and there was a large bed in the second room. The third room was the kitchen, furnished with a table, chairs, cabinets, and a fireplace; and it was supplied with foodstuff and cooking utensils. The fireplace had a chimney that passed through a natural vent above. Beyond the third room, the cave narrowed and dropped to an underground stream. The stream served as a sewer flowing downstream and as a source of fresh water from upstream, and it never froze.

After showing his guests his home, Baruk gathered them inside the room nearest the cave's entrance. He lit three lanterns within the room in addition to one that was already burning. Ample light from the four lanterns made it easy to see one another's faces. They sat in wooden chairs, arranging the chairs in a small circle. Marlda and Zephanoah sat side by side, situated closely together.

Marlda's curiosity about Baruk's furry cohorts launched the group's conversation. "However did you end up living with bears?" she asked, looking at Baruk.

"It's a long story, but I'll try to summarize with as few words as possible," replied Baruk.

Silent regard bid Baruk to continue.

Baruk looked from face to face. "Well then, after hiding out for a while, I returned to the homestead where my family was attacked and erected a stone memorial. Then I trekked through the woods to a farm north of Shareen—I knew the family that lived there. The farmer agreed to help me seek out my missing brothers, namely Zake and Zephanoah. But after a month of searching in and around Shareen, I decided that they fled elsewhere. I had no idea where to search next, and I did not even know if Zake and Zephanoah were still alive, so I decided to pursue the life of a monk."

"A monk?" responded Zephanoah with a note of surprise.

A broad smile formed as Baruk addressed his brother. "I journeyed far south and took up residence at a monastery near the sea. There I studied the classics, the arts, and the Holy Scriptures. I also proved quite an asset in the production of crops, and the other monks hated to see me leave because I could pull two plows at once and I was every whit as smart as an ox."

Everyone laughed, including Baruk, and then the room grew quiet.

"Why did you leave the monastery?" asked Zephanoah.

"Too civilized," replied Baruk. "I missed the wild and the mountains, so I requested to be moved to a remote monastery in the north, and I was relocated to a quaint little place on the southern face of this mountain." Then Baruk's countenance darkened. His gaze dropped downward. "Neb, Bartholomew, and I became the closest of friends, and we all enjoyed serving the needs of folks in isolated villages. But I came home one winter evening after hunting, dragging an elk behind me, and I found the place ransacked. Neb and Bartholomew had been murdered."

All three listeners sat motionless and silent. Baruk raised his face. "I tracked them down, a small party of Vikings, and I killed three of them—one escaped. There was a bear carcass in their camp, a sow, and I had seen a couple of cubs wandering around while I was tracking, so I went back and found the cubs. I gathered provisions from the monastery and moved to this cave, and I named my new companions Gruffy and Nectar. I trained them just like one trains a dog, only I spent a lot more time at it, and I discovered that bears could be trained to a degree that I would have never thought possible."

Baruk paused for several seconds, but the others still faced him in silence. "Vikings savor bear meat," he resumed, "and they have no qualms about murdering mothers. So as time passed I acquired several more orphaned cubs. Now and then I met up with a few Vikings, but I no longer fought alone—my pets fought with me, and it wasn't long before most Vikings avoided trekking through my territory. And it was the Vikings who gave me my title—Bear King."

Zephanoah grinned. "The name fits you."

"I'll take that as a compliment," said Baruk, reflecting Zephanoah's humor. "And now, little brother, what's your story?"

Zephanoah glanced at Marlda and Master Edmond, but then he leaned toward Baruk and addressed him eye to eye. "Zake and I grew up in Glamster."

"Glamster!" exclaimed Baruk, slapping one knee. "I should have guessed."

"We used the names Father gave us," continued Zephanoah, "John and Ferando. I always hoped to someday fight against Pithrania, and my adopted guardian made necessary arrangements so that I could meet with a group of Sheranites."

"Your adopted father?" queried Baruk. "Who might that be?"

Zephanoah glanced toward Master Edmond, and then again faced Baruk. "That's something I would prefer to keep secret. I hope you understand."

Baruk pursed his lips for a few moments, but then nodded. "Fine, but what about Zake?"

"He is well. He ventured to Subterrania in search of Alania, and he lives in Southern Ivoria."

Master Edmond nodded, but Marlda's eyes widened.

"So Subterrania actually exists?" she inquired. "I thought it was just fantasy."

"It exists," replied Zephanoah.

Baruk's brows skewed. "Zake found his way into the underground world? And he went there seeking the only daughter of King Wildon and Queen Aracia?"

"Yes," said Zephanoah. "Alania was kidnapped by barbarous cutthroats, and Zake went after her. It's a long and complicated story, but a wondrous story. I will share it with you sometime. But for now, tell me what you found when you went back to the homestead. My guardian advised me to avoid going there because he feared that my identity might be discovered."

Baruk's expression grew solemn. "The fields and crops were untouched. The house, though, was nothing but a pile of ashes. I could not identify any of the charred bodies, what little was left of them. It puzzled me that I never found the bones of an infant, and that I never found King Wildon's royal leather garb."

"Well, I think I can explain . . ." began Zephanoah, but then his speech was cut short. Marlda grabbed his arm so vigorously that he ceased speaking and faced her. The look upon her face was a blend of shock and curiosity.

"What is it?" asked Zephanoah.

Marlda shifted her gaze from Zephanoah to Baruk. "What did you just say?" she asked.

"About what?" inquired Baruk.

"Did you say that King Wildon died at your house?"

"Quite so, he died right before my eyes."

"King Wildon died at the house of Sir Marticus the builder."

"That's right."

"And that was your house?"

"Yes."

"So then, Sir Marticus the builder was your father, and Lady Monica was your mother."

Baruk paused. A curious expression creased his brow. "That's right."

Marlda turned her eyes toward her father. Master Edmond looked upon his daughter with an amused smile. There were secrets known to certain members of the Sheranite movement that were seldom shared with others. He surmised that Marlda was beginning to guess her newfound lover's origin.

Marlda's countenance changed. She turned and braced both hands on Zephanoah's shoulders. She stared into his eyes. "You're Princess Vayle's, I mean, you're Colesia's brother!" she blurted. "Why didn't you tell me?"

"Colesia?" echoed Baruk. "Our Colesia? Our baby sister lives?"

"Yes," replied Zephanoah, without withdrawing his eyes from Marlda's gaze. "Our sister is known as Princess Vayle, and Marlda is our sister's dearest friend."

Baruk brought both hands to his thighs and straightened in his chair. "How?"

Zephanoah heard Baruk's inquiry, but he first sought to address Marlda's eyes. "I was planning to tell you before we returned to Pithrania."

Seconds passed, and then Marlda smiled. "I believe you," she said. The look on her face became one of contemplative excitement. She released Zephanoah's shoulders and settled back in her chair, permitting Zephanoah to begin the story of how Princess Vayle of Pithrania, who was widely acclaimed as the most beautiful woman in Gaul, was in fact his and Baruk's sister.

Baruk relaxed his posture and listened as Zephanoah reiterated the details that were given by Giralda. Now and then Marlda joined in, especially when it came to describing how Colesia had grown into a decent and noble woman despite being a Pithranian princess. Baruk waited until Zephanoah and Marlda finished all they had to say about Colesia, and then he settled his gaze upon Zephanoah.

"I assume, then, that our sister would like to escape the Pithranian castle. Is that correct?"

"That's more than correct," interjected Marlda. "Your sister abhors the place."

Baruk appeared pleased by Marlda's words. He again addressed Zephanoah. "If I remember correctly, our sister was promised in marriage to Prince Zarkanis. Does the prince yet live?"

Marlda's eyes widened. She stared between Baruk and Zephanoah.

"He lives, yes, of that we are certain. His name is never spoken, but he is mentioned from time to time among the Pithranian warriors. They refer to him as the Captive from Shareen, or as the swine."

"The swine?" retorted Baruk with a note of remonstration.

A troubled wrinkle creased Zephanoah's brow. "It is reported that he eats with zest."

Baruk shrugged. "Then I am also a swine."

Moments passed in silence as Zephanoah contemplated whether or not he should divulge more information. Marlda looked upon Zephanoah's face with curiosity. She had heard rumors of a human swine imprisoned within the dungeon, but she had never heard that such rumors pertained to Prince Zarkanis. Perhaps the princess could someday meet a real prince rather than fantasizing upon a prince that supposedly rescued her from drowning. She followed Zephanoah's gaze as he turned toward her father. Soon three pairs of eyes addressed Master Edmond.

Master Edmond looked from face to face, but then he steadied his eyes upon Zephanoah. "If we cannot trust a young Sheranite who puts her life at risk in the protection of your sister, or if we cannot trust your brother who has saved all three of us from a brutal massacre, then who can we trust? You may tell them everything."

Marlda and Baruk looked back at Zephanoah.

Zephanoah took a deep breath and gazed downward. "Zake honored our father's words, fleeing with me when our home was attacked." He looked back up toward Baruk. "I thought that all members of my family were slain, other than Zake and me. It must have been a miracle that liberated my largest brother, for I have no doubt that he stood his ground and fought."

"I regained consciousness in time to escape the flames," stated Baruk.

Zephanoah nodded and gazed back down. "When Zake and I reached the border of Shareen, Zake's teacher met us. His name was Dametrius. He insisted that we flee south to Glamster, saying that he would remain behind for one purpose—and that one purpose was to somehow aid Prince Zarkanis." Zephanoah lifted his face. "Zake had already fled from his home, and Dametrius was asking him to flee again—this time from Shareen. Zake is no coward, and he found it difficult to abandon the impending battle between Shareen and Pithrania, but he heeded his teacher's request. He took me and fled south to Glamster."

"What happened to Dametrius?" coaxed Marlda.

"No one knows for sure," replied Zephanoah, "but Dragus informed the Sharean people that Prince Zarkanis was imprisoned beneath the Pithranian castle, and it is reported that the Captive from Shareen was placed in solitary confinement with a deaf mute—his caregiver. That deaf mute has since died. It is thought that the Captive from Shareen never learned to speak. No one has ever heard him say a word, and no one is permitted to utter a word in his presence. But we know that the mute caregiver was from Shareen, and no one can recall a deaf mute in Shareen at the time Zarkanis was imprisoned."

"It must have been Dametrius," surmised Marlda.

Zephanoah met her eyes. "We believe that is possible. Prince Zarkanis and his caregiver were placed in a secluded cell far removed from any other human beings. If the caregiver was Dametrius, then Zarkanis may have been taught to speak in secret, and may have been taught to keep his ability to speak a secret from prison guards. That is our hope, and we have a compelling reason to uphold such hope."

"A compelling reason? What reason is that?" asked Marlda.

After another look at Master Edmond, Zephanoah responded to Marlda. "Giralda informed another midwife in Shareen—a woman who happens to be a loyal Sheranite—that Colesia claimed to have been spoken to by Prince Zarkanis."

A look of incredulity sprang to Marlda's face. She stared at Zephanoah with widened eyes, but said nothing.

"I asked Giralda if Colesia ever swam at the western edge of Lake Manassa, near the eastern side of the castle, because the secluded cell where Zarkanis is imprisoned has a window in the eastern wall, but…"

"No!" interrupted Marlda.

Zephanoah fell silent and stared at Marlda along the others.

"Her prince…he must be real after all…it must have been Zarkanis," Marlda spoke with such excitement that she was nearly gasping.

"What do you mean?" asked Zephanoah.

Master Edmond stared at his daughter with an intense look of inquiry.

Marlda addressed her father. "She made me keep it a secret. Otherwise I would have told you, of course."

Master Edmond leaned forward in his chair. "Keep what a secret?"

"The night she was saved from drowning, and we all thought that it must have been an angel that rescued her…"

"Go on."

"She told me she was rescued by a prince who claimed that he would someday come after her and marry her, but I always thought she must have had a concussion or something."

"And she never told you the prince's name?" asked Master Edmond. Marlda shook her head, "No."

"It must have been Zarkanis," stated Zephanoah.

"But wasn't the prince locked up in a dungeon cell?" asked Baruk.

"The well openings are large enough for a child to slide through them," said Master Edmond, "and the princess was barely ten years of age when she was rescued."

"And Prince Zarkanis is only a few months older than our sister," added Baruk.

A few seconds passed before anyone spoke again. Keen interest and anticipation stirred the atmosphere.

Zephanoah spoke next. "So Dametrius must have taught Zarkanis how to swim when he was a child, and they must have seen that Colesia was drowning, and Zarkanis must have saved her. And that explains how Colesia was able to tell Giralda her real name, rather than her name being Vayle."

"How do you mean?" asked Master Edmond.

"I still remember Dametrius and Zake talking about Colesia before Zake and I left for Glamster. So then, Dametrius knew her name, and he must have taught that name to Zarkanis, and he must have taught Zarkanis that Colesia was his intended bride—so it makes sense that Zarkanis told Colesia her real name, and it also makes sense that he told her that he intended to marry her."

"Oh my," said Marlda. "So Zarkanis not only can talk, he was educated by Dametrius."

"That must be true, but I suppose there is only one way to find out for sure," said Zephanoah. "One of us must gain access to the dungeon cell where Zarkanis is imprisoned."

Marlda absorbed Zephanoah's words and studied his eyes. "Couldn't that be dangerous?"

"I'll be cautious," returned Zephanoah. "I have a compelling reason, now, to sustain my mortal existence."

Marlda said nothing, but her eyes pledged all the *reason* that a woman can offer a man.

A stern look mounted Baruk's face. His huge hands rested atop his thighs. "I have heard rumors that Dragus plans to have his son, Borgar, married to the most beautiful woman in Gaul—a Pithranian princess. I have friends who live north of Danvurst, and they have told me this. Could this mean that the great toad wishes to marry his wart of a son to our sister?"

"I do not think she would have it," averred Zephanoah.

Both brothers looked inquiringly toward Marlda and Master Edmond.

"Of course she would not have it, if she had a choice," Marlda stated with a note of dread.

Zephanoah and Baruk both sprang to their feet.

"When is this atrocity supposed to take place?" asked Baruk.

"No one knows," replied Marlda. "The princess is afraid she will be abducted, but I know she plans to escape…or if necessary, to resist. She keeps a dagger in her bureau."

"Why has she not been rescued?" inquired Baruk, facing Zephanoah.

"I, well, I intended to," stammered Zephanoah, "but I did not know that she was in imminent danger."

"Then we must go at once," pronounced Baruk, stomping one foot so firmly that the ground beneath them quaked.

"Yes, we must," Zephanoah agreed.

"I will fetch my pets."

Baruk turned and began stepping toward the door to the room.

"Wait," spoke up Master Edmond. He remained seated. His voice arrested everyone's attention. He had done much listening and little talking, and this lent his words staid respect. He waited to speak again until Baruk stopped walking and turned back around. "I can assure you that the princess will be guarded, and penetrating the Pithranian fortress by force would require a capable army."

The Bear King gave no hint of dissuasion. "Nonetheless, my brother and I must try to liberate our sister."

"We should do more than *try* to free the princess—we should *succeed*," pronounced Master Edmond.

Baruk stood still. He stared downward at Master Edmond as if he were seeing him for the first time. "I quite agree. Do you have a proposal?"

"Yes."

Baruk looked toward Zephanoah.

Zephanoah spoke without hesitation. "Master Edmond is not chief consultant to the Sheranite regime without good reason. His cunningness is unequaled. I think it would serve our sister well for both of us to consider his counsel."

For a few seconds the Bear King studied his younger brother's face. Then, without another word, he stepped back to his chair and seated himself. He folded his hands upon his lap and faced Master Edmond. Zephanoah sat back down beside Marlda.

Master Edmond looked from face to face. "The Sheranites have long been working toward freeing Zarkanis, the Prince of Shareen. I have no doubt that they will also want to free the daughter of Sir Marticus." He turned his regard toward Baruk. "Zephanoah, Marlda, and I are all spies with access to Dragus's castle. Marlda is the princess's personal lady-in-waiting, and Zephanoah has been granted guard duty atop the royal tower. We should be able to devise an escape from inside the castle that would be impossible to accomplish from without."

Baruk turned his eyes upon Zephanoah. "Do you agree?"

"Yes," said Zephanoah. He peered at Baruk for several seconds. "But once we are free, we may be tracked, and we may need your assistance. Do you think that you and your bears could camp on the northwest side of Mount Thrandor for a few days?"

Baruk smiled. "We have camped there several times. How many days shall we wait before coming after you?"

Zephanoah's eyes turned toward Master Edmond.

Master Edmond faced Baruk. "We must have time to formulate a plan of escape—one that will free both Zarkanis and the princess at the same time. Give us ten days. If we have not joined you by then, you have our leave to investigate the cause of our delay. The princess is housed in the southeast tower, which is the royal tower. Her chamber occupies the highest level."

"Southeast tower, highest level...very well," said Baruk, tapping the iron head of his sledge hammer. "Now let us gather your bedrolls and sleep. We can begin our mission in the morning."

Baruk started to rise, but Zephanoah raised a hand and stayed him. "Please...sit back down, just for a little while."

Baruk obliged and settled back in his chair, staring at Zephanoah.

Zephanoah dropped his hand back to his lap. "Yes…we should get some sleep …good idea," he commented, but his manner of speech evinced that his mind was otherwise engaged. "There is something I want to do first, if Master Edmond would be so kind as to grant his permission."

Zephanoah up stood and bowed formally toward Master Edmond. Master Edmond's face bloomed. He had no problem interpreting Zephanoah's intent. Baruk's face drew into an expression of quizzical interest.

"I would be honored," spoke Master Edmond.

Zephanoah turned and knelt before Marlda. He reached forward and took her right hand and embraced it, and then he lifted his eyes. The look on his face and the penetration of his eyes made Marlda forget all else. She felt her heart quicken and throb within her breast. She realized what was coming. It seemed like her favorite fantasies were being withdrawn from a dream.

"Will you marry me?" he asked.

There ensued several moments of suspenseful silence. Marlda ventured more deeply into Zephanoah's eyes. She broke out crying and collapsed into his arms. It was not until after she kissed both his cheeks and wiped warm tears from beneath her eyes that she replied, "Yes."

Baruk erupted into a hearty belly laugh, standing up from his chair and clapping. But then he grew quiet, bolstering his hands on his hips and staring down upon Marlda and Zephanoah. "Very well then, let's get some sleep."

****

The winter evening was cold. There was little activity outside the castle walls as Master Edmond, Marlda, and Zephanoah crossed the icy bridge west of the waterfall and approached the pathway leading to the stables.

"Hail! Master Edmond!" a guard called from atop the southwest tower.

"Hail, Tristan!" Master Edmond returned. He knew the names of all the castle guards and he could recognize their voices.

"It's Master Edmond! He has returned!" Tristan called down to guards stationed at the portcullis to the drawbridge. Word was then passed up rank until Dragus received notification of his majordomo's arrival. The news was delivered to him as he sat behind the great desk in his military conference room in company with several warlords and captains. He was discussing the matter of levying additional taxes against subservient provinces. A grimace crossed his face as he received the news; he had not planned for Marlda to return before Borgar was wed to Vayle. He dismissed everyone from the meeting other than five of his bodyguards, and then he sent two of the bodyguards to fetch the returned travelers.

Master Edmond, who knew Dragus well, was disconcerted when Dragus's bodyguards arrived at the stables and summoned him, along with Marlda and Zephanoah, to Dragus's military conference room. He did not expect their homecoming to elicit such regard from the megalomaniac king. The two bodyguards remained at the stables until the travelers finished tending to the horses, so Master Edmond had no opportunity to relate his misgivings to Marlda and Zephanoah.

As the three returned travelers were issued into the conference room, Master Edmond noted that Dragus appeared more anxious than angry. This settled his nerves, at least in regard to espionage. He knew that Dragus would be fuming over the discovery that the castle's long-established majordomo was a spy.

"You have returned prematurely," stated Dragus. His manner of speech and facial expression were those of interrogation.

"Indeed," replied Master Edmond. "We spotted several Vikings and considered it wisest to retreat."

Dragus nodded. "Not an unwise choice." He looked at all three before readdressing Master Edmond. "From what I have heard, though, it is most difficult to spot a Viking before he spots you."

"That may generally be true," interjected Ferando, "unless one in your company happens to be sharper in mind and keener of eye than any Viking could ever aspire to be. It is a fortunate party that travels with a protector who possesses the vision of an eagle and the judgment of an owl."

It seemed apparent from the inflection of his words and the protrusion of his chest that Ferando relished bragging. This entertained Dragus and caused him to relax his scrutiny.

"Of course," said Dragus. He turned his eyes upon Marlda and noted that she gazed at Ferando with a look of admiration. Such regard toward a Pithranian warrior coming from Master Edmond's daughter pleased him. "Considering your recent loss," he said, peering back at Master

236

Edmond, "I insist that you retain your week of release from duty. Sir Broham shall continue as majordomo five more days."

"Thank you," Master Edmond replied, but such kindness sparked his wariness. He was not used to receiving this sort of benevolence from Dragus.

Next came long seconds of silence. The formal gathering seemed much too preponderant for the simple announcement that Master Edmond was granted more time away from his duties. A stern expression deepened the crevices of Dragus's face. "There is one other thing," he said. "Since you have been gone, Prince Borgar has announced his forthcoming marriage to Princess Vayle." Dragus paused and perused the responses of Master Edmond, Marlda, and Ferando—analyzing each countenance in turn.

The face of Master Edmond showed considerable surprise, Marlda's face revealed near shock, and Ferando's face displayed detached interest. These facial reactions were in keeping with Dragus's expectations. Borgar had informed him that Marlda made it difficult to approach Colesia in courtship, and such interference did not seem unnatural—any selfish wench would shun the possibility that her royal position as lady-in-waiting might be diminished because her mistress got married. Master Edmond was like an adopted father to the princess, so he would be expected to react to major events in her life. Ferando was a newcomer from Shareen, so his having less interest in matters involving the princess was logical. What intrigued Dragus, though, was the interest Ferando seemed to have in the princess's lady-in-waiting…and what was more, it appeared that the majordomo's daughter, whom Dragus had theretofore deemed as prudish, had eyes for Ferando.

"When is this to take place?" asked Master Edmond.

"In two days," said Dragus, turning his eyes from Marlda. "There will be a morning feast with dancing and festivities. The feast will continue until sometime past noonday, and then a priest from Danvurst shall conduct vows."

Marlda tried to control her feelings, but her face paled.

"Are there any other questions?" asked Dragus.

Glances were exchanged, but no additional questions were proffered.

"Very well, I expect all of you to fulfill your duties and encourage the princess toward royal matrimony, even if the great honor overwhelms her. Do you understand?"

"Yes, Sire, perfectly," answered Master Edmond, bowing after he spoke.

"Good…and, Marlda, you may have the next five days off duty to comfort your father."

Marlda was in a state of anguish, but she managed to present a composed countenance. "Thank you, Sire, but I am sure that my duties to the royal Princess of Pithrania must take precedence over all other concerns. I am honored to serve Princess Vayle during this time of nuptial preparation."

Dragus's eyes narrowed as Marlda curtsied before him. He could not respectably decline such an offer. "Very well, my dear, but remember that you must sustain the cheer and encouragement befitting the marriage of a prince and princess."

"I understand, Sire," said Marlda, again curtsying in feigned respect.

Dragus redirected his attentions toward Ferando. "And you, Ferando, shall return to guard duty."

Ferando's mediocre response to the announcement of the wedding had been a remarkable feat—given that a panging knot had formed in the pit of Zephanoah's stomach. Now he summoned every whit of self-control he could muster. "As you command, Sire, and if I may have a few moments in private with Your Majesty, there is something I think merits discussion between us—discreet discussion."

The potential intrigue of Ferando's words appealed to Dragus. With a wave of his hand, he directed a guard to escort Master Edmond and Marlda from the room. Then, as his eyes again focused upon Marlda, an afterthought struck his mind. "Garth," he spoke to the guard. Everyone stopped and faced Dragus. "See that the lady-in-waiting is detained in the grand hall until Ferando is free to escort her to her royal chamber. He will be on duty atop the royal tower until midnight, and I will give him leave to use the inner stairwell."

"Yes, Sire," said Garth, glancing toward Ferando with a look of envy, and then he issued Master Edmond and Marlda out of the meeting room, closing the door behind him.

There were still two bodyguards with Dragus and Zephanoah, but it went without saying that this was as private an interview as anyone might hope to have with the wary dictator.

"What is it you wish to discuss?" asked Dragus.

Ferando stepped forward to Dragus's desk and then leaned forward with his hands propped on the front edge. He spoke in a confidential voice. "I have no doubt that the King of Pithrania considers the cooperation of local women an important asset for his fighting forces."

"Yes," agreed Dragus, and the bodyguards who stood on either side of him flashed malignant grins.

"Well, I have ascertained that many of my comrades consider themselves deprived of available services on the part of Master Edmond's daughter—a situation they attribute to deplorable circumstance stemming from priggish ideals."

The guards grunted in agreement. Their guttural concurrence touched upon Zephanoah's ears like the hedonistic snorting of rutting hogs, but he maintained composure and sustained his ruse.

"This is unfortunate," stated Dragus. "However, initiatives to rectify the matter could prove awkward since the wench is the daughter of my majordomo. We cannot emancipate her through brute force without prodding her father toward illogical and self-destructive behavior."

Ferando cocked his head in feigned indignation. "Of course not, Sire. Your wisdom in making such a statement is beyond questioning. What I advocate, rather, is persuasion—simply compelling the maiden to succumb of her own free will."

Dragus raised his brows with indulgent deliberation. "You presume to accomplish this?"

Ferando lolled forward. "It is on the verge of accomplishment, and I have gained such ground in her father's shadow. Can you imagine what I might attain if granted a greater degree of privacy? If you would merely permit my access to her chamber, I feel most confident of an intimate interlude."

Pestilent flames ignited in Dragus's eyes, increasing Zephanoah's disgust for the tyrant's decadence. "I appreciate your zeal in working for the good and satisfaction of my army," he remarked with self-amusement. "I wish you success." Then Dragus's brows furrowed. "There is a slight complication, though, since the wench serves as lady-in-waiting to the princess. You may accompany her into her quarters tonight, for as long as she and the princess will allow, but hereafter you must entreat her to visit your own quarters. I will see to it that you are issued a private room in the castle barracks."

The bodyguards stared upon Ferando with jealous admiration.

"Thank you, Sire. It will be a pleasure and an honor to carry out your royal edict."

"I am sure. Is that all?"

"Yes, Sire."

Dragus turned toward Kerman, the bodyguard to his right. "Tell Garth to return. You shall then go up to the princess's room and inform Jarak and Vixro that Ferando is granted entrance into the princess's quarters this one time. And let them know that he is given permission to ascend the inner stairwell, escorting the princess's lady-in-waiting."

"Yes, Sire," said Kerman. He stepped around the desk and crossed toward the door, looking back in awe toward the brazen new member of the guard who dared ask permission to enter the princess's chamber. He would have feared imprisonment, or worse, for presenting such a request.

"You are dismissed," Dragus spoke to Ferando.

"By your leave, Sire."

Zephanoah followed behind Kerman and then walked to the door to the grand hall. He opened the door and stepped forward to join Marlda. Her eyes disclosed distress. Master Edmond had already departed.

"Dragus requests your return at once," Kerman said to Garth. Garth strode back through the stairwell chamber and into the conference room, closing the door to the conference room as he entered. Kerman headed up the stairs to the royal tower. This left Zephanoah and Marlda to themselves. Zephanoah took hold of Marlda's arm and drew her back into the stairwell chamber. He closed the door to the grand hall and brought his lips close to Marlda's ear, and then he informed her of what had transpired within the conference room.

Marlda placed both of her hands upon Zephanoah's chest and looked into his face. "What shall we tell the princess?" she asked in a whisper.

"Can we trust her judgment?" Zephanoah inquired, also whispering. He hoped to hear Marlda respond in his sister's favor.

"With our very lives… I know of no human being on earth who is more trustworthy, and she is as cunning as a mother fox."

"Then we will tell her everything. Perhaps she can help us formulate a plan of escape."

****

Nighttime darkness had already befallen when Colesia and Diana detected boisterous conversation outside the stairwell door. Both women were still attired in daytime apparel, and a dagger was still strapped to Colesia's thigh. Not until time to crawl into bed and sleep would she shed the wool dress in favor of a nightgown, and the dagger would remain in place. An oil lantern was burning in the antechamber. Logs were blazing in the fireplace, and all five wall lanterns in the princess's bedroom were aflame.

"Did they say something about Marlda?" asked Colesia. She and Diana were sitting on the elkskin rug before the hearth. It was difficult to hear persons speaking from outside the solid oak door to the stairwell, but the guards had been speaking with loud and excited voices. Diana was seated toward the antechamber and was in a better position to overhear what was spoken.

"I think so," returned Diana. She turned her face toward the princess with a look of empathetic concern. "And…and I think I heard them say that Ferando is escorting her into your room."

The princess's cheeks glistened where tears had crept downward during the dread-filled day—she had difficulty taking her mind off Borgar's visit. Diana's words tightened her throat. "They have returned before they were supposed to, and a Pithranian warrior accompanies the majordomo's daughter to her quarters." She paused, facing Diana with a look of grave concern. "Do you suppose Master Edmond has been slain?"

Diana arose and closed the drapes between the antechamber and the royal bedroom. She stepped back and again sat down upon the elkskin rug, facing Princess Vayle. "Perhaps it was just too cold, or perhaps snow made the northern trail impassable."

Colesia used the hem of her dress to wipe the tearstains from her cheeks. Then she gazed upon Diana's face. She knew that Diana was trying to comfort her, but she doubted that snow was responsible for the early return. "May God deliver us," she spoke.

"He will, Princess… He will," averred Diana. What remained unspoken, however, was Diana's uncertainty as to whether God would grant deliverance during the course of their earthly lives or deliverance through death.

Despite an atmosphere of despair, Colesia managed an appreciative smile. Diana smiled in return. There was no doubt in either of their hearts that they would stand by one another through any degree of mortal affliction. They faced each other for several seconds without additional words.

Crackling sounds from the fireplace drew the princess's attention. She turned her head and watched the embers and flames rise and fall, increasing and decreasing in intensity like the eyes of a sleeping dragon.

The door to the stairwell opened and closed. Both girls turned their heads and fixed their eyes on the closed drapes that separated the princess's bedroom from the antechamber. Slender hands reached through and drew open the passageway.

"Marlda!" cried Colesia.

Marlda rushed forward as the princess and Diana both rose to their feet. All three girls exchanged hugs, huddled at the foot of Colesia's bed.

"Is your father alive? Is he all right?" asked Colesia.

"Yes, he is fine."

"You returned so early," stated Diana.

"I know. It is a long story, and one I must tell you. First, though, I want to introduce a friend."

Colesia and Diana both froze.

"A friend?" probed Colesia.

"Yes, a friend," spoke Marlda, lowering her voice and moving closer to Vayle. Diana leaned toward them so that she could hear also. Their three faces were close enough to feel one another's breaths. "I know about the wedding. There is someone with me who is going to help you escape. He's in my room."

Colesia's eyes flitted back and forth between Marlda and the partially drawn drapes to the antechamber. Marlda had advised Zephanoah to remain out of sight until she explained the nature of his presence. Neither the princess nor her lady-in-waiting had ever invited a man into the royal bedroom.

"Really? Help me escape? Is it possible? Who?"

Marlda glanced toward Diana. "Do you wish for Diana to remain? I trust her, as I am sure you do, but we may involve her in great danger if she lingers here."

"If there is any chance that I too may escape with you, then there is no danger I would not embrace with unutterable gratitude," asserted Diana. Her voice conveyed cool resolve. "I would rather die ten times over than be left behind—I know what my fate would be if the princess were no longer here to draw Prince Borgar's regard."

Diana's words flustered Marlda. "Well...ah...I guess we could."

"We must," proclaimed Colesia.

"All right," Marlda consented, "I am sure the others would not object."

"Others?"

"There are others helping us, but I'll explain that later. First I want you to meet my friend."

Colesia peered toward the opening to the antechamber, and then back toward Marlda. "Who is it?"

"Your brother," said Marlda, lowering her voice even further.

Startled silence ensued. Marlda's words seemed surreal. Colesia stared into Marlda's eyes with a blank look—a look of incomprehension.

"Ferando is not really Ferando. He is really Zephanoah, a Sheranite spy."

"A Sheranite spy?" returned Colesia.

"Yes. The Sheranites are a secret group of people who wish to see Dragus overthrown, and Ferando is a Sheranite spy from Shareen—and he's your brother. My father is also a spy."

Colesia's eyes grew wide. "My brother? Really? What do you mean?"

"Your brothers were not all killed. In fact, believe it or not, the Bear King is one of your brothers too."

"The Bear King!" exclaimed Diana. She had a great admiration for animal trainers, and she had heard stories about the Bear King that captured her fancy.

"Shh..." warned Marlda. "Talk softly."

The princess's head swam. She could feel blood pulsing through her limbs. "You mean, my brother, or one of my brothers, is in your sleeping room? Right now? Ferando is really my brother?"

Marlda smiled. She was tempted to go ahead and tell Colesia about Zephanoah's marriage proposal, pointing out that the two of them would be sisters-in-law, but she decided to wait until later. She turned her face toward the antechamber. "Ferando, come in," she spoke aloud.

When Marlda turned back, Diana and the princess looked like two fawns caught drinking from a spring inside a wolves' den. They drew closer to one another as Zephanoah entered. He closed the drapes behind him. He had already removed his helmet, laying it on a small table in the antechamber. Marlda and Zephanoah exchanged glances, and then for several long seconds, Colesia and Zephanoah stood facing one another.

"There is definitely a family resemblance," Diana whispered to Vayle.

Colesia did not answer. She stepped dizzily across the room, motioning toward the five wicker chairs that were situated before the closed doorway to the balcony. "Would you like to sit down?" Her aqua eyes were riveted upon Zephanoah in wonder.

"Thank you," replied Zephanoah, looking upon his sister with reciprocal awe.

Zephanoah seated himself and Marlda sat beside him. Colesia sat on the other side of Zephanoah, to his left, and Diana sat to the left of Colesia. The chairs were arranged in a semicircle like a horseshoe, so it was easy for Colesia to face all three of the others in turn.

Colesia signaled with her hands and arms for the chairs to be scooted closer together. Even with the drapes closed to the antechamber, it was prudent to speak quietly. The empty chair was pushed back, and the chairs were resituated. Then the group of four sat and faced one another. It seemed difficult for anyone to begin communication.

"Marlda tells me that you are my brother," said Colesia.

"Yes," affirmed Zephanoah. His eyes turned from Colesia to Diana.

"It's no problem," interjected Marlda, "she's one of us. She would rather die ten times over than remain captive to Dragus's regime. She wants to come with us, and we can trust her with our lives."

Zephanoah's eyes drew confirmation from Diana. He gave her an approving nod, and she responded with a smile. Then he turned his face back toward Colesia. "Your name was chosen by our oldest brother, Zake, who used a Euphratian word for a golden-hued dawn—Colesia. He chose that name because of the golden lock of hair."

The princess faced Diana. "It is true. My real name is Colesia. I've already told Marlda." She then turned her face back toward Zephanoah. "So then, our oldest brother's name is Zake. Was Zake killed?"

"No, but he is in a faraway country. It is a long story. After we get you away from here, I will tell you everything I know."

"And the Bear King?"

"His name is Baruk. He was the fourth born, and I was fifth, and you were sixth. There is much to tell, but for now we must concentrate our time and efforts upon your escape."

Colesia's face sobered as she refocused her mind upon her present predicament, but she was not through asking questions.

"And your name is Zephanoah, not Ferando?"

"Yes, my real name is Zephanoah. But since I am a spy against Pithrania, it is important that everyone call me Ferando. Dragus may have some memory of the names Sir Marticus gave his five sons, and Dragus does not know that three of those sons survived."

"I see, but how did you find out about me? How did you find out that I am your sister?"

"Giralda told me."

Colesia gasped. She had not heard a single word about Giralda's whereabouts since the day that Giralda departed. "My lady! Where is she? Is she safe?"

"Shh..." warned Zephanoah, "we must keep our voices indiscernible to the guards outside the door."

Colesia knew how nosey the guards were, and she determined to keep her fervor in check, but she was anxious to hear news of Giralda. She looked toward the closed drapes and then back to Zephanoah, giving him a nod.

"She is safe in Shareen," said Zephanoah. "She is living next door to an old friend of hers, and that friend is also my friend. Before she returned to Shareen and told her friend about you, I thought that you had been killed. Once I found out that you were alive, my comrades and I began making plans to free you. We were already planning to free someone else—someone who is held captive within this castle. Are you willing to risk your life in an attempt to escape?"

The princess did not keep her brother in suspense. "Of course. I would rather be devoured by a dragon than married to Borgar. But, who else were you planning to free?"

For a second time, Zephanoah turned questioning eyes upon Diana. He then looked toward Marlda.

"I assure you," Marlda spoke in reference to Diana, "she will in no way hinder us. She is dependable and shrewd. If anything she will help us. She aided Giralda in escaping from Lady Eldra, even at the risk of her own life."

"All right," said Zephanoah. He turned his face back toward Colesia. His countenance bore a look of staid significance. "We were already planning to free the Captive from Shareen."

"The Captive from Shareen... Who is he? I have heard the warriors making fun of him. They say he is mute and obese."

Zephanoah gazed thoughtfully between Colesia and Diana. "The Captive from Shareen is none other than King Wildon's son, the heir to the Sharean throne, and we have reason to believe that he is much different than what the warriors have reported." Then his eyes settled solely upon Colesia. "Giralda claims that you have spoken with him—Prince Zarkanis."

Chapter 12

The Encounters

It was another odd morning of the capricious winter. Black tiers of clouds shut out the sun like a full eclipse. It seemed that nighttime refused the coming of dawn. Zarkanis noted the bizarre phenomenon with mixed emotions. Environmental variety was stimulating and he usually welcomed it, but this darkness was sufficient to preclude his observing Colesia as she stepped out onto her balcony to offer morning prayers—and he preferred the visage of his princess above any sort of environmental extravaganza.

Three times he strolled past the window and peered out into the darkness. Then he shrugged off his disappointment, stepped to the center of the floor, and began jogging in place. He intended to break a sweat before beginning morning sprints. Several minutes later, after his fourth sprint was completed, his ears detected movement of the latch on the second door in the passageway to his cell. He stopped pacing and picked up his outer garment. It had been over a year since a guard delivered breakfast so early.

When the cell door opened, Zarkanis sat as usual beside the well and rocked from side to side. He intended to fix his eyes on the bucket of food and grunt when goods were emptied onto the floor. His senses alerted him to the fact that a new guard walked through the door—a guard who had never visited before. The guard entered slowly and knelt down before the prince, holding the torch so that both of their faces were visible. As usual, Zarkanis directed his face downward to avoid disclosing intelligence through eye contact, but it was evident that the new guard was visually addressing him. He knew that something unusual was going on. No guard had ever before behaved in a manner that seemed to regard him as a person.

"Zarkanis?"

The rocking stopped. No human being had spoken to the prince since Dametrius died. It would have been less shocking if a hole had opened in the ceiling and water had poured down on his head. He continued looking downward, mentally questioning whether he were awake or dreaming.

"Zarkanis, my name is Zephanoah. I am a spy for Shareen. Colesia is my sister, and she told me about the time you rescued her from drowning. Perhaps Dametrius told you about my brother Zake, his former student."

For a while Zephanoah wondered if the reports about the imprisoned swine were valid. There was no detectable movement within the worn wool blanket that shrouded the prisoner's body. Not even the bushy auburn hair stirred. Was his sister mistaken? Had she only dreamed that a boy told her that his name was Zarkanis?

Then the prince raised his eyes. Before a single word was spoken, any question of intelligence was dispelled. There was no hint of fear; rather, Zarkanis surveyed Zephanoah with engrossed curiosity. "You are the youngest son of Sir Marticus and Lady Monica?"

Zephanoah's heart leaped to his throat. He had guessed the truth, yet to face living proof of his assumptions was astonishing. There was no doubt that Zarkanis was tutored by Dametrius. "Yes, that is correct."

"Dametrius spoke highly of Zake. How does he fare?"

It took a few moments for Zephanoah to collect his thoughts. A few seconds before he was staring at a prisoner who he hoped would be capable of speech, and now it seemed that he was conversing with a family friend. "He fares well. He lives in the kingdom of Southern Ivoria, in a faraway land called Subterrania."

Zarkanis's brows rose with interest. "Subterrania? The world beneath the surface of the earth?"

"Yes," replied Zephanoah, amazed by Zarkanis's knowledge. "But I must get to the point of my visit—I do not have much time. It concerns my sister."

Zarkanis's countenance was devoid of nervousness, but he could not hide his peaked interest when Zephanoah referred to Colesia. "You are a spy?"

"Yes. I am a spy for a group of men and women who hope to free themselves from Dragus's tyranny. We call ourselves Sheranites."

"Sheranites," reflected Zarkanis. "Dametrius would have been pleased. Wait here."

Zarkanis rose and stepped across the floor to the stone bed. There was something Dametrius had asked him to do if someone ever entered the cell and spoke, claiming to be a friend. He leaned over and retrieved a special item from his hidden cache of possessions. Then he returned and knelt back down before Zephanoah, holding up a ring suspended from a chain. "This was my father's ring. Dametrius said that any true Sharean should recognize the engraving."

Zephanoah leaned forward and examined the ring. There was an engraved image of an eagle in flight. "Yes, that is the emblem carved in marble on the outer surface of the west wall of the royal palace in Shareen." He straightened and faced Zarkanis. "But I must warn you…many of our enemies, as well as comrades, would recognize that insignia. I do not think it would be wise to assume that a man is trustworthy simply because he can identity that emblem."

Zarkanis nodded. Dametrius had explained how to use the ring to determine whether a stranger were a friend or a foe, and Zephanoah had passed the test—he had warned that an enemy could also identity the engraving.

"I see," said Zarkanis. He rose to his feet and returned the ring to its hiding place. Then he stepped back before Zephanoah, who had also risen to his feet. He removed and cast aside his blanket, and then he extended his right hand in a gesture of friendship.

Zephanoah stood dumbstruck. He lifted the torch and stared, wondering if his eyes were playing tricks on him. He transferred the torch to his left hand, and then he offered his right hand while his eyes roved over a body of symmetric magnificence—a flesh-and-blood figure that outshone any statue of Hercules he had ever seen. In the hand that clasped his, he sensed sufficient strength to crush bone—if not granite.

"Are you well?"

Zarkanis's words brought Zephanoah to his senses. "Oh, yes, quite. I just thought that, I mean, everyone said that you were…"

"A pudgy pig?" inquired the prince as he released Zephanoah's hand.

"Yes, but you are not. I mean, you have a very fine physique."

Zarkanis flashed a smile. He was aware that his body was different in appearance than the bodies of men he observed outside the window, but he lacked social feedback to ascertain whether his appearance were attractive or disgusting. He meant to rescue the princess, but he had determined to let her go free if she found him appalling.

"So you do not consider me unsightly?"

Zephanoah was startled by the prince's question. It was evident that the imprisoned Captive from Shareen was well educated and introspective. "Oh my, no… you are the very antithesis of unsightliness, my friend, the very antithesis."

Zarkanis's smile grew wider. "Thank you, Zephanoah. I would have you know, then, that I intend to marry your sister—if you think she will also consider me the antithesis of unsightliness—and if she will have me of her own free will."

"Oh, of course, sure, fine," stammered Zephanoah. His mind was struggling to recover from the shock of beholding the prince's conditioned body, and talk of the prince's marriage to his sister did little to settle his nerves. He had no objection, however, to the thought of having Zarkanis as a brother-in-law. His sister had stated that she wished to marry Zarkanis after being informed that he was the Captive from Shareen, and he knew that his father and mother had hoped for such matrimony. "I am quite sure that she will be delighted. That is, if we can rescue her before Prince Borgar forces her to marry him."

The smile disappeared from the prince's face. The look that poured from his eyes caused Zephanoah to take a step backward. "You mean the evil emperor's son?"

"Yes. He and Dragus have summoned a priest from Danvurst."

"I know of Danvurst. Dametrius taught me about surrounding cities and villages. It is one day's march to the southwest."

"Right. The wedding is to take place in two days."

The prince was disconcerted. "But, does the princess wish to marry Prince Borgar?"

"No, she detests the very thought."

"Then he cannot marry her. She will not have him."

"She has no choice. He is forcing her to marry him."

A look of disgust mounted the prince's face, but there were also signs of relief. "You are sure that she does not wish to marry Prince Borgar?"

"I am positive. It is you who my sister wishes to marry—she told me so."

There was no mistaking the celebration in Zarkanis's eyes. "Good. I will free her tonight. Can you tell her this?"

Zephanoah stared. The Sharean prince spoke so matter-of-factly that it was difficult to doubt his words. "You will free her tonight?"

"Yes."

"*You?*"

"Yes. Do you not trust me?"

Zephanoah thought for a moment. Zarkanis had already overwhelmed his expectations and hopes. He nodded. "Yes. I trust you."

Zarkanis told Zephanoah his plan—a plan devised years before by Dametrius— and demonstrated his strength and his ability to climb the stone walls. He also discussed how he and Colesia could seek refuge on the far side of Mount Thrandor, at whatever destination Colesia disclosed.

Zephanoah gave some consideration to the prince's strategy and then nodded his approval. "Your plan is a good one. I would request, however, that you wait until tomorrow night to rescue my sister. The wedding with Prince Borgar is not to take place until the day after tomorrow."

"Why wait?"

"It will give me time to get word to my sister so that she can make ready for your arrival. And in addition to that, I will be on duty atop the royal tower until midnight tomorrow night."

"Good," said Zarkanis, lifting his right hand and again shaking hands with Zephanoah. "Dametrius taught me how to measure time. I will break free from this cell tomorrow night, one hour before midnight."

"Very well," said Zephanoah. His mind was overflowing with questions, but he knew that it would be unwise to spend additional time in the cell. It seemed that plans for the princess's rescue were complete. "By the way, I will see to it that my sister has some winter clothing for you to wear, including some boots."

At the mention of Colesia, a look of concern beset Zarkanis's eyes. "When I enter the princess's room, you are sure she will want to leave with me? Prince Borgar is heir to the throne of the Pithranian Empire. I have seen him on the lake and on the southern banks, and the ladies look upon him with much admiration."

"Have no fear," spoke Zephanoah. He wanted to give Prince Zarkanis the confidence in his sister's allegiance that she deserved, and he was convinced that comparing Prince Zarkanis to Prince Borgar was like comparing a golden eagle to a rat. "She has neither lust for evil plunders nor admiration for evil persons."

Zarkanis's face eased. "That is what I hope and believe. Dametrius informed me of Giralda's virtues as a tutor, and your sister is the daughter of Sir Marticus and Lady Monica. Still, do you suppose that you could deliver a message to her?"

Zephanoah paused, but then he nodded. "Yes. Marlda is now her lady-in-waiting. I am a good friend with Marlda, and with Marlda's father, Master Edmond. They are both Sheranites, and we can trust them."

Zarkanis cast an insightful gaze upon Zephanoah's features. Dametrius had spent long hours teaching him how to decipher the expressions upon men's faces as well as the tones and inflections of their voices. He perceived that Marlda was much more than just a *good friend* to Zephanoah. Then his mind refocused. "I have observed both Marlda and Master Edmond in company with the princess, and I find it easy to believe that we can trust them. If Colesia prefers me over the Pithranian prince, then instruct Marlda to ask Colesia to smile down at me from her balcony as soon as dawn breaks tomorrow morning. I will be watching for her."

"Very well." Zephanoah paused in thought. "I will do as you request, but I will also direct Marlda to have my sister hang a silk scarf from the balcony as a sign that she chooses you rather than Prince Borgar, and to leave the scarf there until the lower edge of the sun rises above the eastern horizon. You can look for the scarf even if the sky is too dark to see my sister's face."

"Thank you," said Zarkanis, again shaking hands with Zephanoah. The food was deposited onto the floor near the well opening, and then Zephanoah departed with the bucket.

A few seconds later the second door to the cell closed, shutting out sounds of Zephanoah's footsteps. Zarkanis was left with his thoughts. It seemed that the world of his imagination was transforming into substantive reality. He performed much less physical exercise than usual, only warming up long enough to break a sweat. Then he stretched. He planned to repeat the same routine the next day, thus boosting his body to physiologic readiness for peak performance. He practiced scaling the cell walls where the stone was smoothest and most difficult to climb. Insofar as he could prepare himself, he was ready. Beyond that, he could only hope and pray.

Nighttime came. Zarkanis lay in his sleeping space and reflected upon a happy childhood, a childhood blessed with a tutor who dared to dream heroic dreams and who worked to make those dreams come true. Now he dreamed his own dreams. He dreamed of tasting freedom in the outside world, and he dreamed of holding Colesia in his arms.

****

Morning came. Past the pale tarnish of iron bars rose an indomitable gaze. A simple mantle hung over a figure of unfathomable strength, a mantle composed of a wool blanket with a hole cut in its center. Silence filled every corner of a cold stone chamber as anticipation swelled within an eager breast. Sunrise shot lucent fingers from the eastern sky and gilded parting clouds. A hopeful prince waited and watched. Seconds seemed minutes, and minutes seemed hours. Finally she appeared, her wistful visage thrust beyond the parapet of her royal balcony.

Zarkanis felt his yearning heart throb against the muscles of his chest. His soul cried out in hallowed adoration. If Colesia did not turn and smile upon him, the sun would blacken, and the skies rend themselves with sobbing. Then warmth flooded the core of his being— she leaned forward and cast aqua eyes toward his dingy den. A myriad of previous dawns had witnessed his surveillance of her heaven-consigned prayers but never mutual awareness. Her face summoned him, and she bestowed a heartrending smile before clinging to the marble parapet and bursting into tears. Feelings such as he had never known permeated every vessel and limb of Zarkanis's body; two powerful hands gripped iron bars, and solid stone cracked like thawing ice.

At the sound of crumbling rock, Zarkanis eased his grip on the bars to his window. Colesia looked long and hard at the little window below her, but Zarkanis knew that his face was barely visible from the high balcony. Somehow, though, he knew that she sensed his presence, and he knew that she was aware that he gazed at her. For a long minute they remained thus—interlocked in cognizance of one another's passionate souls. There was a consummation in their mutual gaze—a consummation deeper and dearer than any act of mortal flesh.

After her enrapturing stare, the daughter of Sir Marticus and Lady Monica reached to her waist and withdrew a long, white, silk scarf. She hung the scarf from the balcony, securing one end to the top of the banister with a marble weight. The noble blood of Dametrius's prime student pounded through his celebrating heart. He watched as she turned and disappeared.

The Captive from Shareen counted away the minutes in what seemed the longest day of his life. Toward evening he shaved, and then he sewed the razor onto the right side of his scant shorts. Before sewing it in place, he wrapped it in tough leather to protect both himself and his princess from its sharp edge. Dametrius had shown him how to extract and cure strips of leather, salvaging them from undercooked chunks of pork and beef that found their way to the prison cell from barbarous feasts in the castle. And in addition to the razor, he attached the ring that had belonged to his father, King Wildon.

Meanwhile, Master Edmond, Diana, Marlda, and Colesia were busy preparing for escape. The princess was forced to waste time in the female servants' quarters on the second floor of the castle, just above the kitchen. She was fitted in a luxurious wedding gown of white wool and golden silk, a gown she was supposed to wear the following day.

Diana was assigned to care for Master Edmond during his time of mourning, thanks to a royal request by Colesia; and Marlda was granted permission to spend nights with her father and Diana. Such permission was not difficult to obtain. Dragus considered it a fortuitous turn of events to have both Diana and Marlda removed from the royal tower. He knew that neither of the girls admired Borgar, and he figured that input from either one of them regarding the upcoming wedding would be negative. Thus, Princess Vayle was left to herself.

Marlda sneaked some male clothing into Colesia's room. The clothing was altered and tailored according to Zephanoah's description of Zarkanis's stature. She brought it in a satin bag, explaining to the guards that she was delivering items to the princess. Marlda and Colesia spoke very little. The two girls communicated with their eyes and through whispers, and then, after an encouraging embrace, Marlda departed.

In the privacy of her room, Colesia peeked inside the bag and examined her prince's attire. She had expected to awaken at any moment after Marlda delivered the message from Zephanoah—a message describing Zarkanis's abilities and his intention to abduct and marry her. Such a message seemed the substance of a wondrous dream. Her heart throbbed in nervous anticipation as she closed the bag. The prince of her dreams was real, and he was coming after her.

Time passed. Master Edmond paid a visit to the stables and brushed down Jasper, Whitefoot, and Moonbeam. He saddled and bridled all three horses and then tethered the two mares behind Jasper. There were no questions raised when he took the horses and headed toward his farm.

Darkness fell. It was another cloudy night, which was good—the darker the night, the easier to evade visible detection. Zarkanis lay on his back, staring upward. His body was keyed after the first two days of abstinence from exercise that had transpired in years. The darkness thickened until the anxious prince felt certain that it could thicken no further. There was no way to judge the time by the stars or moon since they were blocked by clouds, but there was a tiny hole in the bottom of the bucket, and as water slowly trickled downward into the waterway beneath the cell, Zarkanis was able to calculate the passage of time based upon the level of water remaining within the bucket. According to his measurement, little more than an hour remained before midnight. He would wait no longer.

****

The night was still and dark. All was quiet within the castle of Pithrania. Then what seemed the impact of a meteor shocked sleepers to wakefulness. Unsettling vibrations rippled through the structure of the castle. Zarkanis stepped back and clung to iron bars that he ripped through solid limestone as an entire section of the eastern wall crashed downward into a heap of dust, iron, and stone. One massive rock toppled down the embankment east of his cell and tore into Lake Manassa with a splintering of ice and a splash of water. Although the iron bars were implanted into the wall more deeply than Dametrius had postulated, the stone and mortar were no match for the force exerted by the determined Captive from Shareen. Guards on both the northeast and southeast towers bolted to attention—including Zephanoah. There were many widened eyes throughout the castle. Dragus sat up in his bed. Colesia heard, too… She took a deep breath and prayed.

"What goes on there?!" shouted a guard from the northeast tower. He was the first, apart from Zephanoah, to regain his wits enough to execute speech—but Zephanoah had chosen to maintain silence and wait for someone else to speak first.

"Stand fast! I will go down!" Zephanoah announced from the royal tower, hailing loudly enough to be heard by the guards atop the northeast tower.

The other guards knew their new comrade to be zealous and daring; his exploits in courting the daughter of Master Edmond were popular gossip, and his bragging before Dragus was deemed incredulous courage. They were more than willing to let him be the first to investigate the cause of crushed stone.

Zephanoah descended the outer steps of the royal tower, stepping downward to the wall walk atop the southern wall. "I've reached the wall!" he hollered, desiring to keep other guards at bay. He circled around the royal tower to the eastern wall, and then he lowered a rope ladder with wooden crossbars. The upper end of the ladder was secured to the stone parapet, and the ladder had been rolled up so that it could be unfurled to the ground below. He looked upward. Nothing was visible, but he thought he heard faint sounds coming from the tower wall. He hoped Zarkanis was unharmed, and he decided to check out the breached cell.

"How goes it?!" one of two remaining guards atop the royal tower called downward.

"No enemy yet encountered!" replied Zephanoah. "I'm climbing down the ladder! Hold fast!"

****

The outer wall of the royal tower was composed of the same stone and mortar as the inner cell where Zarkanis learned to climb. He ascended the tower to Colesia's quarters within seconds, and then he pulled himself over the northern fringe of the balcony. Colesia stood expectantly just inside the room, facing toward Zarkanis as he entered. She was barely visible to his keen eyes. She wore smartly fitting leather breeches and a leather jerkin with sleeves, both dyed royal blue— though there was insufficient lighting for Zarkanis to decipher color. Beneath her outer garments were snugly fitting wool undergarments lined with silk—the princess was aware that her prince intended to transport her over the top of Mount Thrandor. Such a feat seemed impossible, but, then, so did the fact that he was now entering her quarters. Leather pants and a leather shirt were draped over her right arm—both lined with wool. A thick leather belt was threaded through loops sewn around the waist of the pants.

The princess's room was unlit to reduce chances of being seen, and the drapes between the bedroom and the antechamber were drawn closed to mute any sounds. Colesia could not see Zarkanis as well as he saw her, but she heard him, and she knew beyond any doubt that it was her prince who stood before her. She could sense him...a sensation much like previous sensations that had heartened her soul innumerable times, morning after morning, year after year...but now the sensation permeated her flesh and caused a rapturous tingling to ignite the entire surface of her body.

There were no words spoken. Zarkanis felt the princess's aura envelope him. He stepped forward, and with each step an atmosphere of passion grew stronger. Colesia's silhouette remained motionless. He was able to focus upon two alluring orbs—enchanting eyes that captured the few rays of moonlight and starlight penetrating the overcast sky and then reflected them back as couriers of fervent love.

Colesia could scarcely breathe, but her next breath, with his lips touching hers, was the most marvelous of her life. The clothes she held dropped to her feet. He lifted her bodily from the floor and held her. For a few seconds both she and Zarkanis tasted heartfelt ecstasy beyond anything known to the depraved society that had governed their physical lives. They were together—not just in a dream but in one another's arms, and not just physically but in the unfathomable depths of spiritual communing.

"We must hurry," said Colesia after their lips parted. Zarkanis set her back upon the floor. "The clothes were tailored to fit you, and Master Edmond's daughter taught me how to fasten myself to your back with a blanket."

"That was most considerate," responded Zarkanis. His mind refocused on the present mission of escape.

Colesia knelt and lifted the clothing that Diana and Marlda had custom-fashioned with Zephanoah's guidance. Tied to the right side of her belt was a pair of leather boots lined with wool. She left the boots secured to her waist. Zarkanis donned the clothing without difficulty, thanks to training from Dametrius. Meanwhile, Colesia wound a blanket around her hips and pulled two equal lengths of the blanket forward in each hand. Zarkanis knelt before her. She mounted his back.

"Zephanoah says you use your toes when you climb," she spoke as she positioned herself, "so I will keep your boots until we reach the ground." Her thighs rested atop the thick leather belt that encircled Zarkanis's waist. She looped the loose ends of the blanket beneath his arms and up around the back of his neck where she tied a knot. "Ready," she said.

Moments later a guard's voice sounded from atop the royal tower. "How goes it now, Ferando?"

"No adversaries sighted yet!" answered Zephanoah. His voice was more distant than before. "But there has been a collapse in the wall of a dungeon cell! Send word for a prison guard to unlock the prison doors that lead to the chamber of chastisement, and tell him to bring me a torch!"

"Do you need aid?"

"Me? No! Of course not! How many invincible warriors are needed to guard a swine? A kitchen maid should be able to deal with an overstuffed lard muffin!"

"Very well. I'll get word to Duardo! Hold fast!"

"Do not fret! And remember to have someone bring a torch!"

It was still dark. Zephanoah turned and stared into the black hole before him. There was no sound from within the cell. He leaned forward and felt with his hands, moving his palms over the pile of debris below the breach to the cell. It was large enough to cover a man's body, and this worried him. He stood and turned his face upward toward the top of the royal tower. Almost nothing was visible. For a minute he stood staring in silence, wondering what he should do next, but then his attention was drawn to sounds coming from the frozen surface of the lake...sounds of racing footsteps heading northeastward. The sounds of the footsteps faded away faster than seemed humanly possible, especially for a man carrying a woman on his back. Zephanoah heaved a sigh of relief.

After retracing his steps back to the base of the royal tower, Zephanoah headed east onto the frozen lake and then turned south until crossing the roadway and passing into farmland. From there he coursed westward, heading for Master Edmond's house. The darkness gave way to moonlight. His pace quickened. Master Edmond, Marlda, and Diana were ready and waiting when he arrived. They stood outside the small stable near Master Edmond's home, each holding the reins to a horse.

"It's me," spoke Zephanoah as he approached.

"Are you being followed?" asked Master Edmond.

"Not yet."

"We heard the stone crumble all the way out here," remarked Marlda. "Did they escape?"

"Yes, they're heading north, and they're moving fast."

"Then let's get going," said Master Edmond.

Zephanoah and Marlda kissed each other before Marlda climbed into Whitefoot's saddle, and then Zephanoah pulled himself up and took a seat behind her. Diana mounted Moonbeam. Master Edmond positioned himself upon Jasper and turned the stallion northward, leading the group toward the western reaches of Mount Thrandor. Saddlebags were packed with provisions. Weapons and ropes were fixed to the backs and sides of saddles, including bows, arrows, and swords.

The party of runaways coursed northward in silence as they crossed the frozen surface of the Requain River about two hundred yards west of the bridge. The waterfall rarely froze, and the crashing sound at the base of the falls muffled the sounds of horses' hooves moving across snow-covered ground. With the attention of castle guards directed eastward, the escapees passed to the western side of Mount Thrandor without notice. Then they journeyed onward, hoping to meet up with Zarkanis and Colesia before nightfall.

****

Zarkanis did not experience any difficulty making his way down the royal tower with Colesia fixed to his back. Marlda, following directions from her father, had instructed Colesia to clasp onto the blanket where it was tied behind Zarkanis's neck, thereby decreasing the pressure on his spine. But in actuality the princess's weight posed little threat to Zarkanis's frame.

Colesia was grateful for darkness. Not only did it thwart visual detection by the tower guards, it also kept her from seeing how impossible it appeared for a human being to back his way down a vertical wall with a woman bound to his back. Zarkanis had considered the possibility that he would have to descend the wall directly below the balcony, using the balcony as a shield against spears and arrows launched from above—that is, if any guard dared to release projectiles with the princess secured to his back. But thanks to the dark night, he and the princess were seen by no one.

After Zarkanis dropped onto the snow at the base of the royal tower, Colesia untied the leather boots from around her belt and lowered them over his chest. The prince liked the feel of wool as he slipped his feet into the boots and tied them, but he liked the feel of the princess upon his back much more. He headed down the embankment. The princess did not question his decision to keep her on his back. He stepped eastward until reaching thicker ice, and then he dashed northeastward over the frozen surface of Lake Manassa. Running free outside the walls of the Pithranian dungeon was exhilarating—it brought an irrepressible smile to his lips.

Following several seconds of sprinting, Zarkanis turned due north and was soon ascending gigantic walls of limestone. The clouds passed from beneath a full moon and liberated silvery beams of light. Colesia gasped as the surrounding environment became visible. She dropped her gaze and peered downward—they were nearing the top of a sheer cliff. There were adequate crevices and toeholds for Zarkanis to keep his boots on, but his ascent appeared miraculous.

Colesia drew deep breaths of the fresh nighttime breeze. The feel of her prince beneath her body made the entire world seem wonderful. She looked upward and noted a bank of dark clouds gliding eastward. The clouds moved across the sky like the opening of a colossal curtain, and the departing billows unveiled a canopy of shimmering diamonds cast beyond the figure of a great white pearl. The nocturnal sky had never looked so beautiful, and she had never felt so blissfully alive.

Chapter 13

Feast of Consummation

Marlda leaned back in Zephanoah's arms as he reached around her to take a turn holding Whitefoot's reins. The horses had walked through the moonlit night for several hours. Master Edmond directed Jasper with care, coursing along the mountain trail within a few feet of a precipitous slope. Morning sunlight dimmed the stars and granted a bluish hue to the sky. The pace quickened. There was no thought or suggestion of resting along the way—an unspoken sense of urgency drove the group onward.

There was little talking. Slushy sounds of horses' hooves treading through snow were interrupted now and then by whistling winds wafting through mountain crevices. Scents of cedar and pine flavored the atmosphere. Master Edmond took appropriate heed navigating the horses around Mount Thrandor. He pondered what they would do after meeting Zarkanis and Colesia at the demented king's castle—assuming that the prince escaped, rescued the princess, and journeyed over Mount Thrandor without serious mishap. Diana, whose mind was less burdened by matters of travel, found herself thinking about the Bear King. She wondered if the celebrated animal trainer had a sweetheart. Marlda had told her that they expected to meet the Bear King before passing beyond Mount Thrandor, and Diana cast frequent gazes up the mountainside while she rode Moonbeam behind Jasper.

Dawn was resisted by the high peak of the mountain, but illumination intensified with time. The increasing light brought breathtaking changes. Pines no longer appeared like giant, gray-robed gnomes but rather like forest hosts and hostesses stretching forth vivid green fingers laden with clumps of sugar. Their limbs rose in tiers, dwindling in circumference while increasing in brilliance. Ahead were jagged bluffs—sacred monoliths scattered above the northwest foot of the mountain, and below to the northwest stretched the magnificent Poolglade Forest. Zephanoah had expected Baruk to appear several miles back up the trail, but no sign of him or his pets had materialized. Then, from over a high crested ridge to the northeast, eight dark spots emerged and streaked down an ivory slope.

"What is that?" questioned Diana. She was first to espy plume-like splays of snow that rose in the wake of descending creatures on the mountainside.

All three horses were drawn to a halt. "That's him," stated Zephanoah.

"The Bear King?" asked Diana.

"Yes, he's the one in front of the others."

The dark blotches on the snow increased in size as Baruk and his bears raced downward. They disappeared amidst evergreens when reaching the mountain's timberline, and then reappeared a few minutes later in nearby woods. Their heavy plodding through the snow became audible as they broke into view. At a word from Baruk, the bears gathered in a huddle, lolling and panting beneath a pine tree about ninety yards from the horses and riders. The horses whinnied and shuffled, but Master Edmond's voice kept them from bolting. Baruk, who was breathing hard from his swift dash, approached the expectant clan before him. As if on cue, the sun peeped over the mountain and brightened their meeting.

"Greetings, my brother," said Zephanoah.

"Aye, greetings!" returned Baruk. He drew nearer and perused each rider, and then he approached Diana. "Ah! So this is our long-lost baby sister! I can see that the rumors are most valid… She has grown to be the most beautiful woman in all of Gaul, and that beyond any question of doubt!"

Diana peered into the mountaineer's blue eyes. As the nature of his statement impressed itself upon her, she smiled and reciprocated his regard. She held him with riveting brown eyes, but she did not say a word.

"An understandable error, my brother, but our sister has been evacuated from Pithrania by another route. Prince Zarkanis is with her, and they are to meet us farther north—at the demented king's castle."

Baruk's expression melted. A faint tint of pink rose in his cheeks, showing above his bushy beard. He broke his gaze from Diana and looked toward Zephanoah.

"The young lady is a Grecian maiden who was captured by Dragus and enslaved as a cook in the castle. She is a dear friend to Marlda, and to our sister, and she wished to escape her Pithranian captors."

Baruk turned his eyes back toward Diana. He was nonplussed. "I, um…well ma'am…I thought…"

Diana found herself inspired by the Bear King's demure bearing. "That is quite all right, Master Bear King. I think you must certainly be the most handsome man in all of Gaul."

Marlda's eyes widened. Even Diana felt shocked by the words that had passed from her lips. Baruk looked downward toward his leather-clad feet and blushed more fully than ever. But when he looked back up, his eyes captured Diana and held her in his affection as securely as his hands had often cradled newborn cubs.

"Thank you, ma'am. I hope we have the opportunity for further acquaintance without any significant hindrance from the army tracking you."

"You are too kind," began Diana, but then she realized what Baruk had said, and her speech halted. Baruk flashed a winsome smile. Diana found herself comforted by his calm demeanor—despite his report of enemy forces. She could not help but grant him a smile in return.

"Army?" inquired Zephanoah. "Is there a Pithranian regiment behind us?"

Baruk bowed to Diana and then took a step back so that he could address all four riders. "Yes, about three miles behind. Day has broken, so they will move faster now—they will no longer have to rely on torches to follow your tracks."

Zephanoah and Master Edmond both looked back, as did Marlda and Diana, but the rising landscape and trees prevented distant vision. No pursuers were in sight.

"Can we evade them?" asked Master Edmond.

"Not here," replied Baruk. "On my mountain, though, we could do more than evade them. I could battle ten such companies on the slopes of Mount Zeborah."

The Bear King's claim was prodigious, but Diana had no difficulty believing him.

"How many bears do you have?" asked Master Edmond.

"Several, but Mount Zeborah is more powerful than an army of bears. The mountain will fight for us."

Master Edmond looked questioningly toward Zephanoah, who in turn queried his brother.

"Can we first meet Zarkanis and Colesia at the demented king's castle? They are supposed to hide inside the castle and wait for us."

"Inside the castle? How?" asked Baruk. "Not even a bear cub could climb the cliff that lies below that castle."

"Zarkanis climbed the stone wall of a vertical tower and carried our sister down on his back," stated Zephanoah.

Baruk faced his brother in awed silence. His brows rose and fell. He peered northwest, but then he shook his head and looked back at Zephanoah. "If Zarkanis has not yet reached the castle, or if he cannot scale the cliff, then we would be trapped in the gorge. Our sister's best chance of survival will be for us to draw the army away, destroy the army, and then return and look for her."

Zephanoah was not at all certain how his older brother intended to destroy an entire Pithranian regiment, but it made sense that Colesia would be safer if the pursuing army were drawn away from her. "We will have to trust your judgment, my brother. This is your realm."

After a final look at Diana, and after an engaging smile when their eyes met, Baruk turned and retreated back to his sloth of bears. He took them on ahead and led the way through the southern reaches of Poolglade Forest—out onto the Zeborah plain. The others followed.

****

The journey over the mountain was thrilling. Seated together in natural thrones of stone, looking out from the high reaches of Mount Thrandor's northern crest, Zarkanis and Colesia beheld a sunrise more glorious than any prose or poetry could portray. Dried fruit and cured pork provided snacks during daybreak's debut—Colesia had stowed some provisions in her coat pockets. They conversed like longtime friends, and in their own special way, so they were.

Zarkanis relished the sights and sounds of freedom. Colesia marveled at his physical agility and strength. He scaled almost vertical barriers of limestone and granite with her body clad to his back, and he traversed stretches of rugged terrain like a roaming lynx, and he accomplished these feats with such enthusiasm that she feared he would faint from exhaustion. She had cautioned him to slow down, but he replied by explaining that he was traveling at one-half potential speed, retaining sufficient energy to battle a large carnivore. She merely smiled in response.

When they reached the border of Poolglade Forest, Colesia requested that Zarkanis permit her to walk. He knelt and let her dismount, and then they made their way through the forest, strolling side by side. "It's lovely, even in wintertime," Colesia commented as they came to a halt at the eastern edge of Crystal Pond. The pouring waterfall gleamed in the sunlight.

It was almost noon. Sunlight accentuated the beauty of a virtual winter wonderland. Artesian wells and petite falls spawned ice sculptures that shone like glass statues. Pink-, purple-, red-, and black-dappled, granite boulders rose above smooth blankets of pure-white snow. For a while Zarkanis and Colesia just stood there, holding hands and beholding their surroundings. It struck Colesia's mind that she and her prince had conversed almost continuously during the latter part of their extraordinary journey. It was marvelous that Zarkanis sustained sufficient breath to hike and climb while talking incessantly, and it was also marvelous that he was such a good conversationalist—despite being manifestly male, and despite having grown up in an isolated cell.

He turned and faced her. She motioned toward a nearby pine that held its lowest branches a few feet above the ground. They walked together. Zarkanis removed the blanket that was tied about him and spread it at the base of the pine, and then he and the princess sat side by side upon the blanket. They gazed at the waterfall. It seemed to share their cheer, dancing merrily at the far side of the pond and splaying droplets of water like bouncing diamonds.

"Have you ever seen anything so beautiful?" queried Colesia, turning her long lashes toward Zarkanis. Sunlight glanced from the snow and illuminated the golden lock in her hair. Her aqua eyes conveyed love. She was with her prince; and therefore, she was home.

Zarkanis met her eyes. "This place is more beautiful than any mortal tongue could describe... There are no words to embody such creation," he proclaimed. Then he paused, and his eyes penetrated hers more deeply. "But morning after morning, year after year, I have looked upon more wondrous beauty than all of this—beauty beyond fathoming, beauty transcending the capacity of mortal eyes."

"Wha...?" began Colesia, but her speech faltered. She realized that Zarkanis referred to her. He continued gazing into her eyes. She blushed, but she never disengaged her eyes from his. He smiled, and she smiled in return. The message imparted by their eyes communicated far more effectually, and far more sincerely, than verbal avowals could ever convey.

"I love you, Zarkanis."

The prince's heart throbbed in ecstasy. "I love you too, Colesia."

For a long minute they sat thus...with proclamations of love ringing in one another's ears...and with attestations of heartfelt devotion pouring from one another's eyes. It was Zarkanis who spoke next.

"Will you marry me?"

Colesia leaned into Zarkanis's arms and rested her head against his chest. The chaste dreams and hollowed hopes of a virgin princess had come to fruition. "Yes, my prince...yes."

"I will forever love you," he spoke.

Colesia smiled. "And I you."

He rose and took her by the hand, and then he draped the blanket over one shoulder. They walked through the forest and across the narrow gorge to the demented king's castle. Colesia asked if she could again secure herself to Zarkanis's back and inspect the castle along with him, and he agreed to this so long as she would hold his boots. He had to climb to one side of the castle and then make his way over to the castle wall because the face of the cliff below the castle was sanded so smoothly that even he could not climb upon its surface. Then, when they rose above the upper border of the castle wall, their eyes widened in wonder.

The roof of the castle, stretching out below their eyes, was composed of smooth, red flagstone that contrasted sharply with the gray limestone cliff and the limestone blocks that composed the front bulwark. To either side, resting atop the castle roof and nestled beneath the sloping sides of the domed ceiling of the cavern, were lines of white marble chests. Seven chimneys, all white marble, protruded upward through the roof. Colesia dropped down beside Zarkanis and handed him the boots. She looked into his eyes with an expression of amazement.

"I'll see what's inside the marble chests," said Zarkanis.

"Good idea, and I'll check what's downstairs inside the castle," returned Colesia. She turned and trotted to a nearby stairwell and disappeared down the steps.

Zarkanis walked to one side of the roof and knelt to examine the front surface of a marble chest. "Firewood, Axes, & Gardening Tools," was engraved across the chest in Latin; and beneath the Latin letters were odd symbols intermingled with exquisite depictions of strange birds, weird plants, and bizarre animals. Zarkanis's eyes widened with wonder. The writing on the chest listed contents in both Latin and Subterranian. Lying on top of the chest was a steel wedge. He examined the back and edges of the lid. There were fixed stone hinges at the rear of the lid, and the edges of the lid appeared to be sealed.

Then Zarkanis heard a creaking sound from below. "Are you safe?" he asked.

"Yes. I've just opened a chest. It was sealed with wax or something. I used a wedge. And oh my lands! Oh how beautiful! Wait until you see these!"

Zarkanis looked back down at the wedge and the lid. More creaking sounds came from below. He used the wedge to open the lid, which opened fairly easily once the seal was broken, and then he tilted the lid backward until its hinges held it just past vertical. "Remarkable," he muttered. He picked up a chunk of firewood and examined it—it was in excellent condition.

After setting the firewood down, Zarkanis moved from chest to chest, reading the Latin and Subterranian inscriptions, though some of the Subterranian symbols and depictions were new to him. It was on the opposite side of the roof that he found a chest marked *Bows and Arrows*. He opened the chest and stared downward. The right side of the chest was packed with arrows in wooden boxes, and aligned in front of the arrows were several wooden bows and leather quivers. But Zarkanis's eyes were drawn to marble boxes on the left side of the chest—boxes filled with strange-looking, pale yellow arrows. In front of the odd arrows were a single bow and a single quiver, and they were both the same color as the arrows.

Zarkanis lifted the pale yellow bow and examined it, and then he strung it. He nocked one of the matching arrows and walked to the battlement. In the distance was a small stump. He drew back, aimed, and released. His eyes widened. It was no more difficult to draw back the bow string than it had been with the bows that he and Dametrius fabricated, but the arrow streaked through the air like lightning, striking far beyond the stump.

After putting his boots back on, Zarkanis stuffed the odd quiver with several of the odd arrows, and then he hung the quiver behind his right shoulder. Next, he grabbed an additional handful of the arrows and returned to the battlement. It required three more arrows to adapt to the bow and strike the center of the stump. His years of target practice within the chamber of chastisement permitted swift adaptation to the pale yellow bow and the farther distance. He gazed southward down the narrow gorge. There was no sign of horses or riders.

A faint smell of burning wood touched upon Zarkanis's nostrils. He turned and saw wisps of smoke rising from the nearest chimney. Then came the sound of rapid footsteps, and Colesia emerged from a stairwell. Her face was glowing.

"There was flint, and tender, and some firewood, and oh ...wait until you see!" she exclaimed, rushing to Zarkanis and placing both palms on his chest. She peered into his eyes. "The furniture in four of the bedrooms is all marble, and they all have fireplaces, and the mattresses and tapestries and blankets inside the chests are all in perfect condition. Can you believe it?" She paused and thumped her hands against his chest. "But don't come down yet, I want to surprise you. Wait until I say I'm ready."

Zarkanis took a moment to savor the look in Colesia's eyes. Then he lifted the bow before her. "Have you ever seen anything made of this substance?" he asked.

Colesia examined the bow. "No, how strange. It seems to be flexible glass."

"I've been giving it some thought," said Zarkanis. "I think this bow and arrow were brought to this castle from Subterrania."

Colesia responded with a startled expression. "Marlda told me about Subterrania—a world beneath the surface of the earth—but she spoke of it as an imaginary place."

"I believe it exists," stated Zarkanis.

Colesia gazed into his eyes, saying nothing.

Zarkanis's expression deepened. "I can see far south from the battlement, and I see no sign of the others."

Colesia's expression changed at once. "They should be within sight by now. Where do you suppose they are?"

Zarkanis placed a hand on Colesia's shoulder and held her with his eyes. "I'm going after them, and I want you to continue working here. You may do what you can to get this castle ready for visitors."

Colesia shook her head. "No, I'm going with you."

"I respect your words," Zarkanis responded, "but you would slow me down, and I would have to protect you at risk of my own life. It is better that I go alone."

His words were inarguable. Colesia stared speechless into Zarkanis's eyes until her own eyes grew moist, and then she leaned into Zarkanis's chest. Zarkanis held her and let her cry. A minute later she straightened and faced him.

"I will do as you request. I will work hard while you are gone," she said. Her gaze into his eyes deepened. "Come back to me…please."

Zarkanis nodded. "There is a chain ladder in one of the chests," he said, "in case one of the others arrives before I return. I love you."

"I love you too," returned Colesia.

They both knew that the words *I love you* were the last words that either one of them wished to speak, and they were the last words that either one of them wished to hear. He kissed her once more; and then, despite wearing his boots, he made his way back down to the narrow gorge without difficulty.

Zarkanis traversed the landscape like a wolf on the scent of prey. Tracks were easy to spot, even from a distance. He followed the tracks all the way to the northern reaches of the eastern face of Mount Zeborah. There, the forest gave way to a snowy cove that sloped steeper and steeper upward toward the mountain until meeting the foot of a sheer, smooth, vertical cliff. The cliff was about one hundred yards wide and twelve feet high. On the northern side of the cove was a narrow pathway that led up to the top of the cliff. About fifty Pithranian warriors, all on horseback, were making their way toward the base of the cliff. A lone figure stood atop of the cliff with the late afternoon sun behind him.

Stealthily making his way through thick woods, Zarkanis was able to reach a favorable position at the southern edge of the cove. He peered out over a small boulder, cradled between the branches of evergreens. No one was looking his direction. The man atop the cliff was facing the warriors, and all of the warriors were staring at him.

"Hear me," the man spoke loudly; and upon hearing the voice, Zarkanis recognized that the man atop the cliff was Master Edmond. The words *hear me* resonated throughout the atmosphere, and then Master Edmond continued speaking. "The Prince of Shareen is free, and he is in need of an army. Why not join us? Why not serve a fair and just king rather than being enslaved to an evil tyrant?"

Zarkanis looked out over the throng of Pithranian warriors, and then he looked back at Master Edmond. His brow creased in contemplation. Master Edmond spoke as if he had the warriors at a disadvantage, and yet he appeared to be alone.

Snickers and guffaws erupted throughout the group of warriors. One of them motioned toward the pathway that led to the top of the cliff, and then several others turned their horses in that direction.

"Perhaps I should speak more plainly," resounded Master Edmond's voice. "Join us and amend your ways, or die."

Zarkanis's eyes were fixed upon Master Edmond as he spoke. One of the warriors below him launched an axe. Master Edmond saw the axe flying toward him and ducked beneath it, but then his feet slipped and he fell off the cliff, crashing into the snow and sliding down the slope to the forefeet of a horse.

"No! Father!" a female voice screamed out as two of the Pithranian warriors dismounted and took Master Edmond in hand. But it was not a female who appeared at the top of the cliff and gazed downward, it was a man who held a bow with a drawn arrow.

Zarkanis watched. There were many thoughts racing through his mind, but he took no immediate action. Despite the background sun, he recognized the new figure as the young man who came to his prison cell—Zephanoah.

"Stop where you are! The sun is bright, and I can see all of you," spoke Zephanoah. "If any man draws an arrow or raises an axe or sword, I will put this arrow through that man's heart, and all of you know my skills with a bow and arrow."

The warriors riding toward the pathway halted their horses. One of the warriors nearest the cliff then addressed Zephanoah. He remained on horseback as he spoke. "Ah, Ferando! It appears that Master Edmond has decided to rejoin our ranks. Why don't you follow his example?"

Zephanoah gazed downward with the tip of his drawn arrow aimed toward the man who had spoken. "A fair question, Castor," he finally replied. "What if I trade places with him?"

"No!" Master Edmond yelled out. "She needs you!"

Castor turned his face toward two warriors who had dismounted and were holding Master Edmond. "Gag him, he's interrupting a serious conversation," he directed; and then he turned his face back toward Zephanoah. "I have another suggestion, Ferando. We'll trade Master Edmond for the Bear King."

Muffled sounds erupted from Master Edmond, but the warriors with him were able to keep him from saying anything intelligible.

Then the cove fell still and silent. Zarkanis's eyes became fixed on the third figure to appear atop the cliff—a figure that, to his mind, more than merited the title of *Bear King*. Strips of leather hung from furry garbs and swayed in the breeze, and a huge sledge hammer was toted easily in one hand.

Zephanoah continued gazing downward and continued holding the drawn arrow as he shook his head and begin speaking—but his speech was interrupted.

"Listen all!" roared the living legend that stood atop the cliff like a mountain god. "I will exchange places with Master Edmond as follows. We will lower two ropes, and you must tie one end of a rope securely around Master Edmond's waist and permit him to take hold of it with both hands. You will then permit us to haul Master Edmond three feet above the ground, at which point I will lower myself down the other rope while Master Edmond is drawn upward. If at any point in the transfer you release an arrow or otherwise attack, I will ascend back up my rope. Do we have an agreement?"

The silence deepened. Castor signaled for several warriors to dismount and gather around him. The group of warriors spoke in hushed tones for several seconds, and then Castor stepped back and drew the attention of the two men standing above him.

"We have an agreement," spoke Castor. "But Ferando must permit one of our archers to keep a nocked arrow aimed upon Master Edmond, and he must permit a second archer to keep a nocked arrow aimed upon you."

Zarkanis observed as the warriors who had dismounted scattered to either side of Castor. One of them slunk to a small recess in the lower portion of the cliff where it would be difficult for someone atop the cliff to see him.

"It's me you want," growled the Bear King. "You may have one archer with a nocked arrow, and he may aim the arrow at whomever he pleases. And in return, Ferando will have a nocked arrow aimed at you."

There were a few more seconds of silence. The warrior hidden at the base of the cliff nocked an arrow. "Very well," returned Castor. "But you must leave your hammer behind."

The Bear King laughed aloud. "The hammer will stay above," he consented. Then he turned and spoke something to Zephanoah.

Zephanoah remained in place with a drawn arrow, keeping an eye on the army below. Baruk disappeared for a couple of minutes, and then two ropes dropped side-by-side over the edge of the cliff. Zarkanis was not able to see how the ends of the ropes above the cliff were secured. Baruk placed his hands on his hips and watched while warriors tied the far end of one of the ropes around Master Edmond's waist; but Master Edmond was resisting, and the warriors ended up tying his hands and wrists with a second rope and then securing them to the first rope above his head. They left his gag in place.

"Very well then," Castor called up. "One of our archers will now nock an arrow before Master Edmond is lifted three feet above the ground."

"Proceed," hailed the Bear King.

Castor directed a Pithranian archer to dismount and nock an arrow. The archer positioned himself less than three feet from Master Edmond and aimed the tip of an arrow toward the center of Master Edmond's chest. The rope grew taut and Master Edmond's body was raised three feet. His thrashing and kicking failed to draw Baruk's or Zephanoah's attention to the warrior hidden at the base of the cliff—the exchange was underway.

Zarkanis was now standing with a nocked arrow. He was certain that the hidden warrior planned to ambush Zephanoah after Baruk dropped too low to escape attack from the other warriors, and he was also certain that Castor had no intention of permitting Master Edmond to be drawn safely to the top of the cliff. Baruk turned and backed his great boots over the edge of the cliff. Zarkanis drew back on his bowstring and released the arrow.

"Ah!" cried the archer who had been aiming at Master Edmond. His body crumpled backward and his bow and arrow dropped into the snow.

"Baruk, back up! Pull Master Edmond up!" yelled Zarkanis as he nocked a second arrow.

Everyone heard. Baruk was quick to scoot around and look down over the edge of the cliff. The warrior who was hiding at the base of the cliff stepped out and raised the tip of his arrow upward. "Nah! Nah!" Baruk's voice boomed, giving a command to two large bears that were fitted with ropes around their breasts.

"Shoot him!" barked Castor, pointing toward Zarkanis.

Zephanoah released an arrow into the chest of the first Pithranian warrior to take aim at Zarkanis; and at the same moment, Zarkanis released a second arrow into the chest of the warrior who had been hiding at the base of the cliff. Then Zephanoah ducked down as warriors released arrows toward him, and Zarkanis had to squat behind the boulder as arrows zipped above his head. Meanwhile, Baruk vanished from above the lip of the cliff, and Master Edmond's body streaked up the side of the cliff and disappeared over its edge. "Tor! Tor!" Baruk's voice sounded again.

"Attack!" screamed Castor; and mounted warriors spurred their horses toward the pathway leading to the top of the cliff.

Zarkanis peeked around the boulder to see if any more arrows were being released in his direction. He nocked an arrow and stood; but then he paused in astonishment.

A great copper gong rose into full view above the center of the cliff. To either side of the gong appeared bears—four on the north side of the gong and four on the south side. The Bear King stepped forward and drew back his great hammer.

"Shoot them!" shouted Castor. His voice drew Zarkanis's attention, and Zarkanis rose and released an arrow as the Bear King's voice rose above all else.

"Dollah! Dollah!" hailed the Bear King, and all eight bears rose onto their hind legs and roared—great horrifying specters of beastly savagery emitting terrifying sounds. And then the din of roars was thwarted by a greater sound—a sound that shocked the atmosphere— the huge iron face of the Bear King's hammer pounded the center of the gong like the percussion of titanic bronze rams butting heads. Vibrations shot through Zarkanis's body…great sheets of ice splintered off the face of the cliff and dropped downward…and then the entire cove rumbled.

Castor fell from his horse with a pale yellow arrow through his chest. The warrior beside him tried to turn his horse back to the east while yelling retreat; but his voice was not even audible, and the snow beneath his horse's hooves was shifting.

The Bear King watched with satisfaction while the entire slope beneath him writhed in a lethal avalanche of ice and snow—it appeared as if subterranean gods were reaching upward through the earth's crust and crushing evildoers in gigantic fists of righteous fury. "Natah! Natah!" rose his voice above the dying sounds of the gong; then eight frenzied bears launched themselves from the edge of the cliff—monstrous death angels streaking downward to wreak just rewards upon the ungodly, and the Bear King leapt from the cliff to fight amongst them.

At last the savagery ended. Not one Pithranian warrior survived, but Baruk managed to rescue three of the horses. Zarkanis made his way to the top of the cliff and joined Zephanoah, Marlda, Diana, and Master Edmond. Introductions were made, and many thanks were given to Zarkanis in regard to his timely intervention. The group strode to the cliff's edge and watched Baruk and his bears interact, noting Baruk's affection as he withdrew arrows from the bears' hides and inspected their wounds—none of which were serious.

"Is it safe to come down now?" called Zephanoah.

"Ride the horses down the pathway and try to look nonchalant," Baruk hailed back while flashing a droll smile. Then he set his eyes upon Zarkanis. "Is that my sister's rescuer and our timely hero?"

"Your sister fares well, and she is waiting for us in the castle," responded Zarkanis. "But I think she will fare better when she sees us all alive. You will be coming with us, will you not?"

Diana tried hard to read the expression in Baruk's eyes. Their eyes met. Baruk then turned his face back toward Zarkanis. "My bears have ample cause to remain on our mountain. Take all the horses, and after I've sliced some horse-loin steaks, I'll follow after you with Pugsnout and Charmley. They're my smartest pets, and they'll keep the horses safe in the nose of the gorge while we dine together in the castle."

Diana drew a deep breath and hollered down to Baruk. "Now listen...I'll likely be doing the cooking, and I want to oversee the carving of the steaks. Perhaps two of your newly obtained steeds can stay behind so that we can catch up with the others on horseback."

Baruk stared in wonder at the Grecian woman above him. He smiled and nodded.

****

Colesia was well-prepared for guests. Lamps burned in the dining room and in the kitchen and in four eloquent bedrooms. She was awed to make acquaintance with her brother Baruk, the Bear King; and she was delighted to note the affectionate relationship between Baruk and Diana. She led the way to the bathing room and demonstrated how a natural spring could be channeled through marble fountains. Then, back in the dining room, she explained that the dried fruits and nuts that filled several bowls on the marble dining table were taken from pale yellow pots with sealed lids. No one could identify the well-preserved and tasty victuals, but it was agreed that both the pots and the food must have come from Subterrania.

Baruk and Diana retreated to the kitchen while the others seated themselves at the dining table. Zarkanis and Colesia sat on one side of the table while Master Edmond, Zephanoah, and Marlda sat across from them. Two additional place settings were prepared for Baruk and Diana. All of the settings were furnished with golden plates, silver utensils, and porcelain goblets. Colesia listened as the others narrated the wondrous defeat of Pithranian warriors at Mount Zeborah; and in turn, she described the marvelous contents withdrawn from marble chests. Then wafts of savory scents drew a pause in the conversation.

Diana and Baruk delivered platters laden with steaks, and then they sat down at the table. Master Edmond gave thanks. Honey-colored nectar was poured into goblets, and plates were filled with steaks, nuts, and fruits. Conversation was lively and jovial. After Marlda shared details of Zephanoah's marriage proposal, and after Colesia did the same in regard to Zarkanis's proposal, Baruk announced that he had just agreed to marry Diana while they were in the kitchen; and then Diana poked Baruk in the ribs and described how *he* knelt on one knee and asked *her* to marry *him*.

"Well," commented Zephanoah as the group laughed at Baruk's and Diana's remarks, "I guess we males will have to give our own renditions of our courtships after the ladies go to bed—each in her own private bedroom."

"Oh no!" interposed Marlda. "We just can't permit that, can we ladies?" She looked back and forth between Colesia and Diana; and then suddenly she locked eyes with Colesia…the expression on her face changed.

"What?" asked Colesia.

Marlda did not answer. Instead, she turned her face toward her father.

"Would you not agree, Father, that Zarkanis, Colesia, Baruk, and Diana have all proven themselves worthy of joining our ranks as Sheranites?"

The change of subject was startling, but Master Edmond agreed. "Of course," he said.

Marlda turned her head and looked back and forth between the other two couples. "Would you join us as Sheranites?" she asked. "Would you join the ranks of those who wish to see Dragus defeated?"

Both couples accepted Marlda's invitation. Colesia kept peering into Marlda's eyes—she sensed that her former lady-in-waiting was up to something.

Marlda looked back at her father. "Remember, Father, what you told me about your position among the Sheranites? Do you remember that you have been ordained to perform marriages, so long as both the suitor and the betrothed are members of the Sheranite fellowship?"

No one made a sound. All eyes became fixed on Master Edmond. "Ah…well…perhaps so, but I never actually…" began Master Edmond; but then his eyes met the eyes of his daughter. There was only one response that he could muster in response to those eyes. "Yes."

Marlda's face bloomed. She took hold of Zephanoah's arm and pulled him close. "We wish to be married after dinner," she said, still facing her father.

Colesia and Diana looked at one another. Their eyes communed, and they gave one another a nod. Colesia took hold of Zarkanis while Diana grasped Baruk.

"So would we," said Colesia.

"And we," said Diana.

Master Edmond looked from couple to couple. The women were exuberant. The males wore expressions of utter shock and sheer delight.

"Do the suitors consent?" asked Master Edmond.

One by one, Master Edmond looked at each man's face. Not a single word was spoken, but each suitor responded with a nod.

"So be it," proclaimed Master Edmond.

The remainder of the dinner transformed into a merry wedding banquet; and later that night, after performing marriage ceremonies for all three enamored couples, Master Edmond retired in solitude, enjoying the comforts of his own bedroom. The lonely little castle, having sat desolate for so many years, was transformed into a sanctuary of love-laden mirth.

Made in the USA
Coppell, TX
05 October 2024

38216833R00163